To women in offices, everywhere.

PROMISING

YOUNG

WOMEN

CAROLINE

O'DONOGHUE

virago

VIRAGO

First published in Great Britain in 2018 by Virago Press

1 3 5 7 9 10 8 6 4 2

A CIP catalogue record for this book
is available from the British Library.

Hardback ISBN 978-0-3490-0990-2
C format ISBN 978-0-3490-0991-9

Typeset in Bembo by M Rules
Printed and bound in Great Britain by
Clays Ltd, St Ives plc

Papers used by Virago are from well-managed forests
and other responsible sources.

MIX
Paper from
responsible sources
FSC® C104740

Virago Press
An imprint of
Little, Brown Book Group
Carmelite House
50 Victoria Embankment
London EC4Y 0DZ

An Hachette UK Company
www.hachette.co.uk

www.virago.co.uk

PART ONE

I

When the company grew to over two hundred people, each with their own birthday, each with their own birthday *cake*, the cleaners started to complain. The excess of uneaten cake was attracting rats, and when bodies started appearing – bloated and sugar-filled and, more than once, belly-up in the stairwell – they insisted we downsize.

When I turned twenty-five, Mitchell Advertising gave me an entire carrot cake.

It's a year later, and I have a cupcake.

It's five past nine when I get into work, and I can see my desk cupcake winking at me from the lift, a lone candle sticking out of the middle. Becky snaps into action when she spots me, flicking her thumb desperately over the lighter's metal roll, sparks flying out of her hands.

The girls in my department start singing for me, smiling widely in obligation. The people not in my department blush into their monitors, mumbling along in the shared agony of an office 'Happy Birthday'.

There's a collective wince when they reach the high bit: 'Happy BIRTHday, dear Jane, Happy Birthday to you.'

Most of them know about the break-up.

I expect Becky has found some way to tell them, attempting to be as tasteful as possible but barely managing to control her glee. Not because she's happy I'm alone, but because

women love telling other women new and preferably confidential information. It is a great honour to be a break-up's town crier, especially when the break-up in question is for a relationship as long and as outwardly peaceful as mine and Max's. Most of my team have met Max. Becky herself said how lucky I was to have him.

The birthday chorus ends, and I smile weakly.

I'm expected to say something, or react in some way, but I just keep standing there, unable or unwilling to sit at my desk because if I sit at my desk, another day of work will begin and the shaky tornado of grief will be free to descend on me at any time. I fix my eyes on the wavering flame of the cupcake. In every flame there is a small, black, empty space, and if you look at it long enough, it doesn't seem like fire at all.

'For she's a jolly good fellow, for she's a jolly good fellow ...'

This is not what we do here. We always stop our Happy Birthdays after the third 'to you'. Continuing feels perverted, punk almost. A way of saying, 'Hell, we can stand here and sing "Happy Birthday" on company time all day, who's going to stop us?'

I scan the room for the singer: Clem Brown. His brows are straight and very black, a little bushy where they meet his temples. He's the only middle-aged man I know who lets his hair grow past his ears.

But I don't know him, not really. He works with the copywriters, the graphic designers, the account people. I don't think we've ever spoken. I'm only ever in rooms that he is talking to. But here he is: singing for me. Singing *to* me.

'And so say all of us! And so say all of us!' He smiles, enjoying having so much control over a room that he can add an extra verse to 'Happy Birthday'. I wonder if he's doing this for fun, or whether he knows, somehow, that I need another minute to steady myself.

He's just fucking around, Jane. He doesn't even know your last name.

The two of us are the only people standing at full height – not sitting, not hunched over a printer, but straight and solid as playing cards – and it feels as though we are the only two people in the room. It takes Becky waving the cake in front of me for me to remember where I am, and to blow out the candle.

There is a card in the shape of a champagne bottle, and a bottle of cava on my desk. 'For later,' says Becky. There's a heat coming off her, an agitation that says, *Please, can you start eating the cupcake now?*

Clem is talking to someone else, but we keep making eye contact. He crosses his eyes in a pantomime of boredom, and for a second I feel like I'm back in school, getting tiny white pieces of paper flicked into my hair.

I eat half the cupcake, and hand the other half to Becky. Sometimes I suspect that I'm Becky's best friend. That's not a tragedy, exactly: Becky is a good person, and I like her – but she isn't Darla. Becky was moved to my desk two months ago, after Darla swapped departments to work in PR. Darla's actual job has changed very little, but something about her is shinier. She walks around with a refreshed sense of purpose, a notion that her new job is both one floor up and one level up a class system that she's invented in her own head. She is also wearing a lot of statement necklaces.

She calls me from her desk as soon as I sit down.

'Hey there, Birthday Girl,' Darla purrs. 'Hungover, are we?'

'It's my birthday week. I've earned it.'

I'm rolling my eyes, but she has a point. I have been drinking too much lately, and last night was an unfortunate example of how that can turn out. I reach for the day-old glass of water at my desk.

'There's no such thing as having a birthday week. You have a birthday *day*. You're not Celine Dion.'

'Why Celine Dion?'

'Dunno, just seems like she'd be pretty demanding, birthday-wise. Anyway, how did it go with Max last night?'

Becky is pretending not to listen. Darla misses nothing.

'I take it from your silence that y—'

'Are you taking me out tonight, or what?'

'Didn't we just agree that you've been drinking too much and should stop behaving like Celine Dion?'

'Yes, but today is my birthday day. Today being Celine Dion is appropriate.'

'All right,' she says, laughing. She's used to being the mouthy one, used to me going along with whatever plan she has set in motion. 'Piano Bar. I'll pick you up from your desk at six. And for God's sake, have something to eat beforehand. I don't want you vomming up your wine or bursting into tears.'

I open my inbox and watch the number of unopened emails wind upwards. A moment of hungover anxiety snaps at my ankles. Last night, at the Kasino club, pressed up against the slot machines with one of the Finance boys, the cartoon fruit dancing in my eyes as he stood behind me with both hands on my hips.

Did we dance? We may have danced.

Did we . . . ? I don't *think* so.

No – I was too busy planning how I was going to go home and trick Max into falling back in love with me, and I was only staying at Kasino so I could get drunk enough to work up the courage.

Not that it did much good.

I had taken my shoes off in the hallway, putting on a show of not wanting to wake him up, when that was exactly what I had come home for. I undressed in the bathroom, peeling my tights off, hiking my boobs upwards, tightening my bra straps so they dug into my shoulders.

'Go home,' Darla had said, when I called her in tears outside the club. 'Go home, and show him your lovely big mermaid tits, and remind him what a horndog you can be. You'll be back together by morning.'

He was in the living room, shirtless under a zipped-out sleeping bag. I stood in front of him in an orange bra and knickers that didn't quite match but at least were the same material.

'Hey,' he said.

'Hey back,' I replied, slurring my words a little. *Could he smell the vodka, the cigarettes I've started smoking again since he stopped being the one to stop me? Did he care?*

He looked at his watch. 'One thirty a.m.,' he said, trying to sound amused. 'Happy birthday.'

I lay down next to him, nudging his limbs so they were forced to cradle me, and inhaled the familiar, homey scent.

'Go back to your room,' he said, snatching his mouth away.

'*Our* room,' I stressed.

'Go back to our *old* room.'

I got up, mortified.

'I'm sorry I was a bitch to you,' I said, my voice cracking slightly. 'I'm sorry I am a bitch, but . . .'

'You're not a bitch. You just don't love me any more.'

I felt like he was trying to cut my wrists with safety scissors. I brought my hands to my eyes.

'Go to sleep, Jane.'

I did what he said, but slept naked in case he changed his mind. He didn't.

This is why I didn't want to sit down, I think. That's the trouble with memories: if you're still and sober, they have a better chance of finding you.

The excitement of my office birthday is quickly forgotten, and I try to lose myself in work. I am looking through six pages of focus-group testing to try to find a hook: something all the human lab rats are saying but not saying.

HOW DOES THE PRODUCT MAKE YOU FEEL?
ANSWER BELOW IN THE SPACE PROVIDED

<u>Clean</u>

CAN YOU ELABORATE ON THIS ANSWER?

<u>Very clean</u>

WOULD YOU BUY THIS PRODUCT IN THE SUPERMARKET? WHY OR WHY NOT?

<u>No, wife does washing</u>

On and on like this, someone half-heartedly filling in a questionnaire because they were promised a fiver and a custard cream at the end of it. Unimaginable sums of money are built on these answers. If enough people from the focus group say that it made them feel 'clean' then you can guess that the client will go with 'FEEL CLEAN' as the slogan.

I look around to make sure no one can see my screen, and log into JollyPolitely.com.

Dear Jolly,

My twin sister graduated as a doctor and is getting married next year. I would be happy for her – I AM happy for her – but my mother can't stop comparing us. I have a steady but unremarkable and badly paid job in the civil service, and am single. As you can probably guess, I don't come off that well in these comparisons.

It's not just my mum either: as soon as anyone finds out about my sister, my ordinary life suddenly seems like a massive failure. Do I need to take this as a nudge to improve my circumstances or do I need to stop mentioning my sister?

Yours,

Spinster Sister

When I was a kid my mum used to slip a letter under my door a few minutes after the clock struck midnight on my birthday. Usually it would be about the day I was born: what I looked like, what everyone thought of me, why they decided to name me Jane. (*The nurse said you would be tall*, she wrote once, *like Jane Russell.*) One time, she wrote about the day she found out she was pregnant.

I wasn't ready to be a mother, but I felt ready to have a friend.

She doesn't compare me to anyone because she doesn't have anyone to compare me to. When she married Paul she inherited two stepkids, two blonde bowl-cuts called Polly and Allie. Eight and ten then, fourteen and sixteen now. Their lives are a puzzle to her, I think. It's like she has walked into a living room where a movie is already playing, and there's no space for her to sit down. So, she hovers: *Oh, is that the guy from the Bond films? No? Why is he— Who's that? Okay.*

Dear Spinster Sister,

I couldn't care less about your sister. Honestly, she doesn't sound all that impressive. So she's engaged – anyone can be engaged. So she has a better and more meaningful job than you – do you know what you have? Weekends, and evenings on the couch, and the flexibility to not risk a human life every time you go to work. Meditate for a moment on how fabulous a life that is.

If there's one thing I've learned from answering strangers' problems on the internet, it's that people like to be reminded of how brilliant they are. It is the adult equivalent of going to see a shopping-centre Santa Claus. You have doubts about his legitimacy, sure, but once he's looking into your eyes and telling you that he's heard amazing things about you, you're sold. It doesn't matter that his beard is fake.

> Let's look at the rest of your letter. Here are some of the words you use to describe your life: Ordinary. Unremarkable. Failure. These are not the words of someone who is completely okay with how their life has turned out. Should you improve your circumstances? Maybe, yeah. Take a night class, or tell your mum you're taking a night class. Either will get her off your back for a bit.
>
> Also, if your friends think your sister is better than you, well, they can go be *her* friends. If I were your friend, I would sit on your couch and talk shit about your sister all day. I'm sure it can't be that hard to find other people like me.
> Love,
> Jolly Politely

I don't know if it's the right answer, or even the most appropriate answer. I don't have any qualifications for being Jolly. Some of my readers think she's a retired therapist, and some think she's a fourteen-year-old boy. I don't tell them anything.

After about an hour of answering letters, I start house-hunting on Gumtree. A part of me wants to believe that this thing with Max will blow over, and in the meantime I'm merely window shopping. This allows me to be picky and judgemental. One flat has a shower in the kitchen. There's a house that has six bedrooms and one toilet. A man who says he will let a woman live with him rent free, as long as she is beautiful and quiet and cooks well. I send that one to Darla, gleeful, and pretend I'm going to request a viewing.

I've never done this before. I moved to London when I was twenty-two, lived with some girls from uni for six months, and then moved in with Max three weeks after meeting him. He was twenty-six then, the same age I am today.

I hated our flat when I first moved in: all sharp edges and black furniture and chrome bathroom fixtures. It's near Canary Wharf, and maybe for that reason it reminded me of a high-class prostitute. You are not meant to love this flat. You are not meant to kiss this flat on the mouth. I sat on the hard sofa and I thought: *Someone has paid a lot of money to make you look this anonymous.*

I remember Max, in the doorway, the first time I went over. He had been living there a year, but his face when he saw my shopping bags, bursting with Lidl wine and Arborio rice told me that this was the first spark of clutter the flat had ever seen. I remember his eyes when I told him I would make him dinner, his mouth when he told me he had never had risotto before. His hands when he didn't know how to cut an onion properly.

'If you lived here, would you make me risotto every day?'

'Maybe,' I said. 'If you were good.'

'I would be good,' he said. Then he lifted my bra strap from where it had fallen, between my elbow and my shoulder, and placed it carefully in its rightful place. He kissed me on the curve of my neck. I was skinnier then, with elegant, protruding clavicles. We would both become softer and rounder over the next few years, our lives filling up with risotto and grated parmesan and bottles of white wine. 'Happy-fat,' I called it. We would tuck in our chubby limbs and sleep soundlessly next to one another like two strays who had been rescued and re-homed as a pair. We would discover what it was like to feel full.

A tight little tear falls to my keyboard, hitting the spacebar square in the middle. I rub my face, hoping I can limit it to just one drop. I will not be the girl who cried at work on her birthday.

Becky notices. Like it or not, Becky always notices. But for once, she knows the exact appropriate way to deal with this situation.

She clears her throat. 'Jane, do you have a minute? I need your eye on this.'

She leads me into an empty meeting room, and without one word passing between us, I burst into tears.

A few hours later, Becky, Darla and I are squeezed around a table for two. There's an enormous champagne bucket full of prosecco taking up almost all the table space, so we have to hold our glasses. We each take awkward, second-long micro-sips, our lips pursed tight. The Piano Bar tables are too close to the floor, so we're all sitting sideways, our legs sticking out like we're on a DVD cover for a show about interesting single women.

Darla is annoyed with me for inviting Becky. That's what you do, isn't it, after you've collapsed on your desk neighbour in a fit of vodka-infused tears? You invite them to have a drink with somebody who hates them.

Darla would jump in here and stress that she doesn't hate Becky, she just doesn't want to spend any of her spare time with her.

'Not enough people understand the distinction between work friends and *friends who you also work with*,' she would say. I know this, because she's said it a million times – fag in hand, aghast that not everyone understands the myriad informal social cues that she has invented.

'People need to understand the difference. I'm more than willing to grab a sandwich with a work friend, but there are very few people at Mitchell who I want to hang around with after work or at the weekends. Maybe I need to start handing out badges, to let the work friends know. Not everyone can be a weekend friend.'

'What do you think all that was about earlier, then?' I say to Becky, who has been twitchy since we got here. 'With Clem Brown singing?'

I'm partly trying to make conversation, but I'm also still dazzled by the gesture. After my cry in the meeting room, the image of him standing, singing – to me, for me, at me – was the first one that settled in my mind.

'Sorry, who?' says Darla.

'Clem Brown. You know, he works in—'

'I know who he is. I mean, what was he doing singing to you?'

'He sort of picked up on the "Happy Birthday" song. Did the extra verse. The "jolly good fellow" bit.'

'You know what they say about him?' she says, after a second. 'HUGE flirt.'

'I've never heard that.'

'Well, you wouldn't, would you?'

She has a point. Underneath everyday Mitchell, there's Single Person's Mitchell. The single, glamorous, most attractive members of staff who spend every Thursday night in one of the terrible clubs on Carnaby Street, and who seem to operate via an information black market of kiss-and-tells. I haven't been single since I joined Mitchell, so much of what

happens on these Thursdays is a mystery to me. But something about Darla's tone makes me think that this is less about
Clem, and more about someone else receiving attention that
she hasn't coordinated, and on the floor she used to work
on. Darla doesn't suffer from Fear Of Missing Out so much
as a Rejection Of Missing Out: if she wasn't there, then it
didn't happen.

'When does she start singing?' Becky asks, twisting in her
seat, searching for the performer, the living jukebox who
sings old hits every night while standing uncomfortably close
to you. 'I can't wait to see what she sings.'

'She doesn't start till later, usually,' says Darla, seeing her
chance. 'So if you've got somewhere to be . . . '

With that, the singer stands up and starts belting out 'Life
on Mars'. Becky's face lights up. She looks like the inside of
an orange, the very moment after you cut it in half.

'Oh, I love this one. It's so sad, isn't it, him being dead? I
know he wasn't really our generation, so it feels a bit false to
act very sad about the whole thing. But I remember, when
my dad used to sing "For the Longest Time" when I was
little. And when I heard that he'd died, I just cried and cried,
thinking about my dad singing that song.'

'That's a Billy Joel song.'

'What?'

'The Longest Time.' Darla turns to me, a smile rippling
across her face. She looks into my eyes like a long-lost lover,
grabbing my hand in faux-desperation, and starts to sing.

'Woah-oh-oh, for the longest time.'

We giggle, and Darla – being Darla – takes it as encourage-
ment. She keeps singing, keeps clutching me, and commits
fully to being Billy Joel. She talk-sings about her innocence
being gone, and how happiness does indeed go on. Another
hot, choking cry rises through me like spit before vomit.

She wraps her arms around me, and sings over my shoulder,

her body heavy with devotion. I sink into her, happy to be in the arms of the last person in London who loves me.

I tell her then, with her black hair brushing my cheeks, the thing I have been too afraid to tell anyone. I whisper it to stop my voice from cracking.

'He met someone else.'

Her head moves sharply to Becky, to make sure she's not listening, then back at me.

'What?' she says, disgusted. 'What? Max? That's why you broke up? Because he's fucking somebody else?'

I nod, but even I know that's not the whole story.

'Her name is Kim. He says they haven't done anything yet, but that they want to.'

'Oh, Jane,' Darla says. She's not afraid to hold me for a moment and say nothing.

She pulls away and puts her hands on my face.

'Let's get fucked up.'

With that, Darla drops her coldness with Becky, and Becky's nervous talking dries up as a result. We drink, and we make friends with strangers. We sing loudly, and badly, and happily. There are moments when I think: *This is better. This is better than staying with a man you don't love, just to feel the other side of the mattress sag.*

Every few minutes some newfound friend of Darla's grabs me by the arm. 'So it's *your* birthday,' they say. 'How old are you?' And I tell them, and they shake their heads and say how I'm only a baby, and how it makes them sick to think about it.

We relocate. We find ourselves at a bar, then another bar, and before I know it we're in a burger bar and it's one in the morning. I turn to Becky and Darla, grinning with deep, meaty joy. I want to tell them I love them. I want to tell them I need them.

'I am buying your food,' I announce, gesturing with my debit card. 'Because I love you. And because it's my birthday, and I'm an adult, and when one is an adult, one pays the bill. One entertains their friends. One holds exquisite dinner parties in the middle of crowded restaurants.'

I head to the counter and I see a familiar head in front of me in the queue.

Max.

Without thinking, I pounce. I do that thing when you try to surprise someone from behind by pretending to be a mugger.

'BOO!'

He spins around, panicked, and then relaxes into a new state of unease. 'Jane,' he says uncertainly. *'Jane.'* He tugs a woman into view, and I am dimly aware of her saying hello.

Max is *with* someone. And then, as a dark yellow queasiness rises through my body, I realise that Max is with the woman that he left me for, four days earlier. This is Kim, Kim is real, and mere feet away from me, accompanying my boyfriend to a burger restaurant on the night of his ex-girlfriend's birthday.

'Oh, uh, hello,' I say, and some crude and masochistic element of my emotional make-up forces me to stick my hand out and shake hers. 'I'm Max's ex-girlfriend but we still live together. We don't have sex, though.'

Kim's eyes widen. Did I want her to look like me? Maybe. Maybe so I could say: He couldn't handle me, so he got a no-fuss model. So I could say: Well, he certainly has a *type.* But she looks nothing like me, although she doesn't look enough *not* like me for it to be interesting. I can't say: He must have been sick of my shit, so he went for my opposite. So I can't think: *Well, I was one of a kind.*

She looks like an ordinary twenty-something woman in the way I look like one. She has too many coats of mascara on, so her lashes are spidery and brittle under the restaurant's strip lighting. Her mouth is the kind of mouth that only happens when you apply lip-liner, and an undercoat, and then blot with a piece of tissue paper like grown-up women do. It's a first-date mouth. It's an 'I'm meeting someone' mouth.

'I know,' she says. 'I think it's great how you guys are managing to get on while you sort your living arrangements out.'

'It is.' I smile gamely. 'It really is. So great.'

Silence hangs between the three of us, a moment of mutual appraisal, to size up what role everyone is playing. Who is the drunkest? Me. Who is the most awkward? Max. Who is going to tell her friends later about her horrible date with that new guy she's seeing? Kim.

'I have to go now,' I say. 'For ever. Goodbye. Enjoy your date.'

I whip by my table and bundle my coat and bag into one hand.

'Max is here. I'm going. I love you. I hate me. Bye.'

I run onto the street, lighting a cigarette and tugging my jacket on as I go. My name is being shouted behind me.

'JANE.'

I keep walking.

'JAAAANE. TALK TO ME. PLEASE.'

I turn around and there he is. Hands in his pockets, beard trimmed to a perfect right angle around his jawline. Max has new trainers on.

'Do you want to share a cab?'

Me and my partner have been together for two years and have always had sex with a condom. Now we're moving in together and he wants me to go on the pill. Only thing is I have the herpes virus and I don't want to give it to him in case he gets mad and dumps me. What do I do?

Max may have signed the death warrant on our relationship, but I was the surgeon who butchered us. It's hard to know when it started, except that one day I began to hate him. Or, at least, I acted like I hated him. If I had known how to stop, I would have. If I had known how to push the growing black contempt to the bottom of myself, I would have done it. But it was like I couldn't help myself: when I wasn't criticising him, I was ignoring him. When I wasn't raising a condescending eyebrow at his work stories, I was picking a fight over nothing.

There isn't a court in the country that would convict him for fucking someone else.

I let him get in the cab with me, and we both pretend like Kim was never there. I turn her over in my mind endlessly, though, committing her appearance to memory. *She's thinner than me*, I think. The 'happy-fat' that Max had told me never to worry about — the curves that made me softer, sexier, plusher — seems to expand in the taxi, rising like dough as we sit in silence.

When we get home, I try not to embarrass myself.

'I'm not going to try to have sex with you again,' I say. 'And I want you to know that it wasn't your fault, what happened. I know it's a cliché to say it, and I know it doesn't count because you broke up with me, but — it really wasn't you. It was me. I'm the one who wasn't right for this relationship. I don't know why, but I wasn't. Maybe I'm too young to be in a serious thing. Maybe I'm too young to feel married. I—'

I sway a little, and keep one hand on the door frame to steady myself. I'm confident that I'm doing a good job until, moments after the word 'married', I run to the bathroom and vomit into the toilet bowl.

As I hobble to my feet, I feel another warm pool of spit form in the corner of my jaw. A warning that more, much more, is on its way.

I slump on the bathroom floor, and Max scrapes the hair off my face, rubbing my back very gently. I vomit. We manage to laugh a little, between retches, and I think: if I were a film director, I would use this shot. I would zoom out on us on the tiles, letting the open door frame us, letting the darkness of the flat surround the scene as I zoom out further and further, until we are two dots in the middle of the picture. It feels like the perfect way to signify the end of my relationship with Max, and it is, because in the morning he is gone and a week later I move out.

2

Dear Herpes,

I assume you have already explored the idea of lying to your boyfriend – or partner, as you call him, which is very grown up of you. For this approach, your options are limited: you can say you went to a public swimming pool and picked it up, or sat on a dodgy bus seat, or disposed of cotton buds unhygienically. There are any number of false and disgusting ways you could pick up genital herpes. Be creative!

Why have you avoided telling him this very basic thing about yourself? Nowadays, STDs are incredibly common, even a little glamorous. If I had one, I'd be shouting about it from the rooftops, telling everyone about my adventurous unprotected sex. My guess is that you have always felt on the back foot with your partner: maybe you have always felt like he was a little better than you, a little smarter, a little richer, a smidge out of your league. So, you've been hiding your imperfections from him. You've been putting up a barrier, both physically (TWO YEARS and you're still using condoms?) and emotionally (what, you were NEVER going to tell him about the herpes?), hoping he'll never see who you are. My guess is that you feel a little bit like an impostor, and have never fully relaxed into this relationship.

Let your guard down. Be honest about yourself. Let him see the real you, even if the real you is literally riddled with herpes.

Love,

Jolly Politely

On the second Saturday after I move out of Max's flat, I decide to go for a walk. *I'll go somewhere new. I'll have an adventure.* I walk, and walk, and walk, and try to take deep, long breaths while I do it.

Can you be homesick when your home isn't yours any more? I moved into my new flat two weeks ago, and I can't get over the gnawing feeling that I am in the wrong place, and that whoever is in charge of writing *The Jane Show* is temporarily off sick. The story of my life for the past four years has been a rotation of Max and work, work and Max. Now I live in a two-bed with a woman who I'm only 90 per cent certain is called Shiraz.

'Shiraz. Nice to meet you. Bathroom's here. Bathmat needs hanging up after every shower or the tiles rot. Water pressure is shit but you get used to it.'

'Shiraz? Like the wine?'

'No.'

I've tried looking at her post to determine how she spells Shiraz (maybe it's just 'Shaz'? Maybe it's 'Sharon'?) but it all just says S. COLE. I haven't said her name since because I know I'll say it like the wine and I don't want to, because she scares me. I hang up the bathmat every time.

Shiraz (?) is out almost every night, so on the nights I'm not at the pub I poke around, trying to get used to the place. Her flat looks like the set of a nineties sitcom, in that there are magazines fanned artfully on coffee tables and big, silk flowers in bigger ceramic vases. In essence, it's a woman's flat, but it has a curious lack of personal items that might make it a *girl's* flat. There are no photo collages of friends, no clutter of ASOS soon-to-be-returned items. Everything is neatly tucked away with feminine precision. A man wouldn't mind living here, but he isn't supposed to want to.

I don't even want to live there, I think, the back of my legs straining as I descend Telegraph Hill.

At weekends, Shiraz goes into full nest mode. She cleans out the fridge, scrubs the bathtub, stands in front of a Pilates DVD and does all the things you're supposed to do if you're an adult, except I always assumed that no one actually did them. I've been hiding in my room, laptop under my chest, tackling the large task of watching everything on Netflix. I started with the romantic comedies. That's what you do when you stop living with a man: you watch all the things he's never in the mood for. So I blitzed the classics first, the Nora Ephron ones that even cynics acknowledge are classics: *When Harry Met Sally, You've Got Mail,* that kind of thing. After that, the quality started to drop off. I cried at *Maid in Manhattan.* I went on Kate Hudson's IMDb page and downloaded pretty much all of her movies from the early noughties, the ones where Matthew McConaughey looks like the human equivalent of a cheesy Dorito. Before I knew it, I was watching *Legally Blonde 3* with a bottle of Pinot next to me.

I've been regular with my Jolly columns, at least. I got about a hundred comments on my response to the Herpes Woman. Even though a few weeks have passed since I published my answer, it seems to find life on other communities: it pops up on Tumblr and Reddit, and then debates branch off on their own, like immigrant children of the original discussion. Some of them link back to my blog, and I got more hits that week than any other week for the last year.

I let Jolly's victory over herpes stroke my ego a bit, refreshing the page again and again while walking. *Look, Jane*, I tell myself as I scroll through the fan comments, stopping at the ones that praise me and my wisdom, *these people are talking because of you. You're doing okay, really.*

This is the most useful thing, I think, about having an online alter ego with a somewhat significant following: the readers make the bad days feel a lot less awful.

My legs are getting tired, but I'm impressed at how far I've walked. I'm at Tower Bridge now. A crowd of tourists let out a collective 'ahhhhhh' as the bridge rises to let a boat through. The pigeons, gathered by the bridge and fighting over a chicken nugget, flutter upwards in the commotion, startling everyone.

During my first year of university, an art student fed some pigeons a bag of popping candy until their stomachs exploded. We waited for someone to do something, for someone to get expelled, but nothing ever happened, and for two days the campus grounds were covered in feathers and bird parts. I washed my hands in the Student Union toilets and something wet, round and calloused slipped between my fingers, skidding around the enamel of the bowl. I looked up what it was: *gizzard*. I held it in the palm of my hand for a long time before flushing it down the toilet.

People at my uni were always doing inexplicable things for fun, and if not for fun, then to be ironic, and if not to be ironic, then to just exist. And that's one thing you could say for Jolly Politely: she *existed* to people right away. Her first appearance was in my uni newspaper. I wrote advice columns in response to letters I had written myself. I pretended to be a professor with a madly obsessive crush on one of my students, and I dropped obvious, scandalous hints as to who the professor might be. I invented questions about Facebook etiquette, and one-night stands, and disappointed parents, and

by the time my fifth column had been published, I was starting to get more invested in the answers than the questions.
I invented Jolly in a bid to seem clever, but it was her heart
that people wanted, and it was my heart that people got. It
seemed, at the time, to be more useful inside her chest than
in my own.

I pause at a pedestrian crossing near Trafalgar Square, completely baffled at where to turn next. What was I doing in
Central London? If you're not a tourist and you don't have a
boyfriend to drag around a museum, what was there *for* you
in this city?

A couple stand outside the National Gallery, poring over
an extendable brochure. I wait to feel something, some loss,
but it doesn't come.

Truthfully: I don't miss Max. I don't long for his touch or
call him and hang up or contemplate what a mistake I made.
What I do miss, however, is the space in my life that Max
took up. It's easy to fill a weekend in London when you're
a couple. You wake up late. You lounge around. You fail at
making poached eggs. If you're feeling ambitious, maybe
you go to the Natural History Museum or Columbia Road
Flower Market. Or you see your other couple friends. We had
three other couples that we saw on rotation, and I sometimes
felt like we just met up with them to talk afterwards about
how much superior our relationship was. 'Did you see the
way she orders him around?' 'Did you notice him looking at
the waitress?' 'Do they seem happy?' It occurred to me only
during the final weeks of our relationship that the other couples were probably doing the same thing.

I'm outside the door of my office building, perplexed as to
how I got here. That's the thing about London, I guess. No
matter what you do or how many museums you visit, you'll
never escape the instinct that you are here to work.

I don't know what else to do, so I go inside. They keep it

open twenty-four hours a day, a casual reminder that there's no such thing as being too dedicated. The security guard is Skyping his relatives as he nods me in. I switch on my computer and look at my Jolly emails.

> Dear Jolly Politely,
>
> Last year I had a miscarriage, and ever since I have been terrified of getting pregnant again. My husband still wants to try, and my doctors tell me that there's no reason I shouldn't have a healthy baby. Ever since we started having sex again, however, I've had nightmares. They always start the same: I'm eight months pregnant, and the baby starts eating me from the inside. I think it's cramps, or I'm about to go into labour, but then I realise too late that the baby is eating my heart and liver and lungs and my body goes into shutdown. I am awake before the baby is born but lately the dream has developed. Now, I have an emergency Caesarean section and when it's born the baby is Paul Dano from *Little Miss Sunshine.*

I start laughing at my desk. I can't help it. I Google Paul Dano to make sure I have the right actor: yes, that one, with the bowl cut who was in *There Will Be Blood.* It's all too bizarre and sad, and I'm cackling at my desk when Clem Brown rounds the corner.

'Jane?'

'Oh. Hello,' I say, and minimise my screen quickly. 'What are you doing here?'

'I come in on Saturdays sometimes. Get a jump on the week while it's quiet. Plus I can rummage through everyone's desks for snacks and spare batteries.'

I smile, and he waits for me to explain what I'm doing here.

'Me too,' I say, and luckily there are some printouts of

focus-group research on my desk. 'I was just laughing at this guy's answer.'

'Is this what you do, then? Go through info from focus groups?'

'It's *part* of what I do.'

'What else do you do?'

He is genuinely interested. I stiffen at the memory of his birthday song: *For she's a jolly good fellow.*

'I . . . send a lot of emails? And I try to propose ideas based on what I find in the focus groups?'

'What do you mean, "try"?'

His insistence is making me uncomfortable: like I have suddenly acquired a TED talk that I haven't asked for.

'I mean, no one usually listens to my ideas because I'm only an account exec.'

'Ah. Well. We'll see,' he says, and then bonks me on the nose with the top of his pencil. It's an odd little gesture, because he isn't touching me exactly. But it's intrusive and intimate, like his 'Happy Birthday' song to me. Could the 'jolly good fellow' thing be a coincidence, or is he senior enough to have access to my internet history? And if he does, why does he care?

'Hey,' I say, 'you sang to me.'

'Pardon?'

'You sang me the end of "Happy Birthday" – the "jolly good fellow" bit.'

He looks at me blankly. Maybe he doesn't know about Jolly, then.

'It was a few weeks ago,' I say. 'The second of June.'

'No, no, I remember. So how old were you?'

'Twenty-six.'

'Not so very old, then.'

'Old enough.'

I don't know why I say it, but immediately there's an

atmosphere. Old enough for *what*, Jane? I blurted out the first thing that came to mind, but it came out sounding flirty, almost, and far too forthcoming to a man who's old enough to be my father.

'Right,' he says, and after an awkward pause he leaves me alone and staring at my computer. I blink at it until I'm sure he's gone, and then leave.

Back at my desk on Monday, I have an email from Deb in the New Business department, asking me to be on a pitch for Fat Eddie, an oven pizza brand, and to join their first pitch meeting. Today.

'WHAT?'

'What's up?' Becky asks.

'They've invited me on a pitch, Becky.'

'Oh my *God*,' she says, her hands flying to her face. 'That's huge, Jane. Huge.'

For once, she's not exaggerating. A pitch is how Mitchell feels people out. The obstacle course that usually happens before a promotion or a pay rise.

'Why do you think they've asked you, then?'

'I don't know, Becky, maybe because I'm good at my fucking job?'

I sound like Darla at her worst, and I feel guilty, but I can't help but be irritated.

'I'm sorry, Becky. I'm just on my period,' I say, truthfully. 'I'm a bitch today.'

I wave a tampon wrapper in her face to prove it, and Becky smiles, happy to be friends again.

Period aside: I *am* amazed they have asked me. When I joined Mitchell, I had expected creativity and glamour, and lots of artful slouching around on beanbags with bearded men. I bulldozed into meetings, convinced that the secret to success was having lots and lots of ideas. I realised – maybe because someone told me, or maybe I picked it up from the stony responses to my over-eager suggestions – that while there's no such thing as a bad idea, there is very much such a thing as an unqualified one. And the people who were qualified to have ideas at Mitchell had no interest in adding me to their ranks.

After six months, I stopped trying so hard. After a year, I started phoning in my suggestions. Two years and one break-up later, my work barely scrapes 'adequate'. The pitch meeting is at 2 p.m., and I use my lunch hour to go into Boots to buy some tampons and lipstick. I'm the first person in the meeting room, until Deb walks in. She's the head of New Business, and the only woman in the agency to have her own department. She has been on maternity leave twice in the last four years and somehow hasn't let go of an inch of her power, despite the fact that almost everyone senior at Mitchell is gunning for her job. I want to know how she does it.

A few copywriters – the people, I remember with vague embarrassment, who used to roll their eyes whenever I spoke in meetings – trickle in, heads together, talking about Tinder. I pretend to make notes, but can't think of anything, so I start making lists of everything I have in the fridge at home. This is when David Lady arrives.

David Lady is sexy, but in a specific sort of way. He looks strong, but not the kind of strong that seems practised or self-conscious. He doesn't have any muscle definition to speak of, but strikes me as the sort of guy you would call if you needed to lift a grandfather clock. His nose is a little crooked and his hair isn't complicated, which I like, because men's hair has become far too complicated over the last couple of years.

I have had a crush on David Lady for just over a year. If I'm honest, it started when I fell out of love with Max. 'You're like a monkey,' Mum had laughed, when I confessed my feelings to her over wine. 'You don't want to let go of one branch until you have your hand on another.'

He sits opposite me and gives me a tiny man nod, the kind that's more like a nod in reverse, where his chin bobs upwards and I can see the stubble on his neck. There's something about him that makes me wonder whether I've shaved my legs lately, and whether he would notice or care if I hadn't. I press my knees together, bare under my summer skirt, as if trying to convince an imaginary nun that I'm not thinking about having sex with him.

I try to look anywhere but directly at him, and open up Jolly again on my phone.

> Now, I have an emergency Caesarean section and when it's born the baby is Paul Dano from *Little Miss Sunshine*. I don't know what any of this means but I don't know how to stop it. How can I put my fear aside and just try again?
> Little Miscarriage Sunshine

I start talking to her in my head, and I pretend she's my mum in the days after Dad left: both of her hands wrapped around the blue mug she liked best, hoping for a smile or a joke or the answer. I pretend that she is the one haunted by the ghost of Paul Dano.

> Dear Little Miscarriage Sunshine,
> I can tell by your brilliant sign-off that you're fully aware of how dually tragic and hilarious this all is. That's what makes me think we could be friends. If you don't mind, I'm going to treat you as if we are friends.
> My darling, I'm so sorry. You've had an awful year, one you do not deserve, but one you have got on with anyway. I have never had a miscarriage, nor tried to be pregnant, but I do know what it's like to be one thing

and then very suddenly be another. I was a girlfriend, then I was an ex-girlfriend. I had a beautiful flat, then I had no flat. It takes adjustment. You had a life inside you and now that life is gone. You shouldn't be expected to move along and be cool about a new baby. As I say: it takes adjustment. You are doing fine. You are making jokes. You are dealing with it.

I don't know a lot about the actor Paul Dano but when I go on his Wikipedia page it says that his 'trademark' is that he 'often plays characters who receive beatings'. I don't know how much I believe in dream interpretation, and I don't know who compiles Wikipedia pages, but nonetheless: you are beating yourself up, and you are using the actor Paul Dano to do it. It makes me think that you might blame yourself for what happened, and maybe you're as afraid of the idea of your own failure as you are of miscarrying again. This always sounds like a cop-out coming from agony aunts, but even so: maybe you should talk to a therapist.

Godspeed, pal. I'll be thinking of you.

Love,

Jolly Politely

As I sign off, Clem walks in, which means the meeting has started. Everyone sits up straighter, except Deb, who is still writing an email and hasn't noticed. I look from Clem to David and back again. David is stocky and fair, like the eldest son on a farm. He's very much 'my type', as Darla is fond of saying: sunny, open-faced, playful. Clem, meanwhile, has something that edges, very slightly, into femininity. He reminds me of an old issue of *Jackie* my mum had saved, with a thirty-five-year-old Mick Jagger on the cover. 'Isn't it weird, the way they pushed this adult *man* on teenage girls?' I asked once. 'It was the late seventies,' she said, as if that were the answer to everything.

Clem flicks a presentation on to the screen: a picture of six rather sickly looking pizzas. Pizzas where the cheese sags like melted plastic. I remember these pizzas: they're the same brand that Max and I called 'our guilty pleasure' when we were happy, and what I just called 'guilt' when we weren't. I remember eating an entire one in the bathtub after a two-day-long sulk.

'Ta–dah,' he says.

An audible sigh falls over the room.

'All right, all right. Not glamorous. Fine. I know. But Fat Eddie happens to be a subsidiary of a major Italian food chain, so if we impress them on this, we might get invited to pitch for the whole company. I'm talking penne. Pesto. I'm talking blue cheese, guys.'

It's amazing how many conversations at Mitchell go like this. The agency mainly specialises in food advertising, so we talk about cheese and sausages as though they were fossil fuels.

Deb, having finally looked up from her phone, is ready to speak. 'And once you have cheese, it puts the agency in a brand-new category. It will allow us to go after Big Dairy. Not just milks either. *Yogurt*.' She looks at me, as if to say: *You're the only other woman in this room, and you* will *get off on the notion of yogurt.*

'So this is actually a big one, even if it doesn't seem like a big one,' continues Clem. 'Let's start off with some word association. Everyone's going to tell me what they think of when they think of Fat Eddie.' He gestures to the first copywriter, the one sitting next to him.

'Microwaveable pizzas,' he says, bored and Northern.

Clem writes it on the whiteboard and moves onto the second copywriter, who is beardy and always wears a baseball cap. More mumbling.

It's Deb's turn next. 'They're not mum-friendly. They're stuffed with E numbers and the packaging is so clunky that it makes them a freezer liability.'

The men in the room look at her, puzzled. She lets out an exasperated sound. 'Freezer space is a big thing for mothers. Every frozen item in the supermarket is fighting with a jumbo pack of ice lollies, not to mention frozen meat and fish.'

This is a power play from Deb, and it's beautiful. Deb doesn't apologise for being a mum. I've seen women let slip their children's names and then cover their hands over their mouths immediately, as if trying to grab the words and stuff them back in. When you ask them what they did at the weekend, they lower their voice to just above a whisper, as if they are secret junkies: 'You know, mum stuff.'

Not Deb, though. She uses her motherhood as a point of difference, never letting anyone forget that she is one of the most desirable advertising demographics in existence: the wealthy white mother. She flaunts her motherhood, but she doesn't let it soften her. She invents phrases like 'freezer liability', and she makes them sound like they're something everybody says.

Clem writes it up with a slightly pained expression on his face, as if he's already bored of having to consider 'mum' opinions.

I am too busy studying Deb when it's my turn to say something about Fat Eddie pizzas. Everything about how shit they are has kind of been said already.

'I wouldn't eat them . . .' I begin, and the room takes my pause as a sign I'm about to say something brilliant. Even though I'm only about five or seven pounds over my usual weight, I feel doughier than the pizza I'm trying to pretend I don't eat. The 'happy-fat' I gained with Max in my early twenties – which, let's face it, wasn't fat at all, but hips and an ass – was expanding, settling and saddening. 'Unless I was depressed.'

This is the only comment that is not written on the board. I try not to look hurt, but Clem picks up on it anyway.

'Before we begin,' he says, gesturing to the room but looking straight at me, 'I want to make sure everyone knows Jane Peters. She's worked with focus groups, so she'll be our codebreaker for the next couple of weeks, when it comes to audience insights.'

I can't help but feel grateful. A *codebreaker*. Like I'm one of the women in Bletchley Park, and not an aimless 26-year-old who gave up being interested in this job over a year ago. I want nothing more than to prove that I'm not the jam-faced idiot I was when I joined Mitchell two years ago. I want to prove to myself that I'm not the recently dumped daughter of a broken home, trying to convince herself that she's worthwhile by keeping an anonymous blog. I want to stand up in front of my snobby colleagues and tell them to go fuck themselves. I don't want to tread water any more. I want to be brilliant.

'Oh,' Clem adds, his eyes still on me, 'and she loves it when you sing to her.'

3

Darla still lives with her parents, and she knows how that sounds. She will occasionally refer to her family as 'the people I live with'. I don't blame her for not moving out: I've been to Darla's house, and I'd struggle to leave a fridge with that much expensive yogurt in it. But despite her freedom, and despite her Muslim parents turning a blind eye to what Darla gets up to, she still chooses to do Ramadan every year. This year, it's in June, so Darla starts working through her lunch hour so she can leave a little earlier.

It's Ramadan, then, that is indirectly responsible for me dropping a bowl of soup on David Lady's shoes.

I start bringing lunch to work, thinking that I can save money while Darla abstains. I'm taking my soup out of the office microwave and trying to do it with two paper towels, which I know before I've started is a rookie error. Everything from this microwave comes out either cold or burning hot, and this time it's the latter. I yelp, my fingers slip through the towels, and it's only then that I see David Lady behind me, and only then do I ruin his shoes.

He doesn't say anything, but he has a face. It is not a good face.

'Oh, fuck. I'm so sorry. I'm a tit. I'm a useless tit. Let me help you,' I say, daubing him uselessly with more towels.

'No, no. It's fine. You're not a tit.'

'I am. I'm a useless fucking tit. I'm so sorry. Let me . . . '

'Buy you new shoes?'

'I was thinking more in the buying you lunch territory.'

'Shoes AND lunch? You're very spendy for a useless tit.'

We smile. He takes off his shoes, runs them under the sink and we walk to the sandwich place while he's still in his socks. I can feel myself nurturing the crush on him I had developed when Max and I were still together. I am already turning this whole incident into an anecdote to be told and retold later in our imagined relationship. I would tell him how embarrassed I was, and he would tell me how he wasn't mad, not really, and that he thought it was cute. I would say: *I can't believe you walked shoeless to get a sandwich with me.* And he would say: *I would have walked over hot coals.* I would say: *Or soup.* And he would kiss me and say: *Yes, darling. Or soup.*

In the meantime, however, I can't think of one single thing to say to David Lady. I have our future relationship all figured out, but our present is a total mystery.

'How do you think the pitch is coming along, then?'

'Oh. You know,' he says, while sorting through the rubbish sandwiches. 'They're all the same, really. I only took this one to work with Clem.'

'Is he good, then?'

'You haven't worked with him before?'

'Not much.'

'Well, you must have done something to impress him.' He picks up a falafel wrap and hands it to me, giving me a look like 'are you sure you want to buy this for me?' and I nod and take it. 'He tends to work with the same four or five people over and over again. He's tough, and he makes everyone stay late, but he usually wins the pitch in the end. Good to be on the winning team.'

'I've never been invited on a pitch before.'

'Well, there you go then. This is going to be great experience for you.'

A few people have said this, but it's been a week, and so far I've not had much to contribute to the pitching process. I never have anything good to say, so I take very good notes instead. This is probably for the best, as Clem tends to ask for ideas and then immediately give a bulletproof reason why they would never work.

As we make our way back to the office, we find more to talk about. There's a gentle confidence to David Lady, which is amazing, considering how much a man with the last name 'Lady' might be tempted to overcompensate with his masculinity. I had never noticed before, but he has a slight Northern lilt to his voice, one that lets the middle of his words bubble upwards when he's happy. When I ask him about it, he smiles.

'My mam's from Sunderland. She moved back there when she left my dad when I was small, but I still spent all my summers there. No one ever notices, though.'

'Well, I did.'

'You did,' he says. 'I'd say you notice a lot of things, don't you?'

I don't know what this means, so I just smile back. 'My dad moved away when I was younger, too. To Switzerland. Here's to our broken homes, I guess.'

'And did you go there for holidays? To Switzerland?'

'No.' I wonder how to phrase it without bringing down the tone of the conversation. 'No, I never did.'

He nods, and in that moment, we've started something. We've made our first trade of private information, our first step towards intimacy. He walks me back to my desk. Where, even more surprisingly, Clem is sitting.

'Oh hello, you *two*,' he says. I blush horribly. He nods a hello at David and shows me a thick, stapled document. 'I wanted to give you this. See what you can get from it.'

'What is it?'

'It's a detailed profile of the Fat Eddie customer. What they like, what they don't like, what their wives think of them.'

'Because every person who eats a frozen pizza is a man whose wife has gone out for the evening?'

I mean it in a playful way, but it comes out sounding irate. And maybe I am a little annoyed: after all, pathetic food is a human right we all enjoy. David looks uncomfortable, and Clem looks not in the mood.

'Do you want to go through it, type up the main points of interest?'

It's posed like a question, but really it's an instruction. His tone says: *Do this now, please.*

David goes back to his desk, thanking me for lunch. Clem lingers.

'New friend?' he asks, gesturing to David.

I shrug. 'I spilled soup on his shoes.'

'Ah. That old ploy.' He rolls up the paper and bonks it on my nose, like he did with the pencil before. 'Try not to go spilling soup about too much. We have a pitch to work on.'

I'm in the office until 8 p.m., going through the document for Clem. It's boring work, but methodical in a comforting sort of way, like rearranging your bookshelves. Plus, there's nothing to go home for. Last night I drank a whole bottle of wine in bed with an ease that frightened me. So I highlight, and make notes, and type them up. I feel like a model citizen, and wonder if this new gap in my life – this Max-shaped hole that seems impossible to fill – could be taken up by a dazzling new career. I think: *Maybe it's okay to not be passionate about something if you're really, really good at it.*

And I am capable of being good. I know that, or I at least suspect it. The people who read Jolly seem to trust her entirely, but I've somehow never been able to turn Jolly into a transferable skill. Every now and then, I consider putting her on my CV as evidence that, if nothing else, people listen to me. But I can't imagine being Jolly if I knew people were reading it, knowing I was Jane. It would ruin the whole thing.

I don't think Clem ever goes home. He always wears the same sort of clothes – a black overcoat, a black T-shirt, jeans – and I begin to think his clothes are simple so he can keep a stash of identical T-shirts under his desk. I wander into the kitchen to make myself a tea, and find him at the table, his coat perpetually draped over the other chair, papers in front of him. He orders Thai food and asks if I want any. I say no, still conscious of my Fat Eddie misery pounds.

'You must be starving,' he says.

'I'm really okay,' I say.

Even so, when his food comes he makes me up a plate, a baby-sized portion of Pad Thai with one delicate summer roll on the side. 'It's too boring to eat alone,' he says and I join him, moving his coat off the chair. As I fold it over a nearby desk, I catch the smell of him: cologne on deodorant on shampoo on what must be his natural scent. Spice and citrus and wood, heat and hair oil and skin.

This is what you smell like.

'So,' he says, like a child king waiting to be entertained. 'What's your story?'

'What, professionally?'

He moves his chopsticks in circles in the air. 'Generally.'

'I don't know. I'm not sure.'

I realise, with no small degree of self-pity, that I am telling the truth. 'I'm enjoying the pitch, though.'

He laughs. 'Are you?'

'Sure. I'm not sure why I'm on it, exactly, but I'm grateful to be getting the experience.'

'Why not? You're old enough.'

I blush then, and he smiles at me like he knows that I've been kicking myself for that weird 'old enough' comment. It's not nasty, though: it's more like he remembers how easy it is to say odd things when you're nervous, because he was once nervous himself.

'I see you in the meetings, you know. Hiding. You've been hiding here for two years, by the look of things.'

I must seem wounded, because he touches me on the shoulder, reassuring me.

'Because, you know, you see someone at work on a Saturday, and you think, *Why haven't I heard about this hardworking young woman? Who is hiding her away from me, this girl that comes in on a weekend?* So I found your file – sure you were some kind of rising star – and you've not so much as had a raise since you started here.'

I don't know how to feel, or how to respond. It feels like he's complimenting me and insulting me in the same breath. Jolly would call this kind of behaviour 'negging'. She would say that Clem is trying to make me feel insecure so I'll rely on him for compliments. It's not a bad way to manage a new employee, I suppose.

'Well . . .' I say, groping for some kind of explanation for my uninspiring career. 'I graduated in a recession, so that was a whole thing.'

He waits for something better. I dig down in the weeds and pull something up for him.

'I guess I don't really know what I'm *for*. What I'm doing here, I mean. In this agency. Or in life. Hah.'

He nods. 'I felt that way. For a long time, actually. But you know, if you keep at it, people notice. And once people notice you, things have a way of . . .'

'Falling into place?'

'No. Not that.'

He does this. I've seen him do it with other people. He

leaves his sentences hanging open like an unlocked back gate, and it feels intentional. He wants you to rush in to close it, and feel stupid for doing so.

'Not falling. That makes it sound like an accident, because I worked hard. And as people moved me upwards and onwards I stopped feeling like a fraud. You'll see. It happens to everyone.'

If you're a man, I think while looking into my noodles.

'I mean, it happens *more* if you're a middle-class white guy, I suppose.'

I laugh. 'I didn't want to say it, but I'm glad you did.'

'I suppose you're a bit of a feminist then?'

'Why do you ask?'

'There's more of you around these days, aren't there? And don't think I didn't notice that pizza wife crack earlier on. That got your back up.'

He watches me twist a noodle idly around my chopstick.

'Are you all about Sheryl Sandberg? Are you going to *lean in*?'

Something passes between us. Something small, indistinct, like an animal with glowing eyes. My skin prickles. The way he said 'lean in' makes me all too aware of my body, my breasts, the way I'm bending towards my plate. I'm uncomfortable, but I don't hate it. I don't hate it at all.

Citrus. Wood.

Heat. Skin.

A second later, and it's gone. I finish my food and go back to my desk. I text Darla.

'When is Ramadan over?'

'A week. Why?'

'Let's go out dancing when it is.'

'Ahhhhh. Finally ready to meet your rebound shag?'

I pack up my bag and make for the lifts using the most inconvenient route possible, back through the kitchen. *I'll say I left my lunchbox there*, I think, not totally sure of why I'm bothering to furnish a lie.

Clem is gone, but his coat is still where he left it. I pick it up, formally at first, as if trying to figure out who it might belong to. Keeping one eye on the bathroom door, I pinch the shoulders, bring it towards me and softly inhale.

4

Darla has decided to take my rebound shag mission very seriously. So seriously, in fact, that she's willing to invite Becky out on a Saturday night. They seem to have developed a bond since our night at Piano Bar, and I feel a twinge of jealousy when I see them together, all jokes and easy chat. I resist the urge to dive in-between them and shout: 'But you're both MY friends! You *can't* go off and be friends on your own.'

I know I should take my rebound shag seriously, too: I'm starting to fixate on every man I meet. All week, I've been alternating my fantasies between David Lady and Clem Brown, treating them like snacks I can reach for if I'm feeling empty. I change it up depending on what I want: sweet or savoury, ice cream or salted pretzels. I think about long, romantic moments with David Lady: I think about walks around duck ponds and breakfast and cool white sheets. These are the things I think about during the day. At night, I reach for salt. My thoughts get darker, stranger, stickier. I think about being a different kind of girl, and what it would feel like to be that girl with Clem. The fact that I'm even comparing them in the first place is strange. It's like being a dog person all your life and suddenly waking up with the thought: *Hey, y'know what? Cats.*

You're only doing this, Jane, I remind myself, *because they're*

*the only two men you're in contact with right now. Meet someone
else, for God's sake.*

So I'm trying. We're at a fashionable pop-up bar in East
London, and I am thrilled to find that, for once, I have
dressed appropriately. The secret to dressing up for a night
out in East London is to pretend you're coaching a Goth
baseball team. I have an Adidas vest on with no bra and a lot
of dark lipstick, and I have to admit, I'm kind of into myself.
I'm drinking gin out of a jam jar and hoping that tonight,
at long last, I will ascend gracefully into my role of young
sexy Londoner. The kind of exciting young person who has
infinite disposable income and knows where all the good
clubs are and which night bus to get home.

Becky ruins it.

'Can you believe how expensive these drinks were?'

'Were they?'

'Eleven pounds each. I mean, I know there's elderflower
and rose water or whatever in there, but essentially it's just a
gin and tonic, isn't it?'

'I'll get the next round, don't worry.'

'Oh, no, I don't mind. Actually, I have some extra money
now, anyway. My Girls' Holiday has been cancelled this year.'

Poor Becky. No wonder she's putting so much energy
into being a good friend to me. I know how much her Girls'
Holiday means to her.

'Your what?' says Darla, looking up from her phone.

'Every year me and the girls from school have our Girls'
Holiday. We're all a bit, you know, scattered to the winds
these days and it's an excuse to go somewhere sunny and go
crazy for a week every year. Only . . . ' She rattles the ice in
her glass with a straw. 'This year Tara wants to save up for
her trip to India with her boyfriend, and Emma is saving for
a mortgage, and Megan's job has got so crazy that she can't
take any time off because she's a journalist now and journalists

don't take time off. So we said we'd leave it this year, and go on a mega break next year instead.'

I can imagine the endless WhatsApp conversations that went into this decision, the excuses, the hesitation to book flights, the eventual 'look, let's just not do it this year' conclusion that everyone except Becky knew was inevitable. I want to wrap my arms around her, take her to a place where Best Friends Forever really does mean for ever, and no one grows up, and no one moves in with their boyfriend.

'I don't see any of my friends from school,' volunteers Darla. 'I don't know why anyone would. I had very little in common with them then and I have nothing in common with them now.'

'You don't mean that,' I say, trying to preserve the ideals of female friendship for Becky.

'Yes I do. Do you know what it's like to be the only brown girl in Berkshire? I *always* had to be Scary Spice.'

'You're Scary Spice now,' I nudge her. 'You're fucking terrifying.'

'Yeah, Jane, *you* try being a Muslim teenager after 9/11,' she says, with an exasperated eye-roll. 'It was a total shit show. And the boys who liked me only fancied me to feel different. I have a whole stack of love letters that feature the words "exotic" and "dusky".'

Darla drains the last of her drink, and spies Becky's sad expression through her glass. She backtracks, softens. 'I do still see my uni girls, though. They're ace.'

Every woman is meant to have Girls, or so I've been told, but I'm not sure who still counts as part of that circle. After I got together with Max I disappeared down the relationship rabbit hole of couples' holidays and Saturday-night curries, boxsets and anniversary dinners. The uni friends I moved to London with steamrolled through their early twenties, and I turned down their invitations to go out so many times that they eventually stopped inviting me. I didn't mind, not usually, until I came across a heavily filtered picture of them on somebody's balcony, falling over one another to fit into frame.

Can I even say that I know those girls any more? Can you reconnect with people when all you have in common is that you tottered down Old Street together as twenty-two-year-olds in the wrong dress and the wrong shoes?

The getting ready was always the best part, that I remember for certain. I had a real thing for false eyelashes, the kind you buy next to the barley sugars at the chemist for £3.99. We would smoke indoors, on hard kitchen chairs, while I dabbed craft glue on my eyelids. We drank iced white wine from plastic cups to avoid washing up. We played elaborate card drinking games, the commands for which we never properly remembered. There were never enough plug sockets to go around, not between the iPhone speakers and the hair straighteners and the phone chargers. Time was always getting away from us. There was always a last-minute rush as the taxi waited outside, as we scrambled for our ID and our debit cards, our lips shiny, goose pimples on our legs already.

And then? The bolshie confidence we built up during our five-hour getting-ready sessions slowly eked out of us while we waited in line with a hundred girls who seemed more sophisticated. No matter where we went, nowhere seemed to be *for* us. We didn't know how to dance to house music, and we didn't understand what dubstep was. We knew how to scream along to 'Sex on Fire' by Kings of Leon and we didn't understand why anyone wouldn't want to do that.

We paid incredible amounts of money to clutch our drinks awkwardly and feel provincial. We lived in London but we weren't *of* London, a fact we could ignore most of the time but not during the crush of a night out. We were like immigrants who settle without learning the local language or customs. We had built a Chinatown to our own bad taste. I think part of the reason I got into a long-term, committed relationship so young was to escape those nights, and the feeling of desperation that came with them.

I could have just as easily been one of the women breaking poor Becky's heart, refusing to go on a Girls' Holiday, planning for what I believed to be my future and losing my connection to the past.

We plough on, following Darla's lead from cocktail bar to cocktail bar, and I knock back shot after shot of tequila with lime and salt. Does Clem drink tequila? No – whiskey, I bet. I imagine him at home, drinking expensive Irish whiskey with a single ice cube, reading one of my reports. I can feel the hair on my neck rise at the idea, and then I'm angry with myself.

Why are you entertaining this? Why are you thinking about this man in this way?

I grab Becky's hand, dragging her onto the dance floor. We've ended up at a Nostalgia Night listening to indie guitar hits from the early noughties. We dance to Razorlight and The Fratellis, stomping our feet and laughing at how many of the words we still remember. I look at them and think: *Maybe* these *are my Girls. Maybe these are the women who I'm supposed to build my life around, maybe this is the clique I go into the second half of my twenties with.*

Darla disappears just after 1 a.m., when she gets a text from a guy she's seeing. Becky is sloppy.

'Let's go on a holiday,' she says, hugging me.

'I'm broke, remember? Heartbreak isn't cheap. I don't recommend it.'

'Let's go to fucking ... Scotland. Scotland is cheap. Everyone's poor in Scotland.'

'Okay,' I say and she grins. 'We'll go to Scotland.'

I wonder if she thinks it will happen.

Dear Jolly Politely,

My housemate is an 'early adopter'. This is techie
speak for 'total bell end'. EVERYTHING in our
house has to be controlled by his phone – he boils the
kettle WITH AN APP, he monitors how much water
we're wasting WITH AN APP and now he wants to
buy an Amazon Echo that will automatically order
our shopping. I have read up on Amazon Echo and
apparently it records all of your voice conversations,
which doesn't disturb him at all. How do I make him
understand that privacy is too high a price to pay to
live with a spy who orders your toilet roll???

Exhaustedly yours,

Luddite

By Monday morning I still haven't shaken off my hangover,
which is awful, because it turns out to be a very shouty
morning. The pitch is on Friday, and Clem isn't happy with
anything the team has produced. I'd feel worse about it,
but I haven't really *done* anything, except transcribe some
research data.

We sit in silence while he reviews the proposed artwork.
He slowly flips over each glossy page of Photoshopped pizzas.

A picture of a Mafia family eating pizza.

'No.'

A series of great Renaissance artists painting with
pizza colours.

'No.'

Michelangelo's David holding a pizza.

'Are you fucking serious?'

He puts his thumb and forefinger on the bridge of his nose.

'These aren't it.'

David Lady crosses his arms.

'Well, you could tell us what's wrong with them.'

Clem looks like he is about to punch David, like what is wrong is so blindingly obvious that it is beneath him to explain what is wrong. He turns to me.

'Jane.'

'Yes,' I answer, briefly considering adding a 'sir', and then thinking better of it. I have never seen this side of him before: the 'tough' one David had mentioned at lunch.

'Are you able to explain to David what's wrong with these?'

Everyone is watching me now, David looking horrified at what I've been asked to do.

'Excuse me?'

'Tell me why these aren't right. I know you know. I can tell by your face that you know these aren't right.'

'No, that's just . . . ' I stall. 'My face.'

He is not going to rest until he has an answer, until he has raked someone over hot coals.

I meet David's eye, trying to give him a 'you know I don't want to do this' face. 'Well, the research packet they sent over tells us that Fat Eddie's customers see their food as a guilty pleasure, or a last resort. Something they'll pick up in a two-for-one special.'

'Yeah, and it's our job to change that,' interjects David. 'Which is why we took this Gonzo Italy approach. Taking what you know about Italy and making it a bit cooler, but still authentic.'

'But it's a step too far,' I say. 'I mean, the work you've done is amazing, but people don't associate this brand with Italy, and they never will. And they shouldn't. They're not even Italian-style pizzas, they're American inspired. I mean, it's called Fat Eddie. There are stars and stripes on the box.'

David's face has gone a deep red. The images he and his team have produced are gorgeous, but the Fat Eddie people would never buy it. And I know that, because seemingly I'm the only person who has read a single thing about the client.

Clem smiles. 'Jane, if you're *quite* done nailing David to the wall.'

The whole room laughs in gratitude, glad that Clem has finally decided to ease the tension.

'But you—'

He has already moved on. David looks at his shoes, and Deb repeats her long list of reasons why this pitch is important for us. When the meeting ends, I try to catch up with David but he scoots out of the room like, to borrow a phrase from my mother, a cat with a hot arse. I linger in the meeting room, too embarrassed to head up to the canteen with everyone else.

Clem hangs back too, packing up his laptop and various bits of pizza paper. 'You're welcome, by the way.'

'Excuse me?'

'The team respects you. No one's going to fuck with you now that they know what you know. And that you know everything they don't know.'

'But . . . David's my friend.'

Clem slips his arm into his leather satchel and lets out a long, loud sigh. He goes to the door and places his hand on the light switch.

'Jane,' he says, 'I've seen a lot of women get nowhere because they were too afraid of upsetting people.'

Click. Darkness.

'Don't be one of them.'

And I'm alone.

Dear Luddite,

If you're going to get through to your housemate, strong moves are required. He is a man of the future: you must be a man of action. You have outlined where you stand on having a small robot in your house that secretly records your conversations, and if he cannot respect that, I suggest you respond by wrapping the robot in tinfoil and throwing it out of the window. Perhaps someone, somewhere will mistake it for a baked potato.

Whatever you do, remember this: a lot of good people get nowhere because they're afraid of upsetting people.

Love,

Jolly Politely

5

Clem is right. Within this pitch team, this little universe within a universe at work, he is always right. It's a little like Fascism in the 1930s, in that if you can get with the programme and just accept his superiority, you can do very nicely under the regime. If you don't – well. Things could get difficult for you.

While I'm still cringing about my showdown with David Lady, I seem to be reaping the benefits of having stuck a knife in his back. I have become the Clem Whisperer. People are coming to me with their artwork before they go to Clem because 'you know the client, and you know what *he* likes'. I overhear someone talking about me. They say: 'Talk to Jane. She's your go-to girl.' Clem's announcement on my first day seems to be coming true: maybe I really am a codebreaker.

I have never been anyone's go-to girl. I've always felt that my job, even when I was doing it well, didn't really help anyone: not my co-workers, not the advertising industry, not the entire human race. I thought I just had a job because everyone is supposed to have one. It's exciting to be respected at mine.

I get aggressive. I don't have many ideas but I know when I do, they're the right ones. I come up with Fat Eddie Film Nights, where we include a discount code for a film download in every pizza box. This idea is treated with the same respect and gravitas as Alexander Fleming's discovery of penicillin, and for a minute I am convinced that I *have* discovered penicillin. I stay late. I work on the pitch like it's an endless equation, pulling apart every component and putting it back together again. I feel myself becoming an expert in discounted oven pizza. It may not have been my childhood dream, but it's nice to be an expert in something.

'All right, Russell Crowe.'

It's nine o'clock on the night before the pitch and David Lady has appeared at my desk. My highlighter is still in my hand, trying to see if there's a mistake I might have missed. Everything has to be perfect tomorrow.

'Russell Crowe?'

'*A Beautiful Mind*? I feel like I should give you a stick of chalk to write on the window with.'

'Ha ha.'

'Are you done yet?'

'No,' I say, rubbing my eyes, 'I'm beginning to think I'll never be done.'

'I was going to ask if you wanted to go for a drink. You seem like you're taking this all a bit seriously.'

'I'd love to . . . ' I glance at everything I've worked so hard on for three weeks. 'But I can't. I really need to make sure this is right. Can we go for a drink tomorrow?'

'Sure.' He smiles. 'I'm sure it'll be Sodom and Gomorrah tomorrow night anyway, it usually is after a pitch.'

'I'm glad you're not mad at me,' I say.

'Mad at you? For what?'

'For when I said those things about your work. At that art meeting.'

'Oh, that. Don't worry about that. That's Clem playing his power games. I know you don't really think that.'

I'm annoyed that he thinks I can be so easily manipulated, and that I'm a mouthpiece for someone else. That he thinks I'm too sweet to have an unpopular thought. I smile blandly.

'I should get back to work.'

When Max and I were still together, I would attend Mitchell parties for the mere chance of having a beer with David Lady. I lingered around his department, talking to people on his team, in an attempt to imprint my presence on his mind. I have watched the hair on his forearm as though it were a crop I was personally tending to, and now I was refusing to have a drink with him. It wasn't the pitch, either. Something was making me reject him, possibly the same something that made me reject Max.

'Will you promise to buy me a drink after this madness is over? I feel like I've worked so hard that I owe it to myself to wait until it's perfect.'

He nods. 'All right, well, don't lose your mind over it. I'm off to eat my final Fat Eddie's pizza. Possibly of my entire life. Wish me luck.'

When I eventually do go home, I sneak a look at my Jolly comments. My response to the guy with the techie housemate was rushed, but funny, I thought. Turns out I was wrong: it won't stop getting comments, and they're mostly negative.

Uhhhhhh remember when Jolly used to answer problems with LOVE and not with snide bullshit?

Vacuous and trite.

I'm so tired of people complaining about new advances in technology!!!!! Build a bridge and get over it!!!!!

Lol Jolly giving tech advice when she doesn't even have Twitter

> What Jolly Politely doesn't know about tech could fill
> a barn

On and on. There are a few positive ones. One woman thinks my writing is always 'very enriching', and there's another offer from a gentleman who would like me to watch him masturbate in his car in exchange for a Nokia Lumia. This is not the first time this has happened. The truth is that I don't know whether I'm a very good agony aunt. I never know if my tone is right or my advice is right or whether I'm being too serious or not serious enough. I don't know why so many people read it every week.

I scroll further down the comments, to find a glut of people arguing about whether Jolly is a Luddite or not. I try to suppress a smile when people say they like my 'old school' approach: no Twitter, no Facebook, no YouTube, no names, no photos. Just a lone blog, floating in space. Every now and then a plea comes through to 'reveal' my identity, but I know that, if I do, the role of 'advice-giver' will be irrelevant. Who would take advice from someone who can barely find the right night bus? There have been a few stray requests to do guest columns for bigger websites – some for money! – but all of them wanted a photograph, or at least a little background. They wanted to show a side of Jolly the fans hadn't seen yet, and the idea unnerved me. I look down at my comments again.

> CLICK HERE FOR FREE NUDE PICS OF JOLLY

I smile in silent gratitude for my own anonymity, snap my laptop shut, and go to sleep.

The next morning I get up at 6 a.m. to blow-dry my hair straight and put on my make-up properly. Usually I just slather on a bit of tinted moisturiser and some mascara, but this is pitch day, when appearances are everything. I unwrap a new pair of M&S tights and put my nail through them almost immediately.

'FUCK. NO.'

I do not have a single clean pair of tights, so go through my laundry basket, digging and burrowing frantically through sweat patches and weird brown knicker stains. Every pair of tights I own smells.

I spy a clothes horse heavy with Shiraz's laundry, including a host of perfect tights, hanging down like lazy black jungle snakes. Tights are okay to borrow, aren't they? It's not like borrowing someone's dress or wallet. Nicking a pair of tights is like nicking a tampon. It goes without saying that if you have a surplus you help the sisterhood out. I snatch a pair, run back into my room to wrestle myself into them. Shiraz is smaller than me (all those Pilates DVDs) so by the end of it I feel like a banana stuffed into some sausage casing.

I look pretty good. The crotch is so tight that I will almost certainly have thrush by the end of the day, but I look like an air hostess for British Airways: refined, slightly glamorous, reassuring. As I leave, Shiraz looks at me slyly over the rim of her coffee mug.

I get a text on the bus.

Did you take my tights?

I think about lying, but what would be the point?

Yes! Sorry, dress emergency this morning. Will buy you a new pair on the way home. Jx

She responds immediately.

This is strike one.

Christ. How much are tights, anyway? £2.99? Four quid?

I get another text. I'm all ready for Shiraz to tell me she's going to kick me out, when I see it's Max. Max, who I haven't heard from since the night of my birthday, the night of the toilet sick.

Hey J. Hope you're well. Just texting to say I need the money you owe me back.

I stare at the text for a few minutes, and decide that I don't have time today to wonder endlessly about this. I call him.

'Jane.'

'Max.'

'Hi.'

'Hello.'

A pause.

'So what's all this about then?'

'What do you mean?'

'What do you mean, what do I mean? You texted me asking me to pay back the money that a month ago you said was fine to pay you in instalments. You said a hundred pounds a month was fine.'

The truth is that I had taken advantage of Max's generosity in the past, but we always insisted that there was a 'tab'. The £1,000 he spotted me while I was interning, the rent he paid on my behalf while I was looking for a job, the £200 he had loaned me to buy 'office-appropriate' wear when I finally got the job at Mitchell two years ago. We always knew I would pay him back one day ('when you're famous': for what or how, we never discussed) but we hadn't suspected my tab would go on after our relationship had ended.

'Well . . . ' I can hear him leaving his office, finding a quiet place to chat, probably an empty meeting room. 'The thing is, my circumstances have changed, and I sort of need it back now.'

'Have you been fired?'

'What? Oh, no.'

As if the idea were unthinkable – Max, fired? This is the guy that got promoted to Head Carwasher on the first day of his first job. Coded his first website at fifteen, sold it at seventeen. According to the press releases his office pushes out, he's now 'redefining online finance'. Max is not one of life's firees.

'It's just . . . I'm moving house, and I need to get as much money together as I can. So I'm calling in old debts, so to speak.'

'You're leaving our old flat? Why?'

'It's time to buy. And the market isn't getting any better.'

'You can't afford to buy on your own,' I say confidently. I repeat myself, slower this time. 'You can't afford to buy *on your own*.'

'Yes.' He clears his throat, uncomfortable. 'Quite right.'

There is a long, horrible moment of silence and I hang up.

Who in their right fucking mind buys a house with someone they've been dating for a month? A *month*? I've dated people for a month and wondered whether it was appropriate to buy them a birthday gift. This is unprecedented. This is *nuts*.

Max has always earned more than me, which is sort of the natural conclusion of dating someone a few years older. It made me uncomfortable sometimes, but not in the 'I guess you'll pay for dinner again' sort of way. It made me feel as if he were the key decision maker in everything we did. Most decisions cost money, and he had most of it. We once argued about where we wanted to go to on holiday. I wanted France because I had never been to Paris and had always wanted to go, and had an idle dream of driving along the coast for a week drinking wine afterwards. He wanted beaches, and tall drinks, and a holiday resort manager to pamper us like baby pandas.

Of all the relationship advice I've given over the years, this is the only one I truly believe: you can be with someone who loves different movies to you, or different music to you, or even is a different religion to you. But it will never work out with someone who wants to go on different holidays to you.

Despite this inevitability, and despite my full and complete knowledge of the reasons Max and I are not meant to be together, I am appalled by this development. Well, wouldn't you be? He's buying property with a woman who, only a month ago, he was leaving behind in a burger bar so he could get a taxi with me. They don't even know each other.

It's then I realise three fundamental truths at the exact same time.

1. Max may not have told me the full truth about him and his relationship with Kim.
2. That if he was buying property with her now, then the promise Max had made to me before – the one about them waiting for our relationship to end before doing anything – was a lie.
3. Kim must make a lot more money than me.

The first two truths fill me with nausea, but the good kind, the darkly thrilling, rollercoaster kind. I had been labouring under the suspicion that it was me who'd destroyed our relationship, and had been praying to a shrine for my own guilt ever since. I had thought it was my grumpy, demanding nature and constant low-level dissatisfaction that had ended us, and Max was just an innocent bystander in my path of destruction. But no: he had been playing around. Max had been falling in love. Max had, in all likelihood, been cheating on me for months.

It's the third thing, oddly, that fills me with a peculiar self-hatred. I imagine Kim in expensive cashmere loungewear, drinking an enormous glass of tasteful wine that is definitely not from the corner shop. I imagine her and Max meeting with estate agents and saying things like, 'I think we can stretch to that.' The Kim I met on my birthday – the one that seemed so normal, so nothingy, pretty but not threateningly so – has finally taken her monster form in my head.

The pitch is in Slough, so we're all getting the train together. Instead of buying my ticket, however, I am standing in a Starbucks, downloading the LinkedIn app so I can try to find out how much money Kim makes. I had resisted Googling Kim before, and had been proud of myself for doing so. I had even bragged about it to Darla ('Why do I need to know? I'm happy for him. Happy for them both'), but now, I can't resist. I have to know everything about Kim.

After a few false starts (who the fuck even remembers their LinkedIn password?) I find her. I hold my breath, and hope her job title is 'Idiot Heiress'. But no. She's a barrister at Crown Office Chambers. I don't know what Crown Office Chambers is, but I bet it's something to do with the Queen and it's really important and probably highly paid. I feel sick.

Money both was and wasn't a problem with Max and me. He's a naturally generous guy, and had a conveniently old-fashioned stance on paying for dates. But when we talked about serious stuff – like buying a house – things would get awkward. He would talk about how his parents would be happy to help us out with a deposit, and I would dodge the conversation whenever I could. How could I tell my mum that Max's parents were helping us, when she couldn't?

When I finally get on the train, I find a four-seater table that Clem, David and Deb are occupying, notes spread out everywhere. I sit, and keep thinking about Kim. I bet she's been at work for hours, probably freeing some orphaned children from a bin bag or something.

'Are you okay?' says David. 'You look a bit ... green.'

I nod, but my voice quavers. 'My ex-boyfriend told me this morning that he's buying a house with someone else.'

The men shift uncomfortably. Deb doesn't look up. It occurs to me that I might have disqualified myself from the grown-ups' table by announcing something so vividly personal.

'When did you break up?' they ask, practically in unison.

'June.'

'Fuck.'

'Harsh.'

'Well, London's buying market is so bad right now that they probably won't find a house for months,' says Clem.

'And it will probably be a shitbox in Catford,' chimes in David.

'Also true. I didn't know you were going through a break-up, Jane.' Clem has a hint of something in his voice. Concern, yes, but a glimmer of interest.

'Yeah, he broke up with me,' I say, and then enjoying the pity, add: 'On my birthday.'

Lie. A lie, Jane. It was days before, but I only knew it was over – really over – on my birthday. But I liked the way it made me sound: like someone who had bad things happen to them because they were unlucky and not because they deserved them. David reaches out and squeezes my wrist gently across the train table.

'Fuck,' he says again. 'Sorry.'

He lets his forearm sit a couple of centimetres from mine, and I can see the hair on his arm prick upwards.

Clem says nothing. I wonder if he's remembering my birthday, and how we had looked at one another while he sang to me. He taps his pen on his bottom teeth, reshuffles his papers and, for a moment, I forget about Max and David. Clem is *flustered*.

'Let's talk about the pitch,' I say, and we do. Or at least, they do. Within moments, I'm deep in Kim and Max's world again. I excuse myself.

The toilet water judders and spits as the train rounds a corner. I close the lid and sit on it for a moment, shutting my eyes.

I think about Kim in my old flat. I had never considered this in the last month: that while I was living as a lodger with Shiraz, drinking entire bottles of wine in bed, she had been in my flat. *My* flat. I think of all the things I left behind because I thought it would be too painful or too sad to take them into a new life. I think about her using my oven glove shaped like a crocodile's face, scrunching up her little rat nose in disapproval. What would a barrister for the Crown Chambers (I still don't really know what that is, but whatever) think of such a frivolous oven glove? What would she think of all the egg cups I had collected from museum gift shops? I imagine Kim picking up each one of them between her thumb and forefinger, disgusted by the stale intimacy of it all, and gently suggesting that Max moves out of his shit-heap ex-girlfriend flat and into a new one with her.

They're looking at houses. They're looking at two-bedroom houses, and the estate agent is saying things like, 'Great for a study . . . or a *nursery.*' They are looking at each other and giggling. He takes her into the master bedroom and kisses her and says this is the happiest he has ever been. She agrees. He proposes. She accepts. The estate agent cries and gives them a discount. Kim gets pregnant and looks great in maternity wear. People tell her you wouldn't even know she was pregnant from behind. She keeps practising the law. She wins a huge human rights case while eight months pregnant. People call her the next Amal Clooney. There's a piece about

her in *Tatler*, where Max says it was love at first sight, that
she is the most impressive woman he has ever met, and the
interviewer agrees. The world is built for Kims.

I can feel a hot flush creeping up my face. I put my head
between my knees. This is what the therapist back in uni told
me to do, whenever I felt like I needed to calm down.

I started having panic attacks in my second year, and always
in very quiet places where it was obvious. I would be hunched
over in the library, and suddenly I would be hit with the feeling that I was jaywalking. That everything I did, however
small, was a wilful act of self-endangerment. I stayed inside,
and became obsessed with swine flu. Therapy was free so I
saw the campus therapist.

'Do you know what a panic attack is, Jane?'

'No.'

'It's sort of like a misplaced adrenalin dump. Your brain
gets sent a message that you're in danger, so it gives you the
fear that is necessary for humans to protect themselves. It's
a wiring problem. It's like living in a house where you turn
the bathroom light off and the TV turns on.'

'Oh.'

'It can be brought on by stress. Are you stressed by anything, Jane?'

He said my name a lot, the way telemarketers do when
they want you to trust them. The truth was that I was constantly stressed out, but in a low-level, maudlin sort of way. I
had gone to uni with the hope that I would find the missing
pieces of myself. I would meet my new best friends on the
very first day, and we would challenge each other and know
each other and have intense, enriching experiences with
books and hallucinogens.

Except that didn't happen. I lowered my expectations.
I went to bad nightclubs. I had sex with people I didn't
like. The panic attacks ceased as I gradually learned to stop

worrying so much about what I was, and what was going to happen to me.

What do I do while Max is off living his perfect, Amal Clooney-enriched life? I'll probably carry on working in marketing. It's too late to retrain, really, and I don't have the money to go back to uni. I'll probably keep living in other people's houses in parts of South London that are badly connected by public transport. Eventually, I will be in my thirties, and I will have dithered so long, so absolutely unsure of what I want, that I will have alienated myself from every option available to me.

Then, the thing that I had pushed behind a cloud for so long, the thing that a lovely boyfriend and a stable job and nice friends and good brunch places can banish but not erase, appears again. My heart pounds, and my spine becomes electric with pale, shivering sweat.

I have visions of myself moving home to work in the office of my old primary school, like my mum did after she had me. Sometimes I wonder whether every woman's worst fear is to live her mother's life. Even if there's nothing wrong with that life: even if it is a good, strong life.

There's a knock on the door. For a second, I think it might be Max, and then realise that's insane.

'I'm in here.'

'It's Deb.'

Christ.

'Sorry.'

I smooth my dress down and slide open the lock.

'Hi, Deb.'

'We'll be arriving in ten minutes. We'll get a taxi from the station.'

'Oh. Okay.'

Silence.

'Have you brought your make-up bag with you?'

I catch a look at myself in the toilet mirror. I look a state. My face is red, my eyes are wet, and my hair is frazzled and static from nervously pulling my hands through it.

'Sit down,' she commands.

She unzips her make-up bag – a Marc Jacobs leather pouch, I note, not cheap – and digs through it. It wafts towards me, that expensive, department-store make-up-counter smell. Creams and glosses, plastic and lemon. Deb dabs concealer under my eyes and blots it steadily with a perfectly painted finger. She sweeps some highlighter on my cheekbones and dabs pink lipstick on my cheeks, smudging it outwards. A dusting of translucent powder. The whole thing is relaxing and strangely intimate. Her movements on my face are nowhere near as intimidating as she is: they're tender, diligent, and it makes me think about what a nice mum she must be.

The train jolts forward and her hand slides off my face. We both yelp in panic, then laugh.

'Thank you for fixing me.'

'That's fine. You needed it.'

'I was having a bit of a moment.'

'About your ex-boyfriend?'

'Yes.'

'Do you want to get back together with him?'

She is very matter-of-fact, as if she's asking about a campaign budget.

'No. I don't think so. I just didn't want him to move on quite so quickly. With someone who is so much more impressive than me.'

'Impressive how?'

'Barrister.'

Deb sucks her teeth. '*Barristers*,' she says hatefully. 'Jane, there are always going to be people who make what you do seem less important than what they do. And it's very important that you learn as early as you can how *not* to let them do that. We women are taught to make everything we do seem unimportant. And most of us buy into it.'

She puts on a squeaky voice. 'Oh, I just do the press releases,' or, 'Oh, I just have the children.' It's all bollocks. It really is. Only you determine the asking price. Only you can decide how important you are. Not your old boyfriend. Not the new client. Not *him* outside.'

I immediately understand 'him' to mean Clem. They are both leading this pitch, but there seems to be a struggle over who is the *real* leader. They are oddly curt with one another: never outrightly disrespectful, but never visibly thrilled to be in each other's company.

The trees outside of the toilet window are slowly turning to bricks, and Deb signals that we need to go. When we get back to our seats, David and Clem are packing up.

'Are you ready to go?' Clem says.

'Yes.'

And I mean it.

By the time I'm in the meeting room, hooking up Clem's laptop to the projector, shaking hands with the Fat Eddie client, the make-up Deb put on me might as well have been warpaint.

Only you decide how important you are.

Today, I have decided I am the most important person in the room. I don't laugh nervously or sit too far forward, I don't write down everything everyone says. I sit back in my chair. I once read in a Nancy Mitford book that if you want to look fabulous before you enter the room just say the word 'brush' to yourself: it leaves you with a dreamy, elegant little smile. I think brush without actually saying it.

'And what do you do at the agency?' asks one of the people from Fat Eddie.

'I try not to tie myself down to one department.' *Brush*. 'I get involved whenever I can with Market Research and New Business developments.'

'Jane's been my right-hand woman over the last few weeks,' says Clem, and I give him a smile. *Brush*.

I look at Deb. She smiles. *Brush*.

All this charming brush business screeches to a halt, however, when the laptop we're projecting off freezes. The mouse stops moving, and the presentation sticks on one image of a Fat Eddie pizza. It hovers there stupidly, like a moon watching us all.

Clem chuckles nervously, and jokes with the client while glaring furiously at David. He is trying, very hard, to keep the energy up in the room.

'I'll tell you, this was much simpler in the old days when we used to present on poster boards, wasn't it?'

The Fat Eddie people smile politely and say nothing.

'I remember one time,' Clem is still looking at David, who is now trying to force restart the laptop without much luck, 'when I went to a pitch with the wrong poster boards and had to do the whole pitch on the back of a napkin.'

'Well, couldn't you just do that now?'

Everyone looks to the top of the table, where the CFO of Fat Eddie is sitting. He's one of those sharp, hard men who use fashion the same way Deb uses her motherhood. It's a dare. Wearing a perfect pink shirt and a silk pocket square is his way of saying: Enough people are scared of me that I can wear whatever the fuck I want. He challenges Clem with a sideways smile, the same way I've seen Clem challenge all of us.

Clem pales, and I realise that the only person in the room who knows this entire presentation, inside and out, is me.

All the adrenalin that should be going into panicking right now was mercifully dumped on the train, when I was crying about Kim's graceful future pregnancy. I stand up and take a stack of pages out of a folder in my bag.

'Well, I guess we'll have to.'

And that's that. I stand over the table and go through the presentation as best I can remember it, drawing diagrams in Sharpie on note paper. Even I'm surprised by how well I know this shit: I don't just know it, I Happy Birthday song know it. I could do it in the shower, I could do it backwards, I could do it with a gun to my head. This is my first pitch, and like a child learning its times tables, the information is written on the walls of my brain. When I get to a point that Clem or David or Deb are responsible for, they chime in, and the whole thing soon feels very relaxed. Not like a presentation at all, more like an idle chat. The pizza looms on the screen, which suddenly leaps to life when we only have two minutes to go. Everyone laughs, calls it sod's law, and we shake their hands and leave.

We stumble out of the building and flag a cab. The moment we sit inside, all of us start laughing hysterically.

'All right,' says Clem, clapping a hand on my shoulder. 'Who wants a drink?'

6

'What'll you have?' David shouts at me.

'Helvetica Light,' I shout back, making a guess. I've never actually seen a menu in Font. It's one of those cool bars that does cocktails in chipped teacups and jam jars, and not one of them is less than £10.

'I think that's virgin.'

'No I'm no—'

'I said THE DRINK is VIRGIN.'

'OH. Helvetica then?'

It's a strong, hard vodka thing and within minutes I can feel it rushing to my head. Vodka gives me that confident, manic feeling that most people get when they snort cocaine. We've been back in Soho since 4 p.m., and have more or less been drinking all day since. We met up with everyone who worked on the pitch and Clem took us out for an Italian, promising that we'd need to line our stomachs for the night ahead. This is the first time I actually feel pissed, though: the vodka buzz is cutting through the lazy wine high like a knife.

David and I sat next to each other at dinner, and it was like looking at a brochure for the kind of couple we might be. We were boisterous, swapping food, teasing one another with jokes about who was hogging the garlic bread. Each new movement we made towards each other seemed like a question followed by a guarantee. He would graze my elbow, and

I would leave it next to him. I would laugh into his shoulder, and he would angle his body towards me. By the time our espressos came, his leg had touched my leg a total of six times.

'You did great today,' David says. 'You're a hustler, Peters.'

I want to say 'I know!', but even now, it feels weird to take a compliment. 'Thanks.'

'I mean, you're good, but I didn't think you could perform like that. You were *serious*, Jane. They loved you.' I wonder if he is trying to say: *I loved you.*

'And, y'know, you're really flying the flag for us fellow children-of-broken-homes. Who says that our abandonment issues are impeding us professionally?'

I start laughing. I think how different he is to Clem, the way he wears his heart on his sleeve like this, the way he allows bridges to be built between us out of mutual hardship. The way he lets his vulnerability be a joke. Clem never says anything about himself. He asks arch questions about what my goals are. I wonder if it's a generational thing, or a David and Clem thing.

'You reminded me of Lucy Liu in *Kill Bill*. In that boardroom scene.'

'Doesn't she literally execute someone in that scene? She slices their head open with a samurai sword, right?'

'I feel like you accomplished that figuratively today. If not literally. And the night is young.'

It is, it is, it is! I want to scream. The night *is* young and before the end of it, I will have had my tongue in your mouth. The thought creeps along my nerve-endings, making me giddy. I think about taking his hand, right now, and leading him outside and into a black cab. My house? His house? His house. I don't want Shiraz to hear me having sex, and I don't want to worry about keeping quiet for our first time.

A smile spreads across my face: I am going to have sex tonight. I'm hyper with it. It's like there are little beams of blue light shooting through me, preparing me, excited for me, telling me that everything I want to happen is on the brink of happening. He will kiss me. He will pull me closer. He will stroke my face and tell me that he is so happy this has finally happened, because he has wanted it since the moment he met me.

We start acting out our favourite Tarantino scenes. I do that one from *Reservoir Dogs*, where Mr Pink refuses to tip the waitress. I'm making him laugh now, and the more serious I play it the more fun he has.

'Your memory freaks me out, Peters. How do you know all that?'

Why is it so nice when men call you by your last name? It makes you feel like you're in a club with them.

'I don't know.' I think about the kind of house David Lady might live in. I picture myself sitting on his kitchen counter and beckoning him towards me, wrapping my legs around his waist, our skin separated by bulky denim and the slippery nylon of my underwear. 'I like films.'

'That settles it, then. I'm getting us two more drinks and when I get back, you're giving me your best Samuel L. Jackson. What do you want?'

'Times New Roman?'

'Times Negroni Roman, I think they call it.'

'Fine.'

He disappears off into the crowd, the back of his head bobbing away with a newfound sense of purpose.

Clem appears then, pushing through bodies to get to me. Space is tight, and as his balance falters, my nose briefly touches his chest. That smell again: but woodier, darker, damper. Closer. Not just a jacket in my arms, but close, immediate, real.

'What are you doing over here? The pitch team has a booth.'

'They have BOOTHS?'

'Yes, and they have perfectly good bottles of prosecco going to waste.'

'But David is buying me a drink.'

'I met him. I told him to put his money away and join us. You pair of silly rabbits, don't you know that the company pays for drinks on nights like this?'

He grabs my wrist and leads me to a downstairs bar that I never knew existed, where the rest of the team are roaring with laughter and falling over each other, limbs stretched out, people sitting on laps, people's friends showing up to cash in on the free drinks. I wonder if David knew that everyone would be down here, and was trying to get me alone.

'Now,' Clem says, putting a glass in my hand. 'Hold this.'

He grabs a bottle of champagne and stands on the table. Everyone starts clapping wildly.

'I have, right now, in my inbox, an email from Howard, saying that Fat Eddie has halted the pitching process. They don't want to see any more agencies.'

You could hear a mouse sneeze in this room.

'Because they're going with us.'

Everyone goes wild. Banging their hands on the table, their drinks splashing everywhere, drops of gin spitting on to their clothes. Are pitch wins always like this?

'I want to thank you all for working so hard the last month. I know, for lots of you, it has been a *long* July. Lots of you missed birthday parties and piss-ups and, in all likelihood, a few funerals to work on this. So thank you. The agency couldn't survive without the talent in this room, and cap-italism couldn't survive if we didn't have agencies. So, in essence, you are all saving the Western world from the brink of collapse. Give yourselves a hand.'

More applause, more banging on tables. We all know he's

joking, but a small part of us believes it. That we are the silent, vigilant, clockwork machinery that is keeping society ticking over.

'I want to take a minute to single out one person in particular. Our Man of the Match, if you will.'

I crane my neck for David but can't see him anywhere. Clem's hand is outstretched towards me from the table.

'Jane,' he says, and I let him take my hand. He has spent so long almost-touching me – nudging me with pencils, or tapping me on the head with wads of paperwork – that feeling his actual skin on mine makes me catch my breath. I'm caught off guard by the sureness and the steadiness of his grip. 'Get up here.'

I am being pulled up, above the chairs, above my colleagues, my head inches away from the ceiling.

'Jane has never worked on a pitch before this one, and I think we can all agree that she saved our arses today. She went into that room with her war face on, and according to Howard, was mentioned by name by the client in his reasons for signing with us. Give her a hand, everyone.'

He sticks my hand up in the air like I'm a prizefighter, and I'm mortified but determined to hold on to the moment. *I deserve this. I worked hard and I deserve this.* The thought shines on the tip of my finger for a moment, and then pops, like a soap bubble. I get down from the table bashfully and smile, trying not to make a fool out of myself.

Clem's declaration seems to have rubber-stamped me with team-wide approval. Everyone wants a glass of something with me. There are three more pitches lined up, and I am needed on all of them.

I have worked here for two years, and this is the very first time I have felt seen. Someone brings me a vodka, and that speedy high I had with David earlier comes back to me.

Clem is in the corner, talking to someone, one arm spread

across the sofa and one on his jaw. Listening, always listening. I like the way he smiles when he talks. I like the way his grin always begins sideways, in the corner of his face, and I like the way his stubble is always just one or two days overgrown. I try to think who he reminds me of and when I think of it, I'm delighted. I go over.

'I know who you are.'

He lifts his eyebrows. As if to say: *Well, it's about time some-one figured it out.*

'The dog from *Lady and the Tramp*.'

'Is that so?'

'Yes. Exact likeness.'

'Aren't there rather a lot of dogs in *Lady and the Tramp*?'

'Yes, but you're the main one. The Tramp one.'

He starts singing the most well-known song from it, smil-ing at me the whole time, eyes shining.

We're singing together now, surprising ourselves by know-ing the words, doing our best Peggy Lee voices.

'He's a tramp, he's a scoundrel.'

'He's a rounder, he's a cad.'

He leans in a little closer.

'I am, you know.'

It comes back again. That heat, that pressure, that feeling like I am inches away from the earth's core with him, on the brink of melting. It doesn't scare me this time. I lean into the feeling. I remember what Darla said in Piano Bar, on the night of my birthday. About how he was a huge flirt, and how everyone knew.

'I know.'

We are not touching, but it feels like we're engaging in an indecent public display of intimacy. A dark curl of hair floats to the front of his face. I want to touch it. It looks like it will feel like sheep's wool.

'Why is it,' his voice is low now, but stern, like he's voicing a thief in a radio play, 'that we're always singing to each other, Jane?'

He slides out of our booth, putting his hand up to his face to symbolise a phone call. I'm struck with an intense, almost otherworldly gloom. I sip my drink, the bubbles rising to the top and popping as they meet the air. I try to shake off this strange, new misery. *You'll be over this in a second*, I think. *The night is young.*

Fuck. Where is David?

I search the bar and eventually find him talking to a girl called Liz Stone, who I've never spoken to but now despise. He sees me trying to catch his eye, but moves closer to hear Liz, her eyes huge and focused on him like prey.

I remember then, that the last time I had seen David he was trying to buy me a drink and I was planning to have sex with him. I look at the time – that was *three hours* ago. Wasn't he supposed to join us downstairs? Didn't Clem tell him we were down here?

He untangles himself from conversation with Liz and disappears upstairs. He gives Liz an 'I'll be right back' gesture and she smiles. I hate her. I hate her dark curls and her watery eyes. I hate how pretty and insubstantial she is, like a china figure balanced on the very tip of a mantelpiece. She makes me feel sturdy. I feel my tummy, all wine-fuelled bloat, and looking at her only makes me more conscious of it.

Any other evening, I would have accepted my defeat and allowed the David and Liz romance to unfold. But this is a night – Clem had declared it – where I'm the winner. I had saved the pitch, remember? I was entitled to get what I wanted, so I follow David upstairs.

I do something that, were I any less drunk and over-confident, I would never dream of doing: I wait outside the door of the men's toilets.

All you need to say, I tell myself, *is that you forgot he was getting you a drink. And then offer to buy him one.*

But the person who first comes out of the men's loo isn't David. It's Clem.

'Well. Do you have another song for me?'

It's like the moment you decide to pack up your picnic basket, and then the sun comes back out for one more brilliant hello. I turn my face towards him, his smell, towards the sticky thoughts I've had about him, towards Mick Jagger and *Jackie* magazine.

'You didn't seem this tall,' I murmur. 'When we first met.'

I don't know what I mean by that, or what he understands it to mean, but a moment later I am on my tiptoes, and we are kissing.

PART TWO

7

My first kiss was at fourteen, and happened on the floor of my mum's living room. I was desperate to get rid of my kiss virginity. It was a status I wore like last season's Skechers, kicking it under me and hoping that no one would notice. Or at the very least, that no one had noticed that I had noticed.

My group of girlfriends talked about it like it was a real problem. It was one of the main points of discussion in our Group Meetings. The other points were Sarah Q's period (when? *When?*) and Ashley B's parents' divorce (and how much we could exploit the subsequent freedoms of this). Ranking between these two issues in severity was Jane P's kiss-ginity.

If I didn't kiss someone soon, I was under very real threat of being exiled. So one Thursday (Mum was an Avon Lady around then, and Thursdays were always sale nights) I asked my neighbour, Anthony Burrell, to come over. I didn't really fancy Anthony, but I knew I didn't hate him either. We hadn't been proper friends for years, but we talked on MSN sometimes, and he would tell me about how he wanted to be a famous actor.

We sat on the couch and watched *Gangs of New York*, which he'd brought over.

'Your screen is too small.'

'Huh?'

'Your screen is way too small. I can't see Daniel Day.'

'We could sit on the floor?'

We sat on the floor.

'The floor is too hard.'

Christ, he was whiney.

'I could get some cushions?'

I tossed some cushions on the floor.

'More,' he said, eyebrows furrowing at me for being so stupid.

In the end, I took all the sofa cushions and put them on the floor for Anthony Burrell. He lay down, arranging his plush pen of accessories around him, positioning his head so he could see Daniel Day Lewis pretending to be a butcher.

I lay down next to him. His chest rose and fell, the Ripcurl sticker on his shirt shining under the TV's glare. His hand nudged against my hand. 'You know,' he murmured, 'Daniel Day trained to be a real butcher to do this film.'

'Cool,' I said, knowing that was my cue to lean closer.

Then our mouths were on top of each other, in that sideways, lolling, teenage way. My first thought was how different Anthony's face looked when I was kissing him. How he didn't look like a teenager, or a man, or even a boy really: he looked like a long, stringy baby. He had pale eyelashes that tickled my cheeks and graceful, shell-pink eyelids. I had an urge to both mother him and kick him out of my house.

We dated for four months. That, I think, is when I absorbed all of Quentin Tarantino's monologues, word for word. Rolling around on my mother's floor, miming passion and listening to the director's commentary of *Pulp Fiction*.

I think of Anthony now, for the first time in twelve years, because this is how I feel while I am kissing Clem. He is not the lion of the boardroom, or the titan who, moments ago, took my hand and led me into the spotlight, and pirouetted me senseless and drunk into the praise of my peers.

He is just a man, with a sideways face.

I thought it would feel different to kiss a man in his forties. That men's kisses matured as they did; became dignified, easy, quick-witted.

This moment – his touching me, his tongue hot in my mouth and my legs warm against his crotch – was it a surprise? Yes and no. It was an utter shock and a total inevitability. It would be naive to say that I had never imagined his hands sliding up my ribcage, his thumbs under my armpits. I had felt the dark, sweet soreness of his attention. I had rubbed myself up against it, a cat curling between its legs.

'Jane,' he whispers, his fingers twisting into my hair, holding handfuls of it roughly. 'You're beautiful. God, you're fucking beautiful.'

The trembling cynicism that had been keeping me upright – the vaccine keeping my mind and my heart safe from this, whatever *this* is – gives up. Cynicism floods my bloodstream and bubbles up like a fever, and it makes me crave him. I kiss him, deeper and deeper, falling further and further. It feels good. *He* feels good.

I keep pulling away from him, swirling my neck around to see if anyone is coming. He ushers me under the stairwell and starts to work on my neck, his hands freer now, more curious. He slides a hand into my dress, my good navy dress, the one my mother bought from TK Maxx because she thought it would be good 'for interviews', and I had sneered at because she had never even been to a proper interview. But I had worn it anyway, worn it to three job interviews, and then to this pitch meeting, and now it was being pushed to one side of my chest so my boss could take my tits out of it.

I push him off. 'Stop,' I say, breathy and red and not at all determined to keep this piety up.

'Yes, yes, I know. You're right.' He looks completely different now. He smiles, amused, as I try to fix my dress. 'I want you.'

Three words. Three words that, from a man my own age, would sound ridiculous, try-hard. But from Clem, they are everything. They sound like a man who knows exactly how to order a bottle of wine, because he has been to enough places and drunk enough glasses to know what he likes and how he wants it. I don't know if you can buy that confidence, but I'm curious to know if you can absorb it via osmosis.

No, a tinny, petulant voice within me says. *Not* him. *David. You wanted* David. But what does it matter? David would go the way of Max eventually: David is a boy my own age. David is a nice person. David probably has a house share and party-sized cans of Heineken in his fridge. I failed at Max, and I would have failed at David. It would be like trying to eat a steak with a fork and spoon.

I pull away from Clem again, and study his face.

'You could lose your job.'

He laughs. 'Do you really think so?'

'I don't know. I could lose my job.'

'Oh, Jane,' he says, stepping closer and holding my chin between his thumb and forefinger. He knows I'm making excuses, groping for something, anything, to get me out of having to make a real decision.

'That would never happen. You're one of our best.'

He strokes my hair, then makes a ponytail with his hands. 'One of *my* best.'

It's too much. I let myself be kissed again. I kiss away my past life with Max and my future one with David. I feel my crush on him flow out of me like melted snow. He was too soft, too nice, too good. A fork with a spoon.

Clem snaps back into boss mode.

'Here's what we're going to do,' he says, as if we're planning an email campaign. 'I want you to go outside, turn left, and wait for me in the alley next to Carluccio's.

'Brown leather jacket, right? Is it still in our booth? Jane? Your coat?'

I nod. 'And my bag, yeah. It's a green shoulder thing.'

'Right, I'll grab your stuff and shove it under mine, so no one sees. Now, where did I tell you to go?'

'Left. Alley next to Carluccio's.'

'Good girl,' he says. *Good girl?* 'I'll see you in ten minutes. I need to say my goodbyes, or else it will look strange.'

I go.

8

As I wait for him in the alley outside Carluccio's, I question what it is we are about to do, and whether or not I want to do it.

At uni, they gave us consent classes. There was a lot of emphasis on what a 'yes' was. A yes was a clear statement of intent, and of permission: yes, you can have sex with me. Yes, I want to have sex with you. Yes, I am entitled to change my mind. I hold onto that thought in the alley: *You can change your mind whenever you want, Jane. You could call time on this right now.*

You could flag a taxi, go home, touch yourself, fall asleep, explain on Monday.

Clem would hate me. And even though I'm not simple enough to think that one person disliking you is enough to ruin your career for ever, I desperately want him to like me. And I want him to keep wanting me. And I want to keep feeling this feeling: this magnificent, chosen-one feeling. I want to keep feeling that I – and I alone – have the power to reduce the most confident man I know to a sweating animal. One that could lose himself in my hair and my body and whatever else I decided to offer him.

I miss sex. I miss feeling desired, and feeling desirable. I miss chatty, funny conversations about each other's bodies. And with his hands on my shoulders, I feel small again: thin, light, delicate, loved. Pretty. The bloated, frumpy feeling that I had while looking at Liz Stone dissolves within me. I *want* to keep feeling this way. I'm tired of not feeling it.

Are these good enough reasons to sleep with your boss? Yes and no. They feel more morally pure than the office sex I am used to hearing about: the kind where you have sex to get ahead, the kind where you leverage job promotions with blowjobs.

Besides, I'm already getting ahead at work by myself.

Aren't I?

'Well,' says a man's voice, 'if it isn't Lucy Liu.'

I look up. It's David Lady. He's leaving Font, and he's alone.

'Oh, hey. Are you going home, then?'

'Yep. It's getting a little too – I don't know. Advertising-y, in there. You'd swear it was the eighties, the way they carry on. A few people are already ordering coke to the bar, for Christ's sake.'

'Oh, wow. Okay. So it's just you?'

'What do you mean?'

'I thought you and Liz—'

'Liz Stone? Oh. No. She's a bit—'

I never find out what Liz Stone is a bit of, because Clem appears at that moment, holding my bag and coat.

'Sorry, gorgeous, I couldn't find yours under all those bloody jackets.'

He clocks David, who is attempting to fix his shocked face into one of seen-it-all composure.

'Ah. Lady. Didn't see you there. I just thought I'd take Jane here out for a post-pitch pasta arrabiata, but it turns out Carluccio's is closed.'

'That's . . .' David struggles to find the words, his brain still trying to compute exactly what his eyes are seeing. The pasta excuse is pathetic, particularly considering we all went for a pizza before we went to Font.

'That's a real tragedy, yeah. Well. Goodnight, I guess. Good luck with the . . . pasta.'

He walks away.

Clem thinks this is funny and calls after him. 'Don't worry, Dave! I'll get you a post-pitch penne next time!'

David's pace picks up and he vanishes around a corner.

I am queasy with shame, sickened by what David must now think of me. I hear a door closing: I have slammed it on David Lady for ever. But when God closes a door, He opens a window, and that window is standing right in front of me. The only thing left to do is jump through it.

Clem takes my hand and kisses each knuckle with care, and another realisation pulls slowly into focus, and it's sitting on his finger.

Clem has a *wedding band*. Silver, thick. He's never mentioned his wife once, not in the entire time we've worked together.

'Don't worry about Dave,' he says, cupping my face. 'He'll be professional about it. He always is. He won't go blabbing around the office. He's a good guy.'

I know, I want to say.

'What do you mean, he *always* is? How many office girls have you picked up, exactly?'

He laughs fondly, looking at me as if I am a child playing hide-and-seek, but all of my hiding places were too blindingly obvious to even merit a game. The whole thing is just too *cute* to him.

'Look, Clem, I think this is a bad idea.'

'Jane, stop.' He snatches me back, and holds my face nose to nose with his. 'I meant, he is always professional. Generally. There are no other girls. There's only you. *You*, Jane.'

A shadow of doubt must cross my face as I think about what Darla said: about Clem being a flirt. He steadies my face towards his again, a hand on each temple. I feel like a horse, blinkered by its owner.

'Look, I'll ... I'll level with you. That Saturday I found you in the office, I wasn't ... I wasn't having a good time. My wife had just asked for a divorce, so I was sleeping at Mitchell, hoping she would change her mind. I thought ...'

He waits for me to say something. I don't.

'I thought it was all over for me. Me and women, anyway. I've never felt so old or tired in my life.'

The street light hits his face, and he does look old. I have never been this close to him to tell, but he has faint, branching lines around his eyes.

'And then – you. I don't know, the *you*-ness of you, laughing at your desk, able to have a good time all by yourself. I had to talk to you. You were like this electric current that I needed to get in a room with. So I asked for you. I wanted to work with you. I wanted your energy. I needed it. I didn't think ... or at least, I didn't think you'd ever *want* to ...'

I'm in love with his vulnerability in this moment, in love with the idea of making him happy. Of – what's the cliché again? – *fixing him*.

'If you don't want to be with me, say so now, Jane.' Just like that, he is using his stern boss voice again. 'Don't mess around with me. I'll pay for your cab home and we won't ever mention this again.'

I lace my fingers through his and can only manage two words before his mouth is on mine again. 'I want ...'

On my way home the next morning, I try to remember Becky's Three Good Things tactic.

1. The free shampoo and conditioner in the hotel bathroom was Aveda, which never happens. Not in hotels I'm used to staying in. As I left, I passed an unattended housekeeping cart and filled my bag with tiny shampoos.

2. It is still early, and it is a Saturday morning. And it's a nice day. I could be home by 9.30, and then the whole day would be mine. Maybe I could bake something. Maybe I could go for a run. Maybe I could buy Shiraz a pair of new tights and we'd laugh about the night I had, and today will be the first day of us being lifelong best friends.

3. I did not make a complete fool of myself.

I'd finally felt guilty at the front desk. Clem handed over his credit card. 'King bed or twin?' the woman asked, raising her eyebrows so imperceptibly that the gesture could have only been for me. It was an eyebrow that said, 'I'm going to humour you and try to let you pretend that this is your father, even though I have night managed a hotel for long enough to know what it means when a forty-something man brings in a twenty-something woman.'

Believe me when I say this was a very expressive eyebrow. 'King,' he said.

The passion that had felt so magnetic and inescapable in the bar had an awkwardness to it now that it had reached its natural conclusion. We didn't kiss in the lift up to our room, Clem instead choosing to rub my back in rhythmic circles, as if he were in a doctor's waiting room with his grandmother.

I have had four one-night stands in my life, which I believe to be a respectable number for a woman of twenty-six to have. ('Not that there *is* a respectable number,' Darla would say, threateningly. 'Not that you're a slut-shamer.') All of them had a life-or-death urgency to them, a fierce scramble in case one or both of us suddenly changed our minds. This was not like that.

Clem took his time. He looked at me for a moment before moving a muscle.

'Put your arms up.'

I did as I was told. He eased my dress off over my head and left it on the floor.

'Turn around.'

I would like to joke here, or complain that all these verbal commands were demeaning: I cannot do this. It was hot.

Clem placed his hands on my shoulders, his thumbs meeting at the nape of my neck. He slid his hands down slowly, tracing my spine as if it were a river splitting a map. He eased off my bra in one movement. He drew me closer, so I could smell him, my back touching the cool linen of his shirt. And finally, after an agonisingly sweet time suspended in this state, he inched his fingers into my underwear.

I squint in the morning sun, trying to catalogue the entire experience, trying to decide how I feel about having spent the night in a hotel room with my married boss. Having – well, not the best sex I've ever had, but certainly high on my top five. Top three, possibly, which is remarkable for a first time.

First time? *Only time.*

There were things to be worried about. How readily he had taken a condom out of his wallet and snapped it on – that was a worry. Do married men usually carry condoms? I have no idea, but I'm relieved, because I stopped picking up my pill prescription after I moved out of Max's flat.

As he moved into me, I yelped. He stopped and looked at me, concerned.

'Have I hurt you?'

I tried not to laugh, or cry. No, I wanted to say. You haven't hurt me. But you've done something: you've drawn a very definite line between my old life and my new one. I'm used to everyday sex, relationship sex, sex where no one cared about strange noises or sudden leg cramps. The unfamiliarity of the latex and the newness of your body feels like a confirmation that everything is different now, and will be for some time.

'No,' I said, draping my arms around his neck. 'It feels good.'

And after a while, it did. I fell asleep being held by him but woke up to him putting his shoes on.

'I need to get back.'

'Back where?'

'Home.'

This is the first time I have ever known him to go home.

'Home to your wife's house?'

This irritated him. 'Home to *my* house, yes.'

'I thought she kicked you out.'

'Yeah, no, she did. We patched that up.'

He was really peeved now. I decided not to say anything else. I watched him get ready, and when he was, he knelt down beside me.

'Look, me and Renata, we have . . .'

He was doing that thing again, that thing where he leaves the gate of the sentence open and hopes you will close it.

' . . . an arrangement?'

'An understanding.'

'I've never heard you say her name before.'

'I've never had cause to.'

'Renata. Is that . . . Italian?'

'Her mother was Czech.'

'Ah.'

'Anyway, I want a divorce, and she doesn't want to give me one.'

'You said last night that she kicked *you* out.'

'Marriage is very complicated, Jane. I don't expect you to know.'

'Fuck you.'

It rang out in the room. And even though I was naked, and even though we'd had sex only hours previously, I still felt the terrifying impact of saying 'fuck you' to my boss.

'I'm sorry,' he said. 'I didn't mean to patronise you. But I need to go. Stay as long as you want. Order breakfast. We'll speak soon.'

We'll speak soon.

I mouth the words to myself on the bus, trying to find the exact meaning. We'll speak soon. So swift, so businesslike. Did 'soon' mean Monday? Did 'soon' mean he would call me as soon as his wife wasn't in earshot? Did it matter? Did I care?

'We'll speak soon,' I say quietly. A woman in front of me, a woman with long, untidy grey hair and a big apple face, cranes her neck around to face me.

'All right?' she says cheerfully, and I give her a mortified smile.

'Sorry,' I say, and pretend to look at my phone. The battery is dead, so I just see tangles of my own damp hair and the beginnings of a spot.

When I get home, Shiraz is doing one of her DVDs. She takes one look at me in yesterday's dress, my hair wet, my eye make-up smudged towards my cheekbones.

'Well, hello.'

'Hey.'

'There's a ladder in my tights.'

'Oh, piss off,' I say, and go straight to my room. I brush my wet hair. It's clumpy and filled with knots, the way hair can only get if you haven't brushed it immediately after stepping out of the shower.

'Fuck,' I say, to no one. 'Fucking *fuck*.'

There's a faint ripping sound, and then there it is: a little brown clump of hair in my hand. I stare and stare and stare, and after a long time, I throw it out the window. Maybe a bird will make a nest out of it.

9

I go into work on Monday morning armed with a secret. I am not going to tell anyone what happened on Friday night. Not even Darla. She would kill me.

I'm mostly ashamed because of how — well, because of how *obvious* the whole thing is. Sleeping with your married boss? Really, Jane? Is this what you're doing? Joining a long line of women who have nothing better to do with their youth than have sex with older men they barely know?

I don't think men worry about being unoriginal in their sexual conquests. Otherwise, Rupert Murdoch wouldn't have married Jerry Hall. Otherwise, bikini models wouldn't regularly marry men who can tie their neck skin into a bun. Clem isn't worried. He isn't worried that he's had sex with someone twenty years his junior, and he's not worried about who I might tell. He's not worried about his wife Renata finding out, and he's not worried about whether or not he stays married to her. He is confident that however the chips fall, he will be fine. Because things are always fine for men like him.

Becky is all over me. She has heard about the wild success of the pitch on Friday, and the party afterwards. She seems to know everything that happened: the technical failure, the private tables at Font, where we went for pizza. I try to be casual, uninterested, but I am analysing every word that comes out of her mouth. Does she know? How could she know? Does *everyone* know?

I get an email before lunch, cc'ing in the whole pitch team. We're to go to the boardroom to talk about the Fat Eddie win. When I get there, Howard Mitchell is waiting for us. This is unusual: he's usually off entertaining some Russian clients in a hotel bar somewhere, or pacing in his glass office. He is the only person at Mitchell who has an office, because he comes from a time when everyone had an office. He set up this business by himself and, according to everyone, was fuelled entirely by prescription drugs when he did it.

Clem is there, and he barely looks at me. David is there, and he's looking everywhere but right at me. I've ruined it for ever with him. I wonder if he's disgusted by me, if he thinks I had sex with Clem to get ahead at work. I wonder if he'll tell anyone. I imagine him telling the people on his team, delighted the way colleagues are when there's a fresh piece of gossip to polish. Because that's what this story is now: it's not about sex, or romance, or two adults choosing to spend a night together against their better judgement. It's about gossip. As soon as this story gets into the water supply, it will ripple throughout the agency. Certain people will avoid me out of awkwardness, and certain others will try to befriend me to get as much information as they can. People will say I have Daddy Issues and maybe someone who knows me – maybe even Darla or Becky – will admit that I don't see my dad, and the story will grow from there.

I pray that the news Howard Mitchell has for us is that we've all been made redundant with full pay. But he doesn't. Instead, he congratulates us. He pats Clem on the back for assembling and leading such an excellent team, then nods his approval at Deb for helping. He says we are invaluable assets, the backbone of the business. He is exactly how I imagine Richard Branson to be: repugnant at a distance, but so charismatic in person you forget that he's probably a dirtbag. As we're all filing out of the meeting room, fat on praise, he stops me.

'I'm sorry, Judith?'

'Jane.'

'Jane! Of course. So sorry. Awful with names. There are so many young people hanging about the place that it gets a bit much for me. Old brain, you know.'

I laugh. 'That's okay. I don't know anyone's name until they've annoyed me.'

His smile is twinkly. 'Could you follow me, please?'

I'm sweating with nerves, running through the possibilities of what could be waiting for me at the end of the corridor. I narrow it down to two options.

1. He has heard about my thing with Clem and now he wants to fire me.
2. He has heard about my thing with Clem and now he wants me to give him a blowjob under his desk.

I feel sick. That's how these things start, right? You sleep your way up the food chain until you find yourself jiggling on the laps of oligarchs, telling them to buy you a fur stole.

Just say no! I can just say no. I could have just said no on Friday, too, but I didn't. Why?

I have been mulling this one over since Saturday morning. *Why?* I tried rationalising my own behaviour. *He manipulated you, Jane.* Did he, though? Or did he just present an option that I wilfully fell into? *He took advantage of his seniority, Jane.* Did he, or did I take advantage of him? Did being with someone more powerful than me make me feel powerful, and is there something just a bit pathetic about that?

I have a sudden flash, a deep, humid sex memory, the kind that makes you stop what you're doing and turn crimson, mortified by the powerful recollection. I turn my face to the floor as I trail behind Howard. I remember looking at Clem's body, his hips between my thighs, and grinning. His is the first male body I have seen of this age, of this nature, of this stature, so different to me and to the boys I have known, yet so exactly the same – and I smiled and smiled. It was like breaking into school on a Saturday. Hearing your feet echo, rummaging through the staffroom, feeling the sharp thrill of having seen the building in repose. Looking at your classmates on Monday and thinking, *I know how this place sleeps.*

He kissed my smiling face, tickled me until I begged him to stop. 'I love your laugh,' he said. 'I want to be the one who makes you laugh.'

This was before the morning, before good sense smacked us both around the sides of our heads and scattered us in different directions. But I couldn't deny it, couldn't rationalise it, couldn't tunnel my way out. I had wanted to be with him that night, and the fact that he was my boss, my much older boss, was part of the allure.

The glass door closes behind us and I'm alone with Howard. The only person who can see through is Howard's secretary.

'Have a seat.'

There's a squat cardboard box on the table, like something you would put a bracelet in. Oh God, is this how it starts? Jewellery first, blowjob later?

'Well, open it.' He's grinning now.

I do, slowly, the lid making a soft pop as it comes off.

It's a stack of cards.

I pick one up, unsure. There are perhaps five hundred cards here, and they all say the same thing.

Jane Peters
Account Manager
Howard Mitchell Agencies

My mouth drops open, and Howard starts up his twinkly laugh again.

'Congratulations, my dear. I've heard about your success on Friday, and I looked into all your performance reports, and had a word with your manager.'

I'm startled. My line manager is a woman called Ruth, who has been on maternity leave since December. She's perfectly nice, but she became my manager a little too late in her pregnancy to really invest in what my career was doing. I didn't resent her for it or anything. That's just how life pans out sometimes: not everyone has the energy to be on your team all of the time.

'Ruth?' I say. 'You called *Ruth*? Isn't she still on mat leave?'

'It wasn't easy getting her on the phone, I'll tell you that much. But once I finally did, it turned out you had been overdue a promotion for some time.'

I feel a bubble of pride rise through me and burst in my throat. There's something keeping me from embracing this good news, and it's the image of Ruth on her phone, baby sick on her shoulder, being accosted by Howard Mitchell for not promoting someone whose existence he was entirely unaware of two days ago.

'Thank you,' I finally manage. 'This is amazing.'

'That's not all.' He slides a letter across to me and looks at me expectantly. I take this to mean that he wants me to read the letter in front of him. It is delighted to inform me that I have a pay increase of eight grand.

'This IS amazing,' I repeat. 'Thank you, again.'

'We want to look after young talent like you, Jane. There's so much temptation to leave and go to a new place, and one of our biggest problems is holding on to our brightest girls. Or, young women. Brightest people.'

Did Mitchell have a problem hanging on to female talent? I think back over the last year, remembering all the leaving drinks I have attended. Sophie, the copywriter. Riti, the graphic designer. Aisling, the account manager. All the parties and speeches blend into one long champagne flute. A lot of them, I realise, were women. Howard Mitchell was having a problem keeping women at his company. Was that normal? Did everyone have this problem?

'The role will come with new responsibilities, of course. I know you were doing mostly assistant work, research, analytics, that kind of thing. This will come with a lot more client-facing duties: managing expectations, convincing the client that what you want is what they want. Do you think you're up to it?'

I nod frantically. I want to cry with joy: all those late nights, early mornings, and poring over research papers before the pitch were actually worth something. It's paying off.

'Good. Well, I'm going to set you up with a mentor, then. It's a new programme we're trying. Big in Denmark, apparently. A quarter of your week will be spent shadowing your mentor, going to meetings with them, absorbing their knowledge. We've trialled it with a few people and it's been very successful.'

I nod, although I'm too mesmerised by my new business cards to hear him. *Mm-hm, Denmark.*

'And you work so well with Clem already.'

'Clem?'

'Clem Brown.'

'Oh.'

Do you know? Is that what this is about? Easy access?

'Is there a problem, Jane?'

'No. No, sir.'

He raises an eyebrow. Men who name their businesses after themselves generally do it to avoid the anonymity of 'sir'.

'Jane, Clem is the one who recommended you for this promotion. Other people verified what he had to say, of course, but when I asked him who the standout was from this pitch, he said – do you know what he said? He said you were the most hard-working junior at the company. What was the word he used?'

He drums his fingers on the notepad in front of him, sending his engraved pen rolling. 'Unstoppable.'

Dear Jolly Politely,
 I have been working at my job for nine years, have a decent position and a decent salary. Overall, I would rank my work happiness at a 7/10. However, I recently found out that my colleague who is at the same level as me earns 10% more than I do, despite the fact that we bill the same amount of sales to the company and started at the same time.
 The company we work for sells extremely expensive kitchen units to retailers, and I think that my colleague is earning more because he is a gay man. I have noticed many hints that this might be the case, such as our boss saying that clients take his advice more seriously because of his 'excellent taste'.
 Is this fair? Am I being discriminated against? Is my colleague perhaps being discriminated against, too, it's just working out better for him financially?
 Please help,
 Underpaid Kitchen Aid

Darla insists we go to the pub at lunch.

'Mate. We have to. It's not often that this place actually

wilfully shells out more money. Title changes sure, but you've got a RAISE now. You've got business cards.' She puts an arm around me, adopts a Sicilian accent. 'You're a made man.'

Becky laughs. 'Yeah, you're Maid Marian!'

'Made man, Becky. Christ. Like in the Mafia?' She rolls her eyes at me, and I feel a mean sense of relief. Darla still likes me best. I'm still the main friend.

When we get there Darla insists on buying the drinks. 'You'll be the one getting the rounds in soon enough, babes,' she says, dumping three glasses of white wine on the table. She says 'babes' with a tight band of sarcasm surrounding the word. It occurs to me why she's making such a big deal out of this, and why she's snapping at Becky. She's jealous.

In Darla's head, she was supposed to be the successful one. She's the one who switched departments to work in PR, and she's the one who says 'When I used to work with you' as if it were ten years ago, not ten weeks. She classifies herself as the brightest and best of anyone she knows, and she hates having to reassess that. It must be weird for her, to watch my newfound interest in my own career blossom over the last month. Like if you spent your whole life playing chess and then your little sister turned out to be some strategy genius on her first try.

Not that I'm a genius, obviously. *You're just a slut.*

I can't get this voice out of my head. This white-hot shame that burns behind my eyes every time I get too close to congratulating myself.

No matter what happens now, no matter how far I go or how much money I earn, I'll never escape the suspicion that I got ahead by having sex. I have been trying to imagine Clem's conversation with Howard since he gave me my cards, trying to picture how the whole thing went down. In my head, it was like *Mad Men*, all double entendres and raised eyebrows over the rims of whisky glasses.

'That Peters girl,' Clem says, as if that's a thing anyone would call anyone. 'She's got *potential*.'

In my head, they joke about what my potential is good for, potential to do what, potential *with* what. Jokes about how I'd be handy to have in the boardroom, jokes about how I'd be better off under the table. There are no two men in the history of the world who have had a more disgusting conversation than the disgusting conversation Clem Brown and Howard Mitchell are having in my head. I reach for my wine. It tastes like tin.

'Drink up, Jane,' says Darla, looking at her watch. 'I have to be on a client call in ten minutes.'

She takes a deep, long sip of her drink, watching me all the while.

'So what's he like, then?'

I stiffen. 'What's who like?'

'Clem Brown.'

'He's ... '

What? Sexy, charismatic, fun? Exploitative, selfish, bad at monogamy?

'He's fine.'

She sniffs. 'Seems like he's more than fine, Jane.'

We study each other for a second. What does she mean? How could she possibly know about Friday night already?

'I don't follow,' I say.

'I mean, he's supposed to be this force of nature. Everyone always talks about his pitch-winning skills. You've hardly said anything about him the whole time you've been working together.'

I dither, struggling to say something about Clem that won't give me away.

'That's me. I have to go.' Darla picks up her bag. 'Congrats again, love.'

But there's a woodenness to our hug when she leaves.

'I'll stay,' says Becky loyally, but there's an odd silence between us. I wonder if Becky is jealous too, given how rarely she is lost for words.

'Do you think they'll move you?'

'Hmm?'

'To where the account managers sit.'

'Oh, I don't know.'

'Susie and Ling sit up there. You'll get on with them. They're both super nice.'

'I don't think I've met them yet.'

'Really nice.'

Becky averts her eyes.

'Or maybe they'll assign you to one client, like a car company or something, and you'll sit with all the people who work on that brand. Like, with the designers and the writers and everything. You'll like that. That will be really interesting.' Her voice trembles.

'Becky?' I say, but she won't look at me. I wonder if she is having a very mild panic attack.

'We could still go for lunch when you're able to. When you're not on fancy client lunches.'

'Becky. Stop it with the window.'

'I don't have any friends, Jane.'

This, I was not expecting.

'Sure you do. I'm your friend. Darla's your friend.'

'Darla hates me. And you're going to go sit somewhere else and you won't be my friend any more.'

'Darla loves you, she's just a bitch. And we will always be friends,' I say, immediately fearing what I've committed myself to. 'And anyway, you have loads of mates outside of work, too.'

Her face scrunches up, turning redder and redder. This is a cry she has clearly been holding in for some time. Becky is *due* this cry, in the way you can be due your period.

'No I don't. Those girls don't even care about being friends. Not with me, anyway. No one even thinks about me.'

I cannot think of even one suitable response to this.

'Yes . . . yes they do.'

She is not going to give up on this cry. This is not a cry you are supposed to stop, I realise.

'It wasn't meant to be like this, you know? I got into Cambridge.'

'No you didn't. You went to Cumbria,' I say gently, fearing she has lost her mind.

'But I *did* get into Cambridge. *HE* got into Cumbria. So I went to Cumbria.'

Ah. I know who *he* is.

'He' is Si, Becky's teenage boyfriend, the one that everyone thought she was going to marry until he dumped her at twenty-two. Becky only ever refers to him in a veiled, wistful kind of way. They shared a flat throughout uni, I know they took a road trip of Italy together, I know that Becky learned perfect Italian to take that trip. And I know that when he left her, her father revealed that he had been saving money for her wedding, and that he advised her to buy a flat in London with it. I have always envied Becky her cute studio in New Cross, the one that will probably be worth a couple of million in a few years. But to her, the flat might as well be a Magdalene laundry, a boarding house for the unmarried only-child of two doctors.

'Becky,' I begin, looking for the words that will comfort her against Cumbria. For a minute, I pretend to be Jolly.

'I'll agree that not going to the number-one university in the country to be near your boyfriend was not the best choice in the world, but it isn't the defining choice of your life, either. There are few decisions you make at eighteen that can truly ruin your life, and you haven't ruined yours. You're smart and you're pretty and you're a homeowner, for

Christ's sake, and you can do anything you want to do. You don't have to stay in this job if you don't like it. You could sell your house and do an *Eat Pray Love* if you wanted to. Travel the world.'

'No one would come with me.'

'That's the point! You could go, and meet someone, or meet a ton of people, or meet no one. You could have sex at a full-moon party while tripping your face off on mushrooms, if you felt like it. But you can't give up on yourself. Not now.'

'That kind of thing wouldn't happen to me. That kind of thing happens to you,' she says, her eyes dry now, taking long gulps of her wine, picking up one of my new business cards. 'Things always happen for people like you.'

Dear Underpaid Kitchen-Aid,

I won't pretend that I wouldn't prefer to buy my kitchen from a gay man, because I absolutely would. I trust the taste of gay men implicitly. It may be a stereotype that this man is selling more kitchens than you, but he is making it work to his advantage, so I say: hats off to him.

I will admit, you are probably at a slight disadvantage here. However, 'discriminated against' feels like far too strong a term. Do you know what discrimination is? A black person not getting a promotion because their boss feels more comfortable with white people is discrimination. A gay guy selling more kitchen units than a straight guy is just life.

Get a grip.

Love,

Jolly Politely

10

By the time I had finished listening to Becky's problems, I was kind of spent, so I bashed out my response to the kitchen guy on the way back to my desk. I like being regular with Jolly. There are some people who have millions of followers just because they update every day. I'm not saying I need millions of followers, but it would be nice to flirt with the possibility. It would be nice to be known for something.

People love my response. It hits all four quadrants of things that people on the internet love: it's short, it's LGBT friendly, it's witty, and it has an implied distrust of straight white guys. Lots of people share it through Tumblr and I get a whole bunch of new people on the blog, which is now a hotbed of discussion about positive discrimination, pay rises, prejudice and kitchens.

'You're happy.'

Clem. I hadn't even had time to consider our new future together: me shadowing him, of all things. This was either God's hilarious joke or Clem's way of keeping me close, and I didn't know whose attention I should be more flattered by.

At this moment, it feels like Clem is shadowing me, looming in the background, squinting at my screen. I close Jolly quickly. What do you say to your boss – now official *mentor* – once you've had sex with them?

'Hi.'

'I've been told by Howard that we're going to be working together a lot more,' he says, not a hint of slyness or intrigue in his voice. 'So that you can get accustomed to your new role.'

'Yes, I've been told the same thing.'

'I have a client meeting at three p.m. Are you free?'

I open my calendar, even though I know perfectly well I have nothing on.

'Great. I'll swing by your desk. Go and Google Think Gym in the meantime: I want you on this account, shadowing at first, but doing some of the client management stuff too. Oh, and it's a lunch thing, so don't eat.'

'Lunch at *three*?'

'Early dinner. Whatever you want to call it. Don't eat.'

I nod. I didn't eat anything at the pub, and I didn't have any breakfast, but I don't feel hungry anyway. I try to remember the last time I had a full meal. There was the breakfast I had in the hotel room, after Clem left: two poached eggs, bacon and sliced avocado topped with chilli salt. I had wolfed it down, but that was Saturday morning. What had I eaten Saturday evening? Or Sunday? I have the vaguest recollections of a yogurt and half a Ryvita.

'Did he say Think Gym?' says Becky, fully recovered from her emotional breakdown at lunch, which we are both trying to pretend didn't happen.

I nod.

'Jane,' she says, astonished, like I've secretly been the Count of Monte Cristo this whole time. '*Think Gym.*'

My expression is blank. She almost takes it as an insult.

'Think Gym, Jane. The gym for your mind. It's a huge, huge deal. It's Mitchell's first non-food pitch in like, years.'

'You can go to the gym for your *mind*?'

'It's like, part yoga and Pilates and meditation and stuff, but also like, activities that make you less stressed out. Like origami, and colouring books.'

We Google it together. The website has a lot of stock images of pissed-off, overworked-looking women. A woman juggling a baby and a massive mobile phone. A woman with her head in her hands, and a mountain of paperwork. A woman with a bottle of wine next to her, grimacing into her empty glass. No prizes for guessing who their target market is.

I flick through other pages, these ones with relaxed, heavenly images of women doing yoga on cliff faces. A woman smiling at the camera, holding up her Certificate of Wellness.

Before Think Gym, I had no idea how cluttered my mind was, or how much it was holding me back. Now I've learned the coping mechanisms for dealing with a stressful life – and knowing when to have fun, too!

I wonder, bleakly, if this is my future. I wonder if the best thing about being a woman in the twenty-first century is working yourself so hard that you have to be sent to a gym to feel like a person again. You can work every day and meet the guy and have the baby, and take eight days' maternity leave, and be a CEO and go to yoga and still be told there's something wrong with you. I look at Becky, who is drinking it all in, staring at the yoga women raptly.

I've never thought much about what my late thirties will look like, and seeing this website, I never want to again. How old was my mum when she became a single mother? Thirty-five? Thirty-six?

Becky is doing her stern face again. 'Jane, this is a huge deal. Every woman on this floor wants to be on that account. I heard some of the senior account managers talking about it the other day. It's *the* account to be on.'

By the time Clem comes to my desk, I'm sufficiently read up on Think Gym. I've looked up all the 'research' they've posted on their website, most of which are unreadable sponsored studies about how social media makes you depressed.

He waits until we're in the lift before he starts talking. He has a fresh shirt on, and I can smell him again: that sharp, muddy man smell. It stayed on me all through Saturday and most of Sunday, getting slighter and slighter, but still present in the articles of clothing he had touched. The smell that made me quake very slightly. The amber scent that makes me want to reach over and touch the exposed piece of skin between his jaw and his collar.

'I want you to know that you're only here because you should be,' he says.

'What do you mean?'

'You know what I mean.' He faces me, but looks at the lift buttons behind my shoulder. 'You're on this job because I need you on this job. Not because of . . . ' He waits for me to fill in the rest. I don't. 'Whatever happened between us. That doesn't matter.'

I feel a strange mix of relief and disappointment. On the one hand, it's pleasing to be reassured that I got here on my own merit. But is he really saying that what happened between us didn't matter? Was it that forgettable an experience, for him?

Darla calls me on the way there. 'Hey,' she says, suspicious. 'You're not at your desk.'

'No,' I say, keen to get off the phone quickly so as not to appear unprofessional. 'I just have, ah, a lunch meeting.'

'A *lunch* meeting? With who?'

'With . . . Think Gym.'

'Think Gym,' she says, a sour note in her voice.

'The gym for mindfulness,' I tell her.

'Yes, Jane, I know what Think Gym is. I'm just surprised *you* do.'

Her comment smarts on me, and I can tell she's still furious that I have been promoted above her, so quickly after her own promotion. It annoys me, even though I know these are the roles we wrote for ourselves. I am the dependable, settled-down one with the boyfriend and the nice flat. She is the wilder one, the one who goes for gold every time. The last few weeks have changed that, and I'm not prepared to let it change back.

'You'd be surprised at what I know.' I'm shocked at how much ice I'm able to muster. For Darla, of all people.

She doesn't rise to it. I can hear her trying to sound distracted. 'Anyway, I must go. It's crazy over here.'

She hangs up.

When we get to the restaurant – I have never had a meeting in a restaurant before – the Think Gym people are already there, two of them, men in their late twenties. They look like Morgan Stanley executives who have gone rogue. Suits, ties and precise, fascist-style haircuts. They look like the kind of guys who could be holding a small amount of expensive cocaine at any given time.

'This is Jane, our account manager,' says Clem.

I know they're definitely going to discuss me later. I have met enough of these kinds of men to know that if you're a woman five years on either side of their age, they will discuss you. Maybe they will give you a mark out of ten.

The more dominant youth looks confused. 'But we thought that—'

'Jane's just won a very high-profile pitch for us, so she's really The Girl to talk to at Mitchell right now.'

I know I'm supposed to hate being called a Girl. I know I'm supposed to correct him, and tell him I'm a woman, in italics. But in the moment, I like it. Girl. It's a word that sounds as puppyish as I feel.

He pulls out my chair for me, a gesture that seems to indicate to the other men that there's a lady here now, and we all must behave. I smile a thank-you at him, and our eyes meet properly for the first time today. The sharp shock of attraction hits me like adrenalin: it makes me want to perform for him, to make him so proud and pleased with me that he kisses me again and again.

He smiles back, and the Think Gym guys look at each other again. Oh God. Can they tell?

Despite my grand introduction, I don't get a chance to speak much. The lunch drones on and on. There are graphs about women, what they do, and what they spend their money on.

'Women feel like they need permission to spend time and money on themselves,' says one, who is called either Matt or Mike. 'So we need them to really engage with the fact that there is a problem with how they're living.'

'Sorry, what?'

Even I've surprised myself by saying this, but it's all such unfathomable bollocks that I have to say something.

'Is there a problem?'

'If you want women to focus on what they're doing wrong, I think the market is just a bit crowded, if you know what I mean.'

I laugh, but no one gets it. The three men look at me, The Girl, as if I were a bird regurgitating my own dinner into my baby's mouth. *Necessary, sure, but why do we have to think about it?*

'Okay, so,' I try to break it down, as simply as I possibly can. 'Everyone wants to sell women things, right? Women control most household expenditure. According to your graph, anyway. And the easiest way to make a woman spend money on something she doesn't need is by making her feel guilty.'

There is a silent group nod. It occurs to me that if I hadn't been here, Clem would have come alone, and no woman would have been present for decisions pertaining to a product that caters solely to women. Where's Deb? Surely she would be able to explain all this in crisper, sharper, more authoritative language?

I feel, in a way, like it's my job to be her. My destiny, almost: not just today, but in my actual life.

'You feel guilty about not getting your five a day, so you buy a smoothie. You feel guilty about not sleeping enough, so you buy a bracelet that tracks how you're sleeping. Everyone is trying to corner the market on female guilt and maybe that still works if you're selling Activia but for something like this—' I gesture at the marketing materials on the table. 'This is expensive. You need something bigger than guilt for this.'

The Think Gym guys maybe gave me a 7/10 when I first walked in, but they've certainly demoted it to 5 now. I see the door of the restaurant behind them, and wonder if there's any way I can slither bonelessly under the table and leave here undetected.

'Bigger than guilt,' says Matt or Mike, flatly. 'Let's get the bill.'

We leave, and Clem gives me a brusque, 'See you tomorrow.'

I go home and wait to be fired. Shiraz is flicking absently through every TV channel.

'Hey,' she says.

'Hey,' I reply, thinking it's a trick.

'How are you?' She doesn't look away from the screen as she says it, but that doesn't change the fact that she has never asked me a question as personal as 'how are you' before.

'Yeah, okay. It's been . . . ' How can I sum up today, as succinctly as possible? I spent almost all of it in paranoid fear that I would never work again. 'I got a promotion,' I say.

'Oh yeah?'

'Yeah.'

'Congratulations then,' she says, and I can detect a note of genuine warmth in her voice. 'Do you want to get a pizza?'

I pause, and she rushes to fill it in. 'Because it's cheaper if you order two. I don't get it. One for twelve quid, or two for a pound.'

It takes me a second to realise she's joking. A joke! From Shiraz! About pizza!

We order pizza. Not because I'm hungry, but because I'm determined not to waste this window of friendship Shiraz has decided to open to me. We watch an old episode of *Friends*. We don't chat much, but it's nice. I relax around her for the first time, and I can feel her body language gradually unspool. Her shoulders ease, her legs unfold and spread out on the couch. She's such a tight spring. I wonder what happened to make her this way.

'I love this episode,' I say, and I do. It's the one where the girls and the boys play a game about who knows who best, and in the end the girls lose their apartment.

'Me too,' she says. 'Do you remember when you thought being in your twenties would be like this?'

'Like what?'

'Having a bunch of friends that all hang out in your flat, all the time. Making up stupid games with them.'

I do remember what that was like. I watched shows like this throughout my childhood, and assumed that they were blueprints of how my life would turn out. I didn't think I was being unrealistic. I knew that the friends in *Friends* had enormous apartments and spent an improbable amount of time drinking coffee and not working. But the other aspects – the kinship, the hijinks, the shared holidays, the crazy bets that quickly got out of control – I assumed that was a given. I think of Becky, crying in the pub earlier, so convinced that her life was already over. That nothing would happen to her, that no one would love her, and that things – real things, remarkable things – only happened to other people.

I never suspected that I would find a fit comparison between Becky and Shiraz, but here I am, having the same conversation with two different women in one day. There's a queasiness to the symmetry of it, coupled with a crawling, dry itch on the tops of my thighs.

'You have loads of friends,' I say to Shiraz. 'You're always out.'

She takes the measure of me, this stranger who has come into her life and now uses her cutlery and steals her tights and orders pizza with her. She smiles slowly.

'When I'm out,' she says, 'I'm not out with friends.'

There's a knock. 'Pizza's here,' she says and goes to the door.

I hear a quick tussle of voices, and then 'Jane,' Shiraz calls, 'can you come here?'

At the door there's no pizza guy. There is, however, a flower guy.

'Jane Peters?' he says, bored. I nod. 'Sign this.'

They're not your traditional red roses, or one of those pastel arrangements that you order online and always end up looking like Mother's Day bouquets. They're wildflowers. Bright yellow and lilac and green, tied together with a satin bow in a big mason jar. I have not received very many flowers in my life, but I know that these are good flowers. These are Pinterest-level flowers.

I put them on the kitchen table.

'These are nice,' Shiraz says.

'They are.'

'Do you know who they're from?'

'I do.'

'Do you want to tell me?'

Only a person as guarded as Shiraz would ask like this: *Do you want to tell me?* Cool, therapeutic. Any other woman in the world would shriek and coo and insist you give her the gossip. Something about her non-judgemental reserve makes me want to tell her everything, while also knowing that she probably isn't that interested.

I choose my words carefully.

'They're from my boss.'

I've started referring to him as my boss in my head, even though Ruth is my real boss. But Clem has already done more for my career than she ever did.

'I see.'

'He's married. We had sex on Friday.'

'Well, he certainly seems to want to do it again.'

'Do you think?'

'Yes.'

Shiraz puts the mason jar under the tap, and slices open the packet of plant food with nail scissors. I start scratching my legs. I wish I could call him. I wish his voice could provide some kind of context for these flowers.

'Did you say you got a promotion today, when you came in?'

The relief I felt at telling her is now turning to regret.

'Yeah, but I honestly don't think those two things are related.'

She lets that hang there. This is so absurd and exhausting, this constant layering of money and sex and sex and power and trying to figure out what bolsters what. It's like a game of Jenga.

There's another knock at the door, and this time it really is the pizza.

'Get as much out of this as you can, Jane,' Shiraz says, grabbing her wallet. 'God knows he will.'

I open the card while she greets the pizza guy, and I know why I felt that eerie sense of familiarity when I talked to Howard Mitchell earlier.

The card has three words.

To my best.

PART THREE

II

Dear Jolly
    do not sign for the flowers

The email address is a string of numbers on an AOL account, and it's sitting in my inbox the next morning. I didn't know AOL was still a *thing*.

I mouth the words to myself. *Do not sign for the flowers*, all lower case.

My first thought is that it's his wife. Renata with the Czech mother. Renata who kicked him out of the house. I picture her, black hair and pinched expression, coming across a florist's receipt in his emails, tracking down the recipient, opening an anonymous email account, and then sending an email as limp as 'do not sign for the flowers'. I don't know her, but it doesn't feel like her style, somehow. She did kick her husband out of her house, after all. Why be so passive? Why not tell me to fuck off?

Something about the word 'dear' forces me to consider it in ways I haven't before. I whisper it to myself in bed, phone in my hands. I speed it up, slow it down, say it like a mantra. *Dear. Dear. De-aye-re.* It strikes me that 'dear' is the most formal way you can greet someone in a letter – your bank uses it, your doctor uses it, a funeral director would use it – and yet look how startlingly intimate it is. So soft and tender. To be *dear* to someone. My dear.

My phone buzzes, and my heart lifts when I see that it's Darla.

Mum is thrilled for you.

I type back

Tell her I say thanks.

I add a heart. I love Darla's mum. I've met her only a few times, but she's one of those people who look ordinary from far away, and beautiful close up. I think it's because she's always smiling.

Barely five seconds pass before she responds.

She wants to know how much money you're on now.

I throw the phone on to the bed, determined not to respond. This is so like Darla: cloaking her furious desire to know which of us is winning in something her mother said. The duvet swallows my phone, and I decide to give Darla some space for a few days. To not participate in her unhealthy sense of competition. I will rise *above* it, I think, a little smugly.

And then a thought enters my head, like a snake into Eden. What if *Darla* sent the email? What if the reason Darla is being so unpleasant towards me is because she knows something? I remember what she said on the night of my birthday: how irritated she seemed about him singing to me, how she had dismissed him as a flirt. With who? With her?

And then yesterday, at lunch. All she wanted to know about was Clem. She didn't ask about the details of the pitch, or the party afterwards. *Do not sign for the flowers.*

Clem's flowers are even more beautiful with the morning sunlight shot through them. I think about the way he kissed the insides of my thighs and the backs of my knees, feeling the shiver of recollection. I can no longer smell him on my clothes or my hair; all I can think about is getting it back.

I remember the way Darla and I joked about the underground network of single-person gossip at Mitchell. Does Clem send everyone he sleeps with flowers? Or just all the ones who help him win pitches?

But for Darla to know, she'd have to know about Jolly, also, to contact me at this address. And no one knows about Jolly. Or, at least: I haven't *told* anyone about Jolly. The only people who are aware that I am Jolly Politely are Max and a few people from uni who I lost contact with years ago.

Maybe it's just a coincidental spam message. And in any case, I've already signed for the flowers, so what difference does it make?

I Google 'Renata Brown', and find nothing that could apply to her: a beauty salon in Crystal Palace and some Facebook pages belonging to Americans. She probably still uses her maiden name, and I have no idea what that is. Still in Sherlock-mode, I Google Clem. There's not a lot there, but what is there is impressive. Quite a few trade mags have featured him over the last five or six years, starting with some wins in the catering industry that branched out into bigger stuff. One article from two years ago talks about a highly competitive pitch where six of London's biggest agencies were bloodily duking it out over a skincare brand.

Coming off the back of a six-win hot streak is Mitchell's Clem Brown, whose strong sense of pragmatism and creative eye has quickly made him a titan in the industry.

On and on like this, talking about these normal, work-a-day husbands and fathers as if they were conquerors; as if they were leading men into war with lit cannons, not into board-rooms with dodgy laptops and poster boards. The whole thing is so unashamedly *blokey*, the entire industry reported on as if it were a blood sport. I can't even dismiss the thing because of how attracted to him I am because of it, these constant references to him being a winner and a titan and a pragmatist. It's a cheap trick and I hate watching myself fall for it.

I go to work, itching to see him. It's like a fever, my skin red and hot and screaming to be looked at and touched. And of course, he's nowhere to be found.

I manage to wait all morning before emailing him.

RE: last night's delivery
　Since when do you know where I live?

I guess it was easy for him to get my address, given how he probably had to sign something with my employee records when he agreed to be my mentor. But it seems like a cute opening line regardless.

Do you like them?

I take a deep breath and try to remember Shiraz's words from last night. *Get as much out of this as you can, Jane, God knows he will.* Why did she say that? Does Shiraz have a Clem of her own, and is that where she is every evening?

Do all young women have a married man they attend to in secret? As unlikely as this is, I'm still quietly hurt that no one has told me.

Love them. How can I repay you?

I wince at the horrible cheesiness of my own line, but there's no point doing things by half. My entire body is gnawing for him in a way I haven't experienced before. That sounds unfair to Max, but it isn't. I always wanted to have sex with Max, but the sex was part of a bigger thing: a cog in the big machine of our relationship, a relationship that was filled with Sunday lunches and watching *Prison Break* and visiting his parents' house and the cat we never adopted but talked about getting. This is a hunger that feels bone-deep, one that makes food taste like nothing. I sat on the couch with Shiraz last night and tried to eat pizza, but I may as well have been chewing a handful of buttons. I had spent all of yesterday feeling sick and perverted, but now the sickness has shifted into something wilder. Something clawing and feral and wrong.

Meet me in India.

Mitchell named his meeting rooms after his favourite places in the world, and because of that certain countries have taken on connotations. Paris, for example, is a small room with only three chairs in it, and is located next to the HR department. Last year a bunch of copywriters got made redundant, each one dragged into the room to discuss their severance packages and then escorted out of the building by security. Ever since then 'being taken to Paris' has been our office slang: our Green Mile, as it were.

India is more anonymous. It's just a regular meeting room, only it has a picture of Ganesh in it. The one thing it does have going for it, which I notice as I make my way there to meet Clem, is that it's in a short corridor and the door isn't particularly in view of anyone's desk.

He's already there, his back to me, facing the whiteboard someone else has left in a mess.

'People really love a Venn diagram, don't they?' he says.

'What's not to love?'

This particular Venn diagram's left circle says 'beer' and the right circle says 'social occasions'. The shaded bit in the middle is called 'the sweet spot'. He wrinkles his brow at it, as if the reason he invited me here was to critique this abandoned whiteboard.

'It's just stupid, isn't it? This is not how a Venn diagram was intended to be used. So we can visually represent that when beer meets a social occasion a 'sweet spot' will be born. Probably one of Deb's lot. She's a big fan of stating the fucking obvious.'

I peer at the board, unable to see any trace of Deb.

'You're really bothered by this Venn diagram.'

'I hate,' he says, grabbing the cloth and swabbing it away, 'mediocre fucking thinking.'

I like him this way, when he drops his usual image of detached charm and allows himself to be irritated by things.

'What else do you hate today, then?'

'Oh, not much. I hate the man on my commute who continually misses the same patch of hair on his neck when he shaves. Also: almond milk. I hate the way it tastes. You can't milk a nut. The correct term is "liquidised nut mulch".'

As I laugh, I remember what he said in the hotel room. *I want to be the one who makes you laugh.*

'And I hate . . .' He hesitates, stepping closer. 'I hate that I wake up wanting to hold you, and you're never where you're meant to be.'

'I'm here now,' I say, as softly as I can manage.

He puts his thumb on my bottom lip, pressing it gently, testing it. He holds my chin in his hand very lightly.

'That you are,' he says, a touch of grandness in his voice. 'That you are.'

He kisses me then, letting his hands travel up my neck and

into my hair. I don't know if I'm turned on as much as I am relieved to silence the terrible, itching craving for him. He pulls my face forward, his fingers on the nape of my neck, as if interrogating the inside of my mouth for information. It feels like he is looking for something, trying to lift a stone deep at the very bottom of me. I lean into him, grabbing him, and realise how clear my mind becomes when he's touching me. The paranoia and the nausea and the constant questioning of my life and the lives of the women around me turn to nothing. It's trash, it's dust particles, it's a few brown pennies and some lint at the bottom of a handbag. None of it matters, because all that matters is being here, with him.

And this is how I end up giving Clem a hand job in India.

12

It's amazing how quickly we develop a routine. Once we've traded numbers – I never thought I'd have seen someone's penis twice before even getting their phone number – we're in almost constant contact. On the nights we can't see each other, he texts me from his house in Surrey, his messages radiating with loneliness. They are full of wishing, and longing, and what-are-you-doings. They range from 'I wish I could be with you' to 'I wish we could watch *The Wire* together'. We have long, fictional discussions about places we're going to visit, and the things he is going to show and teach me. The restaurants I simply have to eat in. The countries he knows I would love.

I've decided that I'm taking you to Cadiz x

I've never been! x

You would love it. I'll open a fish restaurant and you can write your memoirs.

Is he asking me to move to Spain with him, or is this part of the fantasy element of having a mistress? I try not to think too hard about it. I play along.

I'll start brushing up on my Spanish, then x

India becomes our main spot, but it's not our only one. There's a room called Nana's House on the third floor that is barely bigger than a cupboard. It has one armchair and is supposed to be a place where you take private phone calls. The walls are paisley, the pattern so close together that when I'm sitting on top of him, my legs on either side of his hips and my head resting on his shoulder, it becomes a Magic Eye painting.

It's easy to get time together because we're meant to be spending so much of our time together anyway. The boys from Think Gym (we only ever call them boys, and only ever while smirking spitefully) come back within days of our lunch to say they liked our ideas.

'But we didn't have any ideas,' I say. 'I just told them I hated theirs.'

He loves telling me about what a brat I was at the meeting. He tells me I'm fiery, stubborn, that I speak my mind, and he says it with a bounce in his voice. He has an idea in his head of who I am, and it's easy to go along with it. He says he's like Henry Higgins in *My Fair Lady*.

'Does that make me Audrey Hepburn?'

'Only much prettier.'

We stay late at the office a lot, like we did with the Fat Eddie pitch, only this time when we eat Thai food we do it while I'm sitting on his lap. We criticise work that comes back from the creative departments, we build strategies to try to sell yoga packages to women who probably already have a weekly yoga class they attend. We talk about 'she': the anonymous 'she' we are selling to, what 'she' needs, what websites 'she' goes to, what compels 'her' to drop huge amounts of money on meditation techniques.

At night the office becomes our quiet kingdom, but we're still careful: we make sure we're never in plain sight, always in a meeting room, and we keep a close eye on where the security guard is. We never, ever leave at the same time. Somehow, we're able to spend three weeks doing just this. I don't know why it never occurs to me to ask for more: to be taken to dinner, or to be given a promise, or at the very least, an explanation of why things aren't working out with his wife.

I know exactly what Jolly would say: I know because I've written words to mistresses before. Hundreds of them. Words like:

You are accepting the love you think you deserve.

And:

Don't allow yourself to be hurt just so you can be someone's hobby.

And:

You are not being easygoing and fun: you are being an idiot.

Why can't I follow my own advice? Well: because I'm not Jolly. Because she's something I invented to feel better about myself, and it's merely a coincidence that she makes other people feel better in the process.

'What are you doing over there?' Clem is peering at me from the other side of the meeting room. I'm on my phone, looking at my Jolly emails.

I make a face, as though I'm being told off by a teacher.

'Won't happen again, sir.'

He smiles, and pats his lap. I move over to him. I can hardly believe how predictable this all is. Is it fun because it's a cliché, or is it a cliché because it's fun?

If Becky suspects anything, she hasn't said it. I haven't kept my promise to her, even though we still sit together. We haven't had lunch once since her outburst at the pub, and I stuff the memory to the bottom of myself every time I see her. Clem hasn't asked me to move desks, though I keep expecting him to. Sometimes I wonder whether it's easier for him to keep me here, in Research, because of how low-profile it is in comparison to the rest of the agency. Hidden away. *His secret.*

Darla, still quietly fuming at my promotion, has decided to snub me as a way of punishment. On one of the rare days that I'm not flanked by Clem or one of the other account managers, I see her in the canteen. She waves at me, but uses only the tips of her fingers. I know this isn't intended as an invitation to join her, but I do anyway. I walk over to her, my energy bar in one hand and my pomegranate-flavoured water in the other, and with every step her expression darkens.

Maybe it's the loneliness, or maybe it's my newfound lack of shame, but regardless, I keep moving towards Darla like a boat to a lighthouse.

'Hey,' I say. And I'm not sure what to say next. To *Darla*. The person I've spent two years referring to as my work wife, as if we were the first ever people to come up with the term.

'Hey, babes,' she replies. Her voice is even, with nothing to hint that we had ever been more than colleagues. I want to shake her by the shoulders and will her to remember what we've been through: how, the night that Max dumped me, I had gone straight to her parents' house in Barking, and her mother had the guest room all made up for me. I had barely been able to mumble a thank-you, instead gracelessly slumping on the eiderdown as I tried to imagine my life without him in it.

Do not sign for the flowers.

'How's it going?' I say, wanting to ask: *Are you taunting me and if so, why? Why now? Why over this?*

The girls at her table look at one another uncomfortably, and a few of them busy themselves with their phones. I have the sickly feeling of having been recently discussed by women I don't know.

Darla had given me a folded package of her pyjamas, buttoned and studded with snowmen, and crawled under the covers as I changed into them. She let me cry on her that night, my tears sliding into her black hair so that strands stuck to her neck in wet clumps.

'Fine,' she says. 'How are you getting on with Think Gym?'

Is this really what it comes down to? I have something that she doesn't have, and doesn't think I deserve to have? That, at the end of the day, I'm only any good to Darla as long as I'm sad and weeping into her hair in her mum's spare room?

'Good,' I say, trying to mimic her smoothness. 'How's your mum?'

I mean it sincerely, or at least, I tell myself I do. It comes out of my mouth like a bizarre, locker-room taunt. She juts her chin towards me sharply, and I remember how few people know that Darla still lives with her parents, and how hard she works to appear independent from them.

'She's good. Worried about *you*, actually.' She picks up her bag. 'We have a meeting,' she says, gesturing to her group. 'Let's catch up later, yeah?'

She pushes past me, and her friends follow suit.

It feels precisely like school again: like I'm her mate who she used to play Barbies with at Montessori but now Big School has made our acquaintance uncomfortable. I fumble with my phone, willing the moment to pass.

My guts curdle when I see what is waiting for me in there.

Dear Jolly,
    She will leave him before he leaves her

What *is* this? The last email was a command; this feels like a horoscope. Does that mean Renata is actively planning to leave Clem? Or simply that there is no point in hoping for him to divorce her, because he never will?

Darla is deep in conversation while she waits for the lift, on a different planet already. There's a small sense of relief in this: so it's not Darla, then. *Or,* the paranoid part of my brain thinks, *it is Darla, she's just not working alone.*

The more I dwell on Darla the more sure I am that she knows something. It's hardly surprising: I flip between being convinced everyone knows and being sure no one suspects a thing. I have managed to avoid David Lady almost completely. It hasn't been hard, because he seems to be yet another person who is deliberately avoiding me. When Clem and I are together, I try not to sound uncomfortable when David's name comes up. Not infrequently, it does. Clem likes David, and he has noted the way my expression flickers whenever his name is mentioned.

Only once does he confront me about it.

'You liked him, didn't you?'

'I liked him well enough.'

'Oh, come off it. I remember that day I caught you together, coming back from lunch.'

'Walking to the shops together hardly constitutes an affair, Clem.'

He wrinkles his brow. 'You wanted to fuck him, didn't you?'

His tone turns harsh. His hand wraps around my wrist, just like it did the first time he pulled me away from David and to the free drinks and the sticky-tabled booths at Font Bar. Only his grip isn't leading me any more. It's keeping me in one place.

'You're hurting me,' I say. Because he is, and he could hurt me further if he wanted to. This is the uncomfortable reality that you have to occasionally face when you're a woman around men. They are able to hurt us, if they want to.

Maybe he wants to.

He is close to losing his temper. It comes out of nowhere sometimes, and while I can read the signs of disaster, I choose not to follow them. I choose, instead, to stay.

'What do you want me to say?' I ask.

'The truth. I want you to tell me the truth. I want you to tell me that I wasn't your first choice.'

My heart swells for him in moments like these, even though I know his temper is dangerous. He is startlingly insecure, and needs to be reminded that he is the best, the most chosen. This is usually where I weave him a story: *But you're married, Clem. But you're so much more sophisticated, Clem. But I never thought you would be interested in a silly girl like me, Clem.* On and on like this until he's satisfied, the crease of rage easing out of his brow, and his arms scooping me towards him again. I rest the side of my face on his chest, and feel the agitated thump mellow to a smooth, strong beat. But I wonder what would happen if I walked out, or shot back, or rose to his anger. Is all this hyper-masculine sensitivity something I can ignore, or is there something else there? All bark no bite. What a silly phrase that is: as if he didn't have sharp, white teeth, and as if they weren't designed for chewing up pieces of meat.

And even if he doesn't hurt you, I think, *there's no telling what he could do to your career.* Every now and then I remember Howard, and how he seemed to be losing so much female talent. Almost every day, I think about what Darla said: the way she coolly dismissed Clem as a flirt. I could clarify any of this with him at any point, but I don't. I keep my lips together and my ear on his chest.

Sometimes, when we're at the office late enough, he takes me to a bar afterwards. Not the pubs where the copywriters spend so much of their time 'working remotely', but pricey, dark wine bars with soft music and high-backed chairs. One night, he leads me into a basement whisky bar on Greek Street, the entrance to which is tucked behind a bookshelf in the shop upstairs.

'I don't drink whisky,' I say, browsing the menu for something gin or vodka-based.

'Only because you don't know how,' he answers, too smug to be charming.

He orders us two Old Fashioned cocktails, and then insists I 'sample' Scotches, ryes, single malts and bourbons. I realise that saying you don't like whisky is like saying you don't like theatre, in that people will keep ramming it down your throat until you agree that it is good, and that they are smart for loving it.

'People get snooty about Irish whiskey,' he says, pointing the waiter to my empty glass. 'But only because they think it's just Jameson. And I like Jameson, but it's nothing compared to a Midleton rare.'

It tastes like every other whisky I've ever tasted in my life: prickly and medicinal, and like it's been under some grand-dad's bed for fifty years. I knock it back, trying not to taste it. I do the same with the next one. My face is hot, and I'm dizzy trying to focus on all this whisky information.

Three 'samples' later, and I am being woken up by a stranger in the toilet cubicle, my face sliding against the cold tile wall. I stumble out, and Clem is sending work emails on his phone.

'How long was I in there for?'

'Hmm? I don't know. Ten minutes?'

He takes one look at me and starts laughing. 'Jesus, Jane. I didn't realise you couldn't hold your whisky. Come on, let's get a hotel.'

He said it like Darla would say 'come on, let's get a McDonald's'. I lean my head on his shoulder and try to match his steps, my legs wobbly. I can't help but feel angry with him: why did he keep ordering all that whisky? Why didn't he notice that I was in the loo for ten minutes? I'm silent, partly annoyed, partly too drunk to speak. When I eventually flop down face-first on the cool, soft white sheets of the hotel bed, he laughs again.

'Oh no you don't, miss. Come on. Drink some water. Get your dress off.'

He unlaces my boots carefully and eases them off, giving the balls of my feet a little massage as he does. I've been hiding my lower half from view lately, since the itchy red rash showed up on my legs. Thankfully, Clem's too tactful to mention it. I tell myself it's because he's a gentleman, but it's possible that he just doesn't care.

Now, though, I'm too drunk to really mind. I let one eye open, and even through my nausea, I can't help but find him adorable. A grown man, rubbing the feet of his girlfriend as though she were an empress.

'All right, Mark Antony.'

He smiles at my toes. 'You can't be that drunk if you're referencing Cleopatra. Sit up, my Queen.'

I do, and he pulls my dress off, and covers me in a towelling robe with the hotel's logo on it. He passes me a bottle of water from the minibar and I take two big slugs out of it. I nestle my head into his chest, enjoying the sensation of being cared for.

'Richard Burton was married when he met Elizabeth Taylor.'

I don't know why I said it, except that I remember Mum saying it a lot. *Cleopatra* was one of the movies we always found ourselves watching on those long Sunday afternoons, when we still didn't know how single-parent families spent Sunday afternoons. Who makes a roast dinner for two people?

'They both were, I think. She had Mike Todd. Among others.'

'But Burton was the love of her life. Burton was the person she was meant to be with. Burton was—'

I'm not sure where I'm going with this, and I don't get to find out, because suddenly, Clem has his fingers on my vagina.

'Oh,' I say, more surprised than anything.

As his head disappears underneath the towelling robe, I try to blink away the whisky nausea, squeezing my eyelids shut.

Dear Jolly,
  I think my husband is having an affair.

It has been four days since the whisky night, and three since we've had sex, but I still take this email personally. I still think it's not for Jolly so much as it's for Jane. I open it, and immediately close it again. Did anyone see?

Becky is on the phone, asking a client whether we're legally allowed to tell women that they should eat a yogurt instead of dinner.

'Of course, you know, *I know* I'll be trying out the No-YoYo Diet,' she says, laughing in an attempt to appease. 'But can we guarantee that one, their weight *won't* yoyo, and two, it isn't technically unhealthy? Only technically, of course.'

My skin is itchy. The itch I felt the day I first met Clem in India, but deeper still, like a nettle that has buried right under my skin and stayed there. It never goes away, just quells a little when I'm near him.

I go to the loo and scratch. It's disgusting, but I have to do it. I sit on the toilet and peel down my tights, and the red rash across my thighs is even bigger now, angrier. It's August and I'm the only girl in the office still covering her legs. I keep looking at pictures of my rash online and almost everything seems to say it's just a reaction to the heat. I keep Googling meningitis, diabetes, and something I have invented called 'leg thrush'. I roll glass tumblers over myself to see what the rash does. When I am alone in bed, there is a voice in my head that tells me I have a terrible disease.

I tilt my head back and scratch as deeply as I can, and like all itches, the need to scratch only grows with the satisfaction of scratching. I try to woo the cool porcelain of the toilet seat into my veins.

I take out my phone again.

Dear Jolly,

I think my husband is having an affair, and I think it might be my fault.

Three years ago, our son died in a car accident while I was driving. It wasn't my fault, not technically, but even so, I was driving.

Since then, my husband and I have received couples counselling and therapy individually. He has told me – again and again – that it's time to move on and that we shouldn't let our son dictate our lives. He says we should try for another child, but I'm not ready, and to be perfectly honest, I don't believe I ever will be.

I'm terrified of sex in case I get pregnant – I have nightmares all the time about having another child and my son walking up the driveway to come home, only to see me with another baby and turning around and leaving again. I won't let my husband touch me, and perhaps unsurprisingly, he has started looking elsewhere. I won't go into how I know, but suffice to say it's the usual, dull kind of evidence that I suspect wives everywhere find themselves faced with – late nights, out-of-town work events, that kind of thing.

My instincts tell me I should divorce him, but I don't want to be alone either – and who would love a woman who can't even keep her children alive?

Tell me what to do, Jolly.

I put my head between my knees. *Do not sign for the flowers.*

Clem and I don't speak about Renata. Every now and then his phone lights up and he leaves the room, and when he comes back, we don't address it. One time I snatched his phone while he was in the bathroom and tried to look for something – *anything* – that would tell me that their marriage was on the brink of collapse, like he told me it was on our first night. Renata, of course, is a proper adult who doesn't text her husband entire paragraphs about her day, the way I used to do with Max. Her messages are rare and desolate. 'Ok' and 'call me' and 'later'. I scrolled through his contacts, amazed at how many people he knows, tingling with jealousy at how many women's names are in his address book.

I sift through Rebeccas and Paulas and Vivs and Janets. I spy a few names of women who used to work at the agency, and am reminded of Darla and Howard Mitchell again. I think: *How many of you are neighbours and cousins and co-workers, and how many of you have fucked him?*

I put down the phone then, slide it face down across the table to the notebook in front of his empty chair.

Even when I'm at the peak of my happiness with Clem, even when he is being funny and charming and sexy, I try to convince myself that this is a brief phase in both of our lives. I put my Jolly hat on: Jolly, who would either tell me to break up with him, or failing that, reassure me to just have fun with him, and to think of the interesting story I could tell afterwards. Whatever mood she was in, she would tell me to look after myself, first and foremost.

This will always be the time in your life when you had an affair with a married man, she would write, as sure of herself as a child with a stick in the sand. *And this will always be the time in his life when he messed around with a girl twenty years his junior. Try to think about it as if it's over already. Think about it in the past tense so you can enjoy the present. Think about the jokes you're going to tell, in a year or so, when this is all over.*

How many glib pieces of advice like that have I given, as Jolly? How many times has she been more concerned with answering someone originally, rather than answering someone well?

Here's what else Jolly would say: she would say that Renata isn't my business. And she isn't. But that doesn't stop me imagining her: in my head she has black hair and a red mouth, and she has lots of sex with relative strangers. Since Clem doesn't seem to have much intention to leave her, I picture their marriage as a relaxed, open arrangement: one where they smile knowingly at one another, and have no urge to explain their mutual whereabouts. I think that's why I'm convinced that Renata couldn't possibly be sending me those creepy emails: because in my head, she's simply too cool. It has to be someone, *something* else. Some reasonable explanation.

And all this hard work – all this creative non-fiction I have established for Clem and his wife – has been destroyed by this email. Logically, I know it could be from anyone, but somehow I can't escape the thought that it must be Renata. I think of the same Renata that I have imagined, deep in grief, clawing at her beautiful dark hair and looking witheringly at her husband, too selfish and too pigheaded to understand the depth or breadth of her sorrow. I look at my stomach, the flattest it has ever been, and wonder what it must be like to feel something grow in there. I remember the joke Max and I used to have – when we would talk about my future pregnancies, and how I would refuse to lift a finger for nine months because my body was growing a human being.

'I'm not cooking,' I would say, already pretending to be pregnant, 'because I'm making a foot right now.'

What if Renata had grown two feet, two hands, a pancreas, eyeballs – and what if she'd made them perfectly, so perfectly in fact, that it resulted in a whole human life?

I rub my hand over my stomach.

What if it died, and it was her fault, and the only person in the world who is supposed to care as much as she does gets over it so quickly that he wants to replace that life? *You want me to make another?* Like ordering a dessert, like cooking a pie, like boiling a fruit so far down it becomes a sticky jam, filling endless jars.

I imagine what I must look like to him. What a young woman with piteously few strings in her life must look and feel like if you've spent three years with a woman who has been stuck in her own endless feedback loop of hating and blaming, blaming and hating.

Could this be from her? Could she know about me, some-how, and be taunting me? Could it be Darla?

Or is this like every other Jolly Politely email I've ever received – a problem from the roots of a lonely woman, pul-sating and growing under the earth until it finds me?

My phone flashes up Clem's name, dissolving the email that may or may not have been from his wife.

'You're not at your desk. Where are you?'

'I was in . . .'

You're in the toilet, Jane, thinking about his wife.

' . . . a meeting.'

'Which meeting?'

'Sorry?'

'Which meeting? I have access to your diary and I don't see any meeting in here.'

He reminds me of a child monarch. Someone who has been given full permission to treat people as chess pieces, and is easily angered when they don't move in accordance with his plans.

'It was a brief catch-up. With one of the girls.'

'I'm taking you for lunch,' he says.

I look at the time. It's only just gone eleven.

'Bit early for lunch,' I say, not that I would really be eating anyway. My appetite is strangely absent, and only seems to return in the middle of the night. I wake up at four in the morning sometimes, eat endless bowls of cereal, and go back to bed.

'Let's give it an hour then,' he says. 'Do you know where the Metropole is?'

'No.'

'Well, you can Google Maps it. Meet me in the bar. At noon.'

There's only one kind of bar that's open at noon, I find, and it is a hotel bar. It's different from the ones I'm used to; it's not a sleek modern one above a restaurant in Soho: it's near Regent's Park, and I'm reminded how a small geographical distance – a mile, a mile and a half – can make such an enormous difference in a place like London. Within minutes the shiny late-night bars and tourist attractions fall away and I'm in dustier, less distinct territory. The shops become more anonymous, and there's a plethora of Lebanese and Italian restaurants trying to attract business lunches with three-course meal deals. For the most part, they're failing. Bored restaurant managers in vests lean against their doors, squinting at the sun. Some of them try to get my attention, promising a free glass of wine with my meal. The rest of them ignore me.

The sun is so dazzling that it keeps catching the hair of a woman in front of me: dry, iron-grey but shot through with gold and silver where the light is hitting it. You don't see long hair like that any more, the kind you could probably sit on. My hand wanders to my own head, my hair barely an inch below my shoulders. But thin: far too thin. I think of the tangle of hair on my windowsill, the wet lump I had left out for the birds. Something for a nest. They didn't want to take it, though: strands were still stuck to the edge of the sill, dancing with the wind. I'm trying not to feel hurt about it.

I've never heard of the Metropole. Then again, there's never been a reason for me to know any hotel, but maybe by the end of this I'll know them all. Thank God I'm wearing something half decent today, even if I do have opaque tights on underneath.

I sit myself at the counter and order a gin and tonic. I should have learned my lesson from the other night, when I woke up at 4 a.m. to vomit quietly in the hotel room, my insides feeling raw from the sex I was certain I was too drunk to have had.

I look at the email again. And again. My palms are sweating, and my phone feels slippery in my hand.

My mum's picture pops up. It's a photograph I've seen a thousand times, because it's the only one of herself she likes. She's on a boat, and the sun is in her hair. She's wearing a bright silk scarf tied around her neck and big sunglasses. She uses this photo for everything, would make it her passport photo if she could.

I mute the call. She disappears, and I feel a pair of lips graze underneath my ear.

'Cleo,' he says. It's always interesting to see what pet name a man will settle on once he gets to know you. Clem has decided on this Cleopatra/Mark Antony thing. Max was a 'honey' kind of guy, and I have an early memory of my father – thin, glasses, a dead ringer for W. B. Yeats – calling Mum 'Peaches'.

'Hello,' I say, and finish my drink.

'Drink slowly. I'm planning quite an afternoon.'

'You know how creepy that sounds, don't you?'

'Well, I'm a pretty creepy guy.'

We both laugh then, that harsh little laugh you give when a joke holds too much unexpected truth, and you both know it.

'Come on,' he says, taking my hand. 'I said I'd buy you lunch. And it's exactly what I plan to do.'

We leave the bar and head to a dining room at the back.

'This looks like something out of Cluedo,' I say. It's a smallish room – about a dozen tables or so – and there are silver cloches, and pink serviettes arranged into fans. They give us a window seat, sunlight from the tidy garden pouring into my lap. I see her again. The small, muscular frame. The iron hair, inhaling the sun's rays. The woman from the street is in the restaurant.

'This would have been the lady of the house's sunroom, you know,' Clem says, pouring from a jug of ice water, a lemon wedge plopping into my glass. 'She would have done all her embroidery and entertaining here.'

The woman has moved her head out of the sunlight. Her hair now seems duller, a wispy moth grey. Delicate. Damaged.

'You sound wistful,' I say, and it comes out snappier than I want it to. 'Dreaming of a simpler time?'

'I think you would have enjoyed it. I can see you in a big house like this, ladies doing your bidding, a little garden to traipse around and write poetry in.'

'What, while you lock Renata in the attic and she goes insane?'

The waiter comes over to fold out a leather wine list in front of Clem. He orders quickly, and confirms that yes, we will be eating.

'Don't talk like that.'

'Mr Rochester starts afresh with Jane even though his wife is still alive, going mental in the attic. I think she burns the house down, in the end.'

I don't know why I keep layering new myths on top of us: Antony and Cleopatra, Jane Eyre and Mr Rochester, Taylor and Burton. We can't be ourselves, because we're too locked into the long history of people who aren't supposed to be having sex.

'Oh, I see what you're doing, there. Jane *Eyre*. Jane *Peters*. Very poetic. Haven't thought about it that way before.' The wine arrives and he doesn't want to taste it, pouring it straight into my glass instead, going way past the halfway mark. 'Are you enjoying this?'

'Why don't you have children?'

'Why are you asking me that?'

Why am I asking him that? Why am I letting an email that could be from anyone convict him of a crime that there's no evidence he has committed? My Jolly voice switches on again: *Because these are the things you've been afraid of all along, and you'll use any excuse to bring them up.*

'Well, why don't you? Most people do, your age.'

A bread basket lands on our table, and a dish of butter. He reaches for a slice of nutty-looking brown bread, and starts spreading.

'You should have some of this. You're getting skinny.'

I say nothing, but repeat Renata's email to myself in my head.

I won't let my husband touch me, and perhaps unsurprisingly, he has started looking elsewhere.

I have started to refer to it as Renata's email even though I have no proof that it has anything to do with her. And then there's the Dear Jolly email: *do not sign for the flowers.*

I look at my menu. I don't want anything. I want to get out of this game I started, the game I am smart enough to know is a bad one but too stupid to know how to end.

'She didn't want them,' he says. 'I thought I didn't, either.'

'What do you mean?'

'When we met, we were in our twenties. Your age. We were at the wedding of a mutual friend, and she seemed like everything – smart, a cynic, so ready to put two fingers up to this whole exhausting rotation of weddings and babies and weddings and babies.' He smiles at the memory. 'We kept meeting at weddings, and we brought each other to them. Taking the piss, of course.'

'We fell in love, and I became one of those wankers that wanted to get married. She didn't want it. I pushed it. We did it, she hated it. She's not the kind of woman who likes a lot of people looking at her at once. She likes to hang back. A watcher, you know?'

This is the most I have ever heard about Renata. I'm afraid to breathe, like any movement from me will throw him off the story.

'But she was firm about kids. She didn't want them, and pretty soon, I did. And then, about two years ago – miracle of miracles – she got pregnant anyway.'

He flops the bread he was buttering on my plate.

'It was an accident. The pill is only so effective, you know. Ninety-eight per cent, I believe. I thought it was fate. She didn't.'

'Did she . . . did she miscarry?'

He shakes his head.

'She sort of took matters into her own hands.'

He talks into his plate.

'And that, Ms Brontë, is why I don't have any children. Do you still want to have lunch?'

'I'm sorry.'

'It's not your fault.'

He picks up his menu again. The woman with the grey hair is getting up to leave, and she lifts her hand in a cheery wave. I flicker my fingers at her in response. I swear she's mouthing something at me. I squint my eyes, watching her small mouth move, trying to tune out the summery string music being played through the PA.

'I think I'm going to have the quail's egg.'

I smile. He smiles. And we're off.

13

The ceiling in the room where I wake up is yellow. Not yellow completely – yellow in circles and splodges, where the paint has stained. Originally, it may have been a sort of cream colour. It occurs to me that the yellow is from a time when it was acceptable to smoke in hotel rooms.

'Have you ever smoked?' I ask. I still have half a pack in my handbag from my birthday night out.

'For a minute, when I was a teenager. I don't think I was very good at it.'

'Hmm.'

'Why hmm?'

'I was just thinking that this whole having sex in hotel rooms thing would be much more photogenic if we could both smoke afterwards.'

'There's a lot of things that could make this more photogenic.'

'Such as?'

He pulls me closer and runs his hand along my bra strap. 'An improvement on THIS would be a start.'

I laugh and whack him away. He's right, though: my bras are terrible. This one I've had so long that the elasticity in the straps has completely gone, so only one ever stays up at a time. Max never cared about things like underwear. At the start of our relationship I used to buy the cheap satin kind in princess colours, marshmallow pink and soft lilac. I would walk around the house, full of new-bra smugness, waiting for him to comment. Eventually I would break.

'Do you like my new bra?'

'Hmm?'

'Bra. It's new.'

'Ahhh. Yes. Pink.'

'Well, do you like it?'

'I like what's under it better.'

I came to understand that nice bras – like Carlsberg, hairless pubic areas and skinny women – are a thing that men are told to like, but aren't actually all that bothered about. Whenever I went on a miserable diet, Max would always say the same thing. 'Men don't love skinny women. Men who love *themselves* love skinny women.'

I loved this, and thought about it often. I think of men whose egos are so huge that there's no room in the relationship for anyone or anything else, only slight, slippery shadow women. Women who love easily and don't ask to be loved too hard back. Women whose needs can be folded away into cupboards, like ironing boards. Max was good at simple metaphors like that. I used to steal them for Jolly columns.

Most of the time, I'm able to submerge our happy memories under a joyless fog of eye-rolling and exhausted 'my ex-boyfriend' one-liners. But every so often, when I am vulnerable, the happy times come looking for me.

I get out of bed and look for my knickers – equally as depressing as my bra – and Clem watches me, propped up on one elbow.

'Throw me my trousers.'

'Say please.'

'Please.'

I toss them over, and he roots in a pocket. He flips open his wallet, and slides out one card.

'Come over here. Please.'

I go over, tugging my tights on in the process.

'Go buy yourself some decent bras.'

'What? No.'

'You need some new bras.'

'No I don't.'

'Look.' He tugs on a cup. 'This is flapping off. It's like a pelican's bill. *Squawww. Squaaaaaaw.*'

'You're insane. It is not a pelican's bill. It is the delicate beak of a sparrow. In any case, I can buy my own bras.'

'Oh, bugger off, Beyoncé. I've seen your payslips. You can't afford nice bras.'

I hate when we're not two people in a hotel room any more, we're two people where one is enormously more powerful than the other. It's then that I realise that our relationship is strained not because he's a good eighteen – at least – years older than me. Plenty of people have happy relationships with more years between them than that. It's the difference in status, not years, that makes our conversations so frequently awkward. That, and the realisation that things could get nasty for me if I were to pull the brakes now. Emotionally, sure, but professionally . . . ?

I didn't want to even think about it.

I walk into the bathroom without a word.

I hate the light in the bathroom mirror, and how big the mirror is. My hair is so crackled and static lately, even though I've been lathering it with conditioner. I prod the puffy rings around my eyes, and pick the chapped skin off my lips. I eventually get too annoyed by my reflection, turn my back on the mirror, and apply my make-up with a compact instead. It's easier to look at my face if I only have to look at it a bit at a time.

He walks in, naked. I wish he'd put something on.

'Why won't you let me buy you things?'

He has his boy-emperor voice on again. Generous, but too insistent.

'I let you pay for this hotel room.'

'That's different. I want to be able to treat you properly.'

I snap the lid of my compact closed.

'Okay. One bra.'

'One bra does not a mistress make,' he says thoughtfully. The utter obviousness of the whole situation is unbelievable. The gap between me and the cartoon Other Woman who lives in my head – the one who spends her lover's money, hides out with him in hotel rooms and carries around a compact mirror – is getting laughably small.

Except for one thing. I have made a deal with myself to never ask him to leave his wife for me. That would be too much. Too obvious.

'How many bras, exactly, do you want me to buy then?'

'What's the collective noun for bras? A bevvy of bras. A suite of bras.'

'A fleet. A colony. A murder of bras.'

'That's the spirit.' He hands over his card. 'Take this one. The pin is 3368.'

'You're going to tell me your pin just like that?'

'I trust you. Don't you trust me?'

I don't know what to say, so I stand up and kiss him for a long time. For once, he smells like me. So few things do, any more. Max smelled like me. Or rather, we both smelled like one another. That smell your house has that is both you and not you, the smell you only notice once you've been away for a while and then drop off your keys to find you missed it in a way you can hardly express. Living in Shiraz's flat makes me feel like I'm living within a showroom. Nothing is really mine, and even the things that are mine – my picture frames, my slippers, my laundry – feel distinctly like a lost and found haphazardly assembled following a provincial Sports Day.

I pull myself into his arms, letting myself become soft. I don't want to go away from him, don't want to head back to my lonely flat. There's a silence growing around me that feels like a dark moss. I wonder where all the people I talk to are. I forgot, with all the drama of my last months with Max, how important he was. More valuable than being loved, I think, is the sense of being known by someone: and God, did he know me. He knew when a wave of darkness was about to descend on my mood, and he knew exactly how to weather it. He knew what made me laugh, knew what private jokes to bring up at what time to make the trouble and the tedium of the day irrelevant.

Clem strokes the narrow space between my shoulder blades. I feel, with him, like a foster animal being slowly rehabilitated in what it is to be around people. I remember a study about monkeys I had read years ago, when I briefly considered studying psychology. The monkeys were separated from their mothers and given a choice between a soft, cloth mother or a wire one with a feeding bottle. The monkeys had to choose which they preferred: the mother that would nourish them or the one that merely comforted them. Overwhelmingly, the babies chose the cloth mother.

And that's how I feel now, clutching him, squeezing my eyes tightly as I breathe him in. I know it isn't a good choice, but at the same time, it doesn't feel like a choice at all. If I were strong enough to make another one, maybe I would.

I put my legs around his waist and we go back to bed, underneath the yellow ceiling.

Dear Jolly Politely
   I think my boyfriend is stealing from me. I gave him my house key a little while ago, thinking it was a forward step in our relationship. Now, little things are going missing: teabags, throw pillows, a sandwich toaster. All fairly inconsequential, but y'know, still a lot of stuff. Should I confront him? Change the lock? Break up with him and ask for the key back?

I was the first girl in my class to do a perfect cartwheel. Everyone was trying to do them one day during lunch break and failing miserably, no one able to keep their legs straight or in the air. I watched them, and when it was my time to go: boom. Perfect.

I was a physical kind of kid, the kind that was always climbing up or jumping off things. I was sporty – not so much that it took over my whole life, but enough so that the other girls wanted me on their team. My proudest possession was a very long ponytail, and it made me very popular in primary school.

It was the kind of charmed, confident childhood that you could assume would lead to a very charmed and confident adolescence, but it didn't. Because when I was eleven, two things happened.

The first thing was that my dad went on a business trip to Switzerland and never came back. Or, he came back much, much too late: I didn't see him again until I was eighteen. He was an accountant for a pharmaceuticals company, which made his vanishing even more surprising. His job was boring, and would never impress my friends, but I had presumed that his dullness meant he could be relied upon. I think Mum assumed that too, so when he started taking more frequent trips to Zurich, she took it to mean that he was doing really well at work. The reality was somewhere in-between: he was sent by work, but while he was there, he fell in love with a Swiss banker called Gaëlle. Mum pronounced it 'Gail', my dad called her *Gyelle* and I only ever said Gay Elle, because apparently being homophobic was the only way I could muster anger as a pre-teen. The second thing was that I started to get tits. I got tits very, very quickly. The symbiosis of it was quite amazing: it seemed like the week my dad left, puberty decided to get off the bus and become the replacement third member of our miserable little family. My boobs, which had previously been hard little lumps, became round and womanly. They were so big that they didn't go away while I was lying down, the way my mum's did.

Mum had become a child – crying and going to bed early, refusing to eat anything that was good for her – and I was turning into a woman at breakneck speed. I felt like the universe was applying some cock-eyed sense of logic to our situation, like every house was supposed to have a grown-up in it and because Mum wasn't able to be one, I had to step up. For the most part, I did okay. I made us dinners of potato waffles and beans. I washed my own school uniform. I made sure she got up for work. The one thing I couldn't do was ask her to buy me a bra, so I went without. The other girls whispered and stared, and suddenly I wasn't this popular kid any more. I wasn't Jane Who Can Do Cartwheels. I was this frumpy child-woman with a fucked-up home life and no bra.

A few months later, my mum dried her eyes and looked up from her coffee.

'Oh my God,' she said, looking at me as I put my neck through my school jumper. 'Jane, you need a bra!'

She started laughing, and I did too. The whole thing was horribly, brilliantly funny. We were incapacitated with how funny my boobs were. It was such a relief to hear her laugh again. She was like a drowning woman who had at last made it to shore, coughing up seawater and gulping the clean air. We went to Marks & Spencer's and she got me measured by one of the nice older ladies who wear a measuring tape as a necklace. There was no one else in the changing rooms so the three of us communed in the big disabled stall, admiring lace cups and flowery patterns. I tried on a dozen bras. I felt like I was being fitted for a ballgown.

'Now, love,' said Mum, shining with mischief, 'if you're anything like your nan you're going to have big 'uns. They skip a generation in our family, or so it would appear. So you're not to go showing off around the house, making me feel bad.'

I giggled madly. Imagine: bigger boobs than your own mum!

'Let's only get two today,' she continued. 'You'll probably outgrow these in another six months, so pick your two favourites.'

I picked the most grown-up-looking ones – one black, one white – and we made our way to the till. We queued up near a display of stockings and suspenders and a sign with loopy Italian writing. I can't remember exactly what it said. 'For the one you love', or something like that.

'Maybe if I had a few more of those, I wouldn't be in this situation.'

I couldn't tell if Mum was talking to me or to herself, and it took me a long minute to figure out what she meant. We paid for the bras and left.

It is a unique experience when, at eleven, your mother wonders aloud whether she was sexually exciting enough for your father. You never quite forget it.

I don't go to Marks & Spencer's this time around. I go to one of those shops where they stock odd-sounding brands and the women who work there are adamant you're wearing the wrong size. There's a veiled section of the shop specifically for sex underwear. Knickers with pop buttons on the sides, designed to be ripped away frantically. Lace basques with panels of silk and matching thongs to go with them. There is even a section within the sex underwear section labelled 'adult play', and this features a small leather paddle, a riding crop and a pair of handcuffs. By the till they're selling a flimsy book called *101 Ways to Be an Expert in Kama Sutra*.

The manager of the shop is folding some French knickers into neat parcels on a display table, so expertly that it looks like she is preparing sushi. She is, I suppose, in her early sixties. I wonder if she's the one who ordered the adult play stuff in. I picture her looking bemusedly at a catalogue of sex

toys and wondering which ones are the most appropriate for
a bra shop. It's strange to me, this constant symbiosis of sex
and boobs, boobs and sex. You can dress your boobs for sport
or leisure or casual BDSM, and you can do it all in this one
shop off Oxford Circus.

'Can I help you?'

I'm so busy looking at the woman folding knickers that I
don't notice the one standing behind me. She's younger, fifty
or so, and wearing a silk scarf looped into some expensive-
looking jeans. She looks like the kind of person that gets
lunch with Marianne Faithfull.

'I just need to buy a few bras,' I say. I don't mention 'with
my lover's money'.

'Size?'

'Thirty-four D.'

She looks at me, doubtful. 'Are you sure?'

'Well . . . ' I have always been a 34D, pretty much. They
settled at that size when I was about seventeen, when Jane
Who Does Cartwheels became Jane With the Tits.

'I think you need a fitting. Would you like to stay for
a fitting?'

I nod.

'Right,' she says, springing into action. 'Pop into the
changing rooms and I'll be there in five.'

I sit on a pouffe in my cubicle, and wait.

Dear Bad Boyfriend

   **You haven't left your name so apologies for having
named you – but at the same time, I think it's a truth
you need to hear. You have a Bad Boyfriend.**

The easy thing to do would be to say 'break up with him!',
but that advice feels obvious. If she wanted to break up
with him she would have already. This is how most of

the 'relationship' questions go: someone, almost always a woman, writes in about her terrible partner, not because she needs advice – she knows she should break up with him – but because she is glad that she finally has a problem that's interesting enough to warrant an audience. I start typing something to that effect, and stop myself. Isn't that what I'm doing, in a way? Experimenting with a situation that is bound to end in catastrophe for the hell of it?

The fitter lady walks in and starts her spiel.

'My name is Rebecca, and I'm fitting you today,' she says. 'So if you're comfortable, can I please ask you to remove your clothes and face the mirror. If you're not comfortable, I can leave and you can put on our store robe' – she gestures to a silky dressing gown hanging on the door – 'and I can fit you over that.'

'No, that's fine,' I say, taking my shirt off. 'God, do people really choose the store robe option?'

'It's cleaned regularly.'

I am standing shirtless in front of her, and she looks at me critically.

'You're wearing the wrong bra,' she says. 'Face the mirror, please.'

In the glass, I see a woman who is skinny. Not slim, not slender, not athletic: skinny. I've always wanted to be skinny, in that private, vain way that all women wish they were underweight. I sometimes imagine myself pale and wan, with big Winona Ryder eyes and delicate limbs and coltish beauty. The reality in the mirror is a rather different scenario and far from coltish. It's alien to me, grotesque. My ribs are starting to show. How much weight have I lost? And how quickly have I lost it?

Rebecca runs her tape around me, and feels the underwiring of my existing bra. Clem was right – the cups do flap open. I'm barely filling them at all.

'Thirty B.'

'Excuse me?'

'Thirty B.'

'I don't think that's right.'

'Even so, you're a thirty B. Maybe a thirty-two in some brands.'

I don't know what to say.

'Are you okay?'

'I've been a thirty-four D since I was seventeen,' I say and my voice catches. Am I really going to cry, here, to a woman with a measuring tape?

'Have you lost weight recently?'

'I wasn't trying to. I just . . . ' I think of all the skipped lunches, all the half-finished meals with Clem. How many nights this month did I have cereal for dinner?

'I'll get you a few different sizes,' she says kindly. 'We'll see what works.'

She leaves, and I pull my jeans down. I look at the insides of my thighs. Is the skin . . . drooping?

Everything tastes different lately. Everything I eat is like orange juice after you've brushed your teeth, tangy and strange.

I have been avoiding mirrors for weeks, but now that I'm confronted with one, I can't look away. I have spots on my jawline and at the back of my neck, little red bumps with soft white heads. I run my hands through my hair, feeling more of the same bumps on my scalp. I go right up to the mirror now, determined to survey the damage. I look at each ear carefully: my nose, my lips, the pupils in my eyes. I scold the shit lighting in the dressing room, which isn't helping at all.

It isn't lying either, though.

I've never loved the way I look, but I do know what I look like. This isn't what I look like.

Men don't love skinny women. Men who love themselves love skinny women.

Is this the kind of foldaway woman I had to be, to be loved by Clem? Is this what you look like when your life becomes about someone else?

She knocks before she comes back in. 'Only me,' she says. 'Try a few of these.'

I lunge for the fanciest styles, the ones I would never normally look at. Black lace and coffee-coloured satin. An emerald balconette that pushes up what remains of my breasts right under my chin. In the right wrapping paper, I can make this work: this new me, with the bad skin and the pinprick pupils. Rebecca, seeing my interest, starts up-selling madly; she must work on commission. My dressing room is filled with sheer kimonos and long basques, night gowns and sleeping masks.

'Beautiful,' she says, as I try another on. 'Just gorgeous.'

'Is this one popular?'

'Oh, yes. It's honeymoon season, so these are selling out fast.'

Honeymoon season. I think of the women coming in here, excited to start their new lives, their new marriages, planning what kind of wife they're going to be. Making pacts with themselves to never be frumpy, to never 'let themselves go' like their mothers did. Did my mother come in here? Did Gay Elle come in here? Did Kim, excited to fuck Max, come in here?

'That's why I'm here,' I blurt out. 'My honeymoon.'

She claps her hands, delighted for me. 'How exciting! When are you getting married?'

'Three weeks,' I say. Why am I doing this? 'In Switzerland.'

When I get to the till, I have bought £285.60 worth of lingerie. I have never spent this much money on underwear, and never thought I would. I fumble with his card. It feels heavier somehow, more dignified than any of the debit cards currently sitting in my wallet. Can I really be the girl who does this? Who racks up hundreds of pounds on things she doesn't need, so she feels like she's getting something out of the bargain? I remember Shiraz's words, my head filled with her Brixton drawl.

'Get as much out of this as you can, Jane. God knows he will.'

I punch in Clem's pin, half-expecting it to not work. It goes through.

Dear Bad Boyfriend,

You haven't left your name so apologies for having named you – but at the same time, I think it's a truth you need to hear. You have a Bad Boyfriend.

I am sorry to say that people, even good people, will always take advantage if they think they can get away with it. I know. I'm sorry. I don't know why your boyfriend is stealing such a random and seemingly useless array of items (throw pillows, for Christ's sake) but I do know that you are letting him.

Your first choice: break up with him. But you would have done that by now, wouldn't you, if you wanted to? I have spent a long time and many hundreds of words telling women to break up with men and I'm pretty sure the majority of them don't take this advice. It is the best course of action, but also, the rarest course.

Your second choice: take something of equal or greater value from your boyfriend. Take his bike helmet. Spend his money. Push this and see how far it can go.

You might not have a good relationship, but you will have a good story.

When I leave the shop it's 7 p.m., but the sunlight almost blinds me. It's August, the hottest it will get all year. I buy a smoothie from a juice stand on the way to the Tube. There is startlingly little change when I give the fruit vendor a tenner, but I tell myself that it will count as dinner.

My phone buzzes in my pocket, and I get ready to silence the call: I can't talk to my mother, not now, not moments after I've spent a married man's money on tit silk. But it's not my mum. It's him. I smile. He never calls me in the evening: after work either he's with me or he's at home, and if he's at home, he texts.

'Oh, hello,' I say. 'This is a surprise.'

'Your voice sounds different.'

'How?'

'I don't know. Lower. Husky. Like Kathleen Turner.'

I laugh. 'You know, for MY generation, Kathleen Turner isn't that big a compliment.'

'Shame. I'm going to have to make you watch *Body Heat*. Anyway, what are you doing on Saturday?'

'I don't know. You?'

It's a cheap, nasty joke and it sticks in my throat. I imagine my father on the phone and hearing the same thing: trailing our 2002 home phone into his study so my mum and I won't hear. Clem just laughs.

'Classy. Anyway, be ready at noon. I'm picking you up. And bring an overnight bag. We're going away somewhere.'

His voice is excitable, like someone who knows they have the perfect gift for the perfect person and can't wait to see them open it. I wonder where he is, right now. Does he have a study of his own that he locks himself into, or is Renata away somewhere?

I take two sips of my smoothie, chew the straw until it breaks, and throw it away. I barely let myself register the new email sitting in my inbox.

Dear Jolly,

Do not worry. I am looking out for you

14

I don't know where he's taking me. He says it's a surprise.

I'm so excited at the prospect of having something to do at the weekend that I didn't even bother to work out the logistics. The whole weekend? Are we going to Cadiz? Where is Renata? I give myself the answer I know he'd give me, and believe it regardless of whether it's true: *She's away for work. She doesn't mind. We have an understanding. Marriage is complicated. Put her out of your head.*

But there is something else, another worry that is pushing across my mind on mounted cavalry. Do Clem and I have a weekend's worth of conversation between us?

It's the kind of thing that's bound to hamper conversation once you start thinking about it, or at least that's what I tell myself when we're sitting in his car, listening to Radio 1. I fidget. It's a novelty, being in a car. I don't know a single person in London who drives, and can't think of the last time I was inside a car sober. Cars are for taxi drivers and grown-ups.

I am used to him at the office. When we're working or getting coffee or kissing in a chair that is pushed up against the handle of a closed door, I can almost believe that we're in a real relationship. Or at the very least, friends. Peers. But now I'm sitting in his Lexus with the self-heating seats and there is an unmistakable air of him being on the school run.

Like he's about to kiss me on the forehead and give me a fiver for lunch. I wonder what we look like to the other motorists.

He smiles. 'What?'

'Nothing.'

'You look like you're planning something.'

'Like what?'

He takes my hand and strokes my knuckles with his thumb, kisses it, and then lets our hands lie together in front of the gear stick. There's an intimacy to the movement, as if we have been getting in and out of this car for years. For a moment, I pretend that we have. Like he is my boyfriend, or I am his wife, and this is just another trip to get away from the city. There are two dogs rootling around in the back seat, and we are going to take them to the seaside. Two springer spaniels and a newspaper bouquet of chips. A stick thrown a half-mile down the beach. A chubby toddler chasing the tide as it retreats inward, and running away when it comes back. I make pictures of things that I don't necessarily want but still enjoy inventing. I allow my mind to get curious about him: *what if?*

Renata doesn't want kids, anyway. No one would blame you for divorcing a woman who doesn't want kids if you do. Especially if you met someone who does want to have your kids. No one would hold it against you, Clem. You could do it. We could do it.

The pressure to find conversation eases. The land around the motorway gets greener. The thick tightness of London slackens and falls away, and I think about how happy I am, to be in this car with this man with no idea where I'm going. I lean over and kiss the right angle of his jaw.

'What was that for?'

'For free.'

He can hear, I think, the fullness in my throat, the pure and uncomplicated affection that is usually hidden beneath a topsoil of flirtation and sex and misplaced frustration.

'Can you—'

And then I stop. He's interested, though.

'Can I what?'

'No, nothing.'

'Don't do this to me, Cleo. What's in that pretty old head?'

'Can you . . . see yourself with me?'

He is considering what I mean or, worse, what I need. I backtrack quickly.

'I mean, can you see yourself doing this again?' I say. Fast, agitated. 'Us meeting up on the weekend, I mean.'

He laughs. For a second, I think he gets it. That he can see the same fantasy that I can, the one with the toddler and the dogs. He kisses my hand again and places it, very tenderly, on his erect penis.

Neither of us says anything. His penis is saying quite enough on its own.

I can see, kind of, why he thinks this is appropriate. This is what we do, after all, and I am wearing at least £100 worth of underwear. The spaniels and the young child are gone. I remember, not with desperation or with sadness but with pure truth, who I am to this man. I am not his wife or his girlfriend or the daughter he's driving to school. I am a girl from work who he has sex with, and who he buys lingerie for. He is taking me to the seaside – and it is the seaside, because I can see its oily gleam in the distance – as a reward for being easy to manage.

Get as much out of this as you can, I can hear Shiraz saying. *God knows he will.*

I wonder, again, what she meant by that. What experience she had that allowed her to say it with such confidence. There's an aching, old loneliness to Shiraz, one that makes it impossible to guess her age. She told me once that her mother was originally from Ghana, but made no comment as to whether her mother was still alive. It's very hard to make sense of a woman when you don't know how she feels about her mother.

Clem's hand tightens on mine. I can feel denim and heat, the rising temperature of blood, the strain of him against his dark blue jeans. Weekend jeans. Without taking his eyes off the road, he zips down his fly, leaving it gaping slightly, his belt buckle still locked.

Is this what it's like for Shiraz? I want to find out who her Clem is. To know how she feels when she touches him, whoever 'him' is. I think of her beautiful Pilates body in the hands of someone old and experienced: someone fifty, sixty, seventy years old. Does she let herself be seen then, and only then? Does she touch him like I touched Clem: with that deep, feverish urge to sink to the bottom of another person, holding their heart in your arms like an anvil?

I snatch my hand away from Clem's lap, and he makes no sign that he has even noticed, although his smile does dampen a little. I fumble with my phone instead, knowing that I need to talk to someone – anyone – who understands. I stare at Shiraz's number. I start to type:

I don't know what I'm doing here

I erase. I try again.

I don't know what to do

I stop again. I pretend to be Shiraz. Direct, factual. I straighten my spine.

He wants to fuck me in his car

I push send. She responds straightaway.

If you let him do that, he will never respect you

I cringe, mortified. But there's something soothing about it too: she's the only person in the world I've been able to tell about Clem, and while we're not exactly friends, there's a strange companionship in texting a woman you know about a man who is being awful.

The text bubbles come up again.

If he thinks you'll do it, then he doesn't respect you

I don't think this is exactly fair, because plenty of people have consensual sex in cars with people they love and respect.

What about doggers?

I send back. She doesn't respond. Shiraz will only entertain my nonsense so much.

We stop at a set of traffic lights, and he extends an arm out behind my neck, nuzzling his face into my hair.

'You look good in those shorts.'

I look down at what I'm wearing. A stripy H&M top, denim cut-offs, and flip-flops from two years ago. My new green silk bra has thrust my breasts – or what's left of them – right underneath my throat, where they await review. I got dressed this morning with some weekend version of myself in mind: not my real self, but the flirty work Jane that he knows. Like a doll with a reversible outfit: *office temptress or beach girl? Pick whichever one you like! Whatever you're in the mood for!*

I straighten up and go cold on him.

'I'm hungry.'

I'm not.

'We'll be there in half an hour.'

I give a petulant little sigh. I notice a new feeling crawling

up through me, and nurse it for a minute. I am sick of being
easy, and relaxed, and uncomplicated, and fun. I am strangely,
silently furious at his penis, and what he presumes to be
normal car behaviour: or at least, normal car behaviour when
Jane Peters is in the car with you.

He has felt the change in my mood, and he is eyeing me
like a hunter does a rearing animal. Cautious, but confident.
The car slows down and eases to the left, and we are in a
McDonald's car park.

'Why have you stopped?'

'You're hungry.'

'Shut up, not for McDonald's.'

'Well, I am starving for McDonald's, so you can give me
your order, or you can be surprised by what I get you.'

I look at him. Clem, eating McDonald's. It's all so wrong
it's funny. He takes my silence as a challenge.

'Fine, I'm ordering for you,' he says, opening the car door.

'No!' I say, and I do it with such panic that we both start
laughing. 'You'll get me some old-person thing.'

'An old-person thing?' He looks at me, the picture of innocence. 'I was going to treat you to a Filet-o-Fish and a hot
apple pie, which is the height of youthful eating.'

I whack him with my handbag and tell him that no one,
no one ever, has ordered a Filet-o-Fish. He winks at me as
he leaves the car, locking it over his shoulder while I shout
'CHEESEBURGER, CHIPS, FANTA' at him. I decide, in
that moment, that he wasn't trying to have sex with me on a
motorway, or convince me to wank him off in the car park
of a McDonald's. He was, like he is now, messing with me. I
watch him through the window, making big, clueless arms to
the man behind the counter at McDonald's, making a 'God,
I don't know, what do you think?' gesture. I can't see Clem's
face, but I can see the smile on the employee serving him.
It's a good smile. A real one.

Clem's a joker. That's his thing. That's why everyone likes him so much. He messes with me because I get his sense of humour. And if he wanted a hand job on the motorway, then so what? Did I have a right to be surprised? I was having sex in my own workplace three nights a week but I was going to draw a line at expensive luxury cars? Get a grip, Jane.

Or don't. Ha ha.

We eat in the car. He reclines the seat a little, placing the bag of fried food on his stomach, and eats out of it meditatively.

'I was going to take you to a seafood restaurant in Whitstable, you know. You could be having a very expensive Chardonnay right now.'

'I'm fine with car McDonald's. Don't you mind?'

'Mind what?'

'Us, eating in the car. That we'll make the seats smell like oil.'

He shrugs, and eats another chip out of the bag. I see a glimmer of something in him: that not only does he not care, he does not want to ever care. Old men care about car hygiene. It's all well and good to have a nice car if your company is going to provide one for you, but to care? Oh, no. Clem is still too Generation X for that. He's still pretending that this corporate identity is something he's doing ironically, despite having done it for most of his adult life.

That, I decide, was why he wanted me to touch him in the car. Not because he wanted me to, but because it seemed like a young man's thing to do, not realising that it was a thing an older man does when trying to pretend to be a young man. If I were in the car with David Lady, it wouldn't have even occurred to him. He wouldn't have felt the need to prove how young he was because he just *was*.

'Did your dad let you eat in the car?'

It's like he's taken my hand and plunged it into a bucket of ice.

'Pardon?'

'Your dad. Did he let you eat McDonald's in the car?'

'Why do you ask?'

'It feels like you got that line about oil on the seats from somewhere.'

I take a long sip on my Fanta and look out of the window. It seems like I am shielding some deep and very dark pain, but I'm not. I just can't really remember.

'I don't ever remember getting fast food with my dad. It wasn't his thing.'

'What was his thing?'

'Why are you asking?'

'It doesn't matter,' he says, crumpling together his now-empty brown bag and reaching for mine. He weighs it in his hands.

'You barely touched this.'

I shrug like a teenager. 'I wasn't actually very hungry.'

Tankerton Beach is mostly stones, but no one minds. People have foil barbecues and lukewarm cans of Heineken. A group of teenage girls in bikini tops are playing Katy Perry on a pair of portable iPhone speakers. I am ten years older than they are, and still convinced that no matter how old or successful I get, there will always be more teenage girls having endless, dreamy, perfect summers.

Did I ever have a summer like that? Did I ever wear an older boy's hoodie with one bare shoulder peeking out? Did I ever force strangers to give me piggybacks, and would it have worked if I did?

I slip my hand into Clem's and loll my head onto his shoulder, moving slowly with him, enjoying the smell of the sea and the feeling of being anonymous. We have never walked anywhere hand in hand, never had any sort of physical contact with the sun right above us.

'We never do this,' I say.

'Hmm?'

He is only half-listening, his eye caught by a little boy crabbing off the pier.

'Go around in the daytime. In public. We're night time, mostly. Like vampires.'

'What did you just say?'

'Vampires,' I say. His eyes flit around my face, as if the word were some kind of racial slur, and he's surprised I have the gall to say it. 'We only go outside together at night.'

I'm not sure what I've done, or said, but he eases off immediately. 'Oh,' he chuckles. 'Yeah.'

We walk on. I slip off my flip-flops and paddle into the water, kicking my legs up so my shorts are speckled with wet. I love the sea, and the cold water, and not carrying a handbag. I don't even mind that the faded pink hues of my rash are still visible. If I could live anywhere on earth, it would be near the sea. After a few minutes, a gang of teenagers gallop in, girls on boys' shoulders, insisting they all play Donkey.

I saunter out of the water, sheepish, feeling a little old. He wraps his arms around me, gently rubbing the water off my legs with his jumper, kissing each knee and pressing his lips together to taste the salt. We sit on the sea wall, his arm around me.

I want to tell him something. It doesn't matter what it is, as long as it's honest.

'I could never be like that,' I say.

'Like what?'

The sun is in my face. I shield my eyes with one hand and point with the other. 'Like them.'

He is trying to figure it out on his own.

'Happy?'

For once, I am the person who has left the gate open on a conversation, and he's the one closing it.

'No, I was happy. But I was never . . .'

Two of the teenagers stagger towards their bags, the stone path doing nothing to diminish their confidence, and disappear together. The boy is holding his hand straight and cupped and crooked, obviously trying to hide a joint in there.

'Carefree, I suppose, is the word. I wasn't the type of girl who jumped in the swimming pool with her clothes on. I didn't kiss one boy and then run off and kiss another. The girls I was friends with were always nice, but I never seemed to be where the party was. It always seemed to happen an hour before I got there, or an hour after I left.'

'Why? Why were you always coming and going? Why weren't you just *there*?'

'Mum. We became a little unit, after he went to live in Switzerland.'

'Your dad?'

'My dad, yeah.'

And it all comes out, just like that. We make our way down the beach and I talk about Dad, and Mum, and Gay Elle. The facts of it have never been much of a secret but the middle years – after the break-up and before I went to uni – are not something I talk about. Because they are lonely, and because they are private, and because talking about the odd world my mother and I forged together feels like a betrayal of her. She did the best she could, but the best often consisted of me stroking her fine blonde hair as she lay on my lap, tears sliding silently onto my legs as we watched *Trisha* on TV.

'You're not mourning him,' I said to her, a teen attempting a sort of seen-it-all world-weariness. 'You're mourning an old version of yourself. She died unexpectedly and your body is in shock. The new you is here, though, and she'll get you through it.'

Being chipper and acerbic and damning became a valuable chip to play in the great game of keeping her sane. I could take nuggets of wisdom from her on good days and sell them right back to her on the bad ones. It was easy, and it was how Jolly began, really. Giving life advice to my own mother was a wonderful way of feeling in control, even if she didn't always take it.

I tell him all of this, and for a second I almost consider including Jolly. But I hang back. Clem can never know about Jolly. It is an instinct without explanation, like opening your mouth to apply mascara.

Clem takes my life story in the spirit it is intended. Telling someone a secret is like asking them to look after your baby for an hour: it's a burden, but there's a certain joy in being trusted with something so precious. He doesn't try to counter my confession with one of his own, and I'm grateful.

We sit on the sea wall together, and the two teenagers from earlier emerge from the rocks together. Slightly unsteady on their feet and giggling. They walk right past us. The boy gives Clem a little captain's salute, and the girl thinks this is the funniest thing in the world.

'Everything you didn't have then has made you everything you are now, Jane.'

He sweeps the hair away from my face. 'And I like who you are very much.'

He kisses me and his mouth tastes like salt.

15

He hasn't got us a hotel. We drive outside the town to a line of pretty holiday cottages with white stone walls.

'God bless Airbnb,' he says, letting himself in with a key hidden under a plant pot.

'*You* know what Airbnb is?' I say, laughing tipsily. Clem barely knows what Spotify is.

His mouth twitches at the comment. I choose not to acknowledge his annoyance.

The cottage glows with luxurious countryside wealth. There's an Aga, cashmere throws over the couches, and Hunter wellington boots stacked by the door. There's a pantry filled with condiments and preserves from the Selfridges food hall, a wine rack that a note encourages us to 'help ourselves' to.

There are a lot of notes. The bookshelves instruct us to read what we like, but not to take anything. The toilet asks us to go easy on the lavatory chain, the shower requests we don't use it after 10 p.m. as the neighbours can hear it. Clem tries to figure out the Aga while I trail around, picking up one note after another, drunkenly challenging myself to collect them all. I feel a little like Belle in *Beauty and the Beast*, having so many household sidekicks willing to offer me advice. I push the patio door open and find myself in a neat yet carefully overgrown garden. It's almost evening now, the honeysuckle yellow and heavy with sweetness, the grass plush underneath my bare feet. There are birch trees, pale and grey and shocking against the greenery.

I'm amazed at how quickly the day has passed with him. We've not done much: popping in and out of pubs, bookshops and small seaside art galleries. We've had dinner, Clem insisting that no restaurant would care if I wore denim shorts at the dinner table, and then laughing hysterically when they so obviously did. It has all added up to a sort of humdrum bliss. *We are good together*, I think. *We do have enough conversation to sustain a weekend.*

The birds are calling out to one another, preparing to roost. I remember my hair and how they refused to take it, and the slimy hard sureness of the pigeon's organ as it slid out of my hand and around the uni sink. A wind rustles through the garden, shaking the leaves and slamming the porch door shut, rattling the house.

'Jane!'

His voice is sharp.

'Sorry!' I call back.

'Get in here; you're letting a fucking draught in.'

I shiver, and slip my shoes back on. So quick to anger, I think. It's not a draught, it's a *fucking* draught, the words shiny and serrated. A note flutters into my hands as I close the door behind me.

Look after yourself.

The emails that I have been trying so desperately to forget come flooding back. What had the last one said, again? *Do not worry. I am looking out for you.*

I have moved through this day with an extraordinary sense of freedom: certain we would not bump into anyone, confident in being ourselves. My vision blurs as I look at the note, the crisp white wine at dinner turning to sour agitation at the front of my head. *What if whoever wrote the emails is here?*

I blink hard and shove it into my pocket as he comes towards me, carrying a newly opened bottle of wine. My stomach turns: it's a heavy red, the kind you have with cheese. As good as my constitution has become over the last few months, even I don't think I can drink this much wine without getting sick. He takes the nape of my neck in his free hand and pulls me towards him, hard. It's a kiss that says: It's night time, and we are adults.

I drag his bottom lip with my mouth, biting softly.

'Go upstairs,' he says, and I don't so much walk up the stairs as fall up them, tripping over my feet as though I'm wearing clogs.

It's only later, when I am slipping my shorts back on in the pale blue light of not-quite-morning, that I see the note again.

Lock up after yourself.

Dear Jolly,

This is not a problem I am comfortable in telling my friends and family, because even admitting it feels like the grossest form of vanity. But even so, I have to tell someone.

I have a good life. I have a great career, a lovely husband, and fortunately I make enough money to afford reasonable childcare. I see enough of my kids to miss them while I'm at work, to be glad of them when I finally see them as I walk through the door. But even as I write all of this down, I know I'm just reminding myself of the facts of my existence, and not enjoying a single one of them. Everything in my life that I know I should be grateful for I instead feel morose about. An

intense depression has started claiming my evenings. I
have invented back trouble so I can stay in bed from
the moment I get home until the moment I get up the
next morning. I have no idea where my depression is
coming from, but what began as an irregularity has
started taking over my life.

I have no idea what to do. Please help.

Miserable Mum

I stare at the email for a long time, a cashmere blanket around
me, a mug of lemon tea in my hands. The birds are waking
up, making lazy calls across the garden to one another, and
my head thumps with vinegar and dehydration. We brought
the bottle of wine to bed with us, sloshing it around the
sheets. I worried about his Airbnb review, but I forgot to
think about how drunk we were getting. Hell, I was drunk
when I came into the house.

I think of all the women I work with who would kill to
be this woman, and all the women who already are. Part of
me has always believed that once it has all worked out for
you – once you have the kids and the house and the man
who really loves you – then you would be done. You would
have used up your lifetime allotment of wants and needs, and
the rest of your life would be spent coasting on your own
happiness, or dealing with small, workable, domestic struggles. Struggles like: 'Who's going to leave work early to go
to parents' evening?' or 'Can you believe how boring other
people's children are?'

These are the complaints the mothers at work have, and
they always confess to them with a confident eye-roll. There's
always a sense that these problems aren't really problems,
but just something to talk about. Whenever I'm with one
of the work mothers, I think how unstable and directionless
my life must seem to them, how frazzled and open-ended. I

remember telling one of them about Max — how there was nothing wrong with him, but it wasn't right, and I didn't know why, but it wasn't — and how she sympathised, and said we had all been there. By 'we', she meant all women, and by 'had', she meant some other, previous life. Pre-husband. Pre-mortgage. Pre-children.

But what if it wasn't a previous life? What if the only difference between me, the morose twenty-something who threw away a perfectly nice boyfriend, and them, the morose forty-somethings who invent back problems to avoid their families, is that they have the determination to make it work? What if some women are built for sticking it out, and some women are cuckoos: stealing other men, other families, never building up enough spine to create something for themselves? Is Clem the first in a long line of men for whom I will be a side-project?

A wood pigeon makes a soft cooing sound outside. I pull the blanket tighter around me, unable to escape Miserable Mum, the woman who has a perfect life on paper but abhors actually living it. My head pounds, my hangover headache truly setting in, and I hold a spoon up to my face to cool myself down.

'How many of you *are* there?' I say to myself.

A minute later, and I hear the sound of his bare feet swinging out of bed and landing. In a moment he's in the kitchen, pulling on a robe that he's found on the back of a door somewhere. He asks me what time it is.

'It's a little before six.'

'Crikey. Why are you up?'

I shrug. He starts slotting bread into the toaster. I answer his question silently to myself. Because even though I love being with you, I can't sleep when you're there. Because the idea of being unconscious next to you unnerves me. Because sharing a bed with you reminds me of a story I once heard

about a woman who bought a snake, and when that snake
started stretching out its long, limbless body next to her, it
never occurred to her once that it might be thinking about
eating her.

'Are you hungry?'

'I've eaten,' I lie. I'd hoped that, like a Victorian child
recovering from consumption, the sea air would somehow
bring my appetite back. I was wrong: I spent dinner pushing
a crumbling salmon fillet around my plate, trying to make
it appear eaten.

'By the way,' he says, kissing me on the cheek in-between
bites of toast, 'can you get me your final thoughts on Think
Gym by Monday afternoon? Email is fine. I'm seeing
the client.'

I laugh. 'This is romantic pillow chat, isn't it?'

He grins and investigates the fancy jams in the pantry
cupboard. 'Hey, I'm mentoring you, remember? That means
I get to tell you what to do.'

I glance down at my phone again, my head still on
Miserable Mum. I start mentally composing my response to
her. Then something in my head clicks.

'*All*,' I say.

'Pardon?'

'That's what the campaign should be called. For
Think Gym.'

'I don't follow.'

'Right, so women are always encouraged to "have it all",
aren't they? The job, the house, the kids, yeah?'

'"Having it all" hasn't been used in an advertising campaign since the nineties, but I'm with you.'

'So we take that idea, and we subvert it. What happens
when the "all" you were told you could have is not the "all"
you actually want? What happens when you've strived for
a thing, and you have the thing, and you're still miserable?

What happens when you have the life of a woman in a magazine but you still feel like dog shit?'

'So what are we selling them? The idea of rejecting luxury mindfulness and doing nothing? That's not exactly high capitalism.'

I fish the note out of my pocket – *lock up after yourself* – and start scribbling on the back of it.

'So we've already talked about mindfulness, right? But mindfulness is everywhere right now. Mindfulness by itself won't work. You need to take that and layer it on top of feminism, but do so with a kind of . . . ' I trail off, drawing a diagram. 'A kind of ironic knowingness. Like "we know that you know that 'having it all' is a stupid concept, and we're exposing it. We're redefining what 'having it all' actually means. At Think Gym, 'all' doesn't mean what you have, but who you are.'"

His eyes light up, and I know I'm on to something. It's perfect in all its cheesiness: it's current enough to resonate on a bus ad, but universal enough to be inspiring. Simple enough to be sellable.

'Jane . . . ' he says, joy and commerce jumping in his throat.

'Wait, hang on.'

I scribble two words: CALL ALL.

He looks confused, and then smiles. 'Like, we're calling all the disillusioned women.'

'Yeah, and also, we're "calling out" the concept of having it all.'

'Like, calling bullshit on it?'

'Exactly. "Calling out" things is very big now.'

We both consider potential drawbacks. There are none.

'Jane . . . I think that might work.'

'Do we have time to re-do everything?' I think about the presentation we have spent the last few weeks putting together, the one that blathered on about mindfulness in a loose, anaemic sort of way. This was different, though. This was a real direction.

'If we get in the car, I can call a freelancer to mock up some designs for us.'

I can't stop grinning. This, I think. This is the *Mad Men* moment that I got into advertising for. Ideas scribbled on Post-its. Driving back to the city at six in the morning. It's a bubbling passion more alarming and more intriguing and more satisfying than sex.

'Well, what are we waiting for,' I say, heading upstairs to get dressed. 'Get the car warmed up, Don Draper. We've got some shit to sell.'

16

We spend Sunday at the office – me still in denim shorts, my lingerie in a beach bag – and by the end of it, we have the fragments of a whole new campaign. He squeezes my hand, impressed by my energy and my stubborn refusal to go home until CALL ALL is exactly right. He orders me to take breaks, to get coffee, to eat green, overpriced Whole Foods hot boxes. I wander around Soho, noticing how different it looks on a Sunday, how slight and tired, a woman without her make-up on.

This. This is the kind of career I was always the most interested in having: the kind that swallows you. When I'm this deep into something, I don't feel like another silly young person who gets drunk in bed. I feel unattached and overdriven, like a brain in a jar. This is like answering a Jolly email on a good day, but even better because this actually *means* something.

We talk to a freelance designer on speaker phone, and he gets some initial designs sent over to us just before midnight. They're exactly what I wanted: breezy and colourful, like Burning Man if Gwyneth Paltrow ever attended. Next to the old, corporate branding it looks almost beautiful. If advertising *can* be beautiful.

'Go home,' says Clem, after we're done looking over the poster boards. 'You need some sleep. I'm sorry this wasn't quite the romantic Sunday I had planned.'

I kiss him on the cheek. Two days' worth of ashy stubble prickle on my mouth.

'This has been perfect.'

And I mean it.

I gather up my bag, stuffing some of the food we've not eaten into it, hoping that Shiraz will appreciate the gesture. As I sling it over my shoulder, he takes me into his arms again.

'All right, all right, what's all this about?' I say, laughing. 'I'll see you in the morning.'

He sighs. 'No, I'm in Manchester, remember?'

'Huh?'

'Only for a short while,' he says. 'Maybe a week. Possibly more. Depends on how stupid they feel like being.'

'Manchester,' I say. 'Why Manchester?'

'It's where Think Gym are based, and they've asked me to spend a few days working from their offices. I told you this. At dinner.'

'No, you didn't.'

'Yes, I did.'

The tone of our goodbye is changing. I run through our dinner: the crumbling salmon, the sharpness of the wine. What did we talk about? It all feels blurry now. *Lock up after yourself. Look after yourself. I am looking out for you. I am locking up for you.*

'I really don't think you told me.'

'Well, I'm not surprised. You were pissed.'

(I was, too. Earlier I found carpet-burn scars on my shoulders. When I pointed them out, confused and craning my neck, he was irritated. 'Yes, darling,' he said, ruffling my hair a little too roughly. 'From when I fucked you on the floor.')

'Why aren't I going?' I ask, and the minute I do, it sounds petulant.

Clem looks at me like I've lost my mind. 'Oh, I'm sorry. I thought you were interested in keeping all of this a secret.'

'I am,' I say. 'But . . .'

I'm a valued member of the company, Clem. I was given a
promotion recently, Clem, one that you assured me had nothing
to do with my sleeping with you, or being drunk with you, or
being on the floor underneath you. But you're my mentor, Clem.
But I've just spent an entire Sunday building you a whole new
campaign, Clem.

'What, Jane? We need to win this. Do you really want us
to work on pizza and cheese spreads for ever?'

'But you're not the target market,' I settle on. 'You're not
even a woman.'

'Yes, I know that. I suppose I'll call you if I need any advice.'

'How long will you be gone for?'

He kisses my temple. 'Oh, I see. You're going to miss me,
aren't you?'

'I . . . I don't know what I'll do without you.'

He likes this, and envelops me in another hug. I'm not
lying, but I'm not telling him what he thinks I'm telling him.
I really don't know what I'll do without him. He is so much a
part of my daily routine that filling my days at the office without him seems strange. I follow him into so many meetings
that I am having trouble remembering what I did at Mitchell
before he took over my schedule. But I can't get past the idea
that he's going to present my work, my campaign, completely
without my input. Doesn't he remember how good I am at
selling things to clients? Do I need to remind him, somewhat
ungraciously, about my pizza victory?

'You haven't even seen all of my new bras yet,' I say, and
he laughs. We both do.

'I love you, do you know that?' he says.

'I did not know that,' I say.

'Well,' he says.

His confidence doesn't flicker under my scrutiny. It burns
stubborn, like a far-off fire, daring me to come forward.

'Well, I love you too,' I say.

I'm being polite, of course.

'If I take you with me, people will talk. They always do. You should be there, you know, and you would be useful to me if you were. But nobody looks at a girl going to Manchester with her older boss and doesn't at least talk.'

Girl.

'I know.'

'I'm doing this for you.'

'I know.'

We kiss again and he lets me leave, this time far more ready to see me go.

Dear Miserable Mum,

Congratulations! You have ticked off not just one Life Goal from the great cosmic Female Achievement List, but many. Well done.

The mistake you have made, however, is thinking that ticking off your Life Goals will make you into a different person. That external success will equal internal joy. That looking like a magazine will somehow translate to the thin, flimsy passive happiness of that same magazine. Success will not change you. Which is great for the people that love you, but terrible if you're trying to escape yourself.

It's too exhausting. When Clem left, he took something of me with him, a non-essential organ that I could live without but winded me nonetheless. Words that used to spring forward sounding charming and quasi-inspirational now feel hollow, awkward. I type and delete, type and delete, the backspace bar feeling thicker and heavier each time I tap it. I consider attaching an online brochure for Think Gym. In the end I close the response window and try to get on with some actual work.

I go home and tell myself that I need to catch up on my sleep. That the weekend and the last-minute Think Gym overhaul have taken it out of me: but even sleep is getting harder. I lie in my bed with the sunlight streaming through the windows, my eyes to the ceiling. I only get out to go to the bathroom.

What are you doing?

Peeing, I think. I am peeing.

I'm not feeling so well :(

I close my eyes and rest my forehead on my knees. There's a jabbing pain in my lower abdomen, a needling left over from our weekend in Whitstable. There're faint spots of blood on the toilet paper, and I wonder if it could be my period. If this is what my periods look like now that I'm skinny.

What's wrong?

Summer cold. You wouldn't find me very attractive just now.

I haven't had cystitis since I was a teenager, and I had forgotten how deep the burn of it is. It's worrying me that I have it now, because I'm still not clear on how drunk I was in our Airbnb, and how much sex I remember having. Like the whisky night, flashes of it come back to me, but it's hard to tell the difference between what really happened and what I assumed happened. Projected memories quickly become actual memories. Why does he always want to drink so much?

As the days slope on, sleep remains a challenge. I feel as though I'm performing them rather than living them. My features are barely visible through a thick layer of stage make-up, but they still move on command. Clem emails me during the day, sometimes on my work account, sometimes on my personal one. It makes me feel even more muddled and implacable: he sets me tasks on my work emails, then follows up with one-line quips on Gmail, sometimes silly, sometimes sexy, always rushed. I picture him shooting them off while bored in meetings, or on the toilet.

How's my girl?

Sent from my iPhone

What's cooking, gorgeous?

Sent from my iPhone

Hope you're not getting into trouble. My spies are everywhere!

Sent from my iPhone

And then:

J,

Can you find some stats around female depression. % of women with PND, % of women with anxiety, etc. Ask data team.

C

Followed by:

> J, need a one-pager on negative representations of
> woman + mental health in media. Look on Daily Mail.
>
>
> C

I feel like I'm ingesting my work: the more facts I find about the vulnerable women who 'need' Think Gym, the more I feel like I need it myself.

> Hey Clem,
>
> Please find examples in PowerPoint attached. Hope it's useful.

The weekend comes like Christmas. Too quickly, but not quickly enough. On Saturday, being 'busy with work' isn't excuse enough to keep ignoring my Jolly readers, who have started to complain.

They feel slighted that I haven't responded to anyone in days, with a few complaining that their 'whole week' has been thrown off. I consider writing a sort of out-of-office for Jolly, but I never get far with it. Jolly Politely will be unable to answer your problems because of . . . Sickness? 'Personal problems'? I think of my mother again, in our first month as a two-person family: how she made me swear to tell no one at school, reminding me how our business was our business, and that keeping a spotless shopfront was the key to keeping a failing business upright. I decide to take the same approach with Jolly. Her business is her business.

My phone buzzes. It's from his personal email again: he texts me on evenings and weekends, he emails me on weekdays. He naturally hops between cbrown@mitchell.com and clem_brown_advertising@gmail.com: the former for work, the latter for flirting and day-to-day critiques of my wardrobe.

Thinking of you in those tiny shorts . . .

Sent from my iPhone

How like him to cover his tracks like this: it almost makes me wonder if he's been caught before. I push the thought out of my mind. I'm doing that a lot lately, avoiding things can be boiled down to two phone calls that I have not made. The first one is to my mother.

My silence hasn't escaped her. She has called me seven, eight times in the last three weeks and every time I silence the call, sometimes following up with a text about how I'm in the middle of a meeting, or on the quiet carriage of a train. I have started overcompensating for my lack of communication with emojis.

Sorry, can't talk right now. ♥ ☹

or

Sorry, I've been busy. ♥ ♥ ☹

Or even

I love you, Mum. ♥ 🐱

She's not an idiot but I can't tell her about the bomb that I have detonated in the middle of my life. Even if I could, I can't stand to face how hideously I have betrayed her. Betrayed *us*, really. I'm flying in the face of everything we went through together in the long months and years following my dad leaving us, the religion we formed together against men who cheated and the women who helped them do it.

Max was the only serious boyfriend I ever brought home. She had liked him, ish.

When he first came he did what he was supposed to do: complimented her, ate her food, presented her with the same expensive hand cream he had bought for his own mother every Christmas. She smiled plainly, accepted him, but kept the breadth of herself hidden while he was there, ducking behind Paul, busying herself with his daughters and their netball practices.

It frustrated me. I wanted Max to know the mother I had grown up with: her humour, her depth, her quickness in measuring up every scenario. There are a hundred thousand things about my mother that I find fascinating, and getting her to reveal even one fifth felt like a monumental task.

'Your mum is nice,' Max said, when we left her house.

'My mum isn't nice,' I snapped, far harsher than I had intended. 'My mum is so much more than *nice*.'

Was she really as deep and complex as I had made her out to be, or was she simply a specialist subject I had studied for so long that everything about her felt intricate? She was like a single drop of water under a microscope, a whole world within a world of pressure intensity and cell formations. And all Max could see was something he understood to be simple. Transparent. A *mum*.

Max is the other phone call I've been avoiding. He's serious about the money thing, it seems. This mortgage he is ready to share with Kim is not something I can wish away, or ignore until it disappears. I can *technically* afford to increase my monthly instalments to him. It wouldn't be hard, with my newly improved paycheque. I just can't bear to contact him. Every break-up has a winner, and he is winning this one. It's not even a contest, though of course, it *is* a contest. He is buying property and has a beautiful, successful girlfriend who in all probability isn't already married, and if his career is going well he doesn't even have to question why. He doesn't have to look at his monthly bank balance and think: *Why do I have this? Why was this given to me?*

And what do I have, really? Expensive underwear and no one to talk to. Fantastic.

It would be nice to think that I would have called Max eventually, or at least replied to one of his emails. I'll never know, though, because when I leave work he is waiting outside the office with his arms folded.

I know why he is here, that he is acting as a debt collector, but I can't help but break into a grateful smile. His familiar face and his mole below his left eyebrow. Max, the person whose body I have seen almost as many times as I have seen my own. I hug him, but his shoulders are stiff.

'Hi, Jane.'

I drop my arms to my sides.

'Hey,' I say, uncertain. 'It's nice to see you.'

'You too. Can we go somewhere to talk?'

I trail behind him, unsteady, not sure what he's going to say. Or rather: nervous of how he's going to say it.

It's a pub we've been to a thousand times before, a Sam Smith's where we would sometimes play darts and drink cheap pints of pale ale. It's early and it's Monday, so the only people around to witness the dissolution of those memories are a couple of rounded alcoholics and a barmaid with long, brown pencilled lines where her brows once were. She hands Max two orange pints and a packet of crisps, which he carries back to our table with his teeth. I laugh, he smiles, and it's almost like before.

I forgot about the way he smiles at everyone without even considering the politics of what a smile means. There's an easiness to him that makes entire rooms exhale and loosen around him. *I never deserved to be your girlfriend,* I think. *I was always meant to be some other man's dirty secret.*

The pint makes me dizzy, but I drink it. It's something to do with my hands. I hope that another sip will cut through the nausea, but it only intensifies, putting pressure on my stomach and leaving my throat tickling. I count the hours of sleep I've had since Saturday, when I slipped down to the cottage kitchen a little before six because the weight of Clem next to me felt too alarming, and Sunday, when I didn't get home until 1 a.m. and was too wired to sleep properly.

'I'm only here because I don't know what else to do, Jane.'

'I know. I'm sorry.'

I don't think he expected me to give up so easily. He's suspicious: he's used to the old me, the argumentative, constantly fed-up one.

'I've tried calling you. A lot, Jay. I thought we ended all right. We said we'd be friends.'

'I know,' I say. 'I'm sorry.'

He raises an eyebrow and I realise I've repeated myself.

'I *still* want us to be friends.' He is making his voice gentler now. 'I mean, no one expects it to happen right away, do they? It's awkward. And I'm with someone else, and I know that's hard for you. I don't blame you for going off-grid. I know I could have handled things better.'

'It's my fault,' I say. The sick feeling in my stomach is spreading through me now, making it hard to focus. 'You were great. I never appreciated you.'

He stretches out a hand to my shoulder, then looks at it, wonders whether it's appropriate for him to touch me.

'Jane, are you okay?'

I nod. 'I'm okay,' I lie. 'Say what you want to say.'

'Your mum called.'

'Excuse me?'

'Your mum. She's been calling me.'

'My mum doesn't even *like* you,' I say, not considering just how awful that sounds.

'Even so,' he says, 'she's worried about you. I'm worried about you. She says you won't take any of her calls and that your texts . . . she says they're *off.* She wants to know if you're all right. I said I couldn't tell her if you were all right, and that the last time I saw you you were on our bathroom floor.'

'Our *old* bathroom floor.'

'Our old bathroom floor,' he says reasonably.

'She asked me if you've been drinking a lot, or if you're falling in with a bad crowd.'

I laugh, harsh and dry, my throat scratching. 'That's such a Mum thing to say. I'm not fourteen. "Falling in with a bad crowd." As if I'm in a knife gang.'

'Well then, what *are* you doing, Jane? Becky says you don't talk to her any more. Darla doesn't reply to me.'

'What the *hell*, Max? Are you starting a WhatsApp group with everyone I know? What's it called? The "Jane has completely lost the plot" chat?'

'*Have* you? Jane, can you accept for one fucking second that while you were vanishing, people were fucking worried? That maybe, yeah, we chatted and traded notes, because we were scared for you? Because for someone to be virtually uncontactable for six weeks is *weird*?'

I think of Clem vanishing, leaving me to rot here in London where everyone I know is suspicious of me. *But I'm doing so well,* I think. *What do they know?* My breath starts to come short.

'And Jane – I know it's not my place to say this, so tell me if I'm being a dick, but – you don't look well, babe.' He places his hand lightly on mine. 'If you're . . . if you're on drugs, you can tell me. I won't say anything to your mum. Or to anyone. But you need to say.'

I heave at this, and my vision starts to blot, my eyes under a thick screen of purple splotches and squiggly lines.

'I need something to eat,' I blurt out, squeezing my eyes together tightly. *You will not be sick here, Jane. You will not be sick in front of Max. The last time you saw him you were sick, don't make this his primary memory of you.*

'Let me get you something.' He fans out his fingers on both hands and brings them down slowly, the international symbol of 'you need to calm down, you mad bitch'.

'No, no, no.'

Something impetuous in me takes over, and I stand up to go to the bar. The dark oak of it blurs before me and within moments, I'm on the floor. The last thing I see are the holes in the wall, pinpricks made from decades of Friday-night darts games. I remember his hand on my shoulder, demonstrating how to throw a dart, how you have to rotate it slightly between your thumb and forefinger so it spins and hits the target. He used to love to show me how to do things.

I see a swish of grey hair at the corner of my eye, and become convinced that it's my own. I grab at a lock, and hold it in front of my face: it's thin, but it's still the same dark chestnut it has always been. I realise then that the grey hair was actually a woman's head from across the pub, and that my depth perception has narrowed frighteningly. I touch a table, and then the edge of the bar, unsure of how close or far away anything is.

I keep looking at the dart holes in the wall, the paint peeling around them. How many holes did I make, here, with Max? How much damage did I do? How much damage can I do?

As my vision starts to empty and my focus starts to drop, I am convinced I can see light pouring through them.

Dear Jolly,

Run jolly, run jolly, run jolly, now jolly, run jolly, run jolly

PART FOUR

17

After that, Max is in charge. I'm an incidental figure in my own drama, being pulled around by the hand, and propped up in chairs. My eyelids are heavy the whole time, and the trance is only interrupted by a few sharp moments, moments mostly posed as a series of options, in a ghoulish 'choose-your-own-adventure book' questions.

1. Whether or not we go to the hospital

The barmaid thinks I'm fine and doesn't want any trouble. The two drunks suggest I walk it off. And wouldn't an ambulance take forever getting down Soho's narrow streets? And isn't there an A&E near Dean Street, and wouldn't we be better off going there?

2. Whether or not we stay at the hospital

I am underneath Max's jacket and shivering on a hospital chair and he is arguing with the nurse on reception. She tells him that the waiting time is the waiting time and that there's nothing she can do about it.

3. Whether or not I am fine

'I'm okay now,' I say. 'I don't know what happened. I just want to go to sleep. I don't want to wait three hours to find out that I'm fine.'

    4. Whether or not it is Max's responsibility to take care of me

'I'm not yours to worry about, Max, just let me go.'
  'I'm coming with you.'
  'Would your girlfriend like that?'
  'Stop it. Where do you live?'
  'You don't even know where I *live*, Max. Did you ever think that you wouldn't know where I live?'

    5. Whether or not I can stay awake in the taxi

'Don't lean your head against the window. You need to show me where your house is.'

    6. Whether or not Max can convince Shiraz that he is not a date rapist

I am heavy on his shoulder, not saying much.
  'Keys,' he says. 'I need your keys.'
  I root around in my jacket pocket. Shiraz opens the door before he can get to the lock.
  'Who are you?'
  'I'm Max.'
  'Max who?'
  He winces.
  'Jane's . . . friend.'

7. Whether or not Max will comment on my room

'Jane,' he says, 'where are your pyjamas?'
  'Bottom drawer.'
  He opens it and I hear the clear clink of empty bottles.
  'Not *that* bottom drawer.'

8. Whether or not he should wait until I'm asleep

'I'm just going to sit here, okay?'
  'Don't go.'
  'I won't.'
  'I don't know what's wrong with me.'
  'Shh.'

9. Whether or not Shiraz knows what's wrong with me

He went into the kitchen after I fell asleep.
  'He asked what you were drinking, what you were eating, if you were on drugs.'
  'What did you say?'
  Shiraz looked at me with one, raised, are-you-shitting-me eyebrow.
  'I told him I had no idea what you get up to.'

10. Whether or not he will call

He doesn't.
  I sleep for the rest of the night and call work the next morning to say that I'm sick. I get a text from Becky around ten.

Are you ok? Max said you fainted

As if her talking to Max was the most natural thing in the world. I appreciate her concern but remember what she told him: *Becky says you don't talk to her any more.*

'She doesn't talk to me, either,' I say out loud, to no one.

I feel weak beyond all recognition. I lie still and wait for flu symptoms to descend on me, so I can go back to work tomorrow and say: *Just one of those summer colds!*

The symptoms never come. There's no snot, no fever, no vomiting. What there is is an exhaustion so profound that it leaks like a poison throughout my body. Clem's flowers are ashen, a circle of withered petals surrounding the jam jar filled with yellow water. The drawer with the empty wine bottles has been left open, and all over the floor are jeans and tights with old knickers stuck in them. I wince as I ease my bra out through the armhole of a T-shirt Max pulled onto me. I'm still wearing my green silk balconette. I wonder if he noticed it? I wonder if he knew where it came from, or who it was for?

The wine looks worse than it really is. On the weekends it's hard for me to see Clem, so I go back to my pre-affair, post-Max habit of watching movies in bed with a bottle of wine, laptop tucked under my chin. It's no more than you'd drink if you were out with your friends on a Saturday night. I'm just not in a position, right now, to have those kinds of friends. Because having friends means telling, and I don't want to tell. *What would I even say?*

And yes, okay, the bottles have stacked up. But only because I don't want Shiraz to see them in the recycling. I don't want her to think, just as she's starting to sort of like me, that I drink wine by myself at the weekends. It's not sad, and I'm not sad, but it *sounds* sad.

I can't sleep. I close my eyes and wait for the exhaustion to creep into my brain and turn it off. I imagine my mind as a huge building full of rooms, and there is one janitor who looks after it. He is walking around, emptying the waste-paper baskets and switching off each light when he is happy every room is tidy and taken care of. *When he turns off every light in the building, I'll be able to go to sleep.* Only the building keeps getting bigger, with more and more rooms added every minute. I get agitated, my heart pounding even as my eyelids are drooping. My phone buzzes from somewhere in the sheets. It's Clem, and his text is the only sign that it's now late evening.

How's my best girl? Xx

Great. How is it going in Manchester?

Fantastic. They say they might keep me here for another few days. A master's work is never done lol

God, there's something weird about a married man saying lol.

I need to pee, but I can't move my legs. Or I can, but the whole endeavour is so depressingly effortful that there doesn't seem to be any point in trying. They're heavy, like bags of wet sand, and I wrap my arms around them to make sure they're still a normal leg weight. When I manage to plonk my feet down on the carpet, each step feels like it's one taken in a dream. I land heavily on the toilet seat, and the short, hot, jabbing pain of the infection seizes me again.

'Oh, fuck *off*,' I say, in the general direction of my vagina. The sip of beer with Max can't have helped.

Run jolly, run jolly, run jolly, now jolly, run jolly, run jolly

I got the email minutes before the incident with Max in the pub, and it comes from the same address as the other messages. Garbled numbers and letters, a hastily created email address to withhold an identity. I decide that I can no longer ignore these emails, or pretend that they're spam, or a joke. I start a reply.

Dear Anonymous and Somewhat Creepy Sender
Much as I enjoy your frankly terrifying messages, I must
admit that I'm dumbfounded as to—

I stop and delete. This is not a situation in which it feels
appropriate to be glib.

Dear Sender,
I must ask that you state your intent before sending me
any mo—

Why am I being formal? They're being oblique and strange,
and dressing up my words like a nineteenth-century gentleman
won't make them any less so. I delete everything, even the 'Dear'.

Why are you emailing me? What are you trying to say?

My phone buzzes moments later and I almost throw it across
the room in shock. But it's a text, and it's from Clem.

**What are you doing right now? Lonely for my
girl ... xxx**

Oh, God. Does he want to sext? Is that what's happening here?
Does he even call it 'sexting', I wonder. I bet he calls it 'phone
sex' or 'dirty talk' or something equally nineties. I am amazed
that a man who still buys CDs – and *listens to them* – can also be
interested in sexting. I'm the young person in this relationship,
and even *I* don't know how to sext properly.
My phone buzzes again.

What are you wearing?

Oh, Christ.

18

The reply comes the next morning, and the email is just two words.

SisterHive Yoga

I was hoping that confronting the ghost through its own medium would force it into retreat.

Did you mean Sister Yoga?, Google queries.

Probably not. These emails are nuts, yes, but they are concise. Whoever wrote them knew I was in trouble and wouldn't say SisterHive if they meant Sister.

I email back.

Why?

I pick up a pen and lay out the facts as I know them.

1. I have been getting a series of troubling emails from an unknown source
2. I have been suffering from some kind of mystery illness for almost as long as the emails have been coming through
3. Both of these things entered my life as Clem Brown did

I add a fourth point in a light, hesitant hand.

> 4. Although I have absolutely no proof of it, I think his
>   wife is after me

I cross it out and rewrite.

> 4. I have some proof that I might be going crazy

I lay out my list of Known Knowns, on the back of a leaflet for genital warts. I am at the GP's office and have been here for almost two hours. When the receptionist finally calls my name, I stuff the pamphlet into my handbag.

The doctor is rubbing his hands with antiseptic when I go into his office. I haven't met anyone at this practice before: the one I used to visit when I lived with Max is too far away, so I registered here on one of the long, slow weekends after I moved in.

He's older, like a proper GP, the kind you get in villages. He has, I imagine, a bright black doctor's bag with a cold stethoscope in it. The only times I've been to the doctor in the last four or five years was to update my prescription of the pill, and on those occasions I almost always dealt with nurses. They were businesslike, but friendly, and sometimes they would say things like: 'Ah. Dianette. I was on that one for a bit, made my boobs enormous.' Or, 'I'm not going to try to convince you to get the coil because I know girls your age are terrified of it.'

'Hello, how are you?' he asks, as I sit down.

'Not so good, I don't think.'

He gives me a weak smile, as if to say: *For the love of God, don't make me prise it out of you.*

'I collapsed on Monday evening.'

'I see. Were you at home?'

'No. I was at the pub.'

It was the stupidest thing I could possibly have said, and his interest in me now disintegrates into a pained fatigue.

'I see. And how much did you have to drink?'

'Nothing. Half a pint, if even that. I sort of . . . Had a bit of a panic attack, I think, and I felt weak and dizzy. I fainted and after I woke up, I couldn't focus. I could barely stand up. I slept for a good twenty hours after that.'

'Like a drunk person.'

'Yes. I mean, *no*. But I wasn't drunk, is the thing.'

I can't think of how to explain it to him, the panic and fear and exhaustion, the way food tastes, the itching.

'There are other symptoms,' I say.

'Such as?'

'I have no energy,' I say, but immediately it sounds stupid. 'And no appetite. And I have a rash.'

'Does the rash fade under pressure?'

'Yes. I've been doing the glass tumbler thing.'

'Ah. Well, let me weigh you and take your blood pressure.'

'Should I take off my shoes?'

He shrugs. 'If you want.'

I step on the scales, and he types my weight into the computer.

As the cuff around my arm tightens and he watches the calculator that measures my heart rate, he tuts audibly.

'Is everything okay?' I ask.

'Is there a reason you came to the walk-in today?'

'I'm sick. I told you. I fainted on Monday night and—'

He points at the door behind me. 'The man who came in before you had to ask me to change his colostomy bag, because he was too weak to do it himself.'

'Are you allowed to tell me that?'

'I'm telling you because people are supposed to use the walk-in facility for emergencies, Ms Peters. *Emergencies.*'

I know I probably have cause to complain about him, or at the very least, to go on Comment is Free and write an incendiary article about this practice. But I remember a woman in the waiting room with her son, yellow crust thickening on his cheek. How long does she have to wait so I can tell the doctor that I am *quite tired*? What am I hoping for? A sick note? A lolly? A pat on the back?

The stubborn side of me fights back.

'So you're saying there's *nothing* wrong with me?'

'I think you're crash dieting, to be perfectly honest, and I think you've made yourself anaemic in the process.'

'I am *not* crash dieting,' I say, baring my teeth just a little.

'I'm sorry, Ms Peters, I don't want to accuse you of anything. You're not on trial. You don't need to be defensive. Try to calm down.'

'I am calm!' I feel like I'm a difficult woman being accused of hysterics. The thing about hysterics, though, is the more you argue against your case for having it the more it proves their point. Hysterical women argue. *Hysterical women starve themselves.*

'I see a lot of young women your age, Ms Peters. It's a bit of a trend, so to speak.' He is saying 'Ms Peters' far more often than I am comfortable with. 'And I realise the pressure on you girls can be overwhelming.'

'Pressure?'

'I have two daughters,' he says, in the way that racists say 'I have black friends'. 'You get stressed out at work. You try to keep up. And you're all very good at it! You are excellent at securing fantastic little jobs for yourselves, and you push and push and push, and you want to keep up with the boys, and you go out every night. It's marvellous. But it *can't. Last. For ever.*'

He says those last four words as if tapping them firmly with a ballpoint pen. 'I suppose you came in here today hoping for a prescription for some antidepressants.'

'No,' I say, and he cuts me off before I can say, *I came in here so you could tell me what's wrong with me.*

'But I'm not going to do that,' he says, like he's doing me a massive favour. 'Because I don't honestly think that's what you need.'

'I *agree.*'

We look at one another with dim satisfaction, like we're two people who speak two very different languages, and we have been trying for hours to find out where the swimming pool is. We're nowhere close, but at least there's water.

'Fresh air. Exercise. Lots of fresh vegetables. Vitamin supplements, if you can afford them.' He leans in, as if he's about to give me a divine secret of the trade. 'I get mine on Amazon. Much cheaper.'

'Thank you,' I say miserably. 'I also have cystitis.'

He leans back in his chair and considers this.

'How bad is it?'

'It just stings.'

'Is there blood in your urine?'

I think for a moment, then answer.

'There was a bit a few days ago, but that might have been just my perio—'

'I'm going to keep you off antibiotics, because I don't think they'd do you any favours in your current state. You also need to eat properly, when you're on medication.' He nods at my body, as if it's a foregone conclusion that I'm not doing that.

'There's an over-the-counter solution that should work fine. I'll write it down for you.' He grabs another appointment slip. 'Give this to one of the girls outside. They'll book you in for an appointment at our sexual health clinic.'

'Do you think I have an STD?'

'No. But it wouldn't hurt to check, give you a once-over. Very common with people your age.'

I get up to leave, irritated by how he's treating me.

'Exercise,' he adds.

'Pardon?'

'Exercise is great for treating these kinds of problems.'

'What kind of problems?'

He waves his hand over in my direction. 'Depression, anxiety, that kind of thing. Yoga is very popular with the younger nurses here.'

SisterHive Yoga. Could he . . . could he know?

'Maybe I will try yoga,' I say, casual but searching. 'Maybe I'll go tomorrow.'

'Very nice, Ms Peters.'

He looks up from his ancient computer. 'And remember, no more than fourteen units of alcohol a week. The nurses have pamphlets on what fourteen units might look like.'

The door is heavy, and while I don't slam it, I don't stop it from closing hard. When I check my phone, I have a response.

I know about him

19

I stay away from the office the next day, but go into work the day after. Any longer I need a doctor's note – and there's no way in hell I'm going back to Dr I-Have-Two-Daughters. I mix up a sachet of Cystopurin in the staff bathroom, reluctant to be caught taking cystitis medication in the shared kitchen. I gulp down half of it in one go and shudder. It tastes like salt and plastic.

Darla walks in, make-up bag already in her hand. She smiles when she sees me, forgetting that she's annoyed. I can't help but smile back.

'Oh, *love*,' she says, when she sees the cystitis medicine on the counter. 'My deepest condolences.'

'Thanks. I feel like I'm passing razor blades through my fanny.'

She laughs. I miss being silly and crass and personal with her. I miss talking to women: sharing, and oversharing, and complaining about our vaginas. Darla unzips her bag and applies a deep plum lipstick. It's beautiful against her skin, a shade I could never get away with.

'I had it a few weeks ago,' she says, and I can feel her trying to say sorry by confessing. 'And I had to hide it from my mum all weekend. I'm not a hundred per cent sure she knows that you mostly get cystitis from unprotected sex, but I sure as shit didn't want to chance it.'

I chuckle, remembering Darla's mum, and how she is a stereotype of an older Asian mother one minute and a savvy Londoner the next. She'll be scolding Darla for her clothes, and will then turn around to give her a lecture on Tinder etiquette.

'So,' Darla says, looking playful, 'who's Señor Razor Fanny, then?'

The question, while not an unreasonable one between two women who are – were? – best friends, stumps me. Do I tell Darla? Here, now, in the Mitchell toilets?

My expression flickers for a moment, and then I smooth it into passive blankness.

'Oh,' I say, forcing a casual tone, 'no one. It's not a sex thing.'

She giggles, as if I'm joking. 'Sure, okay. Come on, Jane. You can tell *me*.'

'No, really. I think I'm just dehydrated.'

We're both perfectly aware that I'm lying to her, and that something between us has changed as a result. We used to have long, boozy lunches when I told her everything: about my parents, my doubts about Max, my concern that I was going nowhere in my career. The only thing I didn't tell her about was Jolly Politely, and even then, that was never a lie. It was an omission. The idea of someone like Darla – my cool friend, my stylish friend, my friend I could never have made when Jolly started – reading my anonymous correspondence made me shudder with mortification.

Darla turns to the mirror, smacks her lips together, and zips her bag closed.

'Well, drink plenty of water,' she says, with a tinge of frost.

'We should get a drink after work. Or, tomorrow maybe: I probably shouldn't drink while I'm still peeing knives.'

'Maybe,' she says. 'See you later.'

She leaves me with half a glass of Cystopurin to drink. I drain the glass.

When I get back to my desk, Becky is all concerned looks, and I'm not sure how to feel about her.

'How are you?'

I know she is being nice. She *is* nice. But I can't get her conversations with Max out of my mind, her back-and-forths with him about *how Jane is doing*. Why couldn't she have asked me if she thought something was wrong?

'Fine,' I say briskly, and her look turns from concern to mild devastation. Then a sort of horror crawls across her face, shadowing her bright, big eyes.

'Jane,' she whispers, 'your hair.'

'What?'

'I think you should follow me.'

She leads me to the ladies' toilets on the fourth floor, so I know it must be serious. The fourth floor is where the engineers sit, so you rarely find many women in the loo up there. It's where you go if you want to get ready for a night out and need the entire mirror to yourself, or you just need a private conversation with someone. I wonder if anyone will notice that I have spent the working day in the loo with other women.

Becky flips out a compact mirror and gently pushes some hairs at the back of my head aside. 'Look,' she says, her voice laced with pity.

I yelp. The sound you hear from a dog that has been kicked in the belly by someone who loves her.

I have a bald spot. The skin is pink and delicate, like a burn that has recently healed. There are slight rough puckers where the follicles once grew, dimples on a rotting fruit.

'Have you . . . ? Have you noticed anything? More hair in your brush?'

The first morning-after with Clem, I walked home and

tried to think of three good things about my life. The free shampoo. The sunny day. The fact that I hadn't made a complete arse out of myself in front of the man who would become my married boyfriend.

There were so many good things, though. Becky. Darla. A full head of hair. A clean bill of health. A whole new phase of my career opening up in front of me. I'd slid my key through the door and snapped at Shiraz because she reminded me about her tights that I had stolen off the clothes horse. I remember my long ponytail in primary school, my cartwheels.

And I remember something else: the clump of wet hair that came when I tried to brush the expensive product out of it. I was shocked, but like all shock, it eventually becomes something to be dealt with. A chore, a nuisance, a thing I should probably have looked at.

Did I tell the doctor about the fine strands of brown hair on my pillow in the morning, and how quickly my hair was taking to dry? Did I notice it myself?

SisterHive Yoga. I keep coming back to the emails in my head, trying to see what the pattern is. They are, I realise, guesses rather than facts. *Do not sign for the flowers* arrived after the flowers had. *She will leave him before he leaves her* seemed to presume that I was talking to Clem about leaving his wife, when I wasn't at all. And 'run Jolly'? Well, that was just advice. It feels as though this person is attempting to forecast my downfall based on a previous trend, and some-how, this is more disturbing than the idea that someone is watching me.

'Becky,' I say, 'I think I should go to the doctor.'

'I think you should too. I'll email HR. Say you vommed up a lung in the fourth-floor toilets.'

In that moment, I almost tell her everything that I was afraid to tell Darla earlier. Clem, and the strange, magnetic, sickening pull he has on me. That I can't eat, and I can't pee, and that it took me thirty minutes to get out of bed yesterday. About Jolly Politely, and the emails she has been getting.

I almost tell her that I feel trapped, as though I have painted myself into a corner of my own life, and it has only taken me six weeks to do it. How lonely I am, and how much I miss her, and how sorry I am to have neglected her. And that despite knowing these things – despite being fully aware of my own bad choices and misguided impulses – I feel powerless to change any of them. Ending things with Clem, right now, feels like the only thing worse than sticking it out. He loves me. *He loves me he loves me he loves me.*

I don't tell her any of these things. The shame and the absolute fear of another woman's judgement, even when it's a woman like Becky, keep me back.

'Thanks, Becky.'

We hug.

On my laptop at home, I have to scroll two pages on Google before I find SisterHive Yoga. If I were a person who was legitimately looking to get into yoga – even someone who lived in the SE27 postcode it's in – SisterHive Yoga would not be my first stop. The website is woefully dated, and unsettlingly purple. There are broken images everywhere, replaced by red Xs and file descriptions of what once stood. 'Savasana. gif' and 'dharma.jpeg' litter the corners of the screen. There's almost no information about upcoming classes on the website, and no way to book a class online. Under contact details, there's one name: Ludmilla Sedlak.

I practise saying the name 'Ludmilla Sedlak' on the way over. *LUD-milla? Lude-milla? Said-lack? Zed-lack?* I whisper it under my breath as the bus heaves forwards, confident that if I pronounce her name perfectly she will know I am serious.

When I get there I don't see a yoga studio. I see a coffee shop instead – the kind where you need at least one mermaid tattoo to work there. It's tiny. More like a cupboard under a staircase than a café, but every wall has a ledge accompanied by a stool, and a clutch of young creative types are working on laptops while struggling to get their legs under there comfortably.

Welcome to the Wait There Cafe, says a chalkboard sign. *Please Wait There.*

Oh, for fuck's sake.

'Excuse me,' I say, flagging down a guy who looks vaguely managerial, even though he's carrying a stone slab of gluten-free brownies. 'Do I have the right address?' I show him my piece of paper.

'You have the right place, but that business doesn't exist any more.'

'Yeah, I kinda figured that.'

'She went out of business, oooh, three years ago? I think she might do private classes in her flat, because I do see girls going up there, sometimes. But she certainly hasn't had a studio since then.'

'Do you know her?'

'Of course I do,' he laughs. 'She's my landlady. She still lives upstairs.'

'Upstairs? Really?'

'Yeah, just go outside and ring the bell.'

I jam my finger on the button for Ludmilla's flat. I have to press extra hard on the left-hand side before I hear a ring. I realise it's the middle of the afternoon, and she's probably at work. I ring once more, for luck, and hear the break in static as she picks up the receiver.

'Hello?'

'Hi. Is this Ludmilla?'

'Yes.'

'You sent me some emails.'

'Come on up, Jolly.'

The buzzer screams its approval, and I'm in.

'Hello?'

'I'm in here,' she calls, and I follow her voice to a brown kitchen that smells of fruit tea. The whole place feels poky, the atmosphere hazy with too many space heaters. Her back is to me, but I see long, long grey hair and a tiny, lithe body. The body of a dancer. It's impossible to age her from this angle: her hands look older, but her arse is nicer than mine.

'I'm making a pot. Do you prefer lemon, Earl Grey or chamomile?

'Which do you like?'

'I like chamomile.'

'That then.'

She turns to face me, and I almost stumble at the sight of her. I know her. I know her the way you know a family member that you only see at weddings or funerals. Vague and distinct, all at once.

'You said we'd speak soon,' she says politely. 'And here we are.'

'Pardon?'

'On the bus. You said "speak soon". And now we're speaking.'

The bus home from my first night with Clem: she is the woman who sat in front of me. She was there at the hotel.

Her hair is slate grey, witchy, wild. There's a reason why she feels familiar. She has been trailing me for months.

I take a step back, alarmed. My eyes flick to the door. Do I really want to be in this woman's *house*?

She smiles, and a few of her teeth are missing. Nothing that would ruin her looks completely: it actually looks strangely pretty. Characterful, like having mismatched eyes. I touch my own teeth with my tongue. It almost feels like there's too many of them, now that I've seen her mouth.

'Let me see,' she says. Her eyes are a faded blue, the colour of the sea in off-season. 'I don't have a lot of guests these days, so I'm afraid I don't have much to nibble on.'

'That's fine. I'm not hungry.'

'Don't be silly. Dreadfully rude to give you nothing. Sit yourself down and I'll make us something, Jolly.'

'It's Jane,' I say. 'Jolly's just my—'

She waves her hand at me, as if it's all the same to her.

The kitchen and the living room are six steps apart, one becoming the other at a line in the floor where linoleum turns into wood flooring. There's no couch, but there are small, rounded beanbags scattered on the floor. They are the shape of kidneys, but in bright, knitted colours. Everything in the room feels like it once belonged to an alpaca. It's nice, though: there's a cosiness to it. A soft, technicolour womb.

It's remarkable how easy I feel in here. Here is a woman who has been following me for months, and I already feel numbed to the fact. It's as though I call around to Ludmilla's house every day. I pop up for tea, she insists on snacks, I sit on a soft kidney and feel the stress of work and sex and strange, inexplicable diseases melt away.

She brings a tray over and sits cross-legged on the floor, her bum resting on the cleft of a kidney. I copy her. On the tray she has arranged two teacups with saucers, a pot of chamomile and a plate of sliced bread, thick with butter and jam, cut into soldiers. It is a child's tea party, and I am grateful for it.

'Here you are, my love.'

'Thank you . . . is it Lude-milla?'

'It is. But I prefer Luddy. To rhyme with "ruddy".'

'Luddy it is.'

We blow on our tea. I notice her hands are shaking slightly as she holds her cup, but it doesn't seem to bother her, and it feels rude to ask.

'Is that an Eastern European name?'

She nods, but makes no attempt to clarify.

It's amazing, the politeness of women. If I were a man, and if this were an action film, I would have hammered on the door and demanded an answer.

'Do you have work today, Jane?'

'I do, technically. I didn't go. I called in sick.'

'*Are* you sick?'

She looks at me searchingly, worried but prepared for my answer.

'Yes, Luddy.'

She lets out a tired, sad sigh.

'I thought that might be the case.'

'Because you've been following me?'

I don't mean it to sound quite so accusatory. Luddy doesn't react, except to lean closer towards me. She traces one cool, crooked finger down the length of my cheekbone.

'How long?'

When was the beginning? When did the weight start falling off? When did the panic attacks start? When did everything start tasting bitter, coppery? When did my hair start falling out?

'About two months.'

'So, we're still early, then.'

'Early in *what*?'

She takes a long sip of her tea.

'What do you do for a living, Jane?'

'I work in marketing.'

'*Just* marketing?'

'What do you mean?'

'You don't ... you're not a potter, secretly? You're not a pastry chef, or a jewellery designer, or something else?'

'Wouldn't you know if I was?'

She tuts modestly, as if I were giving her a compliment.

'Don't give me that much credit. I see a sad girl who walks on her own. I see a mistress out to lunch with her lover. I don't know the full picture.'

I feel a dark, shameful blush crawling up my neck.

'You know about him, then? Clem.'

She laughs. 'Darling, I wrote the book on him.'

I look around, unsure whether this is a figure of speech, or if she's literally written a book. She chuckles again, but seems unwilling to say more. I think of my mother: how, in the long months after Dad left, it was always better to chop and change with conversations, and never to settle on one thing for too long. If she dwelled on any subject, she could find the sadness in it, and if she was sad, she would cry again.

'No, I'm not secretly a potter.'

'Strange. Very strange.'

'Why?'

She takes a finger of bread and tears it in half. She chews on it thoughtfully.

'He looks for creative types, normally.'

'You mean Clem. Why?'

'Because he's not creative. He's not anything, really. He's charming, I'll give you that. He can fill a room with just himself. But he needs people to survive. To lean on, to drain from.'

'Is that why I'm sick? Is it going to get worse?'

She's sombre now. 'There have been others, before you. Other girls. Did you know that?'

I didn't. But it doesn't surprise me.

'How many?'

'I can't be exactly sure. He goes off-grid with them, sometimes. I met three, but there could have been as many as eight.'

'*Eight?*'

She's cross-legged, with the balls of her feet touching and drawn towards her pelvis. A frayed poster on the wall tells me what yoga position this is. *Cobbler's pose.*

'Well, where are the three now? The ones you met? Did he . . . ? Did he break up with them?'

'You could say that. One works in catering. Another went back to university to study physiotherapy.' She cracks a smile. 'It was me, who got her into that. Into healing the body. Into nourishing yourself *through* yourself. I'm so, so proud of her.'

'And what about the third one?'

She untangles her limbs. Her right leg stretches out behind her, and she folds her left one under her hip. I look to the chart again. *Pigeon pose.*

I think of birds. Once your brain settles on a theme, you see evidence of it everywhere. A chocolate-coloured clump of hair that no mother sparrow would make her home out of. The constant chirruping in our Whitstable cottage. *Look after yourself. Look after yourself.*

'This is a great hip opener,' declares Luddy, and I can tell she's hiding something.

'The third girl,' I repeat. 'What happened to her?'

There is a dull, tired pain in her face.

'Have you ever done a yoga class before, Jane? Meditation?'

'No,' I say, determined not to get locked into some kind of yoga pyramid scheme.

'At the end of every class, I always tell my students the same thing: thank you for bringing your energy here today. We say that because in every class, we create a feedback loop of energy between the students and the teacher. It makes the act of it, the community of it, the *prayer* of it, stronger.'

Oh, for fuck's sake.

'Luddy, I'm sorry, but I really don't—'

'The reason I'm telling you this, Jane,' she raises her voice, 'is because I don't have the strength to tell this story on my own. I need both of our energies, together, to get to the end. It's too hard, otherwise. Will you do that with me, Jane? Will you help me tell you this story?'

I want to gather up my things and bolt out the door, leaving this odd little woman and her dark, overheated flat to rot together. I want to tell her about Think Gym, and the commercial work I've done surrounding the notion of 'inner peace' and 'shared energy', and that I am too cynical to be sold on it now. But I know that if I turn my back on her, I may never get to the end of what's happening to me.

'Okay,' I say. 'What do you need me to do?'

20

I don't have anything of my own to wear, but Luddy doesn't see that as a problem. She has a never-ending supply of colourful leggings, and tosses me a pair in precisely my size.

As I put them on, she shuts her curtains, and begins lighting candles. I think she might be lighting one or two for atmosphere, but she starts opening more and more drawers. She takes out stubby, half-burnt dining candles and aromatherapy candles. She finds tin candles from Muji that smell of firewood and mulberries. There's a menorah full of candles, and she lights those, too. I wonder if she's Jewish, or just likes candles a lot.

She lights a series of candy-coloured birthday candles stuck in a brick of green oasis intended for flower arrangements, and settles it in front of me. I almost laugh. This whole thing started, after all, with a birthday candle.

'Jane,' she says, watching me over the flickering light of a hundred candles, 'please take a comfortable, cross-legged position.'

I take a comfortable, cross-legged position.

'Breathe in, feel your stomach expand. Breathe out. Straighten your spine. Imagine the tip of your crown as an extension of your spine.'

We sit for a little while. Breathing in, breathing out. She gives me a few directives, asking me to stretch different parts of myself lightly. I wonder if I'm supposed to feel something, some sort of common energy. Maybe she thinks she's already telling me the story, through some kind of mad yoga mind reading.

I peek one eye open, and Luddy is absolutely still. I suspect that she's forgotten all about the emails, and about Clem, and about the women before me. Maybe, she thinks she's just giving a normal yoga class. What if she wants me to pay her at the end?

The smell of the candles start to merge and stack on top of one another in unusual, unwelcome combinations. Berries and jasmine, charcoal and vanilla. It's oily and dank and making my long breaths in and out more laboured as the sweet, hot air burns in my lungs.

'Deep breath in,' says Luddy. 'Feel the breath fill you like a balloon.'

I feel like an old carpeted bagpipe, wheezing sourly, stumbling through a tune written for a lighter and more tinkling instrument.

'Deep breath out,' she concludes, and I feel my ribs tighten in protest as I try to follow her. The churning nausea in my gut is all I can focus on, my concentration intimately tied to not throwing up on Luddy's floor.

An imperious light-headedness comes over me. My mind isn't clear in the way I know yoga minds are supposed to be, but it's something *like* clarity. I'm drenched in a thin mist, aware only of the parts of my body that are necessary to stay alive.

'She was an artist,' Luddy speaks, and pictures start to emerge out of the mist.

'She was twenty-one,' she continues.

'They met,' she says, like it's one word, something in Sanskrit. 'They met at her graduate art show.'

The girl I dream up is, like Kim, both me and not me. I make her into someone tall, with brown hair and split ends. Someone who blushes too easily and whose skin is oily, and who can't wear lipstick properly because it emphasises the dry skin perpetually folding upwards on her bottom lip.

'Renata noticed her first.'

It's difficult to understand what happens next: what Luddy tells me and what I invent, how much she says and how much I infer. The pictures come to me as ingredients and then cook in my head, heavy buckets of broth spilling over, with detail emerging like unbroken flour.

The girl is alone, and then the girl is not alone.

She is standing awkwardly at her first art show, watching people investigate her work before they move on to something more provocative, more interesting. She is not from London. She is maybe not even from England. I don't know if this point is ever clarified by Luddy, but I do know that the girl is alone in a way that the other graduates are not, adrift in an obvious way and anxious because of it. She shifts her weight from one foot to the other, pleading silently with visitors to notice her.

When Renata approaches her she is a shining pair of scissors, snipping the girl away from her sickening loneliness, and asks her if she's looking for work. 'This is my husband,' she says. 'He's an art fan, too.'

The husband doesn't talk or look at her much, and the girl forgets about him almost immediately. The girl appoints Renata as her new model for modern womanhood, and takes everything she says as gospel. The girl tells Renata that her name is Viv.

'But Vivian is so much more beautiful.'

And the girl's name is Vivian. Vivian is employed to paint murals in Renata's new office space, and Vivian can't believe her luck. She is the first person from her graduating class to be paid for the job she was trained to do, and this alone is enough to feed her confidence. And when the husband – Vivian referred to him privately as Mr Renata, because she didn't get his name, only that he seemed older, fortyish, and frightening – stopped by to take Renata to lunch to find his wife not at her office, he decided that work alone couldn't feed Vivian. He asked her out to lunch, instead.

This next thing, I know Luddy says for sure, and I am not inventing it. She says it in that chanting, quasi-Sanskrit way.

'He orders one dessert,' she said. 'Two spoons.'

One dessert. Two spoons. The mathematical equation for a bad affair.

I can picture her at the table, spiked with nerves, sliding her spoon into something dense and soft and syrupy. I can see his face, his wide rectangle eyebrows and his eyes the colour of burnt sugar, studying her. She is confident, but vulnerable. Naive, but smart, and promising, and twenty-one.

Vivian starts to split her time between Clem and Renata, frantically scheduling herself with them in an arrangement she knows is doomed to hurt someone. She hides from Renata at the office, she calls Mr Renata in the staff loos. I use my story to fill the gaps in Luddy's knowledge, the things she couldn't possibly know. The hotel, the car, the weekends by the sea. The conversations that start off as affectionate and end as accusations. It's all been lived before, by different young women, picked off from the herd because they were lonely and weak and susceptible to compliments.

'We go into extended child's pose,' says Luddy, and the pictures in my head dissolve. I snap my eyes open, and I realise she's talking about a yoga position. She spreads her legs so her knees kiss either side of the mat, stretches her hands out in front of her, and lets her forehead touch the ground. I do the same, feeling the blood rush to my face, raising the temperature of my body. The nauseous feeling comes back again. I spread my fingers on the mat like a paper fan.

'He sends flowers,' she announces to the floor. 'She starts to get sick.'

'Like me?' I say, also to the floor. *Do not sign for the flowers.*

'Yes, but different.'

Heart palpitations and stomach aches. Too many trips to the doctor. Courses of antibiotics that work for a short while and then stop working. Stomach cancer? No, no. Stomach *ulcer*. She is told to cut out coffee, and alcohol, and spicy foods. She is told to eat four or five small meals a day, rather than two or three big ones. She is told to eat slowly, but no one says how slowly, so she starts timing herself. She forces herself to eat for twenty-one minutes exactly, and eases into an uncanny habit of twenty-ones. Twenty-one seconds to brush her hair. Take the stairs in twenty-one strides, even if there are forty-five steps.

Her fascination with twenty-ones envelops her as Clem's fondness for twenty-one-year-olds begins to die out. When she is well she calls this ironic, when she is sick she calls it fate. He distances himself as she weakens, apologising for missing her calls, and then failing to respond to them all together.

No one wants a broken thing for a mistress. One hot, sickly tear creeps off my eyelash, creating a dark spot on Luddy's yoga mat.

'Does he break up with her?'

'He doesn't break up with her,' she says, 'so much as he just disengages with her.'

Her voice is strong now, and I'm reminded of what she said about shared energies at the beginning of the session. 'Her parents came to find her and take her home. To Scotland. They said she had something else. Something she'd had since she was a child. What do they call it? Obsessive-convulsive disorder.'

'Compulsive. Obsessive-compulsive disorder.'

She shrugs. 'She had a few things.'

Luddy taps her middle finger to her temple, the gesture passive-aggressive people use to mean 'crazy'. On anyone else, it would read as mocking, but Luddy's hand is heavy with sympathy.

'Then what happened?'

'She re-enrolled in art school, eventually. I believe she wanted to do a Masters.'

It is the ending I want for Vivian. *Viv.* But I also know, from how Luddy is telling me this, that it's not the end. My head pressed to the floor, I ask her the question I know she has been fearing since I walked in the door.

'Where is she now?'

One of the dining-room candles burns down to the wick and outs itself, its flame drowned in a hot pool of wax. The smoke blankets the room, tickling the edges of my nose.

'She's dead.'

I sit up from child's pose and feel the blood from the top of my head flow back towards my body. It's dizzying, and I reach a hand out on Luddy's coffee table to steady myself.

'She's dead? How? How is she dead?'

'She was in the middle of a sculpture class at the University of Edinburgh,' says Luddy, her previous command of the room shattered by her sadness. 'And reached out to a work-table, and grabbed a scalpel . . . '

Luddy's hand is stretched out in front of her, her eyes blank and on the middle distance.

'And that was it.'

She folds her long, crooked fingers into a fist, and draws it towards her heart. This is when the story stops being a story. It is a wound in Luddy, a cut in the earth so deep that it is impossible to find its base.

'How well did you know her?'

'I met her at one of their dinner parties. Right after *he* started toying with her. I kept an eye on her after that. I knew she was only a small thing, a thing that needed care and attention. She used to come here, after he stopped speaking to her, after she stopped working with Renata. She painted, sometimes, when she was up to it.'

Everything makes sense, now. Luddy trailing me around

London, unsure of whether the pattern would repeat itself, certain that we would speak soon but hopeful that we wouldn't need to. Keeping her distance, but letting me know she was there. When it went wrong. *If* it went wrong. Her emails were vague guesses, easy to dismiss if I were stronger than Viv, but still a simple breadcrumb trail to follow if I wasn't.

Was I stronger than Viv? Did we have anything in common? Yes and no; yes and no. I was like Viv in that I was vulnerable and lonely: I was unlike Viv in that I knew nothing of Renata, and Clem and I were colleagues before anything started between us. I was like Viv in that I was impressed by him: I was unlike Viv in that I had kissed him first. I had sidled up to him in Font, cute as anything, and sung something in his ear. What was it? The words of the Peggy Lee song float back into my head.

He's a tramp, but they love him. Breaks a new heart, every day.

I kissed him. I chose to leave with him. I was not a child, impressed by lunches and silver dessertspoons. I am not that young, and I am not so simple. Every move I made with him was my choice, my silly impetuousness, my desire to see what was on the other side of the curtain.

Curtains. Houses. Dinner parties.

'Why were you going to dinner parties?'

'Pardon?'

'At Clem and Renata's house. Where you met Viv. Why?'

'It was a long time ago. Six years, at least. We used to be in contact. We're not any more.'

She doesn't seem to want to elaborate on this contact. Ashamed of the man she despises so much having once been that close to her. Dinner-guest close.

'Why?'

'Would you like to see one of her paintings?'

I nod, happy to indulge Luddy. She pads her way into her bedroom, the only other room in the flat aside from the bathroom. When she gets back, she is holding a long canvas, landscape-oriented, at least a metre wide.

'Wasn't she talented?' she says.

A rock hits the bottom of my stomach. Viv was talented all right: an encyclopaedic painter, obsessed with detail, texture and precision. I can see why she may have been predisposed to obsessive-compulsive disorder. Each blade of grass has been kissed with care, each flower considered so sternly that you know precisely what time of year it is, and exactly how heavy and over-ripe, almost rotten, the fragrance is.

It is a luscious scene, but not a lovely one. It's aggressive, and intimidatingly fertile. The longer I look at it, the more dazed I become, until finally the long landscape comes together as one image. My heart, calmed by the meditation and the poses, starts to strain against my chest, screaming at me to leave while my legs will still carry me. I try to get up, hoisting myself off the floor, but my ankles give way and I fall heavily onto my tailbone.

Lock up after yourself.

Yellow honeysuckle and birch trees. Emerald grass and a low stone wall.

Look after yourself.

A glass door with a white painted handle, rusting slightly at the tip.

Lock up yourself.

Birds. Three, four, five little wood pigeons, perched on porch furniture, looking quizzically at the painter.

Look up your self.

The carpet burns. The blackouts. The sex that I know happened but don't necessarily remember.

Look up, look up.

look up.

21

Jolly Politely,

I'm writing this even though you seem to be on holiday at the moment! (If you are on holiday, could you please let your readers know? You are PERFECTLY ENTITLED to take holidays (as are all bloggers!!) but I'm sure your fans would appreciate some notice if you are!)

My husband and I have been together for eighteen years and while we love each other very much, we are considering engaging in a threesome. This is not because we are unhappy with each other, but because we got together very young (17!!) and can't help but wonder if we have missed out.

I would LOVE to know your thoughts on the pros and cons of threesomes and if you could provide a link back to my new sex blog in your answer I would MUCH appreciate it.

Love,

SSI xx

(FOUNDER and EDITOR of SalutSalutIntimacy. wordpress.com)

Even as the house in Viv's painting becomes more unequiv-ocally the house I stayed in, I have the peculiar feeling that I am focusing on the wrong things. That I should be focusing on Viv, her suicide and her madness. That I should be alarmed by the parallels between Viv and me – not in our personalities or our talents or our stories with Clem – but in the crucial similarity that our mental and physical health started to suffer after starting a relationship with him.

But as I sit on Luddy's sofa, my hands shivering around a cup of cold tea, the painting is the only thing I can think about.

'That house,' I say finally. 'I've been with him, to that house.'

Luddy smooths my hair back from my face. I straighten up to ward off the swirling indigo spots behind my eyes.

'Does he take everyone to that house?'

'Not everyone,' she says carefully, as if it's important that I feel special. 'Just the ones he . . . He's really fond of, I suppose.'

I hate that I take it as a compliment. I hate that a young woman is dead, and that my health is in danger, and that the man I have spent the past two months working with and sleeping with and obsessing over is using and discarding women like cheap Halloween costumes, and yet all I can focus on is how *fond* he must be of me. He only takes the really good ones to his beachside shag palace, after all.

I think of us in the light, airy bedsheets of the cottage in Whitstable, our mouths tasting of wine and sea salt. My lipstick, falling out of the back pocket of my denim shorts as I stepped out of them. I remember him picking it up, afterwards, on his way back from the bathroom and reading the label.

'Bare Bloom,' he said. 'Well . . . '

He unrolled the stick of it, peering at the triangular head as if it were the first lipstick he had ever seen in his whole life, and I thought about how perfect he was. Not perfect for lack of flaws, because he had plenty of those. But perfect because there was only one of him, and he was so uniquely himself that I couldn't imagine a better person on earth. And I laughed because between the moments of doubt and anger and strangeness and utter, total misery, there were moments of golden bliss. There isn't much I remember about that evening, after we went to bed, but that shines out like a new penny.

'What are you laughing at?'

'You.'

He smiled then, as if he wasn't going to let me get away with that. He pounced, pinning my arms to the bed, the opened lipstick between his teeth, and drew soft, velvety lipstick lines on my body while I shrieked with giggles, begging him to stop, hoping he never, ever would.

Luddy shakes me gently, uneasy with any trance she hasn't directed.

'I have to go,' I say. 'Thank you for explaining everything to me.'

'You don't have to leave yet, Jane. I could make dinner.'

I wonder what kind of dinner Luddy makes for herself, and picture some kind of sad lentil curry.

'No thank you,' I say, anxious to leave this witch's cottage. 'I really should get home.'

'You know where to find me, Jane. If you ever need anything, I'll be here.'

I tug on my jacket. 'I know.'

'I'm usually here,' she says again, her voice tinged with desperation. 'So don't be afraid to pop by. You can keep the leggings.'

I am now desperate to leave, suspicious that the longer I stay here the more Luddy's new-age spinsterhood will rub off on me. But there's one thing I need to clarify.

'Luddy,' I say, slipping my shoes back on, 'how did you find me?'

Her eyes narrow, and suddenly she looks catlike, sly.

'I told you. I keep an eye on him. I check in. I've known him for a long time, where he goes, what he does, who is around him.'

'But my email address. Jolly Politely. Where did you find that?'

'Oh, that,' she says, as though the matter were so trifling she's offended I even asked. 'You know, you're not as mysterious with that as you think you are. You check it on buses. Restaurants. Cafés. All sitting on your screen, open to anyone. You want to be more careful, if you really want to remain *anonymous*.'

She's condescending now, using bunny ears around the word anonymous. I go, and think about how many times Luddy must have seen me when I hadn't seen her.

The street is, somehow, even warmer than Luddy's candle-laden flat. There's a dank grey humidity pressing on top of me, making every step slow and strenuous. Another heatwave is predicted for next week, as though I don't have enough to deal with.

I try to imagine Viv in the cottage. Viv reading the notes, Viv under cashmere blankets, Viv with streaks of lipstick the colour of pink chocolate on her arms and stomach. Jealous that I wasn't the first. Jealous that I may not be the last. Jealous of the poor, mad, dead girl. I'm so jealous of her, in fact, that I start thinking about her in a new way. I go against Luddy: I start sympathising with Clem.

Because surely, if someone decides to kill themselves, then it's their decision, and theirs alone. And how was he to know, really, that the girl – who started as a distraction, as a light hiss of canned cream on the top of an already sweet life – had a history of mental illness, and prompted Luddy to tap her head in sideways sympathy?

What if he had mourned her? What if her death had torn a chasm in Clem as wide as the one in Luddy, and what if the many dents and chips in his personality were down to the slow erosion by guilt and loss, lapping at the surface of him?

'I thought it was all over for me,' he said, the first night outside Carluccio's. 'Me and women, anyway.'

How could he tell Renata about a loss like that? How could he tell anyone? I see him, at his Mitchell desk, finding out. How would he find out? Through Viv's parents? No, of course not. I know better than anyone that Clem is not a romance you tell your parents about.

Through Luddy.

I imagine returning to his life, wild-eyed and iron-haired, uninvited and undesired. A call on his desk phone.

'Mr Brown, there's someone at reception for you.'

He opens his diary, puzzled. No meetings.

'She says it's urgent.'

He finds her in the lobby, ready to pounce.

I'm outside my own door, jamming the wrong key into the keyhole, half-dazed. I've moved so deeply into being a spectator in Clem's imagined grief, that I have propelled myself home. The trance Luddy cast over me drains slowly, like an anaesthetic that you can only wake up from one muscle at a time.

There's post for me on the hall table – bills finally forwarded to me from mine and Max's old address – and I mime going through it, my mind still fixed on Clem and Luddy.

'What are you doing here?'

'She's dead, Clem.'

'What? Who's dead?'

'Viv. *Vivian.*'

I slip my shoes off, and drift towards my bedroom. I lie on my bed, and close my eyes. I try to breathe slowly, measuredly, the way Luddy taught me when we meditated, the way Think Gym teaches women who are on the brink of unknowing themselves. After a few moments, the under-wiring on my bra digs into my ribs, and I realise that this bra – despite being two weeks old – is already loose around my boobs, giving the skeleton of it freedom to pinch my skin. I wriggle it off through my clothes and throw it to the other side of the room.

Luddy's eyes – a soft blue-grey with me – turn to hard flint when facing Clem.

'You killed her,' she shrieks. 'You took everything from her. You *drained* her. You had *nothing* so you took it all.'

Those were the words Luddy had used, weren't they?

He needs people to survive. To lean on, to drain from.

I sit up and look into the mirrored surface of the wardrobe door. My fingers trace my bottom lip: always a little too full for the comparative thinness of my top one. Irregular. The skin there is scratchy and ragged, folding upwards like a crumpled banknote. I pull the skin off, wincing with the pain, letting my tongue trace the raw new redness below. I shake my legs out, and remember him at Tankerton Beach, kissing the salt water off my knees. His face darkening when I called us vampires.

That's a word she would use. She would show up at his work and call him a vampire.

Examining the flakes of skin under my fingernail, I try to parse my new reality. It's too slippery, the facts and the speculation, the probable and the frankly impossible colliding together and separating again, truth mutating like the inside of a lava lamp. I find the birthday card Becky gave me, the one shaped like a bottle of champagne, and start trying, again, to list my Known Knowns. I'm determined that committing everything to paper will make everything logical.

1. I am falling apart. I am physically sick. I am mentally unwell.

It's an odd thing to write – about myself, to myself – and my hand quakes slightly as I do it. It doesn't feel like enough somehow, so I add this.

I am not myself

I underline it.

I am not myself

2. I am not the first person to suffer like this while sleeping with Clem Brown.

I think of Viv's arm opening up and flowering, as though the knife had been stabbed through a pillow.

I am part of a trend

Someone spoke to me about trends before. Someone I didn't like. I wrinkle my forehead, trying to remember. The doctor.

I realise the pressure on you girls can be overwhelming.
You're not as mysterious with that as you think you are.
There have been others, before you. Other girls. Did you
    know that?
I have two daughters.

There's a tinkle of keys and a bristling of shopping bags at the door. Shiraz is home.

I met three, but there could have been as many as eight.

You push and push and push.
You're not as mysterious with that as you think you are.
For she's a jolly good fellow.

She starts boiling the kettle, and there's a faint rustle of a packet of biscuits being unrolled.

Darling, I wrote the book on him.
You push and push and push.
For she's a jolly good fellow.

What did Viv and I have in common? That we both slept with the same man, who was coincidentally a power-hungry succubus (is that what we're going with, Jane? Was 'vampire' a little too *Twilight* for you?) or that we were both young women? Young women, already fragile, pushing ourselves too fast and too hard and bruising our psyches along the way. What do I believe? What does Luddy believe?

My phone buzzes. Three messages from Clem: two asking how I am, and a third, grumpy one, sent just a minute ago.

It's not very polite to ignore your 'mentor' x

I push my knees under my chin and sink my head into the pillow, feeling increasingly unqualified to deal with the consequences of my own life. What if I'm *not* as mysterious as I think I am? What if Clem knows everything about me, and can watch me at all times? What if he's known about Jolly *from the start*?

I feel the panic rising in my throat. I look around me, aware of all the cameras and tiny red lights in my room. My laptop is open on my dressing table, and I close it. The keyhole. The windows. All these small exposing gaps and vantage points, closing in, analysing me, needling me.

What if, like Viv, I just have to keep being pleasant and distracting and sexy, and if I stop, my world will come crashing down around me?

Whatever is happening, I think, while fighting the urge to fall asleep, *or whatever you think is happening, it needs to stop.*

When I wake up in the morning, a heavy blanket of sweat drying on top of me, the words 'end it' are written on my hand in eyeliner. I do not remember how they got there.

PART FIVE

22

Like a machine that is finely tuned to sense its own demise, Clem appears the next day. He doesn't come straight to me. He is working his way around, disappearing into meeting rooms with various people, and striding purposefully with Howard Mitchell like they're in *The West Wing*. I'm not sure whether it's that I've missed him, or whether he's trying some new diet, but he looks incredible. Not handsome: beautiful, almost. He's radiant and charming, like a beam of natural light in the cloistered, anaemic office.

As the day goes on, my disgust for him softens and yields into a queasiness, a worry that he has already found someone else. It's an odd feeling: the dual sensation of feeling utterly finished with someone and being terrified that they are finished with you. I decide that my paranoid frenzy of last night was silly, and largely the fault of Luddy. That's what happens when you go to a witch's house, I think. You come away strange.

I try to keep my nose in my computer so I don't look like I'm trying to catch his eye. It's been days since I replied to anyone on Jolly, or even checked any of the comments. I still get the email notifications to my phone, though. I delete most of them without even opening them: the mealy-mouthed enquiries evident from the subject lines. I hate them the way I've learned to hate Becky's frowning, nosy concern. 'Where's Jolly?' and 'Worried for you' and 'a loving fan' all go in the bin straight away. I take to the 'open thread' section of JollyPolitely.com.

I added this a few years ago. It was at the beginning of me and Max: I had sheepishly declared myself as having an online following, and he had seen it as a sign of latent ambition, some sign that I was about to do something big. An open thread, he said, would engage users and make them more likely to spread the word.

'I'm sorry I'm not the person you *thought* you were getting,' I screeched at him, in the hours after he had broken up with me. 'I'm sorry I'm not *Jolly fucking Politely*.'

But the open thread is still there, giving Jolly fans the chance to interact and advise one another when Jolly is unable to do it herself.

Dear Jolly fans,

I flush a little typing it, but press on, determined that my Greek chorus of Jolly fans will be able to direct me, but only if I'm anonymous.

> **I just found out that my boyfriend's ex-girlfriend killed herself several years ago. The thing is he hasn't told me, but the person who has told me thinks it's his fault.**

A friend in uni – long lost now, scattered to the winds of Instagram updates – had a boyfriend who would tell her that he would kill himself whenever she went anywhere without him. The rest of us would be tottering around her bedroom, snapping on tights, and she would be crouched in the corner, staring at her phone while it charged.

'Dan says he's having dark thoughts,' she would say. 'I think I should go over there.'

'He *won't* kill himself,' we'd all say, in chorus.

'But what if he d—'

'He *won't.*'

But what if he had? Would it have been her fault? Would it have been our fault, for stopping her?

'Jane.' I know it's Clem, and I know he's not alone. This is his 'we have company, dear' voice. I spin around and there he is: black T-shirt, smart jeans, tight smile. The light of my monitor is dancing in his eyes. Howard is behind him, making idle chat with a flustered Becky.

A cold, clammy bolt of panic shoots through me. I minimise my screen, but I can already tell he's seen something. How much can you read at that distance?

'Oh, hey.' I touch the back of my head. I have done a lot of backcombing with my hair this morning, and have just about managed to cover my bald spot. 'How are you?'

'Great. Manchester's mad, of course, but what can you do? We were actually hoping to get your eye on some of this new work?'

'Sure. Right now?'

'Right now.'

We go into a meeting room, and David Lady is already there. My heart judders: he has a beard now. A light, sandy beard with flecks of amber in it. Who grows a beard in this heat, unless they're growing it for someone? I think about feeling the brush of it against my thigh and immediately go red. I want to grab his hand, say sorry for the night at Font, and for avoiding him since. But I know he's lost to me, in the specific way that sleeping with someone's boss makes them lost.

'So to catch you up, Jane, we're getting to a good place with the Think Gym guys. I've spent some real time with them, assessing the way they talk to their demographic, and

David and I have come up with some new creative routes to present them with when I go back up next week.'

David and I. When did this happen? Before Clem went away, it was just him and me working on Think Gym together. When did David get involved? Were they working long-distance from Manchester? Was he on the project the whole time, and Clem intentionally kept us apart?

'The key to this project, really, is mindfulness.'

My mouth hangs open. Clem didn't even know what mindfulness *was* until I explained it to him.

'Mindfulness, for those of you that don't know,' Clem says, although this is clearly for the benefit of Howard, 'is a sort of Buddhism with the religious bits stripped out. Being one with the self. Freeing your mind from material desire.'

David pipes up, as if the whole conversation has been rehearsed. 'So why, then, should a high-earning, high-profile, cash-rich, time-poor woman care about it?'

Clem smiles, delighted to have his new apprentice ask. David looks so fleshy and real in comparison to the remote iciness of Clem. He's wearing a T-shirt, and there are two half-moons of sweat growing under his arms. The heatwave suits him: he looks alive, healthy, like someone bred to work outside.

How did I ever choose him over you? I think.

'We're talking about the generation of women who were sold on the concept of "having it all". The job, the husband, the kids. And the ones who manage to get to the finish line to find it's *not* the finish line, and that Having It All is a bit of, well, a con. And that's why it matters to them: because they've been duped, and they're disenfranchised, and they don't know where to turn. It's about anchoring female ennui to something that feels like a battle call.'

BATTLE CALL is revealed in large purple letters. It's identical to CALL ALL in every way, except now some of the women are holding sticks.

'Are you pitching me a feminism angle, Brown?'

Howard is bored. Bored of hearing about women's problems, bored of the concept, bored of feminism's new place in his beloved advertising. What happened to 'Because you're worth it'? What happened to 'Maybe she's born with it'? Those were concepts he could understand.

'I'm pitching you the *right* angle.'

He flashes a pie chart up on screen.

'One in ten women will be signed off work for non-medical reasons.'

Howard Mitchell's entire body is radiating *not on my watch.*

'Stress leave. Burn-out. Taking a sabbatical. Whatever you want to call it, it costs companies thousands of pounds a year.'

Howard is visibly annoyed now. He's not the only one. I can't believe these ideas, the ones I gave to Clem, are now being fed back to me. And I'm supposed to smile and nod and act as though I'm hearing them for the first time.

'When a woman goes on a Think Gym retreat, she's not just treating herself. This isn't some spa weekend. This is a mission in increased productivity. This is where spirituality intersects with modern feminism. This is her saving her company money, in the long term.'

'So her company pays for this? Theoretically?'

'There'll be schemes. Your overtime will go towards it.' Clem tosses it out as if it's the simplest thing in the world, making women agree that their overtime will go towards mandatory mindfulness.

'This is about safeguarding her mental health, her physical strength, and her ability to connect with herself so she doesn't go . . . ' He flashes the room a wink. 'A little crazy.'

Howard chuckles. He loves Clem again, and he already loves the idea of sending his female employees to Think Gym.

He will be the progressive, feminist CEO who recognises a woman's right to hold in a fart during yoga.

'So we find her on Twitter. We find her on LinkedIn. We target women who use words like "busy" and "sorry" and "stressed" in their Facebook statuses. We get her while she's vulnerable, and we make her recognise that she *is* vulnerable.'

The campaign images start appearing on screen: the ones we briefed together, the ones I began drawing on the drive home from Whitstable, the Gwyneth-Paltrow-at-Burning-Man vibe I carefully outlined to the designer on speakerphone. The images that, when I looked at them next to the original advertising concepts, felt like art to me.

I'm furious, but I'm not sure if I'm entitled to be. Is it because Clem is taking credit for the intel that I gave him? Partly: but he is my boss, and in that sense he has a right to whatever comes out of my brain when I'm with him. But I'm also left with a distinct feeling that I have sold out my entire gender, and I'm not sure I'm comfortable with it. All those studies I found out about women and their mental health. All those screen grabs of the *Daily Mail*.

I hear the doctor's voice again: *You are excellent at securing fantastic little jobs for yourselves*, that was what he said. *You push and push and push, and you want to keep up with the boys. But it can't. Last. For ever.*

This meeting, this project I'm a part of, is basically legitimising his idea of women. I wonder if he'll get word of Think Gym, and push non-threatening informational pamphlets to nervous-looking patients, women who need real therapy and who will instead be given green juices and adult colouring books.

Clem goes on. 'Now more than ever, people are conscious of their mental health. It's like a car: even if there's nothing visibly wrong, you need to open the bonnet once in a while and have a look. We have to understand that when it comes to mental health, it's not *if*, but *when*.'

I go cold. I think of Viv, who spent her life trying to control her mental illness, only to have it unspooled slowly by the man in front of me. *Not if, but when.*

'When you add the stress of childcare, it's inevitable.'

Not if, but when. I try to remember the last time I had to buy tampons. I have a box on my desk, but when, lately, have I used them?

'So, what do you think, Jane?'

The room is looking at me.

'What do I think,' I repeat.

'You are the woman in the room. It would be nice to get your opinion.'

My opinions are welcome, my ideas are stolen. I open and close my mouth, trying to think of anything to say that won't get me fired. I try not to think about the tampons on my desk.

'Where's Deb?' I say. 'She's closer to the demographic than I am. Surely we should get her opinion on this?'

Clem beams at me, as if I've introduced his final act of the night. 'Deb is at Think Gym.'

'In Manchester?'

'No, I mean, she's *at* Think Gym. At one of their retreats. In Dorset.'

'Our Deb?' says Howard.

'Our Deb. I asked her to go as a mole, really get the full experience. I think we can all agree that Deb fits the role perfectly. Right age, right salary, right . . . *stresses.*'

I see Howard nod. Deb is the only woman superior to Clem at the agency, and he has just quietly implied that she is a liability. I imagine her, partially lobotomised, wandering around a country house clutching an origami set.

'Stresses is right,' says Howard. 'All those kids.'

'How many is it now?' asks Clem, even though he knows.

'*Three,*' replies Howard, a wrinkle of irritation appearing on his forehead. 'I don't know how she does it. I keep expecting her to request part-time hours.'

'Well,' says Clem, shrugging, 'you never know.'

Clem wants Deb's job. He is getting her out of the way for a while, securing a relationship with one of the biggest clients we have, with which she is the most qualified to deal, and is casually undermining her while he does it. I look at David, wondering if he can see what's happening, but he's distracted by his notes.

I think of the first day Clem took me to the restaurant with the Think Gym client, and how quiet I was, how stupid I felt as the chat around me outstripped my level of expertise. He had to take a woman with him, and he intentionally took the wrong one. When I met those two young executives, I thought they acted strangely because they were picking up on the tension between Clem and me. But no: they were expecting Deb, and got a total stranger.

It's genius, and it's horrible, and I have no proof he's even doing it.

'Well, I think it's a brilliant approach,' says Howard. 'Well done, Clem. And David, of course.'

Clem winks at me as they file out of the room. *Later*, he mouths. I bolt to the toilets on the fourth floor, my cheeks hot, my fingers trembling slightly. My lips are scabbed and deep brown when I look at them in the mirror: as if I tried to bite right through them in the night. Sitting on the toilet lid, I fumble for the cool, reassuring feel of my phone.

I bring up the latest Jolly draft, when I attempted to ask the fans about Clem. *Did he see? He couldn't have. Could he?*

The tiny spots appear in the corner of my vision, purple splotches clouding over. My hands start moving faster than my brain.

Get out get out get out get out get out get out get out

I don't remember hitting 'publish' on the open thread. I don't remember how I got home, or whether I waited until the end of the day to leave. I don't even remember typing 'get out' until I look at the comments later that night.

23

Is jolly okay???????

Maybe she sat on her phone

Guys ok i no this is cray cray but what if JP has been kidnapped by ISIS and is using these weird messages to cry for help

OMG that is definitely it

Perhaps we should contact the domain manager who may have her name and address

Get cheap page impressions on your site today! Click here: hit.ly/winpageimp

We should call the police!

Okay i don't want to play devil's advocate here but her messages have been weird for ages

^^^^TRUE

WHY is she posting on the #openthread though??
Why not do a blog??

Maybe she THOUGHT it was anonymous

Lol remind me how women are great at tech again

After Clem leaves, it's just me, the fans and the sickening heat of my bedroom. I regard the comments as if they are for and about someone else. Which, I suppose, they are.

I'm sorry I'm not Jolly fucking Politely.

The bruise on my forearm won't last long: it's a potter's orange at the centre, ringed in navy, but edging out in green. My mistake was not clicking 'sign in as guest' when doing my Jolly post. My mistake was writing it in the first place.

My mistake was letting him into my flat.

I don't know when I got home. I'm losing snatches of time lately. The heat isn't helping, and I feel slower and more misty-headed than ever. Work has become a puzzle: what do I do there? Who do I talk to? What happens? Assumptions about what I have done quickly become memories.

I try to piece the evening together, from the moment I walked in the front door and realised Clem was in my flat. Six o'clock? Maybe earlier: five? But what was I doing home so early, and what was he doing here?

'Janey? Is that you?'

They were on the couch together, drinking one of Shiraz's fancy coffees.

'What are you doing here?'

'Well, that's a hero's welcome.' He smiles at Shiraz, to show how considerate he is. 'I wanted to check to see if you were all right. We're all so worried about you.'

Maybe I didn't go back to my desk, after the Think Gym meeting.

'Well, I'm fine. And I think you should go.'

Shiraz raised an eyebrow.

He walked over to me as if he were approaching a feral animal. He seemed tall again. Even taller in Shiraz's living room, where everything is so insistently feminine. Shiraz's eyes narrowed on the two of us like a cat's. She stayed with us a minute longer – watched him put a hand on either side of my face, watched him bump his forehead to mine and smile as his thumbs met my shredded lips – and decided that whatever was happening, it wasn't her business.

'Do you really want me to go?'

Yes. Why didn't you say yes, Jane? Why didn't you shout YES. YES, I want you to leave.

'No.' A small, choked no.

'Shall we go and talk?'

'My bedroom isn't clean.'

'I don't mind.'

As soon as we were alone, he became as gentle as he knew how to be. He kissed my collarbone, my neck, the soft space behind my ear. He made me lie down, my clothes still on, and lay beside me, his arm draped over me. I tried to lie as still as I could, as small as I could, determined to be suspended in time with him, perfectly poised to be little and loved and to never, ever question Viv or Luddy or Think Gym or anything else.

This is so much *better* than sleeping by yourself.

'Never do that again.'

'Pardon?'

'I said, never do that again.'

'I don't know what you're talking about.'

The light, careful arm that had been draped around me turned into a steady grip around my chest. He pushed his leg over both of mine, locking them in so I couldn't move. For a moment, I thought that he was playing with me: but like a finger trap, his control grew with my struggle.

'I understand, Jane, that you don't have anything that equates to a "past" yet, and that the notion of privacy seems to have escaped your generation. But I need you to be respectful of mine.'

He did see my screen, then.

'I didn't want to find out,' I whispered, still locked in his grip. 'I was told.'

Why, I think now, rubbing my bruised arm, did I defend *knowing* something? Why was it me on the stand, not him?

'Who were you telling, then? After you went snooping around on me, who were you going to share it with? That little bitch Darla?'

'*Darla?*'

It's painful to think of him referring to Darla that way, even in his own head. The last time I talked to her, I lied to her about having sex with someone. She wanted to share with me, to go back to our old confessional relationship – she had wanted to tell me about her cystitis, too.

'Darla.' He rolled her name around in his mouth, scowling slightly, twisting my elbow in his hands. 'It's a great bit of gossip, isn't it? Boy meets girl. Girl turns out to be fucking off her rocker. Girl offs herself. Pretty Shakespearian, I think you'll admit. A pretty fun story to discuss over a bottle of Pinot. A pretty nice way to hurt someone, someone who has been good to you. Who tried to love you.'

'I wasn't telling anyone.'

'I saw you, Jolly Politely. I saw your fucking *screen.*'

I audibly gasped at hearing him say it. He loosened his grip then, and allowed me to push away, confident that his words had hurt me enough. *Was Clem just violent with me?* I put the thought away, focusing on his words rather than his actions. His words were the important thing.

He thought *I* was trying to bring *him* down. That I was trying to use Viv as if she were some kind of playing card.

'I would have told you,' he said. 'I would have told you the whole story, if only you had asked.'

And maybe he would have. But the way he came towards me signalled that the subject, no matter how it could or should have been broached, was to remain closed.

'Look,' I tried to keep my voice still, 'whatever you went through with ... with that. It's not my business. I just ... I wanted to—'

He glared at me then, and I knew that whatever I said, I would be met with a snakebite.

'Do I look sick to you?'

'Excuse me?'

'Look at me. Look at my skin. Look at my breakouts. Look at how much weight I've lost.'

'If you're sitting around waiting for a compliment, tell me.'

'No. Really look at me. Look at my hair.'

I tried to bring his hand to my bald spot, but he bristled before I could make contact.

'You look fine.'

'I don't *feel* fine.'

He stood up, all bounce and aggression, a panther circling his prey.

'Well, that's not my problem, is it, Jane? I'm not your bloody dad, am I?'

I can't believe I told him about my dad. Hand-in-hand on the seafront, my eyes pricked artfully with crystal tears. It was a big deal that I told him, or maybe we both just acted like it was. I loved playing the tragic child bride, wounded by loss and the lack of a strong father figure. And he loved listening thoughtfully, and coaxing out my tears, and relished telling me that my father was an idiot for missing out on such a wonderful young woman. It was theatre, and it was not particularly good theatre.

'I don't want you to be my dad. I don't need you to look after me. I want you to *look at me.*'

He doesn't, though. He closes his eyes, pinches the bridge of his nose with his thumb and forefinger, the way you do with a headache.

'You're all the same, you know.'

'Pardon?'

'You. Girls like you. You do a fantastic impression of a grown woman, but it's all smoke and mirrors. All you want is a little story to tweet about, or blog about, or whatever the fuck it is you do with your time. Stick a push-up bra and a blouse on an eight-year-old and she'll fool anyone.'

'Eight? Is that your age limit, then?'

It was dumb, and it was petty, but it felt good. It felt like I imagine it must have felt for him when he called Darla a little bitch.

He grabbed my shoulder and pushed me backwards, where my arm snagged the frame of the wardrobe. I flailed as I lost my balance and my back hit the corner beam.

I screamed, and wondered whether Shiraz would come running in. She didn't.

'If you ever want to work again, Jane,' he said, his mouth contorting, halfway between remorse and *well, that's what you get*, 'I wouldn't talk to me like that.'

His face flickered with pity: he meant to push me back, not for me to lose my balance, and not for me to be hurt. I looked at him from the floor, hoping that, despite everything, he still might change his mind about me.

'I'm sorry,' I said. 'I shouldn't have said that. It was stupid. I'm stupid. And I don't want—'

'I'm not your lord and saviour,' he said. 'See, this is what I mean.' He picked up the rancid jar, his nose wrinkling at what used to be the wildflowers. 'You're a part of my life, Jane. But I'm *all* of yours.'

'I don't know what that means.'

'You know exactly what it means.'

There was sadness in his voice, like he thought he had found something precious but turned out to be mistaken.

'I'll see you at the office, if you care to continue being the Sylvia Plath of the advertising world. But I would be very fucking careful, if I were you. And you can get rid of that blog, while you're at it. It makes you look retarded.'

Was that why he alienated me from the Think Gym meeting? Because he thought I was trying to *get* him?

'Don't go. You can't just *do* this to me.'

The words jumped out of my mouth before I had time to even consider them.

'I have to.'

'No.'

I leapt at him, hungry, determined to forget his arm across my chest, forcing me into one place, the burning feeling in my arm where the bruise was forming. Too seized with the fear of what happens without him to care about the fear of being with him. *If he goes tonight, he will be gone for ever.* And then what will I have? Shiraz. Becky. Sad, lonely women who I have never had more than a dim, surface relationship with.

What about Darla? Would she ever forgive me for daring to do better than her? Could we find some kind of new equilibrium after the chaos of Clem and Think Gym and the senseless bitchiness we've developed towards one another? Why had he mentioned Darla, earlier?

I couldn't take thinking about it. I tried to kiss him, but his mouth wouldn't soften. I grabbed his hands and guided them, hoping that he would remember what it was he liked about me. He pushed me off, wiping his mouth as if desperation were contagious.

'And don't think your sick days have gone unnoticed, either,' he said, seeing a plate of toast from three days ago on the floor. 'If you keep on missing work like this, I can't control what happens.'

'Are you fucking her?' I followed him to the door and down the stairs of our building. 'Tell me you're fucking her already. Tell me before she does.'

A woman in a hair towel popped her head out of her front door and told me to shut up in a different language.

Hours later and I'm still on my bed, in a tight ball. I can't face Shiraz, so I stay where I am, my head tilted to the window, watching the early evening become the night. I fall in and out of sleep, ambient sounds worming their way into me and converting to something strange and gauzy: too thin to be a dream, too slippery to be a thing I can control. I hear a dog barking at a streetlamp outside and then he's there, too, barking at me in the dream. I'm in Whitstable again, except I'm not me, I'm Viv. I'm trying to paint the cottage, but the dog keeps barking, snapping at me, biting my ankles. I push him away with my leg, and instead kick my oil paints over. Paint covers my leg, then spreads up my thighs, covering my stomach. The more I shake it away, the more it spreads, until I'm green, blue, yellow, blood red all over.

I wake up, having smacked my knee into my bedside table. The lamp falls over, sparking and tearing itself out of the plug socket as it goes. I can still feel the paint, the blades of grass sticking to the oil and making a paste between my toes.

I cry out while trying to save the lamp, burning my hand on the bulb in the process. Shiraz does her interpretation of rushing, which feels more like a swift saunter.

'Dude,' she says, eyebrows raised. 'What's going on?'

'It's everywhere,' I say, but it comes out as a gurgled yelp. 'It's all over me, Shiraz. I can't get it off.'

Shiraz puts her hand on my arm, turning it gently over to

see the bruise from when Clem pushed me against the wardrobe. She's cool, soft, like something a lizard clings to in the
heat. There's something overwhelming about the gesture, and
despite knowing that there is nothing she would hate more,
I fold myself into her. I am so grateful that she allows it to
happen. The paint starts to dissolve and fade into my skin,
into my bloodstream, and I'm safe again.

'Do you remember what I said, before?' Shiraz says.

'What?'

'About getting the most out of this thing with your boss?'

'Yes.'

'And that he would use you?'

'I don't think you said that.'

'I think I made it pretty clear. And in any case, you should
know. You're a grown woman, Jane. You know there's a price
on everything.'

This is not the response that women are trained to give
when they see bruises on other women. Maybe, for Shiraz,
being hurt is something that is preferably avoidable, but not
always practically so.

'What do you mean?'

'There's a certain kind of man who has sex with his
employees,' she says, and then stops herself. 'Actually, there
are two kinds of men who have sex with their employees. The
first kind does it because . . . well, because he's basic. Because
he's forty-six and he's finally in a position of power, and the
idea of having sex with a twenty-three-year-old on his desk
is like . . . ' She gropes at the air for a metaphor. 'It's a like a
hot wax seal on his success.'

I have never heard Shiraz talk this much in one breath.

'You know, wax seals? Like what rich people put on their
stationery so you know it's them?'

'I know what a wax seal is.'

'Right,' she says, resuming her lesson. 'So he's doing it

to prove a point to himself, and to everyone he thinks he needs to get revenge on. So he's not fucking her, really. He's fucking every bad manager he's ever had, every school bully that stole his clothes after PE. She's incidental. She's nothing. She'll move on in a few months and have a few nice pairs of earrings out of it.'

'Did you do a thesis in this, or something?'

'Then there's the second kind. The kind where it's not just about your arse. I mean, it is about your arse. It's always at least a little about your arse. But it's also about potential. It's about seeing someone who is still excited to get up in the morning. Who thinks that hotel rooms are cool, who is just getting started and knows it.'

'I think I know what you mean.'

'There's a reason that it's mostly university professors.'

'Why?'

'Can you imagine what it's like to be reading the same shit, day in, day out for years, and then meeting someone who is seeing it for the first time? Who is excited by it? Who thinks you're brilliant, because you know about it? That's the dream, for some men. Like going back in time and showing someone an iPhone, except instead of an iPhone, it's their entire personality.'

'Why are you such an expert in all this?'

Shiraz starts noticing, the way Clem and Max noticed, the abandoned food, dirty underwear and wine bottles.

'You need to clean up in here.'

'I know. I will.'

'The bin bags are under the sink.' She's seen my rotting flowers. 'Not that you'd know.'

After she leaves, I make a few gestures at tidying. I didn't use to be like this. When I lived with Max I was the tidy one. Not just in a make-the-bed way, either. I was what marketing focus groups would refer to as a proactive cleaner. Someone who cleans the shower because it's time to clean the shower, not just because there are guests coming over. It was my way of telling him that I was worth it. That, despite having less money than him and less professional respect, and less of a general idea of how to get on in the world, I was useful, and could do things.

We both aligned ourselves to his trajectory, convinced he was the meal ticket that was going to propel us both to greatness. His parents petted us constantly about it, his mum perched happily on our sofa, eating the cheese scones I made and having the same conversations with me, over and over. Always about how well I was or wasn't caring for him, maintaining him, their prized show pup reluctantly given to a foster home.

'Glad to see you're keeping him fed, Jane.'

'Well, you know what they say, behind every great man is a great woman. With cheese scones.'

OR

'Is he behaving himself, Jane?'

'Oh, you know. I try to keep him in line!'

OR

'I hope you're not working too hard, Max. Poor Jane must get lonely by herself.'

'Well, I have a job too! Who knows for how long!'

Everyone laughs. In my head, I was saying this ironically, laughing at the cliché even if they weren't. But an iron set of back teeth began to come down, and I tasted blood every time I heard myself go meek and mealy-mouthed, knowing full well that my dedicated-girlfriend act was a flimsy pretence, a set of forged work papers that I was using to get through the war I was sure was going on outside.

When we broke up, Max didn't let me stay in the house because he loved me, or because he wanted closure. A normal girlfriend would have moved out straight away. He let me stick around because he worried – we both did, I think – about what was going to happen to me. Just like the night I met Kim: he left her, and he brought me home. Because he was sure she could look after herself, and still questioned whether I could.

I start sticking things in the laundry basket, and try to make the lamp work again.

And this is the answer he got. Jane Peters, his former future wife, living like a homeless teenager. Can't feed herself. Can't look after her own health. Can't tear herself away from a man who uses her and hurts her and alienates her and threatens her.

You're part of my life, Jane, but I'm all of yours.

A bottle of Cab Sav rolls out from under my bed, a third still left in it. It's warm, vinegary, but I need it: I want the dank sweat of shame to evaporate into something giddy and joyful.

Soon, I'm in Costcutter, trying to make up £10 so I can use the card machine to buy a £6.99 bottle of white wine. I'm loading the counter with Crunchies and toilet roll when I get a call from a number I don't know. I almost don't pick it up, afraid that it will be my mum, or Max, or someone else who might want an explanation that I'm not able to give.

'Hi, is this Jolly Politely?'

This is the second time in a single evening that a man has called me by my fake name. 'Who is this?'

'My name is Tom Perrell,' he says. 'I work for Vice.'

'The magazine?'

'The website. Vice dot com. But more people read the website than the magazine.'

Another pause.

'Do *you* read Vice?'

Is he trying to sell me a subscription to Vice? 'I certainly *have* read Vice.'

'You might have seen some of my work, then. Sometimes it's on the homepage.'

There's a queue forming behind me at Costcutter.

'Sorry, Tom, I'm actually at the shop right now. I'm buying some ...' Dinner? No, it's 10 p.m. Some wine? No, it's Tuesday. 'I'm buying some cigarettes.'

'Cool. Do you vape? I just finished a feature on south-east London's vape scene.'

'For Vice?'

'No.' He sighs. 'For my friend's culture zine. Not for Vice.'

'Look, can you call me back? There's a bit of a queue behind me.'

'Of course. When's good?'

'Twenty minutes?'

'Twenty minutes. I'll call. Super excited. Thanks!'

I apologise to the scowling man behind the counter and go home. Why does Vice want to speak to me? More importantly, how does Vice know who I am? I brush my hair and put on some lipstick while I wait for him to call back. I've always suspected that everyone's voice sounds different when they have lipstick on.

'Hi, Jolly?'

'Tom. Hi.'

'Thank you so much for agreeing to talk to me. And sorry about the late hour. News never sleeps, and all that.'

'Tom, I'm more interested in talking about how you ended up with my phone number.'

'Oh, that. I hope you don't mind. I know you prefer privacy, but I found the registered details for your website domain, which had your last address.'

'Are you serious?'

'Mm hm. Then I called your previous landlord and he gave me your phone number.'

'He just gave it to you? Just like that?'

Luddy's words ring in my ears, telling me how I'm not as mysterious as I think I am, and I feel like an idiot. Here I was, thinking that Jolly Politely was couched in secrecy, when everyone who has eyes and a data plan is able to find me.

'Well, I said I had some important packages I needed to deliver to you.'

'So you lied.'

'Hey,' he says, and I can hear him giving a little shrug on the other end of the phone, 'that's journalism for you.'

'It's not exactly noble, is it, though? I'm a blogger, not the fucking . . . ' I grope for an example. 'Watergate Hotel.'

'That's funny,' he says, not laughing. 'I'm going to put that in the piece.'

'*What* piece?'

'About your . . . recent activity. Do you even know how many people are worried about you?'

'Look, Tom, I've been busy with, like, my life, so yeah, I haven't been updating Jolly. But I don't get *paid* to do Jolly. It's a *hobby*. I probably get less users in a year than Vice gets in a day.'

'You don't understand, Jolly.'

No one has ever called me 'Jolly' in real life before, and this stranger has done it three times.

'There are threads on Reddit about you. Hashtag #WhatsUpJolly has had over four thousand impressions. Don't tell me you didn't *know*,' he continues.

'I can honestly tell you I didn't know. I mean, like I said, I don't even have four thousand regular readers. It's more like five hundred.'

Actually, it was 398 the last time I checked. That's how many people had signed up to get Jolly Politely straight to their inbox as soon as I make an update.

'Yeah, but your recent posts have gone crazy. Didn't you know?'

'*What* recent posts?'

'Hang on, let me get my laptop.'

I listen to Tom shuffle around his house.

'Here we are. The last one was from earlier today.'

I cringe. I had forgotten.

'Yeah. That. I was . . . I've been sick lately, and I wrote that after . . . after something happened.'

He acts like he hasn't heard me. 'And this one, from the week before: It just says "why is he hurting me?"'

'Excuse me?'

'Why is he hurting me.'

'I didn't write that.'

'Well, it looks like you did.'

'What else is there?' I look around for my laptop. I need to see this.

'Two weeks ago – this is the one that really attracted some new people to the site, I think – you make a sort of open plea. Aimed at someone called Kim, and someone called Max.'

'Someone called Max,' I repeat.

'"Max,"' he says in a slightly higher voice, as if he were me. '"I was never good enough and I will never be good enough but don't pick her, don't pick Kim, you don't need her, you need me. We need each other."'

This is why Max hasn't checked in since the day I passed out at the pub. He's the only one who knows about Jolly. He even gave me the money to renew the domain, back when I was between jobs.

Max i can't

I start scrolling through the site for the first time since the morning in the rented cottage. There are posts from me: dozens. Dozens of posts that I don't remember writing, sometimes several in one night, looking more like half-formed thoughts than full sentences.

Hair hair hair hair hair hair

Legs legs legs legs legs legs legs legs legs legs

In between, there are questions I know I have asked myself, but none that I have any recollection of posting.

Why do older men get involved with younger women?

'Tim, I think I need to get off the phone with you now.'

Why does he use up use up use up women

why does he make us sick

Who else is there

'Tom. Tom Perrell. And I would really like to get your take on this. I think your readers just want to be reassured that you're okay. That you're not, you know, having a mental breakdown or something.

'*Are* you having a mental breakdown? Because, at Vice, we're big into promoting positive representations of mental illness.'

I hang up.

24

The responses to my question – the one about older men getting involved with younger women – go like this.

Lol cos they expect less

cheap date

They're bored of their wives

OR their wives are fat

lololol who doesnt want to bang a 21 y/o

ANY YOUNG GIRLS ON HERE WANT TO FUCK PM ME THRU WORDPRESS

WOMEN have all the cards when they are young:
then they get old and MEN have all the cards. Who
can blame them for not playing fair??

Tom was right: interest in my site really has gone through the roof.

I pause at this one:

Because they have no idea what they're getting
themselves into.

I laugh, despite everything. What had *I* got myself into?
Who had I become? What happened to the girl that seemed
so promising? The girl who Howard Mitchell called
'unstoppable'?

I look at the time stamps on each of my posts. 2.33 a.m.,
4.01 a.m. 3.44 a.m. I have spent the last month getting up in
the middle of the night to sleepwalk my way through insane
blog post after insane blog post, and my waking self wasn't
strong enough to look at the evidence. The most recent ones
don't have the decency to be in the middle of the night: there
are posts from three in the afternoon, from ten past eleven
in the morning. These are the snatches of time I've been
losing lately.

There are threads and blog posts, some of them comparing me to famous women. I am 'the Amy Winehouse of
Wordpress' and the 'Amanda Bynes of Blogger Bylines'. I
find a discussion about whether or not I will kill myself, and
another sweepstake about when I will kill myself.

**Never used to read her blog but sounds like a desperate
slut who loves old cock**

OLD COCK MADE HER CRAY CRAY

There are emails, at least twenty, from older guys who would
like to date me, take me out to dinner, for coffee, anything.
They're worried about me, and they want me to know not
all men are so bad.

**I think you'll find that with the right, more mature
guy, you could be very happy.**

I tell myself I will stop reading: that I will hit 'delete all', that I will stop Googling my screen name and all the related hashtags that have sprung up: #SaveJolly, #UokJolly and #JPCray. I can't stop. There's too much of it, and all of it is proof of what I have suspected for some time now: that I have truly lost my grip on reality.

There are even emails from Luddy, lost amidst the panic of strangers. There are three:

Are you okay?

Here is my number. Please call me.

Jane, would you like me to contact him? Please respond

Hot spit floods my mouth, the kind that only ever precedes a vomit. I run to the bathroom, and Shiraz scrapes back my hair as I lean over the bowl. I hadn't even heard her come in.

What else was I keeping from myself? What else was being buried, night after night, in my nocturnal activity?

I shudder as the bottle of white wine comes up. Everything tastes like vinegar.

Who was I writing to? And why was I doing it?

As another surge comes from the bottom of me, I think: *Because it has to come out somehow.* Because you can't keep shoving yourself to the bottom of yourself. Because hiding in the shadow of someone else's life is not a life your heart will accept. Shiraz's cool hands clasp my hair.

I make 'hyep' noises as more comes up. It's starting to go clear now: viscous and yellow.

He takes what they have, you see.

What does he take? Everything she said seems like both a confirmation and a dismissal. The more I try to remember what Luddy said the more it fades away from me, until it's replaced with the bright, bold outline of Shiraz's words.

It's also about potential. It's about seeing someone who is still excited to get up in the morning.

As my retching becomes dry and empty, I hear Shiraz padding away and remember what else she had said.

I told you he would use you.

I go back to my bedroom, but it's too hot to sleep. The sheet prickles underneath me, the feeling of mattress too close. I open all the windows, but my skin is still battery-warm, humming with heat. It's too late in the year for this, surely.

I get naked, but there's no amount of naked I can be that will cool me down. I pull off the plasters on my heels, the ones every woman wanders around with when cheap sandals get the better of her. Navy glue sticks to me in neat lines. I pick it off until I scratch the skin open, then feel sick again. I go into the bathroom and find ways to make there be less of me, anything to shed this heaviness, this heat. I cut my nails down with Shiraz's clippers. I sit in the bathtub and shave my legs with water and hair conditioner, going past my knee, shaving my thighs, then my pubes, then the tops of my arms. I fill the tub with cold water and sit in it, at four in the morning, with my eyes closed.

I wonder if I have heat stroke and then I giggle to myself, thinking about him, missing him a little. *Of course you do.*

I regard the razor, and not one bit of me judges Viv for opening her wrist with a scalpel. How freeing it might be, to do something like that. To feel all that pain, and all that heaviness, and then free yourself from it in one swift movement.

I eventually doze off, and when I wake up at eight, Shiraz has left a glass of water out for me and two painkillers. There's a thick strip of sweat at the front of my scalp, making my hair wet and warm. I can taste the vinegar tang of regurgitated wine in my mouth, feel the hundreds of blog comments sitting like a lead weight at the bottom of my gut.

I gaze into the mirror, both hands shaking a little on either side of the sink.

'*You* are not mad,' I say. And then again, a bit louder: '*I* am not mad.'

Shiraz is in the kitchen, reading a Sunday supplement still hanging around from the weekend.

'Hey.'

'Hey,' she responds, looking at me warily.

'Thanks for last night.'

She shrugs.

'I'm sorry about . . . ' I pause. 'Who I turned out to be. You probably thought you were getting a normal housemate.'

She shrugs again, and takes a sip out of her mug. 'You still pay the rent on time. And you're only dirty in *your* room.'

We smile weakly at one another.

'Shi—' I'm about to say her name but then remember she hates the way I pronounce it, so stop. 'When you're away in the evenings, are you with one of these . . . these guys we were talking about last night? These guys like Clem?'

She laughs into her fingernails. She has the type of nails that don't look fake, but they are: I've seen the glue in the bathroom.

'In a way, I suppose I kind of am.'

'What does th—'

'I'm with my dad.'

'Oh.'

'He's dying.'

I put a hand on her shoulder. She removes it without comment.

'I'm so sorry.'

'Don't be. He's a prick. One of those university professors we talked about. We don't get along.'

'What about your mum?'

'Like you. Young woman, married man,' she says. 'Only

younger. Much younger. She pissed off years ago. Haven't seen much of her since. Can't say I blame her.'

'Is he in hospital?'

'More like an assisted living centre. He's got a woman who washes him when he can't do it himself. But he doesn't have anyone, except me, so I see the bastard after work.'

Shiraz's hyper-feminine, interiors-obsessed life starts to make sense.

'That's a lot to deal with. I had no idea.'

'It's not so bad. And he's not so bad either, now that he's old. But he's alone, and he knows he's alone, and he knows it's his fault. I think that's what gets to him most.'

I try to imagine Clem like that. No wife, no girlfriend, no friends. No one who thinks he's impressive because he was once good at advertising. It's comforting, in a way, to think that however desperate I am now, I might get better, and he might get worse.

'Are you going to work today?'

'He pretty much told me I would get fired unless I went in.'

'Fucker.'

'Yeah.'

'You're done with him, aren't you?'

'I am,' I said. 'I'm done.'

It is only a lie until lunchtime.

I am prepared for my inbox to be spilling over with messages. My Jolly emails aren't the only thing I've been ignoring lately, after all: in Clem's absence I've been putting off anything non-urgent, just in case I am needed on the Think Gym account suddenly. I say hi to a concerned yet strangely quiet Becky, make a green tea, and go back to my desk to see if my inbox has stopped updating. It has.

I have twenty-six emails.

They are almost all emails addressed to the whole staff. I blast through them, trying to find any that are actually relevant to me.

The cleaners have kindly asked that staff do not remove
hand soap from toilets

FREE BEERS ON 1ST FLOOR

We request you complete this short survey on Mitchell

The cleaners must insist that ALL STAFF refrain from
stealing hand soap from the toilets

MISSING: 1 X PAIR RAYBANS BLACK

And then, one quick, cold email from Darla.

Hey girl. Can you forward me any of your Think Gym
info. Thanks

'Becky,' I say, attempting to remain calmly uninterested,
'why is Darla asking me for Think Gym stuff?'

'Oh,' says Becky, in a similarly bogus attempt to appear
neutral, 'she's working on that now.'

'Oh,' I echo. 'Instead of me?'

But why not Clem? If I could be attracted to him, than so
could she.

'I think so.'

My computer pings again.

J,

I need bound printouts of the attached. Single sided, in
booklet form. 250 copies by 3 p.m.

C

I wonder if it's code for something. Mitchell doesn't have a print department big enough to do a job like this. I would have to arrange an independent printers to cover the job, and I have zero clue who does that.

Another ping.

J,

Can you also look through KFC's twitter followers and compile a report on gender/age/location split. Tx.

C

Social media isn't part of my job, any more than arranging print jobs is. And KFC isn't a client of ours.

This is Clem's revenge for last night, or perhaps his elegant, brutal way of resigning as my mentor-slash-boyfriend. He's giving all professional responsibility I once had to Darla, and he's overloading me with pointless, thankless tasks to push me out of the company. This is the end of client lunches and long nights in empty offices, and the beginning of something else: a slow, painful death-by-admin.

I could take everything else: the printouts and the Twitter followers and the abrupt emails. But not Darla.

After an hour of chewing my bottom lip and failing to concentrate, I go to her desk. I push Jolly and the depths to which she has fallen out of my head. I will not be the girl who fades into obscurity. I will not be the girl who tries to kill herself with a scalpel. I am not Viv.

I remember myself in the bathtub, staring at my purple razor. *Aren't you?*

Darla is on the phone, and puts one finger up. She is more than another minute. I make my best bored expression. *Come on,* I mouth. She smiles and turns her back to me.

As I'm about to walk away, she puts down the phone.

'Hey,' she says coldly. 'What do you want?'

This is new. Before, Darla had been distant, but never outrightly dismissive. Something has changed. Some*one* has changed her.

'Did you see my email?' she asks.

'Yeah. That's why I'm here. I think we should talk somewhere in private.'

She sighs. 'I have a meeting in two minutes.'

'With Clem?'

'Yes,' she says sharply.

I lower my voice and move closer to her. 'Look, Darla – I don't know what he's told you, but I think you should stay away from him.'

'Okay,' she says.

'Okay you're going to stay away from him?'

'Okay, I heard what you had to say.'

'Look, I'm trying to help you here. If you knew what he's done to me. What he's done to other women.'

She looks bored, but she's still listening, and I know I'm going to have to say it. Out loud. At work.

'He makes women sick, Darla.'

Her eyebrows disappear under her fringe completely.

'He uses girls, Darla. Girls like me. Look at me. Do I look okay to you? Do I look healthy?'

I stand back from her, will her to look at me properly. My greying skin, breaking out in red, soft pimples along my jawline. My tired, lined eyes. My hair that's become so thin that my ponytail is no thicker than a felt-tip pen. And then there's everything else: my clothes that don't fit me properly, and that I haven't had the energy to wash in weeks. My bra strap sloping off to the side. The eczema that started on the tops of my thighs and is now circling my wrists.

Darla does something painfully typical of her. She laughs.

'I'm sorry, Jane. I really am. But you know what's going on here, don't you?'

I shake my head.

'You're going through a break-up.'

'That was months ago.'

'Grief comes in stages. Everyone knows that. What is it? Denial, bargaining, anger, depression and acceptance.'

'I think it's anger, then bargaining.'

'Denial, anger, bargaining, depression and acceptance, then. We had denial. Remember denial? We went out and got pissed every night for two weeks, and hey, we had fun. It was a blast. Then you found out about Max's new girlfriend, and anger set in.'

Without even meaning to, I start nodding.

'Bargaining. You went to the pub with Max. What was that? Just a friendly catch-up between two people who used to share a lease? Something tells me it was bargaining.'

'How did you know about the pub?'

'Becky told me. And then you stopped coming to work. How many days off have you had in the last fortnight? Five? Six? Sounds a lot like depression to me. And, look, I'm not judging, I'm really not, but you know you've had mental health stuff before.'

Why had I told her about the therapist in uni? Why had I trusted Darla with my most private miseries?

Her tone is careful now. 'And it makes sense that . . . that you would rebound with someone like Clem. Again, not judging. But you know, Max used to look after you so much, I don't blame you for becoming a little dependent on him and falling apart after he leaves. And now you're trying to depend on Clem. Like, all that stuff with your dad, I guess it's probably normal.'

'What do you know about *someone like* Clem, Darla?'

Her gaze travels over to my right shoulder.

Clem is waving at her from the lifts.

'I have to go.'

'Darla, no.'

She makes her way across the office, and I follow her. A few people who sit nearby take their headphones out, interested in the drama we're creating.

'Darla, *please* just listen to me.'

'Fuck *off*, Jane. You're crazy, do you realise that? You're off your fucking head. Don't think I haven't read your shit-eating blog, either. Don't think I don't know what you said about me.'

I try to remember which, of the many poisonous comments I had written about my loved ones, pertained to Darla. I had deleted so many in a rush that it was hard to recall.

'Hello, Jane.'

I have never seen Clem and Darla in the same space before, and it strikes me now how much they could suit each other: all ambition and serrated edges.

'Can I meet you in Copenhagen in five?' he says to her. 'I need to speak to Jane.'

She obliges, grateful to be rid of me. As she turns away, I remember what I wrote, or at least, what crazy-middle-of-the-night-me wrote.

who do u talk to when your best friend is a selfish cunt

'Whatever you're doing with her, stop it,' I say to Clem.

'*What* am I doing with her?'

'You're trying to sleep with her. Or maybe you have already, I don't know. But your shit won't work on her. She's too good for you.'

'Jane, you've become unreliable. I need someone who knows market research and PR for this part of the project. It's not a big deal.'

'And what about this,' I say, gesturing at nothing. 'This fucking bullshit in my emails this morning?'

'Excuse me?'

He waits for me to hang myself, holding the noose up for me. I dip my head into it.

'You want me to trudge across London on a print job, Clem. You'd give that to an intern. And the KFC thing? We're not pitching for KFC.'

People are gaping, open-mouthed, from their desks. They're not trying to pretend they're not eavesdropping.

'We are, actually. Not that I expect you to know. And I'm sorry you're not willing to be a team player. I'll make a note of that in my mentor report.'

My eyes fill up with tears. All I can think about is Darla, waiting in Copenhagen for her life to implode, like I waited in India for mine.

'She's not as tough as she looks, you know.'

'Well,' he says, 'neither are you.'

25

I leave the building as soon as Clem disappears from view, and just walk. Past the gay bars, past the twenty-four-hour Thai massage places, past the frozen-yogurt chain that only hires models on zero-hour contracts. It's October now, and the tourists are mostly contained in M&M's World or Ripley's Believe It or Not. People are starting to relax again. The irate, bloated heatwave seems to have broken overnight and soon, the smoky evenings of autumn will start to hug closer.

I sit down on a powerbox, and – whether it's out of habit or because I truly have become a glutton for punishment – I check my email.

Jolly Politely

Sat with her psyche

Eating her curds and whey

Along came a spider

Who beat her and fucked her

And frightened dear Jolly away

I've never been at the centre of an online hate campaign, but I've read blog posts from enough feminist writers to know that it gets worse before it gets better.

The comments on my post titled 'Why do older men get involved with younger women?' are still going. The conversation seems to have moved on from whether I'm okay, and is now a kind of turf war between 1) the men who think I'm a desperate, crazy slut; 2) the women who think that my erratic behaviour is down to an abusive relationship, and are mad at the men for trivialising it; and 3) the women who insist they are not feminists and don't have to sympathise with me just because I'm a woman.

It's easy to view it with a degree of distance, because it doesn't even seem to be about me any more. I've become a symbol for a couple of hundred people to argue over, like global warming on an infinitely smaller scale.

I open a new draft.

Okay, so everyone knows why older men like younger women. But: why do younger women get involved with older men?

I don't know why I click 'publish', or why I need to know the answer. Or why I need to keep this blog running. These people know the very worst of me: the darkest, most illogical places my mind dares to go. Maybe that's what makes it so compelling: I couldn't possibly make it any worse, so why not watch the fire?

Closing my eyes, I remember a group of girls asking me to sign their petition to remove Ted Hughes from the English Lit curriculum. They pushed pictures of his two dead wives under my nose, and I felt guilty for not recognising Sylvia Plath immediately.

'They killed themselves,' one insisted, 'because of what he did to them.'

'What did he do to them?'

I don't remember what she said back, but when studying Hughes a few weeks later, I decided that they were wrong. That his tragedy was one with the two women who had decided to kill themselves on his behalf. That if he had burned Sylvia Plath it was only because they were both on fire. Was this like that?

I was accusing a man – at his place of work, no less – of sucking the lives of innocent women dry. And what proof did I have?

Why do younger women get involved with older men?

I get an alert when someone writes their first response.

for the story

I get back to my desk to a worried-looking Becky. It occurs to me just how much responsibility she takes for my happiness. Her concern is as deep as it is legitimate, and forces me to consider how vague the hearts of others are when compared to Becky's. Her emotions are pure, like expensive olive oil or uncut cocaine. It overwhelms people who don't know its value, and is taken for granted by those who do.

'Are you feeling better?'

'A little, Becky. Thanks.'

She shrugs, and I touch her arm.

'No really,' I say, determined that someone see me today. 'Thank you.'

How many times had she covered for me, listened to me, forgiven me? Why had I always put her on the back bench?

Why was it so hard for me to overlook Becky's social oddities, yet so easy to ignore the boundless kindness she has shown me?

'There was a call for you while you were . . . out,' says Becky, chewing her mouth again. 'They want to see you in Paris.'

God dammit, Becky.

My friend writes for Vice and spoke to jolly and said she was really fucking odd but also not in any immediate danger

He *spoke* to her?

Cindi Crane is the only person called Cindi I have ever met, and is either South African or Australian. She's worked in HR ever since I started, but I've never had cause to speak to her. I've only ever seen her in the canteen, picking through the fruit with a pinched expression, squeezing peaches to test their ripeness.

I watch jealously as she threads her waterfall blonde hair through her fingers underneath a framed photograph of the Eiffel Tower. I remember my own hair, rich and thick and brown, and – despite everything – I remember Clem's gentle tugs on it when he kissed me.

'Right,' says Cindi. 'Do you have any idea why you're here . . .' she pauses to look at the piece of paper in front of her, ' . . . Jane?'

'No.'

'Could you *guess?*'

'Well, I have been ill lately.'

'You've been ill a lot, I would say. And that's not counting the days you've just *left* the office during the day.'

I try to account for these disappearances. How many *were* there?

'I've been very sick,' I say uncertainly.

'Have you been to the doctor's?'

'Yes.'

'And they didn't provide you with a note?'

'He . . . ' *He didn't believe me.* 'He didn't, no.'

'Am I to understand that he didn't think your illness was as serious as you did, if he wasn't able to provide you with a sick note?'

'I . . . uh, I suppose you could put it that way.'

'How would *you* put it?'

'I'm sick,' I say. 'But not in the usual way.'

She looks at my stomach, and I can tell she's filling out maternity leave paperwork in her head.

'No, I mean . . . this isn't your typical illness. I'm weak. My hair is falling out. And I think . . . ' I pause for a second. 'It's work-related.'

Cindi stiffens, now imagining a whole different set of papers. Paperwork marked 'stress leave'. She looks at my folder again.

'You were recently given a promotion, I see. Congratulations.'

'Thank you.'

'Would you say you were unprepared for the increased workload that came with the promotion?'

I want to laugh. 'The workload is fine, but the conditions in which I have to work are less than ideal.'

I don't know what I'm saying, or what I want to say. This is what Paris does to you.

'Jane,' she says, in a way that makes me think she's definitely Australian, 'can you tell me why that is?'

'Uhm . . . '

'It would really help me if I could understand why you are unhappy at work.'

I think of Darla. I think of Viv. I think of the women who had lost the very idea of themselves to a man more than willing to devour them whole.

And then something rises in me, and I briefly think it's more of last night's vomit.

'Clem Brown is using me,' I blurt. 'And I can't make him stop.'

I put both my hands to my face, a sad, strange attempt to make the tears stop.

Cindi's composure falls for a second, but recovers. Without taking her eyes off me, she reaches for the phone and puts it to her ear.

'Howard, I think I need you up here.'

26

Howard Mitchell asks Cindi to take me to his office, and she wrinkles her nose at the insult.

'We're going there,' she says, lifting her blazer from the back of her chair and tugging it on. 'Although I can't see why. It is an HR *issue*, after all.'

When we arrive Howard and Clem are opposite one another. Clem is taking up a huge amount of space, his foot stretched across the floor, his hands on the back of his neck.

'Ladies,' says Howard, 'please sit down.'

We sit.

'Good to see you again, Jane,' he says, smiling at me with a hollow warmth.

'And you,' I reply. I don't look at Clem.

'Cindi, can you please repeat what Jane said to you a minute ago?'

This time, Cindi sounds South African. 'She said that Clem Brown was using her. And that he wouldn't stop.'

'Is that what you said, Jane?'

I nod.

'And what did you mean by that?'

I can't think of a way to frame this that doesn't sound completely insane, but I am in too deep to say nothing. 'I mean that Clem is deliberately pushing me off an account that I helped secure. And he's trying to flood my workload with menial, entry-level tasks to get me to quit.'

There. That, at least, is true.

Howard Mitchell looks almost scolding. 'I'm sorry, Jane, by my recollection the only account you've helped secure with us is Fat Eddie pizza. And for that, you were rewarded *quite* generously. Isn't that right?'

'But that's not wh—'

'I remember it very well. We were in this room, and I gave you your new business cards. I rush-ordered them because Clem said that it was imperative that we promote you quickly, to make an example of how hard work and initiative is rewarded here at Mitchell.'

I finally meet Clem's eye, and he smiles tightly at me. There's a glimmer of: *I hope you know where you're going with this, because I am going to fucking bury you.*

I clear my throat. 'I'm talking about Think Gym, sir. The gym for mindfulness.'

Now Howard looks legitimately puzzled.

'Jane,' he says gently, 'I've only ever seen you in one Think Gym meeting.'

'That's true,' I say carefully, knowing how unstable my grasp on reality has recently become. 'But Clem and I, while working together, covered the client quite extensively.'

I am walking myself down an alley that I know ends in a brick wall, but I can't seem to stop.

'Clem has taken my ideas and deliberately took me on client meetings to undermine Deb. He's trying to get rid of her. And now he's trying to get rid of me.'

'Our Deb? Deb Hughes?'

'Yes.'

'She's not in this meeting.'

'I know.'

'So why are you bringing her *up*?'

Clem speaks for the first time in the meeting. 'Howard, I think we both know what's happening here. I think, in Jane's case, it was a case of too much too soon. I don't think she fully understands how an agency works.'

Howard nods.

'Jane, let me lay it out a little clearer. When a person is appointed your mentor, it's a two-way street. This desire you have to be given credit for every little thing that comes out of your mouth, it's very – and this isn't just you, I see this a lot – it's very *millennial* of you.'

'That's not what I'm talking about.' My voice is starting to get high and desperate.

'I think,' begins Cindi, 'we're not talking about intellectual theft here.'

'What does that mean?' asks Howard, when he knows exactly what it means.

'Jane, as a woman, I understand why you're struggling here. And if this disagreement is about something else, you need to say so now. If you and Clem are having a romantic relationship, you need to tell me.' She reaches across and touches my hand. 'Let me be your friend. Human Resources is here for *you*.'

Emboldened by Cindi's sympathy, I finally say it.

'We had a romantic relationship. It's over now.' I look across at him briefly. 'But I have reason to believe that Clem bears professional ill will against me as a result.'

If, in this moment, I think I am making things better for myself, I am relieved of that notion very, very quickly.

He said she's just some chick in south london, young like, 24/25/26/27??

Not trying to be a dick but have you noticed how ALL white girls in their 20s now are fucking batshit

How do you know she white

Her name is 'jolly politely' ffs

It becomes clear that Cindi and Howard have played good cop/bad cop many, many times before. The minute I admit to our relationship, pieces begin shifting around the board.

'And was everything in your relationship consensual, Jane?' Cindi asks.

I think of the night in Whitstable again, and the dull ache of my cystitis for days afterwards. The floor sex I don't remember. I shake my head. He was a lot of things, but he wasn't *that*.

'Yes. Of course it was. We're two consenting adults. But that doesn't mean that there's not . . . ' I stumble, looking for the right words. 'A power imbalance.'

'Jane, were you aware that we have a policy at Mitchell forbidding romantic relationships within the company?' asks Howard.

My mouth falls open. 'No, I was not.'

'It was in your starting contract,' chirps Cindi, 'which you signed.'

'Usually we're happy to look the other way. Lord, there have even been Mitchell marriages. So really, it's more of a best practice thing than a hard-and-fast rule.'

'Except in this instance.' Cindi again.

'Yes, except in this instance,' clarifies Howard. 'In this instance, because it's a relationship between a high-ranking member of staff and someone significantly junior to him, we have to take the matter quite seriously.'

'It's not nice,' says Cindi gravely. 'But it is necessary.'

I want to believe that this is when I watch Clem lose his job, but something tells me that isn't going to happen. Even the walls feel slanted towards me, accusing me.

'You will both be issued written warnings.'

Clem smiles benevolently.

'I think that's fair. For my part ...' He looks into the middle distance now, terse, his jaw tight. 'I want to accept responsibility for what I've done. I engaged in a relationship with someone whose hero worship of me was confused, temporarily, with lust for me. Had I been in the right frame of mind, I would have been able to tell Jane that her feelings towards me weren't appropriate.'

'*My* feelin—'

He puts a hand up to silence me.

'As the senior person, I should have taken it upon myself not to indulge Jane's fantasies.'

I can't believe that a real person is saying these real words in real life.

'We have been overworking you lately,' says Howard. 'I understand how these things happen when expectations of you are so high.'

Howard and Clem look at each other with a kindred respect, as if they have both survived the same kind of rare cancer.

'Cindi, if you want to take Jane back to HR and commence with her warning, I would appreciate that. I need to wrap up a few things with Clem.'

'I'll come get my warning later,' says Clem helpfully.

I am quaking with rage by the time Cindi and I get back to Paris.

'Cindi, you can't really believe all th—'

She isn't listening. She is typing.

'Jane, this is difficult. But because of your new role as Account Manager, you are still technically on probation.'

'Excuse me?'

'Do you know what that means?'

'I've worked here for two years. I can't be on probation.'

'You have only been on this contract since July, though.

And when you're on probation, two written warnings equate to a suspension without pay.'

'But I haven't got two written warnings.'

'You do,' she says. 'Because the first written warning is what I initially called you in for.'

She pushes a printed A4 sheet across at me. Words like 'continued unexplained absence' and 'decline in quality of work' appear several times.

'You know this isn't fair, Cindi. Please.'

'It's not my job to think about what's fair, Jane. It's my job to run HR. These are our rules, and they exist to protect both the company and the staff.'

'I was honest with you. I was honest, and I was afraid, and now you're punishing me for it.'

'I'm afraid that it's protocol for you to leave the building immediately, Jane. You're suspended for a week without pay.'

27

She said immediately, but actually it's worse than that. They make someone from security walk me to my desk first, watch me pack up my things, and then escort me downstairs.

'Is this really necessary for a suspension? I *do* still work here.'

'People get angry about suspensions,' the security guard says. 'They're afraid you're going to run into a meeting room and scream in front of a client.'

'Does that kind of thing happen a lot?'

'Oh, no. Not for a long while. But protocol is protocol.'

Becky attempts to follow me out, failing to keep pace with the security guard's charging step.

'Jane! What's going on?'

'I'm being suspended,' I say. And then remember the other bit. 'Without pay.'

I realise, while saying the sentence out loud, exactly what this means for me. This will come up in performance reviews for at least a year afterwards. If I move to another agency, it will come up during my reference checks. And even in the short term: I may have had a raise, but I still can't afford to lose a quarter of my monthly salary. I do the numbers quickly. That's almost four hundred pounds! My rent is seven hundred pounds. Trying to get to the end of next month is going to be miserable, and what's worse is that it's a misery I know I don't deserve.

'Becky,' I say, 'he *fucked* me.'

'Clem?'

I nod.

'Oh, Jane. I'm so sorry.'

'Have you known this whole time?'

'I suspected, only. So, what? Did you break up? Is he mad? Is he trying to push you out of the company now?'

I break away from the security guard quickly, and go to give Becky a hug. I shoot him a mean 'can't I hug my friend?' look over her shoulder. 'I need you to get two phone numbers for me.'

'Sure,' she says, always glad of a mission. 'Whose?'

'I need you to get me Deb Hughes' phone number. And I need you to get Renata Brown's.'

She's about to say 'Who?' until it dawns on her. And then, with a brevity rare of Becky, she puts both her hands on my shoulders and says, 'Done.'

The flat is empty. I'm initially relieved not to have to explain to Shiraz why I'm home in the middle of the day, but the long afternoon stretching out ahead of me soon invites anxiety in. Her place has never felt less like my home. It feels wrong to watch TV, to flick through her magazines, to do anything else other than slump on my bed in all of my clothes. The action, which is how so many of my evenings, afternoons and nights conclude lately, quickly becomes not enough.

Because it's my only option, I finally tidy my room.

I strip the sheets, and both pillowcases. Everything is marked with orange and black streaks of make-up, not to mention the occasional food stain. I have been living my life from bed lately, and in the process it's become more of a nest. Hairbrushes are stuck within duvet folds, along with more incongruous items: an unopened bottle of brown sauce, a shower loofah, books I had bought years ago and never read. I wonder whether I have been collecting all this during my late-night blogging sessions, the memories of which still escape me. They are just another thing I have forced myself to accept, using the same exhausted logic that has accepted that my hair is falling out, my boss is trying to destroy me and that I may have lost a permanent grip on my sanity. It's too draining to remain incredulous, and with so much being drained from me already, it's my responsibility to safeguard any remaining energy I might have left.

When the sheets are done in the washing machine, I put on another load of clothes. I hang up what's clean. I throw away the flowers, the water reeking, brown and sour. I open both windows. I remember that actually, this is a nice room, and that this is a nice flat. This is not a bad place to end up. Not just as a refuge after a break-up, but in general. The ceilings are high, the windows wide, and the furniture a slightly more upmarket Ikea range.

'I like this room,' I say to no one. It feels stupid, but it feels good.

I dust down the dressing table, and remembering that there are still boxes I haven't unpacked, fish one out from the back of my wardrobe. I pull out things that I had forgotten I owned, immediately putting everything Max-related in a black plastic bag. I'm flushing as I do it, knowing that I've been avoiding this job since I moved in, too aware that it plays like a bad romantic comedy. Like throwing away his hoodie is going to be the answer to my problems.

My decorative options are pretty limited after I make these eliminations, but what I have left, I like. I like my carved stone candle holder, shaped like a cart horse. I like the picture of my mum and me at the Jane Austen museum. I like the tiny, brightly coloured clay bowls that I bought at a Scandinavian design fair for way too much money.

'I like my stuff,' I say out loud, because it felt good the first time.

I find my old jewellery box, and remember that I am a woman who owns a jewellery box. Investigating it while cross-legged on the floor, I throw away the mismatched earrings and Freedom by Topshop bracelets that have been following me around since my mid-teens. And then I pull out something I had forgotten about: a lone, pink pearl on a long silver chain.

It was a birthday present, but I got it at Christmas. I was supposed to visit Dad in Switzerland for my twenty-first birthday, but when the moment came to go to the airport – my bags packed, my boarding pass printed, folded and tucked into the back page of my passport – I didn't go. I made a big show of sitting down and picking up a magazine when it was time to leave. Mum, standing in the doorway with her keys in her hand, realised that I had no intention of leaving the house. She didn't force the issue. It was, for me, a way of swearing fealty to my mother: my way of saying, 'What, you *really* thought I'd get on a plane to go see that guy? After what he did to you?' So we spent my birthday together: we drove to the coast, ate chips on the beach and talked about everything I was going to do once I moved to London. She read out my birthday letter, and a page of it almost blew into the sea.

Dad showed up two days before Christmas and the rift between us had become deeper. He wisely thought twice about bringing Gaëlle, but made up for her absence by mentioning her constantly. 'Gaëlle studied English literature too!' and 'Gaëlle would love that dress' and 'Gaëlle was only saying the other day . . . '

It was hard to know whether he thought the best way to install Gaëlle as my stepmother was to mention her a lot, or whether he just didn't know what else to talk about. I rarely let us be alone together, preferring to carry on my conversations with Mum as if he weren't there. I thought she had been magnanimous in allowing him to sleep on the couch, but I had no interest in sharing in her kindness.

I never sympathised with him much before, but looking at his pearl dangling between my wrists in my south London bedroom, virtually friendless, practically jobless, teetering on the brink of non-existence, I feel sorry for him for the very first time. Yes, he abandoned us. Yes, his attempts to reconnect were bumbling and awkward. But did I need to punish him the way I did?

'It's your birthstone, Janey. Pearls are your birthstone.'

It was startlingly at odds with me, this ultra-feminine piece of jewellery, like something a Christian teenager would wear on her wedding day. I liked chunky silver rings, dangling turquoise earrings, stacked bangles. Or at least, I did then. I thanked him, visibly incredulous, then snapped the box closed and didn't put it on.

'When you were born, your eyes were grey.'

I was determined to give him the last shreds of my teenage insolence before it ebbed away. 'My eyes are green.'

'Not then. Most babies' eyes are blue, but yours weren't. They were dark, stormy. You were the most *serious*-looking baby.'

I didn't like hearing his version of my birth, because I was reared on my mother's version. My mother's version of my birth was a story for just the two of us, and having to include my father in the narrative – especially now, post-Gaëlle, post-Switzerland, post-betrayal – was too much for me.

'Lady Jane Grey,' he said fondly. 'Queen for nine days.'

'Jane Russell,' I corrected. 'Mum named me after Jane Russell.'

He shook his head, determined not to settle on this one. 'Jane Grey. I remember, because the Helena Bonham Carter adaptation was on TV a lot at the time.'

'I don't think you're remembering it right. I think Mum is the one who's the authority on me and my birth, actually.'

It wasn't the worst thing in the world to say, nor the most untrue. But it was the way I said it, with sloping, accusatory italics, that made him drop the subject entirely. I didn't see much of him after that: we speak on the phone twice a year, and had one painfully awkward lunch a few years ago, at Max's insistence. I wasn't ready for sympathy then, but I feel strangely equipped for it now. He left us. But he tried until the constant rejection became not worth the effort. I put the pearl on, fiddling with the clasp. It suits me now, at long last.

How long was I queen for? A little over nine weeks? For nine weeks I felt the sun on my face, success and sex and the joy of being chosen, and now it was over. It's idiotic to think that my career at Mitchell will be going anywhere after I get back from suspension, or that I won't be axed during the next round of redundancies. The remainder of my time at that company will be spent trying to evade the notice of Clem, Howard Mitchell and the scores of people who must by now know the whole story: my showdown with Darla will have helped that.

Shiraz comes home, changes her clothes, and leaves again. I find it strange that I know where she goes now, and wonder if I would ever extend the same courtesy to my own father.

Becky calls.

'Are you okay?'

'Uhm . . .' I take a look at my newly clean room, my fresh sheets. 'Yeah.'

'At least you weren't fired.'

I think about how this, in many ways, is worse than being fired. A firing would be a clean break, rather than the slow death I am headed towards.

'Do you want me to come over? I can come over. I don't have anything on tonight. I mean, I have spinning, but I can skip it. They don't charge you if you cancel in advance.'

'No, Becky, that's okay. I guess you know everything now.'

'Everyone's saying that it's a mental health thing,' she answers awkwardly.

'What kind of mental health thing?'

'I don't think I should tell you.'

'I think it's important that you do.'

'That you're mad and that you kept it a secret, and then when you got promoted the pressure became too much, and now you're making up stuff to make it everyone else's fault.'

'Is that what you think?'

'No.'

'What do you think?'

'I don't think it sounds like you. It doesn't sound like my friend.'

'No?'

'You're not perfect, Jane. But, you know, everyone's got edges, that's what my dad says. And I know you. You don't just make things up.'

I am so stirred by her loyalty towards me, and surprised to find out Becky thinks I'm not perfect.

'And what about Clem?'

I can almost hear her shrugging.

'I saw him walking around, he seems fine.'

'What about Deb?'

'Hmm?'

'Deb. Did you get her number?'

'Oh. Right. Yes. Not Renata's, though. I don't know how you expected me to get that.'

'Me neither,' I say, grabbing a pen. 'Call out Deb's number to me.'

When we hang up the phone, I stare at Deb's number and wonder what I can really do with it. Or if Deb will remember who I am: the girl she eased out of a panic attack on the train to Slough. I still think about her, though.

'Only I determine the asking price,' I say. 'Only I can decide how important I am.'

What's the American word for this? Affirmations. I walk around the house, repeating the phrase. I wash up the mouldy mugs that I was hoarding in my bedroom, and I say the words into the sink. I hoover the carpet, and I shout them over the noise. It's silly, but it makes me feel better. My spine straightens, my shoulders broaden. An idea, a resolve, forms in my head, the chant emboldening it. It's like a sickly kitten begging to be nurtured. Afraid of losing my slippery grip on this newfound confidence, I dial Deb's number.

'Deb speaking,' she answers brusquely.

'Hi, Deb. This is Jane. Jane Peters.'

Silence.

'From Mitchell. The pizza pitch?'

'Jane,' she says, with clearly no fucking clue who she's talking to. 'How are you?'

'I'm okay. I was wondering if we could meet. I have some things I think you need to hear.'

'Can't you tell me in the office?'

'I . . . can't.'

'Do you still work for Mitchell?'

'Technically. I don't know for how much longer.'

'I see.' She pauses.

'Hello? Are you still there?'

'I'm looking at my schedule. I have an opening between eleven fifteen and eleven forty-five tomorrow morning. Do you know Reynolds café?'

'No.'

'Well, Google it. It's close to the office, but not the kind of place we'll run into anyone.'

'Fine.'

'Great. Goodbye.'

'By—'

She's already gone.

It occurs to me as I'm walking to meet her the next day that, if you work in London long enough, you develop a roster of

places to go where people will not see what you're doing or
who you're with. Clem has the Metropole hotel – a place, I
wonder, if he plans on taking Darla – and Deb has Reynolds,
a café with high-backed booths promising relative privacy
and expensive eggs.

'Jane?'

She peers at me.

'Hi,' I say, and I'm not sure how to greet her, given that
we're meeting semi-socially. I launch myself towards her and
give her two inelegant pecks on the cheek. Her body stiffens
underneath her cream blazer.

'Good day?'

She nods, and orders a cappuccino from a waiter who has
appeared over my shoulder.

'You're not at work today,' she says, noting my hoodie and
messy ponytail.

'No.'

'Why?'

'I, uh, I got suspended.'

A look of silent, but not appalled, surprise.

'And I suppose you want me to help you in some way?
Move into my department?'

'No.'

'Well, *what* then?'

I drop my voice low. 'You once gave me some advice, on
a train, that I found helpful. I want to be able to help you in
the same way.'

Her coffee arrives, and she shakes a sugar packet, looking
at me expectantly.

'I think there's someone at Mitchell who is trying to steal
your job.'

A short, barking laugh. '*Everyone* wants my job. New
Business is the most important department for an agency like
Mitchell. No secret there.'

'No, I mean, they're trying to take it from you. Someone who is undermining you. To Howard.'

'Go on.'

I tell her about Think Gym, and how I was taken on the meeting instead of her. Clem knew she was the perfect person to handle the client, but knowing how high value it was, purposefully took along someone younger and lesser qualified to make himself look better. She wasn't sent to the Think Gym retreat to gather information, she was sent to be put out of the way. I tell her that, while she was away, Clem undermined her at every turn: implying to her boss that women were likely to suffer from 'burn-out' and would eventually take 'stress leave', that she didn't have what it took to be in such a high position of seniority.

'Oh,' she says when I'm done. 'Is that everything?'

'Everything that concerns you, yeah.'

'And why are you telling me?'

'What do you mean?'

'From what I can tell, you had everything to gain from going along with it all. You could have become the account manager on a highly desirable account. You could have been promoted again. And Clem would have been *very pleased* with you, I'm sure.'

She gives me a wry smile as she says his name, and I know she knows.

'Do you know about me and him?'

'You, I don't really know anything about. Him – everyone knows about him. Everyone knows he's a Venus flytrap when it comes to young women. Always has been.'

'A Venus flytrap,' I say. 'Why do you say that?'

'Because it's true. His wife can't stand him, or so I hear, and he has a lonely life. He hops from project to project, from woman to woman, making his women into projects if he can be bothered. He never rises, you know. Always stuck somewhere in upper-middle management. His pay must be enormous, especially with no family to spend it on, but in terms of real *status*, there's no real respect there,' she finishes, and then nods at her own point. 'Admiration, fine, but not respect.'

'I don't understand. Howard loves him. And his name has been in *Campaign*.'

'It's not hard to get your name in a trade mag. Especially if you're tacky about it, and he is *tacky* about it.' She chuckles. 'He's never quite at the top, but always near it, hovering over a bigger boy's shoulder. Always grasping. Always wanting more. This fascination with being the winner. They think everyone loves them for it, and people are impressed, for a while. But men like Clem don't have the patience for anyone or anything they don't think is "winning". So they ditch things.'

I flinch. For not winning, for being a bad investment, for being ditched.

'When a whiff of difficulty comes their way, they head for the hills. And that's why Clem is the guy you send to the meeting, the guy you employ to win over clients. But would you actually put him in charge of anything? Anything that lasts longer than a few weeks? Would you let him run a major department, like I do?'

I shake my head. 'So you're not worried about what he's doing to you?'

'Worried?' She laughs. 'Jane, I don't *care*.'

The idea, the sickly kitten from earlier that mewled in the back of my brain while I tidied the flat, takes centre stage.

What if only I was responsible for what happened to me?

What if bad people exist, and what if Clem is one of them. What if he is draining my energy and making me sick, and what if he is sabotaging my career as punishment for acting out of line. What if all that was true, and I wasn't crazy, but I could still decide how much it affected me. What if I *was* crazy, and I could still decide how that affected how I felt about myself, too.

Because yes: he did have a pull on me. But I made the decision to be with him, and I made it because I was lonely, and frightened, and unsure about what my life could look like if it was just my life, and not one that was adjacent to my mother's, or my boyfriend's, or my friend's. I was afraid, really, of being the main character in my own life. I choose to be someone that things happen to, because it was easier than being someone who made things happen.

'I suppose that answers my question, then,' says Deb.

'Huh?'

'Why you told me. You're trying to get back at him.'

'No,' I say. 'I wanted to warn you.'

'Why?'

'Because I like you.'

'You're the girl from the train.'

'Yes. I told you that.'

'Yes, but I'm only remembering now. Your ex-boyfriend lives with a barrister.'

'That's ... that's me, yeah.'

'How did that go, then?'

I fainted on top of him in a pub. I made him bring me to my shithole bedroom. I accidentally slammed him and his girlfriend online without knowing it.

'Fine.'

She picks up her bag, and gestures for the bill.

'You'll be fine. It might not seem that way now, but you'll be fine,' she says, counting out coins on the table. 'I guess you've probably heard this before, but women have to work twice as hard as men to get to the same level.'

'My mum says that.'

'Well, she's right.' She stands up to leave, looping her handbag to the crook of her arm. 'Fortunately, most men don't work all that hard.'

28

Dear Jolly Politely,

Hope you're well. It was a pleasure speaking to you last week regarding my article for Vice.com. However, I'm a little concerned that since our phone conversation was so brief, you didn't have a chance to properly have your say re: the online controversy surrounding your blog. Please call me at any time: you can reach me on 07733444732, or simply call the reception at Vice and ask for me by name.

Thanks,
Tom Perrell

This jolly thing is borrrrrrrrrrrrrring now

Yeah i don't know why i still even check this site i guess she's not posting any more or whatever

I just want to know she's not dead

Dear Jolly Politely

Following my last email, I would really love if you could give me a comment for my article on Vice.com. The piece will now feature other bloggers who have suffered publicly with their mental health. It may significantly improve your profile as a blogger if you were to have a quote on the site, as many people have heard of and respect Vice.com.

I would be happy to link back to your blog or any other online projects you're currently working on.

Best,
Tom Perrell

Sometimes i come on here when i can't sleep just to see if Jolly is online
She never is

I feel him before I see him. I leave the café a few minutes after Deb does, and feel prickly, tender. My boobs – still unusually small – are heavy and sore, as though I've been lying on them. My eczema starts itching again, and there he is: walking down Brewer Street, a few yards ahead.

His hair is longer in the back now, touching the neck of his T-shirt. I follow him, always keeping behind.

It's amazing to watch someone who has become the centre of your life go about their daily business as if you had never infringed on them at all. His hands swing with the jaunty pace of his walk. Two young gay guys in surf vests double take as he passes, looking at him and then each other, laughing at having both thought the same thing.

Huh, I think. *I guess he does look a little gay.*

As I get closer, I view his body with something close to objectivity. He's unusually ... healthy looking. I don't mean eats-three-square-meals-a-day-and-jogs healthy. I mean *Men's*

Health healthy. His body looks taut and defined, his teeth — even from across the road — look whiter, his skin golden. When I met him, I would have guessed his age at forty-eight, and now I'd put it closer to forty. Maybe even thirty-nine. He looks like Robert Downey Jr, all Californian wellness, on his way to promote a new movie. I think of Viv, who put his age at about forty when they first met. I wonder how long he has been 'about forty' for, whether his persistency with his prey has been keeping him in a suspended state.

A sharp pain slashes through my side, winding me. I fold over, placing a hand on each thigh, heaving inwards for breath. He dips down a side-street, and I catch up soon enough to watch him enter a restaurant. Twelve thirty. Just like Clem to eat early.

I remember our day at the Metropole hotel. I ordered every starter on the menu, and he laughed as I tried every one. We'd had a bottle of wine each before 2 p.m. His chair edged towards me as the garden room got emptier and emptier, his hand sliding from my knee to the inner edges of my thigh, his thumb extending to stroke me softly. He opened my purse and placed a room key there, and he told me to go upstairs, take my clothes off, and wait.

'Can't we just go up together?'

'We could,' he reasoned, placing his card inside the leather bill book. 'But I like the idea of you waiting.'

I liked the idea of it too. I liked his ideas, which makes it so hard to hate him fully now. I despise him and I want him. He's killing me and he's feeding me. I don't want to see him again, and I want to have sex with him right now.

The pain in my side spreads across my stomach.

I lean against a wall and take long, deep breaths. I remember the tampons on my desk. I haven't had cramps this bad since secondary school, and I haven't had a period like this since . . . since when, Jane?

I remind myself that I have lost almost two stone in three months, and not even a menstrual cycle can keep up with that kind of rent.

I take one more deep breath, and follow him into the restaurant. He's sitting at a two-person table facing the window, so there's no chance of him clocking me. Only when he moves his head slightly do I see who he's sitting with.

I know her, somehow. I try to remember if Clem had ever showed me a picture of her, but even if he had, the familiarity doesn't feel like something surface level. It's something *else*.

It's Renata.

Renata Brown is dark haired, just like I thought, but shorter than how I pictured her. Her face is everything I expected: strong red lips, big dark eyes, pointed chin. But there's something else to her. She is in a permanent state of almost-leaving, and looks away, while his mouth moves, preferring to focus on something else. Her boredom never seems petulant, the way mine does. It's more like a frank admission that there are bigger, better and more pressing things to think about, and it is her responsibility to give them credence while she can. She meets his eye only occasionally, but smiles in an abstract way most of the time. She never puts her coffee cup down, always balancing it between her thumb and forefinger, one elbow on the table.

I had tricked myself into thinking I knew this couple. I thought I had something to do with their future. And here they are, having lunch as if I'd never existed.

When he gets up to leave, she's still pushing something around her plate. She's the kind of woman you can't imagine having a digestive tract. They appear to have an exchange about whether it's okay for him to leave, and she reassures him that it is. She points to her laptop and her notebook and says something like 'Go! I'm fine!' and he gives in. He looks sorry to leave, but kisses her on the cheek. She closes her eyes. A waiter asks me if I would like to see a menu, and I wave him away like he's standing in front of the TV.

Clem leaves his wife, and the decision of what to do next doesn't feel like a decision at all. Within moments, I am at Renata's table. I slide into his empty chair, already installed before she has time to look up from her laptop. She looks past me to see if it's too late to call Clem back. He's gone. It's just the two of us, now.

'Can I help you?'

She has an indefinable quality that makes it seem that she has something that no other woman has, yet is somehow lacking in humanity. She's got an Isabella Rossellini look of elsewhere, and now that we're face-to-face, I can understand why a man like Clem would marry her. Why marriage would feel like the key to unlocking a woman like this, and why a string of predatory affairs would be a satisfactory balm when it didn't work out.

'Maybe,' I say. 'I'm not sure.'

If Renata knows everything I think she knows then she can't be surprised that something like this would eventually happen. I wouldn't be surprised if this exact thing has happened before.

'Do you know who I am?'

'No,' she says smoothly.

'Can you guess?'

'No,' she says again, and I know she's playing dumb. It's not that she can't guess, it's that she doesn't want to.

'Use context clues.'

'You're the latest, then,' she says finally.

I nod.

'Well, what do you want?'

'I want to know why your husband destroys women, and why you let him do it.'

'He doesn't "destroy" women, don't be dramatic.'

'I know about all those girls,' I say. 'And I know about Viv. The girl who killed herself.'

She smiles at me then, a sharp one that doesn't move any of the other features on her face. 'I understand now why he's worried about you.'

'He's *worried* about me?'

'He threatened my sister to stay away from you.'

'*Who?*'

But of course, it's obvious. 'Luddy.'

Luddy, who I hadn't spoken to since the yoga class. Luddy, who had emailed me gentle, concerned messages, and who I had ignored. Luddy, sister of Renata, sister-in-law to Clem.

Renata had refused to let Viv have a nickname, insisting she go by Vivian. It must irritate her that Luddy doesn't use Ludmilla. That the two sisters go through the world with awkward names, foreign names, names that you have to spell carefully over the phone, and Ludmilla chose the easy route out, smiling her big apple smile and saying, 'Call me Luddy.'

I wonder what Clem calls Renata when they are alone: whether she has a pet name in any language. Whether she could ever allow herself to be a pet to anyone.

'Yes,' says Renata. 'Her.'

In the same way my kiss with Clem was both a surprise and an inevitability, the Sedlak sisters feel like something I had always known. They are two of the most dangerous types of women on earth: the one who lives so far outside of society that one backwards, laughing kick could shatter everything, and the one who is so far up the female hierarchy that she could blink and put it back together.

In any other era, they would be hung as witches.

'So Luddy met Viv at one of *your* dinner parties,' I say, still putting it together in my head. 'Because you're her *sister*.'

Renata is attempting to make eye contact with the waiter, but it's just hitting 1 p.m., and the restaurant is busy.

'I had been trying to help her. Back when I still thought I was capable of helping. But she doesn't have a *life*,' she says, all hollow pity. 'She doesn't have a job. Or a husband. She doesn't belong to anything, any schedule. She *has* nothing. She *is* nothing.'

Renata sees herself as the ideal: a married woman with a successful husband, an enviable career and a stylish wardrobe. She has worked hard to reach the absolute pinnacle of expectations for being a woman, for being a person.

The less a life has in common with hers, the less she considers it a real life. There was the root of her disregard: for me, for Luddy, for the string of brittle young women who came before and will come after me. We don't truly exist to her.

'The women in our family don't do so well alone,' she says, a twinge of regret in her voice. 'We become . . . well. A little transient. A little nothingy. We need partners. I know that's not very feminist, but for most women, it's true. And I worried for her, back then. She is still my sister, after all.' She looks to the restaurant window, distracted by herself again.

'And she's been on her own for so long,' she says, not to me, but to a past she had tried to throw behind her.

'Is that why you don't leave him?'

She shakes off my sympathy like a horse refusing a bridle.

'I don't expect you to understand what married life is like. You don't leave someone because they have a hobby. Plus, you know, it keeps him honest. In a way. I always know what's going on. I bet your mother couldn't say the same thing.'

She gives me a glinting, shark smile, and another cramp seizes me by the abdomen, resonating in my lower back.

'I am not a *hobby*,' I say. 'He got me suspended from work. He's trying to ruin me.'

She waves her hand. 'That's just a game he's playing with you. Sometimes he leaves them for a little while and then comes back again. Don't worry.'

'I don't want him back,' I say, but it sounds unconvincing.

'Okay.'

'I really don't.'

'Suit yourself.'

'Why don't you *care*?' I screech at her, and the people at the other tables look up.

'Darling, can you *not*?' She says in a hushed voice, giving the other tables an apologetic look. 'I do *like* coming here, you know.'

'Look,' she says, 'I know this is unpleasant for you, and usually he moves on quite quickly, but he does seem to be getting a lot from you. Well,' she reasons with herself, 'I suppose you could say we *both* are.'

Another tinkling silver laugh. Renata puts a hand on her stomach. My insides turn to slush as I watch the self-satisfaction envelop her. The chic shirt dress and the high table were hiding it.

Renata Brown is pregnant.

'Three months,' she says. 'Well, three and a half. I never thought I'd be one of those women who show so early on. But I'm small-boned, so.' She knocks back the last cold dregs of coffee. 'How *long* have you and my husband been working together, again?'

I am determined not to cry in front of her. I force out the shortest statement I can manage. 'But you don't *want* babies.'

She chuckles lightly. 'Is *that* what he told you? Well, I'm not surprised. Men get so prideful about that kind of thing, don't they? No, no. Bad sperm,' she says dismissively. 'Or slow sperm? I don't know. Wrong sperm, anyway. We went to see some specialists a few years ago and nothing seemed to work out, so we decided to shelve the whole idea. But then you come along,' she says, reaching out and patting my hand gently, 'and he's a new man.'

'Do you know what,' she says thoughtfully, taking out her iPhone, 'give me your address. I need to send you some flowers to say thank you. You'll love my flower guy. He does them in jars.'

I stand up from Renata Brown's table, knocking into a waiter as I do. On the street outside, the knot inside me tightens and snaps, and a warm, thick feeling spreads through my underwear.

In the toilets of a McDonald's, I wrap thin toilet paper around the crotch of my knickers in an attempt at a makeshift sanitary pad. The blood is dark, currant-black, and coming out of me in penny-sized clots. I roll one between my fingers, the blood spiderwebbing across my hand. I remember the bird parts again, falling into the sink of the Student Union.

I put my hand inside myself, squinting with effort, and more gluey blood comes free into my palm. I remember the spots of light pink blood in my pee and telling myself that this was what my period looked like, now that I was loved.

Renata's grin. *How long have you and my husband been working together, again?*

When Ruth, my absentee line manager, left work to have her baby. I had to sign a card. I never know what to say with those baby cards. Sometimes, if I sort of know the woman, I'll make a joke about how I don't have the balls to push a watermelon through a straw. Or, I'll say something about the free drugs they give you during labour. But mostly, I'll just sign, 'Congratulations Mama! Good luck with everything. We'll miss you. Jane.'

Darla, her face cool, her lips heavy and painted and purple. *You mostly get cystitis from unprotected sex.*

I always felt sorry for them, the mothers. I acted like I was impressed, or jealous, but truthfully I was horrified. I think almost all the girls my age are. We talked about how lovely it would be, and how gorgeous she looked, and how shiny her hair was from all the folic acid. And while all of this might have been true, I don't think I ever believed it. Not one of us would have traded our bodies or our time for the life and well-being of a baby.

We used a condom, the first time we were together. It had felt sterile – formal, even – compared to the easy, thoughtless intimacy Max and I had had. Did I forget, ever, about condoms? Did I assume he was taking care of it?

I zip up my jeans, walking like a cowboy out of the toilet cubicle, my crotch puffed with paper. Washing the blood off my hands, I try not to catch my own eye in the mirror.

I look, instead, into the plughole. I think of him: his body, his face that so quickly turns from agitation to satisfaction.

Yes, darling. From when I fucked you on the floor.

The blackberry clots turn into outstretched fingers as the water begins to wash them away.

'Were you something?' I ask out loud.

But just then the hand dryer goes, so no one hears me.

29

I prepare for my first day back at Mitchell like it's the first day
of a brand-new job. I get up early. I blow-dry my hair. I eat
a proper breakfast. I have a new lipstick: it's a deep, autumn
red. Almost a Christmas red. My clothes are hanging up now,
so I'm able to find something clean and unwrinkled quickly.
I do not need to steal tights from the clothes horse.

I try not to think about her baby.

I've spent a lot of time at Becky's this week. It's funny,
all this time I've known her, and I've never been to her flat.
She's a different person there. Relaxed: cool, even. The first
evening I call over she comes to the door in soft indigo jeans
and a Pretenders T-shirt, with her nails painted a different
colour on each foot. Every inch of her little flat reveals something about Becky I didn't know before: how many books
she has, for one. The walls are filled with artfully arranged
shelves that have gaps for display items: an aloe vera plant, a
jewellery stand, framed photographs. An Angela Carter print
hangs where a TV would usually be.

She invites me into the kitchen, and gives me a glass of red
wine while she stirs a chilli. I don't have a lot I want to talk
about, so mercifully she chatters on, careful to avoid subjects
she knows might upset me. She talks about how she used
to hate living alone, and now she loves it. How her parents
never bothered with cooking, but she had taught herself, and

how good it felt to be able to do something that her mother couldn't do. I wonder what kind of mother Renata plans on being, and what gifts her baby will have as a result of being formed from such a desperate pair. How would Clem Brown raise a baby girl, after everything he has done to the countless, wasted young women of his past? How would Renata Brown raise a baby boy, when her permissiveness with her husband borders on sociopathic?

I remember I am trying not to think about her baby.

'Do you not like your mother, then?'

'Oh, I don't know,' Becky says, adding a square of dark chocolate to the pot. 'I think it's more that she doesn't like me.'

'Why do you think that?'

'I think I make her anxious. I don't have a boyfriend or a fabulous career, and I think she'd like some better adjectives to describe me to her friends with.'

I think how awful that is, and how I've never felt anything close to the same. My mum tells everyone what I'm doing, and she doesn't need me to do anything to be proud of me. Even when I broke up with Max, she was proud of me. Proud that I would leave a man because our love was an average and small one, not the grand and sweeping one she thought I deserved.

'You're not disappointed?' I had asked Mum.

'Why on earth would I be disappointed?'

'I thought you wanted me to get married or something. I don't know.'

'What, so I can be mother-of-the-bride and feel *ancient*? No thanks.'

I felt so many urges to call her during my suspension, but every time I reached for my phone I was reminded of how much we had to catch up on, how much she'd be confused and angered by. I knew I had already made everything much worse simply by shutting her out, but trying to break the silence now felt like a bridge too big to mend. I was scared of her having to revise her opinion of me.

I went back to Becky's house two more times that week, to get tipsy and eat meaty, delicious dinners off our laps. Carbonara with two packets of lardons. Curry with a naan bread each. It was joyous, big eating, the way women eat only when there are no men around. She watches me when I go to the bathroom, clever enough to know that skinny girls don't eat platefuls of carbonara unless they have an exit strategy. But miraculously, my appetite is back. There's a familiar, satisfying tightness around my waist after we eat, and I wonder again about the blood in McDonald's. I get 'Fairytale of New York' in my head, but change the words to the dull pain in my stomach: *you could have been someone. Well, so could anyone.*

More than once, I fell asleep on her couch and woke up to see her getting ready for work. That's when the anxious Becky came back. She became flustered in the morning, changed her outfit too many times, worried about tasks I knew she knew how to do. It occurred to me then that Becky, in all likelihood, had some kind of anxiety disorder that she used obsessive small talk to cope with.

'Becky,' I said tenderly, 'does work make you nervous?'

'Uhm,' she said, re-doing her blouse after getting the buttons wrong. 'I don't know. Why?'

'I've just noticed that you seem so much more comfortable at home than you do in the office.'

'Isn't that everyone, though?'

It's better to think about Becky's problems, especially when my own frighten and confuse me. Renata never sent the flowers. Part of me was terrified that she would ask Clem for my address. I had assumed that meeting her would evaporate the mystery that surrounded her, but it made me more afraid of her than ever. Had I really helped her become a mother, in some sick way?

My period lasts the whole week, coming heavy and purple for the first day, easing into a brick red. By the time I'm back at work, it is beginning to look like rust.

I'm coming back to Mitchell on a good day. There are three holidays that the agency celebrates: Christmas, Howard's birthday and the agency's one. Today, Mitchell Agency is sixteen years old and emails about the party have been flooding everyone's inboxes for weeks. They're renting out a space in a hotel to host it, and the theme is 'Sweet Sixteen'. A costume is encouraged. This doesn't always end well. Last year the theme was 'Indian Summer' and some boys from the IT team dressed up in saris, which became an HR issue. It split the agency for a while, with half the company failing to understand why dressing up as someone's immigrant mother might be considered offensive.

I'm not doing a costume this year. My mission for the evening is to have a couple of drinks, talk to everyone, prove I'm not crazy, be home by 10.30. I feel stronger now. I'm not alone, for one: Becky promised she would be at my side all night. My appetite has come back, and a sense of order and logic has returned to me. On three of the past seven nights, I woke myself up saying his name: chanting it, even. I think of my body as working out a tropical poison, and it's my duty to take care of it while it does.

No one pays attention to me as I walk to my desk. People are taking their costumes out of bags, ironing wigs, or milling around talking about tonight. It's always like this on party days. People will be drinking at their desks by 3 p.m., getting ready by four, and frantically calling cabs by six. A few people will vomit before they leave the building. At least two won't make it to the party at all.

I switch on my computer. I'm not surprised that there are almost no emails for me this time, and within half an hour of coming to work I have nothing to do. I log onto my personal emails, which I've barely checked in the past week. I've forced myself to go on a no-tech diet, putting my phone and laptop in the kitchen cupboard to stop myself from any further sleep-posting. I don't wake up with my hand on my phone. I get to sleep earlier. And the Jolly fiasco doesn't make me burn with shame quite as much as it did. I'm getting better at compartmentalising it as something that happened, something that evidenced a glitch in my mental health, something I am dealing with. And then, I see three emails, all from women I barely talk to any more. Two from girls who went to school with me, and one from Rachel Shine, one of the uni girls I moved down to London with. All three have essentially the same message: *is this you?*

I click on the link to the Vice article, my stomach flipping.

WHEN AGONY CALLS FOR THE AGONY AUNT

By Tom Perrell

Who do you trust with your problems? I mean, really trust? All of us have problems we are comfortable sharing with family and friends, and problems we'd much rather confess to complete strangers. Would you, for example, tell your friend that you have been hiding an STD from your partner for years? Would you broadcast that your colleague is getting preferential treatment for being gay? Of course you wouldn't. And I wouldn't either.

Enter the agony aunt: the often anonymous,

generally female semi-professional who has been
helping society with its most private woes since Mrs
Eliza Haywood's work debuted in a 1744 edition of
The Female Spectator. She is usually elderly and known
to type maternal, soothing solutions out on a pink
typewriter, offering folksy wisdom to hundreds of
readers a week.

Jane Peters is not elderly. In fact, she's twenty-
six years old. Her website, JollyPolitely.com, has
been a bit of a cult favourite for a few years now,
with 'Jolly's' tone tending to be as unreliable as
her frequency. She could (to the applause of many)
insult five people in a week with caustic replies to
their problems, or leave long, emotional essay-like
responses twice a month. Her fan base has always
been small, but dedicated. In the spectrum of internet
agony aunts, she has always been in the comfortable
middle class. Respected, if rarely considered. Known,
if not celebrated.

Until, of course, agony came for the agony aunt.

My hands start to quiver on my mouse. I look around, hoping
that no one can see, that no one has already seen. Could
he name me like that? Was it legal? Did he care? I vaguely
remember the *Mail on Sunday* printing Banksy's real name
several years ago, and no one being able to do anything
about it.

Jolly Politely's figures have quadrupled over the last
few months when, quite without precedent, she began
posting eerie, nonsensical blog posts, usually between
two and five in the morning. Her posts seemed to
suggest she was in trouble, and fans immediately began
trying to assess the problem. A discussion emerged

over whether it was a mental health issue or whether
Jolly was in physical danger. Not since *Serial* has
an internet community argued so vehemently over
such flimsy evidence. Onlookers became familiar
with certain characters Jolly/Jane was continually
addressing: a 'Max' she wrote pleading messages to,
an anonymous older man readers seemed to think was
holding her captive.

I whip urgently past the reprinted rants from my Jolly blog.
I still can't look at them, these shards of my mind that were
both me and not me, the ruined, wet towels from a fever I was
not permitted to sweat through in private. I had deleted the
sleepwalker posts and the accompanying comments during
the first days of my suspension, but Tom had clearly screen-
grabbed them long before that and this one is given lots of
space – my comment about Darla. I feel as though I am naked
and tied to a pyre, a captive online audience waiting to see
me go up in flames. My stomach tightens as I scroll down
and see Max's name.

While Jane herself declined to speak with me, I
did manage to track down the famous Max: a
figure so often spoken about in the Jolly comment
threads that he has become a somewhat romantic
hero, the prince we all began counting on as her
eventual saviour.
    In person, Max has all the charm and countenance
of a Prince Valiant, but unfortunately, little of it
extends to Jolly or Jane.
    'This isn't the girl I knew,' says Max, pushing my
phone back to me before peeling the bottle sticker off
his beer. There's a pang of sadness in his voice, one
that he quickly covers with resentment for both Jane

and Jolly. I am not the first person to get in contact with him, it seems.

'I'm in a new relationship. I have a girlfriend who loves me, who respects me, who I want a future with. And now I have to worry that my ex is staging some kind of online drama? That she wants us to break up, that she wants my girlfriend to fuck off? It's not a nice way to go into a new relationship.'

I feel for Max, but dually, I worry for Jolly. Didn't he want to at least see if she was all right?

'I hope she's all right. I really do. But I can't be in that any more. I can't talk to her. We're not good for each other.'

I press Max, conscious that it's a delicate issue but eager to learn more.

'She's got some fucked-up feelings about men, and needs to learn to be on her own. I'm done.'

It hits me like a physical blow. It's every woman's nightmare: reading the worst things she's ever feared about herself in print, ready for the whole world to see. How pathetic I sounded. And Max. I read his words again and again, hoping he was misquoted, hoping that, on top of having zero respect or common decency, Tom Perrell had just made up what he had said. But the more I reread it, the more sure I am that this was in fact what Max had said, and more importantly, how he felt. His resentment of me wasn't just because I had attacked him on the internet, but had started long before that.

'You're not a bitch. You just don't love me,' he had said. He was so brisk and businesslike that I didn't even consider that he had suffered. That he had lived with me at my most callous, my most immature. I used to pick fights with him for no reason. Shut him out when I resented being so coupled-up at such a relatively young age.

I knew what it was like now, to have someone use you to fill a hole in their heart, and then tire of you.

I think that's a little dramatic, says the Jolly who lives permanently in my mind. *You didn't use Max. You loved Max. You just fell out of love with him. It's normal.*

But why did I treat him so badly?

Why did you let Clem treat you so badly? You're touching the stove, babe. Seeing how bad it can get, how much you can stand.

I can stand a lot.

And we know that now, don't we?

I look at my colleagues, wrapped up in their own worlds, gluing sequins to each other's faces. Do they know? How many people will have read an inconsequential article on a sprawling website, which probably posts a hundred new things a day? How many people see a headline about an agony aunt losing her mind and think: *You know what, it's important I click that, in case one of my co-workers is leading a double life.*

'Becky,' I say, 'can I please help you with something?'

She gives me some of her work to do, and I'm grateful to do it. It feels good to lose myself in the reliable boredom of basic admin. By the time I look up, the room is filled with Molly Ringwalds, Judd Nelsons and Ferris Buellers. Nowhere on the invite did it say that Sweet Sixteen equalled 'vague eighties theme', but that's how it's being interpreted. A couple of all-female teams have done their take on the MTV show *My Super Sweet 16*, and are using it as an excuse to wear filmy, cheap club dresses and a lot of fake tan.

Becky disappears to put on her costume, and comes back nervously tugging at herself. She's wearing a baby-blue tulle dress with white silk gloves and a tiara. She has captured the 1950s Sweet Sixteen look with astute and vigilant correctness. She looks wonderful, and is still worried about getting it wrong.

'Is it a bit much? Just like, I read "Sweet Sixteen" and I thought, y'know, prom night? It's a weird brief because no one in England has Sweet Sixteens. Or, I didn't. Did you?'

'You look lovely. And exactly what I think of when I think about Sweet Sixteens.'

She grins. 'You don't have a costume.'

'Yeah, I thought, given my recent suspension, it would be a bit weird if I went gung-ho with the workplace frivolity.'

'Well, you can't have *nothing*.'

'I'm really fine.'

'I think we can get you some body glitter.'

As she dabs it on my face, I try to figure out if she knows about the Vice article, but her features are smooth and untroubled. We walk to the party together, after we decide that the cabs are taking too long. There's the slightest nip in the air, and as I zip up my jacket, I feel an immense sense of gratitude that the summer has passed. That the heat and the sticky closeness of it have finally broken, and now a new season can reign in its place. Scarves soon. Then hats. Autumn, then winter. Frantic, last-minute present buying for my mother's new family; careful, considered shopping for her. I make the decision to get her something really nice this year, and in fact, to get everyone I love something nice. Becky. Shiraz. Even Darla. I will start saving money now. I will make something small but beautiful for everyone I know. I will use my time as a single woman artfully, making Christmas cards and festive jars of popcorn.

I laugh to myself: in a way, I'm back to where I started. Clueless, manless and planning Pinterest projects that will probably never happen. Clueless, manless, holding on to notions of the kind of person I could be if only I tried harder. In another way, I am further along than I have ever been. This will always be That Year: the one when I dangled over the edge, and mangled my hands and feet trying to get back over it. A hardened sense of security floods through me, like I am now versed in a subject that my contemporaries won't touch for another decade, or possibly ever. I have escaped Clem. I have gone toe-to-toe with his terrifying wife, and I didn't let what she had to say knock me back into another downward spiral. I had lost control of my drinking, my thinking and my ability to maintain my own body. Slowly, I am beginning to feel the parts of myself I had lost come back to me in newer and more evolved forms. I've passed through a forging fire, and now I am gilded.

I am ahead in a game that, six months ago, I wasn't even aware existed.

Becky pulls at her gown, attempting to cover herself with a coat. People are double-taking as she tries to manage her tulle.

'What are you doing?'

'People are looking.'

'Becky, you're in a costume.'

'I know but *they* don't know that.'

'Yes, they do.' I spy a little girl, hanging around outside the Nickelodeon shop, eyeing Becky as if she'd do anything to touch her. I walk over to her, giving a friendly nod to her parents.

'Do you want to take a picture with my friend?'

Her eyes fill up with awe. 'She's your *friend*?'

I grin over at Becky, who is mouthing a frantic 'what are *you doing*?' at me.

'Yeah, she is.'

I take her by the hand and lead her over to Becky. The little girl is convinced Becky is Elsa from *Frozen*, and bursts into a round of 'Let It Go'. Her parents laugh apologetically, and explain that yeah, she does this sometimes. Becky laughs too, and she and the girl take five hundred pictures together, some Japanese tourists slow down to take some too. A light fills

Becky, one that so few people get the chance to see, and one I've only recently learned to appreciate the power of. When we leave the family and carry on to the hotel, she's grinning, her coat stuffed in her bag.

'You were great with her,' I say, an arm draped around her shoulder.

'Yeah. Kids are cool, aren't they?'

'I'm sort of neutral on them.'

We walk on a few paces, until I speak again.

'Becky, have you ever thought about maybe . . . not working in marketing?'

'But I don't know how to do anything else.'

I tell her how she shouldn't waste time on things she isn't passionate about. I tell her how relaxed she is when she's away from the emails and phone calls, over-air-conditioned meeting rooms and complimentary finger buffets.

'I could say the same about you,' she says, and I think about the Vice article again. *Does she know?* 'Why don't you go do something else?'

'I might,' I respond.

I think about what makes me happy. Being Jolly used to make me happy. The notion of helping strangers and of having the correct answer made me feel useful. I liked feeling useful. That was the problem with marketing, really. You could do a good job, and you could enjoy the perks and free beer, but you rarely got the impression you were helping. What could I do? What would I do, if I had the option?

The answer comes to me all at once: *you could listen.*

I would listen to people. I would listen to people like Becky, who had every right to live a happy life but always seemed to be a few pennies short of living one. I would listen to people like Viv, who wasn't strong enough to survive the people who wanted things from her. I would listen. I would try to help.

You could go into real therapy, Jane. You wouldn't have to fake it any more.

As I'm deciding this, we arrive at the hotel.

The room, you can tell, is usually reserved for weddings, christening parties and the occasional retirement. Faded party streamers and deflated balloons are still on some of the lighting fixtures, Mitchell Agency ones hanging over them rather than replacing them entirely. The DJ is in full swing, except the DJ isn't a DJ at all, it's Michael Mahoney from the design team in his regularly assumed role of 'guy who gets over-involved in company events'. He, too, has interpreted the night as an eighties John Hughes party, and is playing 'We Don't Have to Take Our Clothes Off' as we walk in. It's too early in the night for mass dancing, but at least a dozen people have taken to the floor. Girls are miming modesty, grabbing their own clothes protectively on the chorus line. Boys are pretending to beg them for sex. Someone presses a cold flute of prosecco into my hand.

Except, they're not boys and girls. They're men and women. Some of them are married, some of them run departments. Some of them are managers of the people they're dancing with. They're dressed like teenagers, drinking like college students and acting like the thing that binds them together isn't also the thing that feeds and clothes them. Like we are a big gang of friends who only happen to work together, and in this environment – where, we have been told, management have agreed to have a *generous* open bar all night, that extends not only to wine and beer but liqueurs and spirits – our jobs and our roles and our struggles do not matter one iota. A junior copywriter is spinning a senior account director around the dance floor, both of them giggling and clutching one another, trying to stay steady.

How many work parties like this have I been to, if you

add them all together? Six? Eight? Only now does something about it feel uncanny. In an environment like this, it seems inevitable that people would have affairs almost constantly. Unavoidable that they would start drinking alone. Yet here I am, fresh from a week-long suspension, for having spoken up about an affair it feels like I was coached to have. It feels like I'm getting an aerial view of a street I have lived on my entire life, and only now do I realise the plains are uneven, the ground unsure and the flora deadly.

'You're back.' It's David Lady. He's got rid of the beard, but added a trench coat.

'Hey,' I say, and then don't know what else to add. 'Yep.'

He gives me a tight smile.

'I like your costume,' I say. 'What is it?'

'Oh, you probably don't get it. My boombox is over there.' He points to a massive cassette player leaning against the wall. 'If I were holding it over my head, you'd get it.'

'Ahh. Lloyd Dobler.'

'Right you are. And extra points for getting the character name. Everyone else has just said "John Cusack from that thing".'

'Well,' I shrug, 'I watch a lot of romcoms, drunk and alone in my bedroom.'

He laughs, assuming it's a joke.

'I used to have the biggest crush on you,' I announce.

It seems silly to bother hiding anything from anyone. Most of the office must know the reasons for my suspension, and have probably drawn even worse conclusions for themselves. Whatever Becky has deemed fit to tell me must be a watered-down, Disneyfied version of what the truth must be.

'I know,' he replies. 'I did on you, too.'

We watch the dance floor fill up, people coming and going in gangs of four and five. Darla rocks a Madonna in *Desperately Seeking Susan* costume in seventeen necklaces. She's not dancing with the wild abandon I usually expect from her: the hands-in-the-air, head-rolled-back-to-the-ceiling dancing that terrifies crowds as much as it draws them. This is a muted dance of a much simpler sexuality. She's writhing and slippery, but detached. She's still beautiful. She'll always be beautiful, but there's something missing. There's an absence to her that I'm not familiar with. I remember, then, that we're technically fighting, and I probably shouldn't be watching her as closely as I am.

'How come you went off, then?' he asks.

'What do you mean?'

'With Clem. There was a night when I was getting you a drink, and we were having a great time, and then you disappeared. You went somewhere with Clem. I didn't get it. I didn't even know you liked him.'

I don't have an answer. I wish I did. He is right: there had been two options in front of me. The handsome, age-appropriate, kind, funny guy, or the married despot I had kissed. I had let him take me to a hotel room, and then I let him take me to much worse hotel rooms. I could hate Clem for who he was, but I couldn't ignore the part I had played in my own downfall.

'My life kind of sucked,' I say. 'And I think I needed to see how bad it could get.'

'Why?' he asks, genuinely puzzled.

'I don't know. Sometimes you need to see how bad you can fuck up to find out how much you're able to recover.'

We stand there for a while, trying to figure out whether what I had just said was total bollocks or wisdom worthy of a TED talk.

'Well, I'll talk to you later,' he says, and disappears into the crowd. I wonder what kind of romance we could have had if I had liked myself enough to go through with it.

I mill, talking, guessing what people's costumes are. People look at me a little strangely, but no one is rude. No one asks why I decided not to dress up. No one mentions Vice. Two people note that I'm looking 'well', where 'well' means something between 'healthy' and 'not as unhinged as I had initially suspected'. Becky checks in with me, and we get on the dance floor. In my effort to look like I'm having a good time, I start having a good time.

When we're halfway through the *Grease* megamix, I see him. He looks like a game show host, wearing a sparkly green suit jacket and a dickie bow, dancing in Darla's group of friends. Darla's former vivacity now seems robotic and empty.

He sees me, clouds passing over his eyes briefly as he scans me from head to toe. He is surprised, I think, that I am here. He would have assumed that I'd skip the party in an effort not to see him. I head to the bar, and order a bottle of beer. I'm not surprised when he follows me, a few minutes later, even feel a little flattered by it.

'Feeling better?'

His voice is an oil slick, dangerous and capable of too much colour.

'Much, thank you.' I grin at him. 'I hear congratulations are in order.'

'Thank you. My wife sends her regards. I know she does enjoy your lunches together.'

'I prefer her sister,' I say, all innocence.

'You're the only one.'

I'm about to turn away, happy with how I've performed in this conversation, when he says my name.

'Jane.'

He places his hand on my wrist, stroking the soft bed of blue veins with his thumb. The bruise from the wardrobe is just a whisper of green now, with a little jaundice yellow circling the sides.

'I want us to be friends.'

The warm familiar rush shoots up my arm, and my body tries to tell me that it misses him. I can feel it pining and scratching, asking me to let him back in again.

'I'm sorry about how all that went down with Howard, and the girl from HR. But it's just business. There are rules. Why can I never make you see that? People get punished when they break the rules. And you didn't help yourself by acting *so* erratic . . . '

'I have to go, Clem,' I say, unravelling his hand from my wrist. 'And I think it's better that we don't talk again.'

He mouth twists, and his jaw tightens. Then he remembers something, and smiles.

'I know you're lonely, Jolly Politely.'

He knows, then. Maybe he has a Google Alert set up on me. Maybe the article travelled throughout the agency and everyone knows. Maybe it's such old news that people are too awkward to bring it up with me. He leans closer to me, his mouth a hair's distance from my ear. I can smell him, and it's suffocating.

'You need me like I need you, and it's silly to pretend otherwise.'

I feel his finger on a notch in my spine. Do I need him, or was I past him? I had worked out the poison. I had passed through the fire. I had fulfilled a thousand terrible metaphors about rebirth, and I was here, and I didn't need him any more.

'No,' I say. 'I think you need me.'

His face contorts with annoyance, and I see that it's true. He's tired, drained. He needs a fix of something. He is nothing without people around him.

'Suit yourself,' he says. He takes a swig of his beer, and gazes out onto the dance floor. 'There's a lot of choice out there, Jane. You're just one.'

'What if it's a girl, Clem?'

His nostrils flare a second as he squints at me.

I break away, determined not to hear the answer. As I search for Becky, I'm forced to consider what he said. There is a lot of choice, here. Our company is teeming with women under thirty, and men approaching or over fifty. That is how the food chain works. Dozens of attractive young women do the grunt work for a handful of men, and the women get filtered out by motherhood. It is the corporate version of natural selection. No wonder Deb makes so many men nervous. Darla isn't dancing any more. She's in a gang of girls, all of whom are taking pictures of their cocktails, but she leans against the wall behind her, and closes her eyes. Her posture, always so spiky and erect, softens. Her shoulders slump, her hands look aimless at her side. There's a sad, exhausted beauty about her, her dark hair flicked over her face like it is beginning to give up.

I go to her, knowing that whatever unpleasantness has passed between us is neither as great nor as deep as the genuine affection I feel for her.

'Darla,' I say, touching her shoulder. 'Darls.'

'Hey,' she says. Her eyes are glassy, unfocused.

'Are you okay?'

She nods insistently. 'Mm hmm. Are you?'

'Yeah.' I signal to one of her new friends, a blonde girl I had seen the afternoon I confronted Darla. 'Is she okay?' I ask.

'Oh, D?' she says, barely looking up from her Instagram. 'Yeah, completely. She gets like this when she's pissed sometimes.'

'No she doesn't.'

Darla gets bigger when she's drunk, not smaller. She smokes more, has more objectively terrible opinions, swears at bartenders for giving her shitty gin. We have had enough nights out together for me to know that. This Darla is a changeling, a creature I haven't seen before.

'DARLA,' I say again loudly. I click my fingers in front of her face. All she can do is smile at me. 'Darla, what's my name?'

'I'm *fine*,' she says, like I'm a parent interrogating a badly disguised hangover.

I turn to her friend. 'Look, I'm going to get her some water, okay? I don't think she's all right.'

'I think you're overreacting,' she says, unimpressed by my trying to take her attention away from her phone.

'Just watch her, okay?'

She rolls her eyes at me, but agrees. I fight my way across the dance floor, now thick with eighties icons, hands bringing me deeper into the crowd. Tom Harrison, the boy I almost kissed on the fruit machines way back in June, pulls me into 'Video Killed the Radio Star'. He's one of those guys that try to turn every dance into a stunt routine, whether you're in the mood for it or not. I try to prise myself off him, but my laughing just gives him more reason to torment me with *Happy Days*-inspired dance moves. As the song changes to 'Come On Eileen', Tom finds a fresh surge of energy and decides to fireman's lift me over his shoulder, and spins around in circles. Tom is the kind of man who will carry on doing something to make you feel uncomfortable if you tell him it does.

Too-ra-loo-ra, too-ra-loo-rye, aye

As he turns me around, I see Darla talking to Clem.

Too-ra-loo-ra, too-ra-loo-rye, aye

Her head is low. She's talking into her own neck. He has one arm extended on the wall, his back blocking her from most of the room. He is the only thing in her field of vision, the only thing he is allowing her to focus on. I wonder what he's saying to her, and whether he has a nickname for her already.

We are far too young and clever

I wrestle myself off Tom, punching him in the shoulder a little too hard to communicate as quickly as possible that picking up girls who don't want to be picked up is not cool. He scowls, mouthing an insulted 'Whatever,' at me.

By the time I make my way through the crowd, Darla and Clem are gone. I expect to see them whispering closely in a corner. *Never in public*, I think. Clem would never let it happen somewhere like this, at a work party, in full view. I leave the function room, the last bars of 'Come On Eileen' following me as I close the oak-panelled door behind me.

The rest of the hotel smells like gravy. They probably do a profitable side deal in Sunday lunches: oversized Yorkshire puddings and jelly ice-cream desserts. I rush to the cloakroom, trying to imagine which of Darla's two jackets she was likely to have brought this evening.

'Hey,' I say to the woman at the counter, bewildered by my sense of urgency. 'I, uh, lost my ticket. I have a leather biker jacket with studs on the collar. And a sort of belted waist thing?'

She shrugs at me. 'Lots of jacket like that,' she says, in broken English. 'Need ticket.'

I feel guilty for trying to con her, so instead try the honesty approach.

'Did you see an Asian girl leave with a man in the last five minutes?'

She's still confused.

'Woman,' I say. 'Brown skin.' I point to the table, and then my own arm skin. 'Very pretty.

'Like Madonna,' I continue. She comes alive at that.

'Like Madonna,' she agrees, and points to the corridor to the right of her. 'Down there.'

I follow her direction and end up in a small foyer containing the lifts and the toilets. This, bleakly, is where the trail ends. My beautiful, fabulous friend has been taken to a hotel room by my worst enemy, ready to unleash on her whatever it was he deemed appropriate to inflict on me. It could be one of three hundred rooms, and I don't see myself getting far knocking on every door. I slump into a chair opposite, and put my head in my hands.

I think about the last time I talked to Darla. Her fury. Her relentlessness. Her barely concealed triumph when she had taken the Think Gym account from me, her satisfied glare when she told me that my hatred for Clem was just a symptom of my break-up with Max. The way she had used our friendship against me, citing things I had told her in private to accuse me in public. I knew she was jealous when I was promoted before her, and I knew her intense sense of competition would lead her to say things she would often regret.

The Darla at this party was someone I didn't know. Someone who wasn't in their right mind and was in no position to consent to sex. I think about that word again: consent. How many times had it been bleated at us in uni, and how often had I really thought about what it means? If there's sex I don't remember having with Clem, did that mean I was unable to give consent? Had I been passed out, or simply glazed over, the way Darla is tonight? Was it drink, or something else? Something stranger, the same something that made Renata a grinning mother-to-be, and me a bleeding mess? The Zen feeling of accepting and forgetting Clem bubbles into fury. *No. Not her.*

I pace the foyer, phoning her, waiting for it to ring out, and then calling her again. Do I call the police? Her parents?

How would I even get their phone numbers in time to stop whatever is happening in one of those upstairs rooms? As her phone is about to ring out I hear something: a low, barely audible buzz. I freeze, hardly allowing myself to breathe. A phone is ringing, and it's coming from the ladies' toilets.

30

I push the door open. There's something in front of it — a sanitary bin jammed under the handle — but it's been placed there so sloppily that it's easy to push out of the way in one fluid motion.

Her eyes are open, but she doesn't see me. Her head is resting mutely on his shoulder, her legs on either side of his hips as she sits on the cold porcelain of the sink.

Even in a rushed, drunken incident like this, his partner numb and unfocused, he is still a foreplay guy. Her right breast is hanging out of her dress, her cheap costume necklaces rattling against the buttons on his shirt as he jams his fingers rhythmically inside her. He is utterly absorbed by her, amused by her, fascinated by the new toy he alone has the right to unwrap. As I reach for the discarded bottle of Corona on the floor, he finally notices my arrival and turns around. His face is red, contorted, disgusted.

'Get the fuck out of here, Jane,' he snarls.

Darla, without the support of Clem's shoulder to rest on, has slumped back against the mirror. I had called her, cried on her, loved her, hated her, but she was still my friend.

I wrap the neck of the bottle tightly in my fingers, and as he turns back to his new doll to fix her upright, I leap. Within seconds I'm on his back and screaming, screaming without meaning to, screaming so hard that it is reaching the depths of the world Darla has disappeared to.

My arms go straight for his windpipe. He wheezes for a moment, but within seconds has grappled his hands to the back of my head. He's tearing at my face, my ears, his hands pulling at my hair. His fingers find their way into my mouth, behind my bottom teeth, where he finds his grip and pulls. The pain shoots through my face, the tender spot below my tongue yelling out in agonised protest. My feet cling to him, my heels digging into his ribcage, but my legs aren't strong enough to crush the breath out of him.

My thighs eventually slacken around his middle. He feels my muscles let go, and seizes his opportunity to get me off him. He flips me off in one movement, hurtling my body into the mirror, cracking it against my spine. He presses one hand on my throat and holds me there. Even as I'm gasping for air, I'm amazed at how much stronger he is than me. How physically ill-equipped I am to match him. How desperately unfair it is that every day, fights like this end with a woman being held up against a broken mirror while she curses herself for thinking she had a chance.

I keep waiting for him to say that I had overplayed my hand, that I had missed my chance with him, that I deserved what I had got. And what I will get: the job I will lose, the sanity I will struggle to maintain, the friends I will alienate myself from.

He just holds me there, and watches my eyes bulge as I splutter. He won't let me lose consciousness, but we both know if he pressed a little harder, I would. He pushes his cheek next to mine, and drags his face slowly down the curve of my body, breathing deeply as he goes. It's an action that, between two people who loved one another, would appear remarkably tender.

Here, though, it is proof of ownership. Proof to himself, that it doesn't matter what I want, what anyone wants. All that matters is that what belonged to him are still the things that belong to him. That if he wanted to, he could make me love him again. He is convinced of this. He is a man whose confidence exists solely in the arena of his ability to control other people. He will hold me and touch me and inhale me and love me and use me, even if it is by the throat, even if he must slowly kill me to get it. He pushes his forehead onto my sternum and leaves it there, resting, breathing, his hand still wrapped around my neck. Hot, damp drops fall down between my breasts, out of him and onto me. He is crying on top of me, crying while the bruises form on my oesophagus.

He did love me, in his way. Even now I can't fully bring myself to hate him. The thrill we got out of one another was real, deep in a supremely shallow way. There was a possessiveness to him that enjoyed keeping things, there was a domesticity to me that enjoyed the sensation of being kept. He liked watching his bird, even if she was beating her wings bloody on the sides of his cage.

He lifts his head, and as though in a trance himself, starts kissing the places on my body where his tears had fallen. Tender, thoughtful kisses, kisses you give a child's finger if it has been slammed in a door.

'Jane, Jane, Jane,' he says, sorrow heavy in his throat. 'I'm sorry, Jane.'

Darla is sleepily trying to adjust her dress, still not connecting with what is happening in the room. There are red teeth marks on her nipple and lace underwear curled around her ankle, daring to escape to the floor.

My hand still gripped around the beer bottle, I take one last swing.

As the glass bursts at the side of his head, the woman from the coat room walks in with two men in bouncer's uniforms.

'Madonna,' she says.

31

There're not a lot of people who journey to rural Sussex on a Tuesday afternoon, or at least there aren't today, because there are only two of us in the train carriage, waiting to leave the station.

'Do you want to go to sleep?' Mum asks, folding her jumper in a neat rectangle, ready to prop it under my head.

'No, I'm okay,' I say. 'I can never sleep on trains anyway. Or planes. Anything moving, really.'

We've been talking like strangers this morning. The drama of last night has worn off, allowing for old business to crawl in. Part of it, I know, is distance: I have avoided her successfully for three months, longer than I've ever gone without hearing her voice in my ear. But there's something else under the silence too, a throbbing new hurt that she can't dismiss, even though she knows it is her job to. If she were the kind of woman who was able to put resentments aside quickly then perhaps I would be the kind of woman who kept in contact with her mother when there was something to be resentful about.

'I'm sorry I didn't talk to you.'

She shrugs with a certain cartoon cynicism, her palms turned up to the sky.

'What are you gonna do?'

It's rhetorical: the kind of 'what are you gonna do' that says: It's done now. You've hurt both yourself and me in a way neither of us will permanently recover from, and there's nothing you can do to change it.

When the police station called her, she had been asleep. Paul had answered. I would have given anything to know how long it took him to realise who they were talking about: *Jane? Jane?* And then: *Oh, I see, Barbara's Jane. Wake up, hun, your daughter is in some mess.*

They came down together. I was in no position to complain, but my mother's husband was the last person I needed to see. He has two daughters of his own, and has always regarded me as a possibly endangering influence, always fearing that one day I would take an interest in them. He looked at me, caked in blood, my face swollen, and sucked air sharply through his teeth.

He didn't matter, though, because there was her: *her.* Five-foot-three and the biggest thing in my life, even when she wasn't in it.

The police let me go home. They didn't want to, at first, but after two hours of questioning the case seemed clear to them, if messy and convoluted. Woman A is sexually assaulted by a man in a hotel toilet. Woman B jumps to defend her. Man attacks Woman B. Woman B bottles him in the head to escape him. But there were other factors to consider: Woman B's motives, for one. Wasn't she professionally and romantically snubbed by the Man in question? Was Woman A on drugs, and if so, who gave them to her? Was the assault an assault at all, or consensual foreplay? Was it provoked by jealousy? And on and on. It felt like they were just ticking boxes, exploring every possible angle. They believed that Darla's sluggishness was proof that she was on some kind of date-rape drug, and they said that Darla had gone to hospital. They talked about forensic evidence. I chewed my swollen mouth, unsure of what to interject with. I agreed that Darla may have been drugged, but I knew that something else was at work here: that Clem is a cuckoo, and that his newfound beauty and glowing health was coming from somewhere.

Eventually they let up. They assured me that Darla was safe, that Clem was being kept overnight for questioning, and that I might be called at a later point to give more evidence in the very probable case against him. A policeman took down my mobile number and Mum's house phone number.

Mum came back to the flat with me, sensing that there was no way I was going to talk properly to her while Paul was around. He dropped us at the front door, nuzzled my mother goodbye, and said he would see her soon.

It was a little after 4 a.m. when we got in. I was afraid to turn the lights on in the kitchen, afraid to wake Shiraz up and have to explain the evening to her, too. We sat on stools and drank black tea because there wasn't any milk, ate stale Jaffa Cakes because there wasn't any bread. And I talked to her. She didn't say much. She likes to do this: to chew on words slowly, methodically, swallowing only when she's broken them down as small as she can. I talked, and I talked, and when I couldn't keep on talking, I handed her an oversized T-shirt to sleep in, and we got into my bed together, a cool blue light creeping through the shutters. I leaned into her shoulder, felt the soft, biscuit warmth of her, and started to cry.

She kissed my hair and put her arm around me.

'I don't know why it had to happen the way it did, Mum.'

'I know, darling,' she said softly into the darkness. 'But it did.'

By morning, we have a plan. I tell Shiraz that I am leaving my job, leaving London, and that I will pay next month's rent using my last pay packet from Mitchell. I tell her that she should feel free to advertise the room, but that if I were to move back, I would be happy to live with her again. I tell her that I am only taking a few things with me now, but I will be back with my stepfather later in the week for everything else. I thank her, for everything.

She shrugs.

'It was interesting getting to know you,' she says. She does not comment on the bloodstained clothes in the kitchen. 'I hope it works out.'

'You too,' I say. 'And I hope your dad is okay.'

Another shrug.

'I'm going to hug you now,' I tell her.

Shiraz allows herself to be hugged.

Mum's coldness on the train is impossible to ignore or work around. The only way to tackle it is head on.

'Mum,' I say, 'I'm sorry I shut you out. But . . . ' I struggle for the gentlest way to say this. 'If you were your mother, you wouldn't tell you either.'

She attempts to correct this grammatical nightmare in her head for a moment.

'But why? You talk to me about everything. About Max. About your job. Your friends. You were never secretive about sex before. I would have understood. Or I would have tried. And then we wouldn't have had to . . . '

She puts her arms out, as if trying to hug the whole world into her. 'Go through all this.'

'You would have understood?' I say. 'You would have accepted that I was having an affair with an older guy, when you lost your husband to a younger woman?'

'What? Where are you getting *that* from?'

'Come on, Mum. After Dad left you made it pretty clear what kind of woman sleeps with another woman's husband.'

Had she? I remember the underwear shop, her eyeing the stockings and suspenders like they were mounted cavalry charging her way. We used to watch *Desperate Housewives* together and made a game out of hissing at Eva Longoria or any other character who was acting badly in their marriage.

Her eyebrows shoot up in surprise and she's about to protest at this, but stops.

'He came back, you know.'

'Pardon?'

'Your father. He came back.'

I look around, the way people do when they suspect they're being punk'd.

'*When?*'

'About eight months after he left. You were away, thank God. School trip?'

'What did he say?'

'He told me he had made a mistake. He said he was stupid and impetuous, and that he loved me, and he loved you, and that we both owed it to ourselves to give our marriage another go.'

'I can't believe you never told me that.'

'I didn't want to make life even more complicated for you,' she says. 'Just like you didn't want to make it complicated for me.'

'What did you say?'

'I said yes.'

'You said *yes*?!'

'He wore me down. He made me believe that it was the best thing for everyone. That you would . . . ' She laughs drily at the memory. 'That you would have a fucked-up relationship with men unless I took him back.'

'Well,' I say uneasily, 'he wasn't wrong there.'

'We went out. Dinner, then the pub. Everyone was so glad to see him, so ready to put the whole thing behind us. Women kept congratulating me in the toilets, on my grace. My ability to *give it another go*.' She says that last bit with malice, and with air quotes.

'He stayed the night. In our bed. Like nothing had happened. I woke up the next day and accepted that this was what my life would be. That I would be a woman whose husband briefly left her, but who managed to win him back. Even though it didn't feel like a win. It felt like the opposite. It felt like another decision I wasn't making, just a thing that was happening to me.'

I remember her birthday letters. *I didn't feel ready to be a mother, but I felt ready to have a friend.*

'And then you called. From wherever you were.'

'France.'

'France, yeah. And you sounded so . . . ' She smiles broadly at the memory. 'I don't know. Like nothing could hurt you. Like nothing could stop you. You were gabbing on about all your friends and all the things you'd seen and I thought, This girl, she's going to be *fine.*

'And I realised that if I was going to stay with him, it would be unfair to pretend that I was doing it for your sake. I had to admit that I was doing it for mine. And that's when I asked him to leave.'

'You asked him to *leave?*'

She nods proudly, happy to be sharing this information with me at last.

'I asked him to leave. He couldn't believe it. It took me throwing his wallet out of the window for him to get that I truly did not want him or his money in my house. And he went. And I was fine.'

It's like I've discovered a deleted scene from a film I'd watched so many times I could perform it from memory. I can't believe that my mother and I had both narrowly escaped such desperate fates with men we had no business being involved with. I had spent so long defining my life by how it was different to hers, and now I felt a sharp sense of pride in how the same it was. How like her I could be. How much more like her I wanted to be.

'And you were *fine,*' she says, putting her arm around

me. 'And you know what? You'll come home for a little while. You'll think about what you want to do next. You'll *work* on what you want to do next and we'll figure it out together.'

I smile at her, hoping it really is as simple as all that. I fiddle with my phone, checking if Darla has answered any of my texts, if Becky knows yet about what went down. We were ushered out of the hotel so quickly that I wonder if anyone caught wind of it. There is a text from Becky at half past midnight asking if I had gone home, slightly hurt that I didn't say goodbye.

I finally voice what has been brewing in my head since that evening at Becky's house, when I watched her morph from someone brimming with confidence into someone who struggled with her shirt buttons.

'Mum,' I say cautiously, 'I've been thinking about therapy.'

'I think that's a good idea. I'll make an appointment for you to talk to someone when we get home.'

'No. I mean, yes, I do want to talk to someone. But I mean . . . ' I grope for the words, and picture Darla waking up in a hospital bed, wondering who to talk to and what next. She might even have bruises on her body, and only fragments of memory from the night before. She will pin the guilt to herself like a bad brooch. Her shine will always have a brassy tarnish from last night, no matter what she tells her friends.

'I think I would like to work in therapy. As a therapist. Or maybe not a therapist, because I know that can take a long time, but as a caseworker or something.'

She looks at me askance.

'Really?'

I nod. Lightly at first, and then with more definition.

'You know that means going back to school, don't you? You can't just walk into a new career.'

'I know. I haven't looked into it, but it's possible, right?'

'I think so. I don't know much about it either. You won't be able to live in London again for a long time, you know that? It will take a while for you to be qualified. And after that I don't know how much money you'll stand to earn.'

I watch Victoria Station fall into the distance. I could say goodbye to molten paninis and overpriced drinks and a lonely life. I could say goodbye to a job I didn't love and to a man I never needed to see again. I could call this a chapter of my life, and not my entire one. I could try for a different kind of happiness, one that wasn't an endless game of follow-the-leader. It could be one I defined for myself.

'I think that would be okay,' I say. 'Maybe I could live somewhere cheaper. Like Edinburgh. Or Manchester. Or Leeds.'

'Good cities.'

'Do you think I could do that? Start again and be okay – even after everything that's happened? Is it too late?'

She laughs at me.

'I know it's hard to imagine, but trust me, it's not too late. Believe me when I say that things might hurt for a while, but you *will be fine again*.'

'Do you think so?'

'Babe,' she says, and mouths 'two coffees' at the coffee cart man. He obliges, steam coming out of two paper cups.

'You're twenty-six. I know so.'

I smile at her.

'I think I will sleep.'

She takes her jumper and places it across her shoulder, and I fold my legs underneath me and lean into her. It's funny how small she is, but how strong, how sturdy, a pit pony dragging me through life no matter how heavy I get. Of all the love stories I have attempted to mould myself into, hers is the one I was born with. Her love is the shred of cosmic luck that made me strong enough to survive the cheap spells of adulthood. Clem was a snake oil salesman, but my mother is the real deal.

I close my eyes, listen to London slide away, and think about what I am going to do tomorrow, when my life starts.

Acknowledgements

This book is about women and work, and how women work together. Fittingly, it could not exist in its final form if it weren't for the involvement of some very hardworking women. Chiefly, my agent Bryony Woods, who believed in Jane's story from the start, and my editor Sarah Savitt, who convinced me that the uglier, darker, stranger parts of this book were the ones worth fighting for. And everyone at Virago Books, too.

Thank you to my parents, Noelle and Peter O'Donoghue, for maintaining the careful balance every writer needs: that is, supportive and loving enough so that you never doubt yourself, but bonkers enough so that you're never short on material. To my older sister, Jill, for her endless support: from giving me books (that were, on reflection, way too old for me) to wiring me money from Ireland so I had enough to get the bus. To my brothers, Shane and Rob, for providing consistent chaos throughout my life. I don't think I would be a writer at all if I hadn't spent my childhood in my bedroom, writing about how much I hated you. I do not hate you. I love you all.

To my grandfather, John Fahy.

To Sam Baker, CEO of *The Pool*, who kicked my arse every day for two years and made me a better writer because of it.

To everyone who read early drafts of this book and gave me feedback: Natasha Hodgson, Alexandra Haddow, Laurier Nicas Alder, Harry Harris, Matthew Tindall, Richard Wallace, Amy Jones, Ryan Farrell and (very likely) lots more people who I'm sure I'm leaving out. Thank you for allowing yourself to be bothered with texts like 'but what did you REALLY think?' and 'if it's shit, you can tell me'.

Special shout out to Ella Risbridger: the smart pig who read more drafts of this book than anyone else. She is also the founding father of Jane's period, so thank her for that, when you see her.

To all of the brilliant people who worked with me at various advertising agencies: thank you for being completely unlike the people at Mitchell.

To all of the brilliant women at *The Pool*: every single one of you is a lesson in determination, compassion and work ethic, and I feel privileged to know all of you.

To all of the brilliant women who have given me chances, looked after my dog, given me work, bought me lunch, loaned me money, written me that LinkedIn recommendation, whatever: thank you. Special mentions go to Hannah Varrall, Lauren Laverne, Ellie Cowan, Daisy Buchanan, Jennifer Cownie, Janina Matthewson, Helen O'Hara, and I don't know, probably every woman I've ever met.

To everyone who ever contributed to Work in Prowess: two things. First: WHY? Second: thanks.

To Tom McInnes, who did nothing useful at all, but who would be incensed if I didn't include him.

To Tom and Salt Anchell, my pretend parents, who are real proud.

To John Underwood, who cheated death more times during the writing of this book than I can count.

To Gavin Day: there is an alternative version of this book,

perhaps, where Jane meets the love of her life while working at an advertising agency, moves in with him, adopts a puppy and spends every day thinking of things to tell him when he gets home from work. It would not make for a very interesting book, but it is an absolutely fantastic life. Thank you for giving it to me.

Credits